plus size player

other books by
DANIELLE ALLEN

Curvy Girl Summer

plus size player

DANIELLE ALLEN

BRAMBLE

TOR PUBLISHING GROUP
NEW YORK

PLUS SIZE PLAYER

A Bramble Book
Published by Tom Doherty Associates / Tor Publishing Group
120 Broadway
New York, NY 10271

www.torpublishinggroup.com

Bramble™ is a trademark of Macmillan Publishing Group, LLC.

The Library of Congress Cataloging-in-Publication Data is available upon request.

ISBN 978-1-250-33118-2 (trade paperback)
ISBN 978-1-250-33119-9 (ebook)

Our books may be purchased in bulk for promotional, educational, or business use. Please contact your local bookseller or the Macmillan Corporate and Premium Sales Department at 1-800-221-7945, extension 5442, or by email at MacmillanSpecialMarkets@macmillan.com.

First Edition: 2025

Printed in the United States of America

0   9   8   7   6   5   4   3   2   1

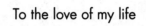
To the love of my life

1

"My friends call you 'which one,'" I told Russ with a laugh.

"I know that's a lie," his deep, velvety voice replied good-naturedly. "They know exactly which one I am."

Heat crept up my neck and flushed my face.

His confidence was just as sexy as everything else about him. He was exciting and with each date, I found myself more and more drawn to him. It wasn't just the fun we had. It was the way he opened me up and lived in the moment with me. He was charismatic, charming, and irresistible. If I wasn't careful, he would have me admitting as much.

Switching the phone to my other ear, I stared out my parents' living room window with a huge grin on my face. "And what do your friends call me?"

"You really want to know?"

"I really want to know."

"My girl."

My stomach fluttered.

"Oop! They call me your girl?" My smile grew, even though he couldn't see me. "I think you like me a little bit," I teased.

He let out a light chuckle. "I'll see you tomorrow."

We exchanged goodbyes, and it took me a few seconds to realize I was still smiling.

"I found it," my mother yelled from upstairs. Jogging down the steps carrying a vintage designer bag, she grinned. "This is the one I was telling you about."

My eyebrow quirked with interest. "This is cute." I took it out of her hand and held it against my red floral dress. The black rectangular bag with the gold handle really was gorgeous. "But it's not going to work because of my shoes." An image popped into my mind. "I know just the thing this would go with! You know those gold shoes I sent you a picture of? That would be perfect!" I looked at her with pleading eyes. "Can I borrow this for a photoshoot?"

"You can have it!"

My eyebrows shot up. "Oh, wow, really?"

My mom loved her bags.

"Yes." She nodded. "I got a similar one a couple weeks ago, so this one is for you."

"Thanks, Mom!" The grin crept across my face as I posed. "How do I look?"

"You should be a model," my mother commented as she stared at me from across the room. "You really should."

She was honest and direct—that's where I got it from. My mom and I always had a good relationship, but we didn't see eye to eye on my career. She thought I was wasting my talents, while I knew I was enterprising.

"I *am* a model," I replied, rolling my eyes.

She sighed. "No, Nina . . . a real model. Not an internet model."

"What's the difference, in your opinion?"

"Respect. Stability. Money." She looked me dead in my face, her hand on her hip. "Need I go on?"

"I have all of those things now."

She squinted her eyes and gave me a questioning look. "Do you?"

Oop! No, she didn't!

I wanted to have a snarky reply, but I cracked up.

"Mom, I can't even get into this right now. I have plans, so I have to go."

"Where are you going?"

"I have a date."

She smirked. "When don't you have a date?"

"Don't be a hater because I get taken out on dates." I pointed at her. "You're just mad because your man doesn't take you anywhere."

"Hey! I heard that," my father yelled from the kitchen.

Mom and I burst out laughing.

"Then take Mom out so she doesn't have to live vicariously through me," I responded, loud enough for him to hear me clearly.

"I take your mother out plenty," he replied indignantly as he appeared in the doorway. "We just went to the movies not too long ago. Didn't we, Diana?"

Mom and I looked at each other with shocked expressions on our faces.

"Michael, that was two months ago," my mom pointed out calmly.

"No, Di, that was only a couple weeks ago," he argued.

"It wasn't," Mom and I said in unison.

He looked perplexed. "Diana, we saw that comedy you wanted to see. The one with the actor you like."

"That was at the beginning of June. It's now the beginning of August," she explained.

I put my hand over my mouth to contain my snickering.

He stared me down, only making me laugh harder. He folded his arms over his barrel chest. "Now why are you all in married people's business anyway?"

"She's making a good point though, darling," Mom defended me with a light, musical giggle. "You haven't taken me out in a while."

"Did we or did we not go to church last Sunday?"

"That doesn't count," Mom and I said in unison.

"Of course the two of you would gang up on me. I'm going back to finish making my sandwich!" He swatted his hands at us. He started to turn around and then stopped. "Nina, do you need a few dollars? You said you were going out."

I smiled. "I'm good, Dad, but thank you."

"In case of an emergency," Dad stipulated. He shifted his eyes to me, and a concerned look flashed across his face. "Do you need emergency money? Let me go get you something."

"Dad!" I called out to his back as he made his way to his office.

He ignored me and I turned to my mother, who shrugged.

"You know how your father is," she reasoned with a pleased smile. "He always makes sure his girls are good."

"This is true."

I glanced at the clock over the television and made a face. "I have to leave in the next few minutes if I'm going to make it on time."

"Where are you going?" My mom eyed me suspiciously. "And with whom?"

"Going to a lecture. With The Smart One."

"Oh! A lecture!" Her eyebrows flew up and a flash of confusion crossed her face. "That sounds . . . fun."

Laughing, I shook my head. "I don't date him for fun. I date him for what I can learn from him. We teach each other things and I enjoy that."

"The way you're dressed, I was expecting something else. But I think a lecture sounds nice."

"Yeah, Tyrell is my smart guy," I replied, pulling my phone out of my bag.

"Is that the one you went race car driving with last month?"

My lips curled into a smile as I reflected on that date. "No, that was The Fun One."

My mom's eyes lit up. "The Fun One? What does that mean? And who is this mystery man?"

I rolled my eyes again. "Russ is The Fun One. And he's not really a mystery man. He just doesn't live locally."

"Ohhh, yes, I remember! I liked that you enjoyed yourself with that one, but I'm partial to the one who took you to that French restaurant in the city. Very romantic."

"Dru is very romantic, and I like that. Tyrell is incredibly smart, and I like that. James is hilarious, and I like that. And Russ is so much fun, and I like that a lot," I explained.

"I understand fun, but the race car driving was a dangerous date—especially for the first date," she complained.

"It was our second date," I corrected.

She quirked an eyebrow. "I see that look in your eye. But don't discount the romantic. I didn't, and look how lucky I am."

"Yes, but you also don't go on dates anymore."

Mom's head fell back, and a laugh erupted from her. "The dates may have slowed down, but the romance hasn't. Wait until you find you a man who gives you everything you've ever wanted and needed. That's when you settle down. You're young. You're only thirty. You have time."

"What if I don't ever want to settle down?"

She put her hand on my arm. "Then don't. When you find exactly what you want, you will want to and it'll feel like home. What I found with your father when we were twenty-five is rare. It happens when it happens and it'll happen for you, too. But in the meantime, live your life for you first and then find someone who fulfills you like life fulfills you. Don't worry about settling down. Worry about settling in."

"Settling in?"

"Settling in to your life." Her smile widened. "Enjoying what God has blessed you with."

On cue, my dad appeared in the doorway with a handful of cash.

"Now take this"—he counted two hundred dollars—"and make sure you can pay your own way."

"Aw, thank you," I replied. "But I don't need it, Dad."

He stuffed it into my hand anyway and then smiled at me. "Take it. Keep it. And if you need to, use it."

I smiled.

Michael Ford always made sure his girls were good. I never had to worry about anything because if I let him, he'd handle it. One thing about my dad was that he didn't just take care of me, he taught me how to take care of myself. I loved and appreciated him for it—even when he was being extra.

Shaking my head, I accepted the crisp bills. "Thank you."

"And here's something for you," he said, handing my mom a note. "While I was back there, I made reservations at Chez François for us—tonight at seven, my queen."

My mom giggled. "Michael!"

The giddiness and lovestruck looks on their faces made me smile. My fifty-eight-year-old parents were a youthful couple, and the way they made each other light up was the most beautiful thing. They found a home within one another. If I ever settled down, it would have to be in a relationship like the one those two

had. And since what they had was rare, I was content being fulfilled in other ways.

Speaking of . . .

"Okay, well, I'm going to head out now," I announced.

"Remember when all Nina wanted was to go off to Magic
World?" my mom asked my dad with a mournful sigh. "I miss
when she was that age, and we could keep her with us all the time."

I lit up. "I haven't thought about Magic World in forever!"

Magic World hadn't crossed my mind in years, but I loved that
place. It was an all-ages amusement park with so many things to
do. It wasn't that far—almost two hours away—but I hadn't been
as an adult.

"We used to take you every summer," my dad reminisced.

"I haven't been there since I was a kid. Maybe we should go one
day soon, for old time's sake."

My mom stopped pretending to be sad to give me a look. "With
these knees?" Pointing to herself and my dad, she continued. "Only
in a magical world are we going to be able to walk around Magic
World."

"Speak for yourself," Dad replied, folding his arms over his
chest. "My knees are good. I still got it."

"Yes, you do," Mom flirted before looking over at me and shaking her head. "He doesn't," she mouthed.

My dad gave her a look. "Hold on, now."

"Yeah . . . I'm going to head out," I repeated, stifling a laugh.

Giving them a big hug, I said goodbye and exited my childhood
home. They walked me out, then stood on the porch watching me
as I backed down the driveway.

I looked like a younger, bigger version of my mother—syrup-
brown skin, thick head of hair, extra-wide smile, and dark, almond-
shaped eyes. She was stunning, quick-witted, and had lots of style.
And while I might've looked like mother, I got my work ethic and
business acumen from my father. He worked hard to create a life
he was proud of and on his own terms. He used his resources and
ingenuity to build wealth and grow his company from the ground

up. Together, I was the perfect combination of my mom's straight-forwardness and beauty and my dad's hustle and charm.

Pulling away from the large brick home with the manicured lawn, I waved to my blissfully in love parents. As I made my way out of the gated community in the Northern Virginia suburbs, I couldn't help but wonder if I'd ever have what they had. It sounded good and looked good on paper. But it was unrealistic to think one man was going to fulfill all my needs.

Unrealistic and a lot less fun.

As if she heard the thought, my best friend called.

"Nina!" Aaliyah James cried as soon as I answered the call.

"What's wrong?" I answered, navigating my way toward the highway.

"I'm done with dating. Done!"

I laughed. "What happened?"

"This man sent me a message a few days ago and we were making small talk. I wasn't sold on him enough to agree to a date, but I entertained the conversation. Today I got a message from his wife stating that she was surprised to find a dating app on his phone and let me know he'd be available in six months because she's divorcing him."

"You dodged a bullet," I told her. "So really, this is a win."

"A win?" she screeched, causing me to snicker. "How is this a win?"

"Because it means that you don't have to waste your time with him and it frees your schedule for someone like that sexy-ass bartender—"

"Absolutely not! That's not going to happen," she interrupted me.

"It should . . ." I replied in a singsong tone.

"I don't know how you do this. How do you keep going on dates? I mean, seriously, how are you going on a date after last night?"

Last night, I'd planned to meet up with this light-skinned, green-eyed man with pretty teeth, but he didn't show up. We were supposed to get drinks before I went to the India Davis concert with Aaliyah. I waited for twenty minutes and then left.

"It was supposed to be a first meetup," I explained. "There were no feelings or emotions involved. He blew his opportunity, so he's blocked and doesn't get another chance to waste my time. And him not showing up worked out because I got to spend more time with you at the concert. Win-win."

"But my real question is how do you have the emotional bandwidth to keep dating after bullshit keeps happening? Howwwwww?"

"Because I'm having fun," I answered with a laugh. "And when I'm not having fun or when I'm ready to end the situation, I end it. It's really that simple."

"Each time one of these dates doesn't work out, I'm ready to stop trying altogether."

"Do not let someone else's bullshit stand in the way of what you want."

"You're right. I'm just . . . frustrated." She sighed. "Enough about me. When is your date?"

"I'm on my way to meet him now," I told her.

"And which one is this? The one you like?"

"Who?"

"The Fun One."

My lip quirked up. Pushing down the feeling the thought of him stirred inside me, I replied, "I don't know what you mean."

"You know exactly what I mean." She sighed dramatically. "That's the one you get excited about. That's how I know you like him."

"I like them all," I corrected her.

She giggled. "Something is wrong with you."

"There's nothing wrong with me," I told her. "I'm doing dating right."

My dating roster consisted of four primary men. Russ was The Fun One and as his nickname indicated, we had fun and did exciting things together. James, The Funny One, made me laugh so hard the entire time we were together. Dru was probably the sweetest and most romantic man I'd ever met. And Tyrell, The Smart One, was so informed and knowledgeable.

The four of them made the perfect man, so I didn't have to worry about not getting what I wanted out of the situation. I had all the bases covered. They each had their own lane. They didn't have to be anything other than what they naturally were. They didn't feel any pressure; I didn't feel any pressure. We played our parts and enjoyed our roles. There was a lot of freedom in not having expectations.

"Yeah," she sighed. "I mean, you're clearly doing it better than me. I can't find one I like, and you like them all."

"Scouting takes time."

"I'm running out of time."

"You're being dramatic. But seriously, it took time and effort to build a solid roster."

"So, since you have . . . let me think, Dru, Tyrell, James, and Russ, why are you still on the dating app?"

"Because scouting has to take place year-round. I'm still open to adding to the team. Anyone can get cut at any time, and I have to be on the waiver wire to pick up new talent. It's always draft season, boo!"

Light laughter rang from her end of the line. "You know you almost lost me with the sports metaphor, but I get your point."

"Well, then, get back out there and stop letting one bad date—"

"It's been more than one," she interjected.

"Don't let a series of bad dates keep you from doing what you want to do. If I'd let a bad date keep me down, I wouldn't have the elite starting four that I have now."

"How do you have the time and energy?"

"I only spend time with people I enjoy. I only do things I want to do. I only have sex with people who get me off. So, my time is never wasted, and my energy stays high."

"If I don't have a man by my thirtieth birthday, I'm going to start living my life like you."

"You'd be a lot less stressed if you did," I confirmed. "And you would actually enjoy dating. You're so focused on finding a man. You're not enjoying the men."

She laughed. "You're right. You're right. You found four good ones—"

"Four and a possible," I interjected. "Someone slid into my DMs, and I might let him take me out, too."

"See? I love this for you. I can't find one worthy of a second date and you've found a roster full of eligible men."

"Yeah, but each serves a purpose. It's easier to find exactly what I'm looking for when I'm looking for it in different men."

"What are you going to do when you find that one man who has everything?"

"One man?" I scoffed. "Nah. Not gonna happen."

"You know you believe in love," she argued.

"I absolutely believe in love. I spent my life witnessing love."

"So, you really don't want what your parents have? What my parents have?"

"Only if I found everything I wanted and needed in one man. And let's be real . . . that's not going to happen."

"It could," she argued.

I knew that she hoped it would happen for me because she needed to believe it would happen for her. And I knew why it was so important to her, so I let her down gently. "It's very unlikely."

"But it's still a possibility. You can't say never."

"Yes, fine. It's a possibility," I relented. "An unlikely possibility."

"But a possibility, nonetheless. My work here is done!"

She sounded pleased with herself, and I laughed.

"No, but seriously, I'm curious how you're going to handle it when you meet your match," she mused.

"You're talking about meeting a man so perfect for me that I'd drop all the men I'm dating now." I shook my head as I switched lanes. "That's funny."

"Why is that funny? You've basically done that with The Fun One over the last couple of months."

"I have not!" I argued indignantly.

While that realization got under my skin, she had a point. I had such a good time with The Fun One that whenever he was in town, I made time. Any opportunity to spend a couple days with him, I took. It wasn't just the sex—although the sex was incredible. It was the way he lived in the moment with me and experienced life with me. He challenged me and explored my mind and my body. He spoiled me with time and attention as much as he did with money and adventure. While I had no intention of admitting it, he was my favorite.

"You've prioritized him because he's your favorite," Aaliyah teased.

With wide eyes and a tight grip on the steering wheel, I shifted the conversation since I couldn't deny her claims. "Let me tell you something . . . over the last few weeks I've gone to a festival, watched an improv group, taken a salsa lesson, attended an art gallery opening, got my oil changed and my tires rotated, went to a live taping of a show, and took a boat ride across the lake just to end up at a picnic specifically created for me. You can't get all that with one man."

"I can't even get one of that with one man," she whined jokingly.

I laughed along with her. "Dating is what you make it."

"So what's The Fun One's name again?"

"Russ," I answered.

"Yes, Russ. The traveling businessman. What exactly does he do?"

"We don't talk about work. We focus on fun. But I do know that he travels, and he handles business. So that's why I call him a traveling businessman."

She laughed. "No details, just vibes."

"The only one who talks to me about work is The Funny One and that's because he's hilarious and he wants to be a stand-up comedian. So, it makes sense for us to talk about it. The Fun One . . ." I smiled, thinking about him. "We decided on the first date to talk about who we are, not what we do."

"Interesting . . ." she responded suspiciously. "When are you seeing him again?"

"Tomorrow."

"And tonight you're going out with who?"

"The Smart One. We're going to a lecture."

She giggled. "You don't even talk about him with the same energy. Does The Smart One know he can't compete with the others?"

Her teasing tone made me laugh along with her.

"Stop it! He's doing just fine!"

She exhaled loudly. "I know what I want. But sometimes I talk to you and I'm like, Nina has this shit on lock."

"And do!"

"I have to get it together."

"Then join me in these streets!"

She laughed. "I'm looking for the real thing. I'm not going to find it looking in the streets."

"News flash, Liyah . . . if you're on a dating app, you're already looking in the streets."

"Oh my God, you're right," she groaned.

"You spent months self-reflecting and abstaining and that's . . . a choice. But you did it, and now you know you're ready for a relationship. Congratulations! But the dating part is where you figure all your shit out with an actual person. So have fun with it!"

"You make it sound so easy. This shit is effortless for you," she sighed. "Give me some advice to carry me through my search. Please."

"If out of nowhere a man explicitly says he's not a player, it's because he's the coach." As she cackled on the other end of the line, I continued. "Don't trust anything that muthafucka says."

"Nina!" she screamed. "I'm so weak!"

"No, but seriously, enjoy yourself. I just pulled up to our alma mater. I'll let you know how tonight is."

We said our goodbyes as I searched for a parking spot. The lecture was being held at Hamilton University. And since I'd driven as fast as legally possible to make up for the lost time, and because every light was green, I was only five minutes late.

Hopping out of my car, I approached the building quickly. A big man with long locs in a ponytail almost collided with me because he was staring at his phone.

"Oh, sorry about that, shawty," he apologized, holding his hand up.

"No problem," I told him, continuing at a fast pace. "But watch yourself."

"My bad."

We were heading in the same direction, but he was damn near running. I slowed down because I saw my date.

Tall, slim, and undeniably handsome, Tyrell slid his glasses up the bridge of his nose as he waited for me to arrive. When he saw me, a smile crept across his face. His dark skin, high cheekbones, and light brown eyes were so distinguishingly beautiful. He would've stood out anywhere.

He checked his watch and then pulled me into a hug. "I thought you were standing me up."

He always seemed so nervous when we'd get together. He'd made it to the roster a few months ago. But because of life and work, it was only our third date. And even though we'd enjoyed each of the dates, he still seemed so shocked that I was interested.

Rolling my eyes before pulling out of the hug, I looked up at him. "Hello to you, too."

"Forgive me. You look beautiful."

"Thank you." I checked out his khaki-and-olive outfit combination. "You're looking good." I touched his green shirt. "This color really complements your complexion."

"Thank you." He opened his arms and grinned. "I just wanted to make sure I matched your fly."

"And you do," I complimented.

"Let's head in." He anxiously glanced at the people walking inside.

"Yes, let's get this philosophical show on the road."

He offered me his arm. "I think you're going to like this. Dr. Reynolds is an astronomy expert."

Two hours later, we were walking out of the auditorium, and I was stifling a yawn.

"How did you like it?" Tyrell asked me as he walked me to my car.

"I thought the beginning was really good, but that last forty minutes felt unnecessary." I made a face. "I love the sky but that last part felt like it was dragging for no reason."

His eyes widened. "What? You didn't like his breakdown of the evolution of galaxies?"

"The birth, life, and death of stars intrigued me. He had a strong start. It just seemed like it started dragging at the end."

"I did notice you kind of sit back once he went on that tangent about the big bang theory."

We talked for thirty minutes outside of my car, recapping the stuff we loved about the event. We shared our favorite moments and he became sexier with each educated point, every insightful question. His mind was just as sexy as his face. Even though I was tired, the allure of his intellect was undeniable.

Tyrell seemed pleased with himself. "I knew you'd like it."

"Yeah, I love learning new stuff."

"Maybe we can talk about some more stuff we can learn together over dinner . . ." He looked at his watch. "It's still early. It's just a little after nine o'clock. There's a lot of restaurants around here."

"I'm actually tired," I told him, feeling my phone vibrate in my bag. "It's been a long day so I'm going to head home."

His eyebrows shot up. "Really?"

I checked my phone and saw a text message from Russ. A flurry of butterflies swirled around my belly. Shoving my phone in my bag, I nodded. "Yeah."

"I would say that the stars aren't aligned for the night to end the way I was hoping, but . . ."

Cocking my head to the side, I looked up at him. "But it would take hundreds of years for us to see stars move," I quoted the lecturer.

Even with disappointment dulling his eyes, a smile tugged at his sexy lips. "You were paying attention."

"Of course."

His face lit up as I answered. "So, I'll see you soon?"

I giggled lightly. "When you have something specific planned, call me and we'll set something up."

"I really like spending time with you, Nina."

"I like spending time with you, too."

He grabbed my hand and kissed it. "Until next time."

"Until next time."

He dropped a swift kiss against my lips before he opened my car door and helped me inside.

"Thank you for coming to this with me," he said, staring at me adoringly. "Get home safe, okay?"

"You too, Tyrell."

He closed my door, and I lifted my hand.

He gave me an awkward yet cute wave in return before making his trek down the sidewalk.

Shaking my head, I couldn't help but smile.

Tyrell was a pleasure to look at and our dates were nice, educational, and interesting. But I needed to rest up for the unexpected, last-minute date I had lined up for tomorrow.

2

Pulling up to an upscale Mediterranean restaurant on Monday, my brows crumpled with confusion. I was looking forward to seeing Russ, and it honestly didn't matter what we did. But since I was expecting something fun and exciting from him, I had to assume we were going to be extras in a movie that was filming at the restaurant.

"Because we can't just be having dinner," I murmured, looking at the stone building he'd picked for our date.

The restaurant was tucked away in a nice subdivision just outside of Richland. I was unfamiliar with the neighborhood, but the restaurant and surrounding stores and homes appeared expensive. It looked to be a high-end establishment, and the people I saw walking in were well-dressed. The classical music became louder as I killed the engine.

Checking the time and then my reflection, I stepped out of my car. Tugging at the formfitting black dress that hugged my curves and accentuated my large breasts and plump ass, I made my way to the entrance of the restaurant.

"Nina Ford," a deep, velvety voice called out to me as soon as I stepped up onto the sidewalk.

My name rolled off his tongue, and his voice cascaded down my back like a chill. A smile tugged at my lips as I slowed to a stop. Brushing my thick, blown-out hair over my shoulder, I turned my head toward the voice. As soon as our eyes met, I felt it.

Russell Long and I had more than just sparks between us. From the moment we met at that party at the beginning of June, we just clicked. I wasn't sure if it was the ease with which we connected, or that when we were in each other's presence, we were our most authentic selves. But the fact of the matter was that he was irresistible.

And not just because the sex was mind-blowing.

Our energy was electric, and as soon as we were in the same space, we were drawn together like magnets. Our conversations were effortless and it took willpower to keep our hands off each other.

"Nina, Nina, Nina . . ."

Licking my lips, I eyed the sexy man in front of me. Letting my gaze travel up and down all six feet, three inches of him, I admired the way his black suit fit his tall, muscular build. His full lips spread into a blindingly white smile, and his thick brows hovered over beautiful brown eyes. He was always well-groomed, and his low-cut fade with deep waves and well-kept beard were a testament to that. His dark caramel complexion was flawless, except for the tattoo that peeked from the collar of his shirt. I knew that particular tat ran from his neck over his shoulder and down his arm.

And I can't wait to trace my fingers over it later.

The man was physical perfection.

He had the face of a model with the build of a professional basketball player, and my body always seemed to react to the sight of him.

"You look incredible," he breathed as he approached me.

"As do you," I returned, checking him out one more time before locking eyes with him. "This suit is fire. You clean up well. I don't think I've ever seen you in a suit before."

He brushed his hands down his lapels and did a pose.

The man knew he looked good.

He reached his hand out and grabbed mine. "I had to step my game up because I knew you would be coming correct." Lifting my arm in the air, he licked his lips and took me in again slowly. "And like always, you didn't disappoint."

"Well, you said to dress up because we had dinner reservations so"—I did a turn so he could get a view of the back as well—"I dressed accordingly."

He let out a low whistle. "You wore this to tempt me, didn't you?" He put his free hand on my left cheek and gave it a little smack. "You know how I feel about your ass."

I feigned ignorance. "Oh, you like this?"

He yanked me forward until my body was flush with his. I had to look up because even in my four-inch heels, he was still a couple of inches taller than me.

"You know I do," he whispered before placing a kiss against my lips. He grabbed my ass with his big hands and jiggled it. "You know you look good as hell."

I kissed him again. "And I taste even better."

"That's the truth." He moved his hands to the small of my back and then smirked. "And I look forward to tasting you again."

"Sooner rather than later," I promised as a car crept by us. Assuming we had an audience, I pushed away from him and quirked an eyebrow. "But first, I believe we have reservations."

He adjusted himself and let out a little chuckle. "Yeah, let's go before you start something we don't have time to finish."

I turned toward the restaurant's front doors, but Russ grabbed my hand.

"Not that way. Follow me," he instructed.

"Is there another way in?" I wondered as I allowed him to usher me toward the car that had stopped nearby.

"No," he answered before opening the back door for me. "We're making a quick stop before dinner."

I noticed the rideshare sticker on the windshield and I looked back at him. Narrowing my eyes suspiciously, I put a hand on my hip. "Russ, what's going on?"

"Do you trust me?"

"As far as I can throw you."

He laughed. "Nina, get your sexy ass in this car."

With a wide smile and not another word, I slid into the back-seat. He closed the door for me and then walked around to the other side. As soon as he got in, the car pulled off.

I turned to him. "Where are we headed?"

"When have you known me to ruin a surprise?" There was a twinkle in his eyes.

I felt the rush of excitement and a flutter in my belly that I always got before a date with Russ. We'd met two months ago, connected instantly, and had eight memorable dates together, seeing each other one or two days a week since we'd met. I had no doubt date number nine would be something to remember. I was a little worried when I thought we were just going to have dinner. But as always, Russ came through.

And has further piqued my interest.

I stared out the window, looking around for clues. "So how long are you in town for?"

"Just a couple of days. I have to head to Toronto on Tuesday," he answered. "Tonight is my only free night."

I turned to face him. "So you only have one free night and you wanted to spend it with me?" I nodded appreciatively. "I get it."

He let his head fall back and chuckled. "Yo, what is wrong with you?"

"Nothing! I'm just saying I get why you'd want to spend your only night off with me!" I smirked. "I'm kind of a big deal."

"See, you play too much," he told me, still amused. "And if you didn't need what I got you, I wouldn't be giving you this gift, because you're already feeling yourself too much."

"Feeling *myself*?" I cocked my head to the side. "You're the one spending your only day off with me."

He patted his pockets theatrically. "Let me make sure I have my receipts to take this shit back."

I put my hand on his shoulder. "Are you denying that I'm a big deal?"

"Driver, I'd like for you to let her out right here, please," Russ joked, causing me and the driver to both burst out laughing.

"Well, we're just about here," the driver stated, turning down an unmarked paved road.

"Excuse me, sir," I called to the driver. "Can you tell me where I am?"

The young twentysomething man definitely knew the plan, as he gave me a sly look in the rearview mirror. "I'm under strict orders to not say anything and to enter the establishment through the back entrance."

I gasped and then pouted. "So, you're not going to tell me?"

He shook his head. "I cannot."

I lowered my voice to a stage whisper. "Am I being abducted? Have I been taken?"

"No!" He glanced at Russ in the mirror. "Maybe you should tell her."

Russ tried to hide his snickering behind his hand. "Naw, she's good."

"Good and missing," I teased with a straight face. "The abduction started the moment I was supposed to eat at that Mediterranean spot but ended up at an abandoned warehouse. Wait until my dad hears the news that Russ and his accomplice"—I located the driver's name on the front dashboard—"Matt snatched me in broad daylight."

"What? No!" Matt yelped from the front seat. "Dude, tell your girl what's going on!"

Russ burst out laughing. "No, it's cool. It's cool. She'll find out soon enough." He looked over at me. "And I wouldn't call this broad daylight. It's technically early evening."

"Snatched me up in broad dusklight."

"Dusklight isn't even a thing."

I pursed my lips. "Semantics. The sun is still out. It's almost dusk. And I've been taken." Turning my attention to the driver, I leaned forward. "Have you seen the movie *Taken*? That was inspired by my dad."

"She's playing with you, man." Russ chuckled. "You're giving her an audience so she's going to keep going."

I tried to stop myself from smiling but I couldn't contain it. Russ's laugh was infectious, the situation was hilarious, and I was impressed by how well he knew me and my humor.

Even though I wanted to crack up, I held it together.

"You want to take your chances believing this kidnapper with all the secrets, or me, a certified big deal with a dad who has a particular set of skills?" I questioned.

Snickering, Matt shook his head. "I mean . . . he's the one paying for the ride, and I don't think he wants to ruin the surprise."

"This is not funny," I grumbled, still grinning at the two amused men. I craned my neck to see if I could make out a sign or a marquee that indicated where we were. "Let me pay attention so I can know what clues to give my father and the authorities. Where—?"

"This is for you," Russ interrupted, pulling a bag from seemingly nowhere.

"You got me a gift for real?" My voice softened and my eyebrows flew up. "I thought you were bullshitting." I took the bag from his hands and saw a shoebox inside. "Russ . . . is this why you asked me my shoe size a few weeks ago?"

"Open it."

I pulled the box out of the bag and then flipped open the lid. "Oh, wow."

I wasn't a sneakerhead by any stretch of the imagination. But I loved fashion, and I loved anything that looked good on me. And the black-and-white abstract two-tone high-top sneakers that were in the box were hot.

"You like them?" he asked expectantly.

There was a hint of nervousness in his question that forced my eyes to his immediately.

"I love them," I gushed, pulling one of them out to get a closer look. "These are so cool." Leaning forward, I planted a swift kiss against his smiling mouth. "Thank you!"

He sat back in his seat, a self-satisfied grin on his face. "You're welcome. You can dress them up or down. They even look good with what you have on."

I put the shoe next to my thigh and nodded. "Yeah, it does," I agreed. "Where did you get these? I've never seen them before."

"I designed them."

"What?" I gasped. "You did?"

Grinning, he looked down at the shoe, almost bashful for a moment. "I like to design. So, I grabbed a pair of all whites and created this. With you in mind." He looked up, locking eyes with me. "I don't get to design as much as I'd like, but I've been inspired this summer."

My stomach flipped. "Any particular reason you've been so inspired?"

He licked his lips. "Yeah. One."

The heat crept up my neck and flushed my face.

"I'm glad you decided to wear black tonight," he continued before I could respond. "You're going to need these in a few minutes."

"For what—?"

"Here you are," the driver announced, slowing to a stop.

I looked around, at first only noticing the warehouse building and the minimal foot traffic. I saw about a dozen cars—including Russ's—and still no signage.

"Thank you, man," Russ said to the driver before jumping out of the car.

I'd put the shoe back into the box and returned the box to the bag by the time my door opened.

"I'm not getting out of this car until you tell me why you brought me to an abandoned warehouse," I stated, crossing my arms stubbornly. Turning to the driver, I leaned toward the front seat. "Are you in on this, Matt? Is he paying you to pretend you never saw me?"

The man's eyes bulged, and a panicky laugh escaped him. "What? No!"

"Sir, is this a setup?" I pointed to Russ with conviction. "Are you working with this man to abduct me? Why did he just pop his trunk?"

"Oh my God, Nina, stop fucking with Matt and let him leave." Russ ducked his head back into the car. "I'm going to increase your tip for having to deal with her bullshit." Russ extended his hand to me. "Let's go, Nina."

"Sorry, Matt," I giggled as I was pulled out of the car.

"Y'all are funny," he commented. "I hope you enjoy your anniversary, ma'am."

Surprised, my eyebrows shot up.

"Thank you," Russ called out, closing the door behind me.

"Our anniversary?" I questioned as the car drove away.

"He assumed I was doing all of this for our anniversary, so I just let him believe it." He shrugged, still holding my hand. "Let's get you into your new shoes."

I bit my lip as he led me the few steps to his car. "Oh, I need to wear these now?" I eyed him suspiciously, yet my smile grew. "What is going on?"

"You'll see soon enough."

"You lied to me. You lied to Matt." I shook my head. "Mm, mm, mm."

He opened the passenger-side door for me. "Matt assumed, and I let him believe what he wanted to believe. And now that I think about it, didn't we meet on a Sunday? It could be our anniversary." He helped me sit sideways in the car, my feet still on the ground.

"We did meet on a Sunday, at the beginning of June," I confirmed. "It's been two months. I'd have to pull out my calendar to know the exact date."

Crouching in front of me, he gently pulled my shoes off. "So, I didn't lie to Matt." He replaced my pumps with the sneakers he'd gotten me. "And you . . ." He looked up at me. "I've never lied to you." As he laced up and tied the sneakers, he continued. "I'm going to always keep it real with you."

"So does that mean you're going to tell me what we're doing here?"

He tossed the box with my heels inside them to the backseat. "Hell no."

"Wow."

He stood, helping me up along the way. Bringing his face close to mine, he whispered, "Enjoy the surprise."

"I always do."

"I got you the shoes for the date . . ." Licking his lips, he bypassed me and reached back into the car. Opening his glovebox, he pulled out a small velvet-covered box. "But when I was on my way from a meeting, I saw this and thought of you." Popping it open, he presented it to me.

I gasped at the white-gold bangle with the twisted hook clasp. "Russ. This is beautiful. Thank you."

"You like it?"

Ripping my eyes away from it, I stared up at him. "I love it."

"Good." He took the bracelet from the box and clasped it around my wrist. "Because it looks good on you."

"Yes, it does. And it goes with almost everything." Lacing my fingers with his, I gazed up at him. "You know what else looks good on me?"

"Everything."

Grinning, I let him lead me toward an entrance. "You better stop flirting with me."

His eyes danced and the excitement was teeming from his body. "Let's go." As we approached a door, he shook his head. "Oh, let me tip extra for the ride since you pulled that abduction stunt."

I laughed. "He knew I was joking. If he didn't, I would've immediately told him that I was a willing participant in anything having to do with you." I checked him out. "I'm ready and willing, you hear me? Ready . . . and willing."

He adjusted himself. "You better stop teasing me," he warned.

"Or what?"

I saw his eyes flash.

He opened the door to allow me to enter first, but he caught me by my waist before I could breeze by him. "Remember this moment," he whispered, sending a chill down my spine.

"Welcome to Sky High Tours!" a young woman greeted us, stealing my attention. "How can I help you?"

My skin was still heated from Russ's warning, and since my mind was consumed with nasty thoughts, it took me a second to realize we weren't in a random warehouse. We were in a hangar.

I gasped.

I wasn't completely sure what was going on, but I felt excited. I loved the beauty, the colors, the perfection of the sky. And my intuition was telling me I was going to see it up close.

"Yes, we have reservations for seven forty-five," Russ replied.

She checked the papers in her hand. "Mr. Long and Ms. Ford?"

"Yes."

"Follow me. I'll get you to Bruce."

Two women who looked like they'd just had the ride of their lives were speaking to a man dressed similarly to the employee in front of us. There was someone working in a small office to the side and a couple sitting on a leather couch outside of that office. And since the big sliding doors on the opposite side of the building were opened, I saw a helicopter parked in the distance.

". . . and the couple with the seven thirty reservation is getting briefed and will be taking off shortly," she continued. "You can have a seat on the couch they just vacated. Bruce will be with you shortly with your forms."

"I got them right here," an older man announced, coming up to us from the side, waving clipboards in the air. "I just need you to fill out these forms and then we can get you squared away." He looked me up and down before handing me my clipboard. "Have you read the rules and requirements?"

"I haven't yet, but I will," I assured him.

"I've read them and made sure we were in accordance before I paid for the experience," Russ said firmly.

His curt tone caught my attention. I glanced up at him.

"Very well. We may have to verify," the older gentleman stated before turning on his heels and scurrying away.

"Let's have a seat," Russ suggested, pointing to the leather couch. His tone was back to normal, but his expression was still perplexing.

"Are you okay?" I wondered as I took a seat.

"Yes, of course. How are you feeling? Are you surprised?"

"I'm so surprised. And I'm excited. How did you even come up with something like this?"

"I know how much you love the sky, so I've been planning this for a little while now."

My heart skipped a beat.

"This is . . ." I let my sentence trail off as I shook my head. "I had no idea what to expect, and you just continue to blow my mind."

He slipped his arm around my shoulder and leaned over to me. With his lips against my ear, he whispered, "I plan to do that repeatedly over the course of tonight."

My lower body clenched. Turning my head so our lips touched, I let out a soft whimper that I knew drove him crazy. "Promise?"

He cleared his throat and placed the clipboard in his lap to cover the growing bulge. "We need to sign these consent forms before they'll let us fly and then I'm taking you home."

I smirked. "What about dinner?"

"Fuck dinner."

Laughing, I focused my attention on the rules of the aircraft. Everything seemed pretty standard, and I signed the waiver.

"I'm going to run to the restroom before we take off," I told him after we gave our clipboards to the man who'd greeted us when we walked in.

"Yeah, I should probably do the same." He rose to his feet and then helped me to mine.

The restroom sign was not far from where we were. The men's room was first. Russ disappeared through the door. Around the corner, the women's room was waiting for me. It didn't take me very long, and after washing my hands and lathering on lotion, I exited. I'd barely gotten out the door when I was stopped by the older Sky High Tours employee.

"Hi, Ms. Ford. Just wanted to catch you while you were alone."

Instantly, I was uncomfortable. "Oh, really?" Continuing to walk until I was in the main part of the hangar, I waited until I could be seen by others before I turned to him. "What's up?"

"I've reached out to my supervisor. He should be getting back to me at any minute now. I just need to verify something—you wrote down that you weigh two hundred fifty pounds. Is that accurate, or would you like to use our scale located in the women's room?"

"I read the rules and regulations and I wrote down my height and weight. I don't understand what the issue is."

"Well, I know a lot of people round their weight down, so I just wanted to double-check. If you're two fifty, we shouldn't have an issue. It's still on the heavier side, but if you're well over that number, that's when we run into problems. We don't want to overload the aircraft. That's why I wanted to touch base with my supervisor to make sure you can fly with us."

My eyebrow quirked. "Why wouldn't I be able to fly?"

"What's going on here?" Russ asked, coming up beside us. He

put his hand on my lower back and assessed me. "Is everything okay?"

I cocked my head to the side. "This man was about to explain why I might not be able to fly today, even though I qualify."

Before Russ could say anything, the man tried to explain himself. "Our tours have a weight and size restriction due to the helicopter's design. My supervisor should be calling me back in the next couple of minutes to let me know if she can fly. I'm just verifying that the helicopter assigned to you is one that can accommodate her size."

I made a face. "No—"

"I spoke to your supervisor and made sure everything was good before booking this tour," Russ informed him in a low tone. "Maybe you should've waited on that call before coming over here and saying anything without all the information. Not knowing what you're doing and then not getting clarity first is a problem. And I don't like problems."

"I wasn't trying to make a problem," the man explained. "I was just—"

"Overstepping," Russ interjected.

"The aircraft can only accommodate passengers under two hundred seventy-five pounds. I just wanted to make sure she was in line with our guidelines."

"Did her form say she wasn't?"

"Well, no. B-but she looks—"

Russ stepped up. "I'd tread very lightly before finishing that sentence if I were you."

"She's beautiful." He turned to me. "You're beautiful. My wife is also a bit heavy. So I meant no disrespect. It's just that people lie about their weight, and it's my job to make sure the aircraft doesn't exceed the maximum weight of two hundred seventy-five pounds per person." His phone rang and he pointed to it. "It's my supervisor." He answered the phone, and I could see the defeated look on his face and the change in his tone. "Yes, sir. Okay. Yeah. Yes. Okay."

"Are you okay?" Russ asked me. "I'm sorry he's on some dumb shit."

I shook my head. "I'm fine. He just took me by surprise, that's all. I'm cool. I mean, he basically told me I was going to bring the helicopter down."

His eyes darkened. "He said that shit?"

"No, no." I fanned the thought away. "I was exaggerating. But he did come with that energy though."

"Well, first and foremost, that's some bullshit. Second, I would never put you in a situation that wasn't safe," he assured me.

"This is an amazing date idea. Even with his"—I gestured to the employee—"bullshit, I'm excited about this."

"Have you ever done this before?"

I shook my head. "Never." I reflected on why I hadn't ever done it and the weight restriction crossed my mind. "You called and told them how much I weighed?" I wondered.

"I read the guidelines, so I called and asked some questions. No big deal."

"But how did you know what I weighed?"

"I guessed. I know how it feels when I pick you up. I know how it feels when I pick up weights at the gym. I did some quick math." He shrugged. "I knew you weren't at the max, so I called and talked to the owner of the company."

"Oh, wow."

I was impressed.

Before I could say more, the employee cleared his throat. He refused to make eye contact as he beckoned to us. "You two are cleared. Let me introduce you to your pilot. Follow me."

"Let me get your name," Russ requested. "I want to make sure your supervisor knows the type of bullshit you're on."

Staring up at Russ, I'd never wanted him more.

After a brief introduction, the pilot launched into a safety overview of what to do and not to do. Once he answered our questions and felt confident that we understood the directions he had for us, we followed him to the helipad. I took everything in, and excitement ran through my entire body as we approached.

"You ready for this?" Russ asked me.

"Absolutely."

"Let's do it."

The noise-canceling headphones were slipped over my head, and then I was strapped into my seat, Russ next to me. We had a shoulder harness and a lap belt connecting us to the backseat. I tried to move around, and while the straps had enough give that I could lean to the left or right to see out of the windows, I was securely in my seat. It gave me peace of mind knowing that I wasn't going anywhere. The pilot got himself situated on the right side of the helicopter—right in front of me.

"Are you ready for the ride of your life?" the pilot asked, his voice sounding different in the headset.

"Yes," we said in unison.

"We're going to be traveling about one thousand feet above ground, so the views of the sunset over the city will be incredible. Get your phones out and take as many pictures as you'd like. You can talk to each other freely through the headset. Hit the red button to get my attention and I'll switch to your channel. Otherwise, I'll be back and forth between being on your channel and being on the channel with the control center. Neither of you are afraid of heights, correct?" He waited for us to confirm before he continued. "Because there's a mute button if you start screaming. The entire trip will take about fifteen minutes, but it'll feel like longer if this is your first time. Any questions before we begin?"

"No," we said in unison.

We looked at each other, and I felt like my cheeks hurt from smiling so hard. I gripped the seat belt straps and closed my eyes to say a quick prayer.

"You nervous?" Russ wondered.

The pilot started the engine, startling me. I gasped before answering his question. "A little."

"Just relax," he said softly. "I got you." Reaching over, he placed his long, thick fingers on my knee, just below my hemline. Gripping me reassuringly, he gave me a nod. "I got you."

My lips parted but words didn't come out immediately. The heat of his touch against my bare skin was disarming.

I wasn't scared of the flight. I was just startled by the powerful blades whirring overhead. Even with the protective headphones, the sheer force of the propellers was loud. But I wasn't about to remove his hand. I wasn't scared, but I definitely felt better with his hand on me.

The pilot started communicating with air control or the ground crew, and I could only concentrate on the way the pads of his fingers caressed the skin just inside of my knee.

"You got me?" I murmured, turning my body so that our knees touched. My slight movement forced his hand to move up slightly.

"Yes." He licked his thick lips slowly and his fingers were right below my hemline. "Just let me know how I can make you more comfortable. I want you to enjoy yourself."

The throbbing between my legs was so intense that I had to close my eyes. "Russ . . ."

"Yes?" He paused. "Nina, look at me."

I opened my eyes.

Toying with the hem of my dress, he held my gaze with a quiet intensity. The vibration throughout the helicopter only added to the feeling that washed over me.

"Tell me what you want," he demanded quietly.

I let out a couple of heavy breaths. "Russ . . ." I squeezed my legs together to try to alleviate the pressure.

"I told you I got you, and you know I mean it." His hand was trapped between my thighs. "So, talk to me, Nina. Tell me what you want."

"I want to see the stars." I opened my legs fractionally. As my legs spread, his fingertips grazed my inner thigh. "I mean, I'm looking forward to the sunset and the ride itself. But I really want to see the—oh!"

His fingers climbed up my thick thighs until he brushed against my lace panties. And even though he'd just barely touched me, my entire body felt a jolt.

His eyes bored into mine. "You want to see the stars?"

"Yes," I breathed. My dress rode higher as my knees fell farther apart. My whole body was on fire. "I do."

He dragged his finger across the damp area of the lace.

His eyes closed and his fingers stilled. "Well . . ." He opened his eyes and the lust in them caused me to get wetter. "We should be up here long enough to give you what you want."

"Prepare for takeoff," the pilot announced.

"I'm prepared." Russ slipped his fingers under the front my G-string. "I'm good and ready," he reported. "What about you, Nina? Are you good and ready?"

His fingers ran down my slit, rendering me speechless.

"Nina," he coaxed with the sexy way he said my name. "Are you good?"

"Yes." I managed to choke the words out as the pads of his fingers brushed the hood of my clit.

The helicopter jolted as it started lifting into the stunning sky.

"Oh my God," I cried as his fingers slid between my wet lips.

He exhaled roughly. "Yeah, here we go."

Adrenaline moved through my veins, and I was hot all over.

His finger slid up and down my slit. As he was teasing me, he started moving in a circular direction, stimulating my clit.

I grabbed his bicep and tried not to scream. "Russ," I moaned, a little louder than anticipated. "Look."

I had to pretend I was talking about the view.

My heart pounded with the fear of being caught and the excitement of getting off.

I hoped the pilot couldn't pick up on the neediness with which I said Russ's name. I didn't want us to get caught. I didn't want us to get arrested. I didn't want any trouble. But as he slid a finger inside of me, I cared about getting off more than any of that other stuff.

"Do you see that?" Russ asked huskily.

"Oh my God," I groaned. The fluttering I felt in my core intensified with each of his ministrations. "Yes."

"The lake looks good, doesn't it?"

"So good." My eyes closed, and each time he slid in and out of me, I felt jolts of pleasure. "So fucking good."

"All that water. I wish I could take a dip in it . . . feel it all over my face." Russ caught himself and cleared his throat.

"Dowdy Lake is . . ." The pilot spouted some facts about the lake, and I didn't hear one thing he said.

My hips moved as much as they could with the lap belt restraining me. Grinding against his fingers, I started chasing the high of the release Russ was building. I rocked into his hand as I stared into his eyes. The slight choppiness of the ascension only aided in getting me off. But when his thumb passed over my clit while his fingers were slowly pumping inside me, I gasped loudly.

The tension within my body centered itself right where he was touching.

"Oh my God," I panted.

"We haven't even really started the tour yet, and it's already an amazing view," the pilot remarked.

"It sure is," Russ agreed. "Absolutely beautiful." His eyes were fixated on me as the helicopter dipped. "You think so, too, Nina? You like it?"

"Yes, yes." I nodded, clenching around his fingers. "Russ!"

"Oh, I see it," he groaned, twisting his fingers and finding my G-spot.

I was breathless.

My arm flew around his neck, and I brought him as close as possible. Because of the shoulder harness, he wasn't able to get as close as I wanted him and still keep stroking me the way he was stroking me. So, our kiss didn't last long, but our lips met long enough to set me off.

"Shit!" I hissed, bucking against his hand. I forgot all about the mute button or the fact that the pilot could hear everything. "Russssssssssssss."

His thumb rubbed circles against my clit while his fingers remained inside me, skillfully teasing my spot internally. "The pilot knows what he's doing," he assured me as the helicopter tipped to the side as it turned. "Open your eyes and look at the view, baby. Open your eyes."

I opened them long enough for my body to surrender to him.

"That's it," he growled. "That's my girl. That's my girl."

My eyes rolled to the back of my head. Heat radiated from his touch, and I let out a muffled moan as my thighs began to quiver.

"Russ," I whimpered.

I'd reached the point of no return. His voice, combined with the way he skillfully played with my pussy, collided with the situation and the way he was looking at me. He was the match to my fuse, and it took restraint for me not to scream as the explosion erupted within me.

"That's it," he rasped as I spasmed against his hand. "You're doing so good. That's it."

Pleasure emanated from my core.

My body jerked, straining against the seat belt as my hips rose off the seat. For a few seconds, none of my other senses worked. All I could do was feel. My skin tingled, my heart raced, my nipples hurt, and my entire lower body felt weak.

Russ slid his fingers from within me, and when I opened my eyes, I found him smiling at me. "Now that we've reached flying altitude, do you feel better?"

"I feel so much better," I answered honestly, tugging my dress back down. I noticed the bulge in his pants and smirked. "I'll have to repay you for taking such good care of me."

He grabbed his thick bulge. "I look forward to it."

A shiver ran through me.

Glancing at the pilot and then back at Russ, I made a face. "I didn't expect the ride to feel like that, so I hope I wasn't too loud."

He reached over and kissed me again. "I think you held it together very well."

"I've had people up here screaming and crying," the pilot chimed in. "You sounded excited and nervous, maybe a little alarmed. A few outbursts calling for your boyfriend is nothing."

My eyes bulged as I stared at Russ. He looked like he was trying as hard as I was not to laugh.

"Okay, thank you," I finally replied.

Feeling warm and tingly, I relaxed into my seat and smiled at Russ. "And thank you," I whispered.

He licked his fingers and smirked. "No, thank *you*."

3

"It just bothers me that he's asking for prayers and privacy," I concluded as we finished our meals. "I'm sorry, no. I need details. I need facts. You can get my prayers, or you can keep your privacy. But I won't be reaching out to God about the release of your homeboy, who might actually be guilty."

"Yo!" Russ put his fist in front of his mouth to disguise his laughing fit. "What is wrong with you?"

"Nothing! But imagine God deciding between my prayer to be a millionaire and my prayer to release the guilty homeboy. And then when I circle back and ask God for a status update on the financial blessings, he tells me he already answered my prayer when the homeboy got released." I shook my head. "Nope. Not blocking my blessings for that."

Russ's laugh was one of my favorite sounds. It was deep, hearty, and musical. It had a soulfulness to it that always managed to make me feel good and full. We always had fun, so I heard it often when we were together. And somehow it never lost its potency. It always filled me.

"So, I hope that helps with the situation," I concluded.

"That didn't help at all, but I'll tell my brother to delete his social media post." He shook his head and took a big gulp of water. "You really are funny as hell, you know that?"

"I was being deadass serious, but thank you."

"That's what's so funny about it. These are just your honest thoughts. It's dope. It's . . . refreshing. I watch you when we're together and you are always you, and it never fails to make the people around you smile. I meet people all the time and their default is to pretend to be something they aren't and to lie about who they are. But with you, it's real and raw. That shit is sexy."

"My main takeaway from what you just said is that you think I'm the sexiest and realest person you've ever met."

Grinning, he nodded. "Oh, you already know that."

"Luckily for you, I feel the same way about you," I admitted. "You are honest . . . fearless . . . authentic. You have a strong sense of self. And you live in the moment. All of that is incredibly sexy. I mean, it doesn't hurt that you're fine as hell. But people don't know themselves, and I love spending time with a well-adjusted man who knows who he is."

"That might be the nicest thing you've ever said to me."

"I say nice stuff all the time!"

He lowered his voice and leaned forward. "I'm talking about when my dick isn't inside that tight pussy of yours."

"Valid."

We both laughed.

"Do you remember how I approached you the night we met?" he asked.

We'd met at a Richland Fashion Weekend party, and those events brought out all the fashionable people in the city. But there were a lot of men who showed up with no interest in fashion. They were just trolling for women. I'd just gotten hit on by one of those, when five minutes later, Russ showed up.

Licking my lips, I nodded. "You told me you started out screen printing before you joined the corporate world, and that you liked my shirt."

"Do you remember what happened next?"

"You asked me if I was a girl boss, so I asked you if you were a boy boss." I smiled at the memory. "Yeah, I remember."

"In my defense, you were standing next to the sign that said *girl boss,* so I put two and two together."

"You put two and two together and got five, because if you don't like being called a boy boss, why would I want to be called a girl boss?"

Smirking, he continued, "And then I asked you if I could take you out as an apology, and you told me it depended on what I had in mind."

"I was leaning toward yes because of your outfit. I liked your style," I confessed. "But inviting me to the Soul Festival was a unique choice. I liked that it was something different."

"I was already going by myself to get away from everything, and something about you made me want to get away with you. I watched the way you were with everyone you crossed paths with, and it made me want to know you. I was surprised when you said you were single."

"I wasn't sure if I believed you when you said you were."

He laughed. "Because you don't trust shit."

"You're not wrong! But look at us now. Two months later."

"Two months later, and you're the only person I want to spend my free time with." His stare lingered on me as he reminisced. "I'm glad you were down for that first date."

"Something about you always makes me ready to be down."

"You're a good time." He brought his glass to his lips and paused before taking a sip. "You make everything better."

My lips parted in a smile. "Likewise."

Grinning, he shook his head. "When was the last time you had a man?"

"I had a boyfriend in high school." I lifted my shoulders and scrunched my nose. "But as an adult, I just date. It's easier for everyone."

"What does that mean?"

I smiled. "My parents have this completely complementary relationship, and that's always been the standard for me. A perfect fit. But perfection is rare. It's a burden to put on someone who isn't. It's a burden to search for it. And since I don't want to burden anyone or myself, I just enjoy life and date."

A waiter cleared our plates away and informed us that our waitress would be there shortly.

"That was delicious," I commented. "I meant to take a picture of it when it came, but I forgot. I'll snap a photo of dessert."

"I like that you take a photo of everything we do."

"I take a photo to commemorate everything I do," I clarified. "I like to live in the moment, but I like to stop and take a picture of the highlights so I can have that tangible physical evidence to hold on to. I don't ever want to forget anything."

"Oh, I thought I was special and that's why you wanted a picture."

"No."

He laughed. "Ouch."

"I'm not saying you're not special. You are." The minute the words left my mouth, my heart stammered. Ignoring the reaction, I continued, "I'm just letting you know that I take pictures all the time."

"Well, you've influenced me to do the same." He pulled out his phone. "I've gotten a picture from every one of our dates. But this might be my new favorite picture of you," Russ told me as he showed me a photo on his phone.

I leaned over my empty plate to get a better look. It was of my profile and the orange, pink, and purple hues of the sunset behind me. "Oh, I like that! Will you send that to me?"

"Yeah." He clicked a few buttons. "Done."

"What was your favorite before this one?"

"The one of you when we went ice-skating." He chuckled, amused with himself. "It was the look on your face that made it my favorite. The fact that your camel toe was on display from that angle was a happy accident. I didn't plan it like that. It just happened."

I tried to keep a straight face as he laughed through his explanation. "You took the picture. You didn't crop the picture. And then you proceeded to call me Kristy Yamacoochie," I reminded him. "It didn't just happen. *You* just happened."

When our laughter subsided, he sat back in his chair.

"This is exactly what I needed," he pointed out.

"The laugh?" I guessed.

"All of it. The escape. With good food. With good company. A good time."

I tilted my head to the side, running his words over in my mind. "This is an escape?"

"*You* are my escape. You are my fantasy—"

"Can I get you two some dessert?" the waitress asked, interrupting

Russ. She smiled politely at me before turning her attention and obvious attraction to him.

"Yes," he answered quickly, shifting in his seat. "Crema catalana."

"Chocolate-and-tahini date bars, please," I requested.

"And I'd like an order of Greek cookies to go," he added.

She looked between us. "Anything else?"

"No, that's all. Thank you," he replied.

As soon as she left, he gestured to the restroom sign. "Excuse me a minute."

"If your dessert comes before you get back, I'm tasting yours," I warned him.

"No worries." With a smirk, he stood. Before passing me, he leaned down and put his lips on the shell of my ear. "I plan on tasting yours, too."

He walked away and I still felt his breath on my neck. I squeezed my knees together, his words stirring something inside me. Staring at my bracelet, I twisted the gorgeous piece of jewelry around my wrist.

I noticed there was a word engraved near the clasp.

Fantasy.

I got butterflies.

"Here's a refill," a different waitress said as she interrupted my thoughts. She poured water into our glasses. "Are you two celebrating something?"

"No, it's just a date," I replied.

"Oh! Really? Are things serious?"

"Why do you ask?"

Her face became flushed, and she shook her head. "Oh, um, no reason." She scurried away.

I watched as she seemed to report back to the waitress who'd been serving us.

Interesting.

It was clear our waitress had a thing for Russ the moment she approached our table. I went to the restroom earlier, and I came back to find her giggling and flipping her hair over her shoulder. When she saw me, she quickly exited. Every time she'd come to the table, she was nice enough to me, but she was gawking at him. I was debating whether or not I should be concerned about her doing something to my dessert when Russ returned.

"I decided to take your suggestion after last time and got a suite downtown," he told me.

"First the picture taking, and now the hotel suggestions. I'm glad you've finally recognized how resourceful I am."

"Oh, I'm *well aware* of your resourcefulness. I'm appreciative of it, too. After dessert, you want to get out of here?" he wondered. "I'd like to thoroughly show you my appreciation."

I wiggled my eyebrows. "Yes, please. I have a few ways I'd like to show my appreciation as well."

A smile tugged at his lips. "I like the sound of that."

"The amazing gifts. That helicopter ride. Your magic touch. This delicious dinner." I bit my lip. "I'm going to make sure you feel every ounce of my appreciation."

His eyes darkened. "Don't give me that look, Nina . . ."

"I love the sky and you found a way to give it to me." I tilted my head to the side. "And when we get back to the hotel, I'm going to give it to you."

His tongue ran from one side of his mouth to the other. "Nina," he warned quietly.

Our waitress came up with our desserts. "Here's something sweet for you," she said as she placed Russ's dessert in front of him. "And yours." She damn near threw mine in front of me. "Can I get you anything else?"

Her back was to me but when I saw her friend, the nosey waitress with the questions, what I'd suspected all along was confirmed.

This bitch is trying to poach my date!

Smirking, I shook my head. I didn't like it, but I respected the game.

It wasn't my style, but Russ didn't have a wedding ring on his finger, so he was technically a free man. Personally, I wouldn't approach a man while he appeared to be on a date. I'd wait until he was alone and then make my move. Or better yet, I'd slip a note in his to-go box.

I took a bite out of one of my date bars. *Amateur.*

"Can we get the check and my Greek cookies, please?" Russ requested.

"Right away," she answered.

"How are your date bars?" he asked, shifting his focus back to me.

The waitress took a second to get her feet in motion, but then she rushed away from the table.

"Pretty good. I didn't know what to expect but I like them." I licked my lips. "You want a taste?"

"I want more than a taste."

"And I'll give it to you." I slipped the dessert into his mouth. "I'll give you all of it."

"Mmm," he groaned as he grabbed my hand. Kissing my fingers as he chewed, he nodded. "That's the second-best thing I tasted tonight."

"What was the first?"

"Your juices while we were flying over the city. It was good from my fingers, but I'm ready to drink from the source."

"Here's your check," the waitress said, interrupting our back-and-forth. "And here's your to-go bag. Anything else?"

Russ tore his eyes from me and looked at the bill. "I'm going to need two boxes because we're taking these to go, too."

"Oh! Crema catalana is best when eaten immediately," she informed him.

He handed her one hundred and fifty dollars. "We have plans so we're going to take this to go."

"Oh, okay. I'll be right back," she said.

As soon as she was out of earshot, he pulled out his cell phone. "I'm going to call the hotel and have them deliver a bottle of wine to the room before we get there." He started dialing numbers. "Once we get up there and close the door, I don't want any interruptions."

"I like the way you think," I told him, popping the last piece of the date bar I'd started into my mouth.

"Hi, yes, I'm in suite 1151 and I'd like to order your best white wine to be delivered to my room . . ."

"Here's your boxes," the waitress said before realizing he was on the phone.

"I'll take that," I told her, taking them from her hand.

I put my dessert into one box, and then I tried to put his in the other box. He got off the phone and attempted to help me. It came out in pieces and completely lost its appeal.

I made a face. "Ummmm."

He shrugged. "It'll still taste good." He stacked the boxes into the bag and stood. "But I'm going to be honest." He slipped his jacket on. "I'm more interested in tasting you than anything in this bag."

"Then, let's go."

He grabbed the bag and then reached out to take my hand. Helping me to my feet, he checked me out. "Yeah, let's get you back to the room."

"I'm right behind you. I'm just going to check on something real quick."

"I'll wait for you."

"It's fine," I assured him. "Put the stuff in the car. I'll be right out. Give me two minutes."

He hesitated and I gave him a look.

"Please," I whispered, knowing how much he liked hearing me beg.

His breath shook as he exhaled. "If you're not out in two minutes, I'm coming back in."

"Deal."

He headed out and I searched for our waitress.

". . . I just don't understand it. She's like twice his size and he is fiiiiiiiiiiiiiiiiiine. Maybe she's giving him the rest of her tax money, or he's between homes. I mean, she's pretty for a fat girl, but there's no way he's really into her. It doesn't make any sense. She's too big for him. They don't fit," she complained as I walked up. Her complaint ended when the nosy waitress widened her eyes and gestured for her to stop talking.

"Not according to him," I chimed in, causing the waitress to turn. "Let him tell it, I'm the perfect fit for him."

"I wasn't talking about you," she said quickly, her face turning red.

"You were. But I came to give you a little advice. First and foremost, if you're going to try to step to a man while he's on a date, at least have the decency to wait until she's in the bathroom or at the bar."

Her eyes widened. "I didn't—"

"You did. But you didn't do a good job and you weren't smooth with it. Which brings me to my second point." I moved closer to her. "If you step to a man who is on a date, make sure he's not all about her. Because he is into every inch of me. And you may not understand why he likes all this"—I ran my hands over my belly for emphasis—"but just know, he likes it a lot."

"I'm sorry, I don't—"

"And third," I continued, interrupting whatever bullshit she was going to say, "don't step to a man who's on a date with a bitch like me. You're small, and I'm big. And I don't just mean in size. So, you can continue to talk shit but just remember that you can't compete where you don't compare."

A mixture of indignation and embarrassment twisted her features, and I knew my work was done.

"I wasn't going to take your man," she sputtered.

"The only thing you could take from me is notes."

Turning on my heel, I sauntered away with a huge smile on my face. Even though I wasn't jealous and would never fight over a man, I meant everything I said to the waitress. And if there was one man who was worth the confrontation, it was Russell Long.

He was The Fun One. He was the one I could live in the moment with. He was the one I related to the most. He was the one who seemed to understand me best. He was the one who matched my energy. And all of those reasons were exactly *why* he was the one who was so much fun.

As soon as I exited the restaurant, I saw Russ leaning against the trunk of the car, waiting for me. I would be lying if I said there wasn't something special about him.

"What's that smile about? What did you do?" Russ asked.

"I spoke to the waitress and gave her some pointers," I answered.

His brows furrowed and he eyed me suspiciously. "What do you mean?"

"I gave her pointers on how to shoot her shot."

He grabbed my hips and pulled me into him. "You know I wasn't checking for her."

"It wasn't about whether or not you were. It was the way she went about things. And then, when I heard her talking shit, we had to have a little chat about the disrespect."

"I can't tolerate disrespect." He shook his head. "I see red." He cocked his head to the side. "She didn't say or do anything to make you see red, did she? Do we need to leave the scene?"

I cackled. "No. It wasn't that deep. I could've let it go, but I didn't want to." I lifted my shoulders. "I might be fat, but I'll never be the bigger person."

His head fell back, and a loud, sexy, rumbling laugh burst out of him. "Yooooooooooooo!" He bent down and pressed his lips against mine. "I fuck with you hard."

"I know. And I look forward to you fucking with me hard in twenty minutes."

"You look at me like that again and I'll take you in the backseat."

"Nah, after the way you teased me on that helicopter, I need you to stretch me out and take care of me."

His hands slid over my ass before he smacked it. "Then let's get you to the hotel so I can do exactly that."

We kissed and I felt it throughout my entire body. I was so ready for the night we were going to have. When he pulled away and looked at me, I felt that shit everywhere.

He opened my car door for me and ushered me in.

"I'm going to tease you, and then I'm going to fuck the shit out of you," he said before closing my door.

For the second time that night, my panties were soaked.

The trip to downtown was normally twenty minutes, but we got there in twelve. I didn't remember speeding. I just kept thinking about him spreading me out and getting me off.

I dropped my car off with the valet and then met Russ on the sidewalk.

"When they finish building my place, I'm going to miss valet parking and room . . ." His sentence trailed off and his brows furrowed. "Where's your overnight bag?"

"I'm going to have to leave in the wee hours of the morning," I told him. "I have to be at work early tomorrow."

He slipped his arm around my shoulders and walked me to the elevator. "I wish you were off so we could maximize the time in the suite."

"Maybe you should take off and not go to Canada on Tuesday and we can."

"I wish I could."

"Well, since I have plans, we will make the most of the time we have now."

"Oh, I plan to make . . ." He kissed the top of my head instead of finishing the sentence as we entered the crowded elevator.

With a smile, I turned my body into him, and we rode to the eleventh floor with our arms around each other. As the amount of people dwindled, Russ's hand shifted from my shoulder to my back to the top of my ass. When the door opened on the top floor, his big hand gripped my ass, and we were the last to exit.

"After you," Russ said, gesturing for me to go in front of him.

I walked out and it didn't take long for him to pull up behind me. Gripping my hips, he pulled my ass into him, forcing me to feel his erection. The tension in my belly spread to the apex of my thighs. By the time we got to the room, we were damn near grinding on each other.

Reaching around me to swipe his keycard, he pushed the door open, letting it slam against the wall. The moment we crossed the threshold, he grabbed my face and crashed his lips into mine. He kissed me hard, yet soft at the same time. It happened so fast that at first, I wasn't sure if we were still moving or not. But my body was fully aware of what was going on and reacted on instinct.

Grabbing ahold of his jacket, I pulled his body flush with mine. That small move propelled us backward and my back hit a wall. The kiss deepened and his mouth overtook mine with a gentle force that consumed me.

"Russ," I moaned as he parted my lips with his tongue.

I wrapped my arms around him and allowed myself the pleasure of indulging in him, in his touch, in his kiss. Endorphins flooded my system, and the knot in my belly unraveled. His hard dick pressed against me, letting me know that he wanted me just as bad as I wanted him. I ran my hands up his chest and then pushed his jacket off him.

I was tired of being teased.

I was ready to be taken care of.

He broke the kiss abruptly and took a step back. "Do you know how many times I've thought about fucking you since the last time we were together?" he asked as he unbuttoned his shirt.

"Every day?" I guessed.

"Every. Fucking. Day." He pulled his shirt off and then started removing his belt.

My body clenched at his words. "Good."

"Do you know how bad I want you?"

"I think so."

He smirked. "You think so? You *think* so?" Licking his lips, he took another step back. "Strip," he demanded.

I didn't waste any time. Holding his gaze, I peeled off the black dress until I was standing in just my matching black bra-and-panty set.

"Take it all off." He pointed to my feet. "Except your shoes. And then slowly go to the bed."

I released my heavy breasts from the push-up bra that held them high. He broke our stare to watch them drop. And then his eyes followed my every movement as I removed my G-string. Stepping out of the damp fabric, I held on to the wall to brace myself.

Feeling sexy in just jewelry and heels, I did a little pose for him before I walked across the sitting room area to the bedroom. Swaying my hips, I made a show of moving my naked body for him.

"You know how much I love your ass, don't you?" he growled from behind me.

He was closer than I thought, and that sent a chill down my spine. I didn't look back until I made it to the bed.

"Stop right there," he commanded roughly.

I stopped, keeping my ass facing him as I looked over my shoulder. "Why?"

He was taking off the rest of his clothes and when our eyes locked, he licked his lips. "Since you won't stay all night with me, I have to take it all in and commit every inch of you to memory."

My eyes dipped.

Good God.

I exhaled audibly when I saw his muscled body and the tattoo that ran down the right side of his neck, shoulder, arm, and torso. And as sexy as his physique was, the nine and a half thick, veiny inches that hung hard and heavy between his legs had my attention.

He ran his hand over it as he watched me watching him.

"Russ . . ." I breathed his name, turning all the way around to face him.

"You want this dick, Nina?"

I forced my eyes up to meet his and nodded. I wanted to speak, but the way he looked at me temporarily rendered me speechless. His eyes dropped to my lips and then my breasts, and when I saw the hungry look in them, I was on fire all over again.

His chest rose and fell faster as we watched each other. He was the first to break our trance, slowly moving across the room until his body was flush with mine. My breathing was ragged as I gazed up at him, wishing, waiting, wanting.

With no more words exchanged, he crashed his lips against mine, kissing me with enough passion to take my breath away. Butterflies spread across my belly. I knew that I craved him, but with that kiss, I couldn't deny the connection we had. My body buckled as I gave in to every emotion I felt. I melted into him and his kiss.

When he pulled away, he sat down on the bed and looked up at me. "I want you to come on my tongue." He licked his lips and scanned my body with a heated gaze. "And then I want you to come on my dick." He put his hand on my hip and situated me in front of him. "Can you handle that?"

My stomach flipped as I looked at his thick dick protruding from his body. Breathing heavily, I nodded. "Yes."

Slowly, he lay back, never taking his eyes off me. "Then come sit on my face."

He didn't have to ask me again.

I bit my lip as I climbed onto the bed and straddled his handsome face.

"Don't tease me, baby. Sit," he growled. "Let me taste this pretty pussy."

The moment I got my legs comfortably under me, he wrapped his arms around my thick thighs and pulled me solidly onto his mouth. His nose nuzzled against my clit as he adjusted me.

"Mmmm," he groaned before his tongue ran up and down my slit.

I gasped.

Grabbing my breasts, I tweaked my nipples as I gave in to the sensation he was causing within me.

"Yessssssssssssssssssss," I hissed as he flattened his tongue when I started grinding against him. "Russ, that feels so good."

He sucked and flicked as I rode his face. His skilled mouth found my most sensitive spot and I felt the orgasm building. I couldn't make out what he was saying, but the sounds that came out of him drove me closer to the edge.

"Russsssssssssssssssss," I moaned his name wantonly. "Please don't stop."

His fingers dug into the fleshiness of my thighs as my body started giving in to the attention he was giving my clit.

"Oh shit!" I cried out as I came hard.

My body quivered with pleasure as I writhed above him, until I tipped forward and collapsed on a pile of pillows.

"You taste so fucking good," he said breathlessly.

I was in a heap, and my skin hummed with the second orgasm of the night. As he got up to grab a condom, my body shuddered with satisfaction and anticipation for more. Watching him roll the latex over his thick dick, I stretched my legs out as I slowly regained the ability to move.

The bed dipped as he crawled over to me. Situating himself between my legs, he caged me with his arms. He hovered above me, his muscles flexing under his weight as he balanced himself.

"How are you this beautiful and this sexy at the same time?" he asked me quietly, pushing my legs open wider.

I caressed his shoulders and up his neck. When my hands moved to his face, I pulled him closer until our lips touched. "Magic," I breathed.

The kiss was sensual and soaked in desire, with my juices coating his beard. I could taste myself on his tongue and that reminded me of the pleasure he'd just caused me. His touch, his kiss, his scent sent chills from my head to my toes and incited the fire between my thighs. The pull deep in my belly caused me to clench tightly and throb with anticipation.

"Oh, you're definitely magic . . ." His voice broke sexily as he moved his body forward. "You kept me thinking about being inside you every day since I last saw you . . ." He rubbed his dick against my wetness. "And not just because it feels so good sliding into you . . ." He rubbed himself against my clit. "And not just because this pussy is so wet . . . and tight . . . and fucking perfect . . ." He held my hips to keep me still and lined himself up at my opening. "With you, everything else disappears." He let my wetness suck the head of him in and we moaned in unison. "And that's what makes you fucking magic."

"Ohmigod," I moaned.

I knew it wasn't going to take much to get me off. I was already primed for it and when I looked in his eyes, I shuddered.

What he said was sexy as hell. But combined with his thickness spearing into me, my mind and body were in sensory overload. Hearing his voice break from lust, smelling his cologne on his skin, feeling his body weight on mine, tasting the sweetness of his kiss, and watching the pleasure on his face as he filled me inch by inch was everything.

"Russ," I whimpered, already on the brink of another orgasm. I dug my fingers into his shoulders as I felt him adjusting to the tight fit. "Russssssssssss."

He was buried inside of me, but he didn't move. "Fuck," he swore. "This fucking pussy is perfect."

Moving his hips slowly, he pulled almost all the way out of me. A rumbling noise erupted from the back of his throat.

"Please," I begged, needing more. I ran my hands up his arms and tried to pull him to me. "Please fuck me."

"Fuck . . ." The word was almost a whisper as he slowly eased back into me.

Stretching me out deliciously, he groaned from somewhere in the depths of him. The sexiness of that sound and knowing I caused him to make it made my heart and my pussy flutter.

"You okay?" he asked as he pulled almost all the way out of me again.

"Yes," I answered softly, trying to focus on my breathing.

"I don't want to hurt you."

"You're not," I assured him breathlessly. "Please. I need it. I need you."

"Say it again."

"Please," I begged. "Pleeeeeeeeeease."

"All of it. Say all of it . . . Tell me you need this dick."

"Please fuck me"—he grabbed my ankles—"Please. Pleeeee-ase"—he pushed my legs open wider—"I need this dick. I need your dick inside me"—he watched himself move in and out of me—"Russ, please"—he rotated his hips, giving me a firm thrust—"oh shit!"

I gasped, clenching around him.

His eyes flew up to meet mine. "You okay?"

I nodded. "Oh yeah," I groaned.

"Good," he growled as he dragged his fingers down my legs.

His fingertips danced across the fleshiness of my belly until he reached my breasts. I relished in the feeling of him playing with my nipples. So much so that it caught me off guard when he started driving his dick into me.

He used my wetness to glide in and out with a steady rhythm. With each stroke, I got louder and more responsive. Holding on to his biceps, I rocked my hips to meet him. The more my body reacted, the rougher his breathing became.

"I love watching you bounce on my dick. You're so soft. And so wet. And so tight." His low, restrained voice caused my stomach to flutter and my heart to race.

"You're going to make me come," I told him.

"That's all I want." He grabbed my hips and pulled almost all the way out again. "All I want is to feel you get yours on my dick the way you did on my tongue."

"I want that, too! I want it all."

"This pussy feels like mine. Is it mine?"

"Ohmigod yessssssssss!"

"Fuck . . ."

Before I could formulate a response, he slid into me in one swift stroke. He hit something deep inside that caused pleasure to ripple through my entire body.

"Oh shit," I panted as he started fucking me with the perfect combination of methodical strokes and reckless abandon.

Leaning down to cover my body with his, he kissed me passionately. Our lips were needy and insistent as we moaned into each other's mouths. I could feel his accelerated heart rate as it pounded against his chest. I could feel the rapid bursts of air from his ragged breathing. I could feel his dick seeming to grow even larger while inside me.

Breaking the kiss, he put his lips to my ear. "That's it . . . that's my girl. I feel it. I feel you, baby."

Grinding into me, he hit a spot so deep that it triggered me to clench tighter.

"Russssssssssss."

"Yeah, say my name like that as you take this dick. Make that pussy talk to me. Give it to me," he demanded hotly.

My body's reaction to his commands caused him to groan loudly. "If it's mine, give it to me, Nina. If it's mine, come all over this dick for me."

My orgasm was already at the brink, but hearing his words and feeling him struggling to hold back pushed me over the edge.

Incoherent words rolled off my tongue as he slammed himself into me repeatedly. I didn't know how he knew my body so well, but he did. He strummed my clit with one hand and pinched my nipple with the other.

"Fuck," he uttered, closing his eyes for a second. His voice was low and thick with want. "That's it, Nina. Give it to me."

And I did.

My eyes shut tight, and I climaxed hard. Clamping down around his dick, my entire body quaked from the sheer force of my pleasure.

He grunted, fucking me through my orgasm.

Just grunts and moans poured out of us as he continued taking care of my needs while succumbing to his own. Feeling him lose control pushed me over the edge again.

A silent scream left my mouth as my toes curled and my back arched violently. I had no control over my pulsating body. The intensity of my orgasm incited his as he bucked against me, cursing under his breath. He stiffened and shuddered as he came just as hard as I did.

My heart was pounding in my chest and both of us panted, completely devoid of energy and juices. He collapsed beside me in bed and after a couple of minutes, our breathing had slowed. He reached over and squeezed my breasts. Then his fingers danced across me, making circles around my belly. After tracing his way over every roll and crevice of my body, he wrapped his arm around me and pulled me close, my back to his front.

"It's getting to the point where I can't stop thinking about you," he whispered.

"That's interesting because I find myself thinking about you a ridiculous amount as well," I murmured.

We were both quiet until he spoke again. "I don't just mean the sex."

Swallowing hard, I scooted my ass back into him. "Me either."

He kissed the back of my neck.

That exchange blanketed us in the quiet stillness of the night. His fingertips caressed my skin, writing a message in cursive I couldn't decipher. His lips moved with silent words across my flesh that I couldn't hear. And in response, I pushed the intrusive thoughts out of my mind.

My heart thumped loudly in my chest.

Post-sex thoughts and feelings couldn't be trusted when dealing with the likes of Russ. His touch, his tongue, and his dick were hypnotizing, and I was under his spell. I felt things I'd never felt with anyone before, and it was thrilling and scary all at the same time.

His lips trailed kisses along my shoulder. "You sure you can't stay the night?"

"I mean, you made a really convincing argument as to why I should stay," I murmured.

"Is there anything I can do to make you to stay?"

Smiling into the pillow, I closed my eyes. "Russ . . ."

He kissed my neck, nuzzling his nose into my skin. "It was just a question."

Sucking my earlobe, he held me tighter.

"I'm not staying the night," I told him, even though I didn't make any attempt to get out of the bed. "I'm getting up in a few minutes."

4

"Well, well, well!" Charlotte Webb yelled out as soon as I rushed into her boutique on Tuesday morning.

"So sorry," I apologized as I locked the door behind me.

"Inventory Day is an important day each month." She shook her head, her shoulder-length locs swaying from side to side. She finished cutting open the huge box in front of her and then pushed her oversized glasses up the bridge of her nose. "And you're late."

"I know. I'm sorry."

Charlotte and I met three years ago at a party during fashion week. We had a similar eye and found ourselves voicing a like-minded opinion in a group discussion. That discussion turned into further conversation, and before I knew it, she was asking me if I was interested in modeling some of her merchandise.

She was looking to grow her brand and wanted to partner with a model. I was looking for an opportunity to model and dive full force into the fashion world. We developed a great working relationship and friendship that only grew as the time went by. My social media presence blew up, and because I was wearing her pieces, her online boutique, Charlotte's Webb, blew up, too. I never wore the same thing twice and I paid very little for the items I actually wanted to keep. So a year ago, when she was just about to make the transition from an online boutique to a storefront in Richland, she asked if I wanted to work part-time—twice a month—in exchange for clothes.

Of course, I said yes.

So even though I only needed to come in for a five-hour shift to help with inventory today, I was almost an hour late.

"I overslept," I explained, joining her at the opened box.

"You've never been late before." She paused, cocking her head to the side. "Who was it?"

My eyes widened. "What do you mean?"

"I know you had a date, and then you come in late, with your skin glowing." She pursed her lips. "Which one was it?"

Snickering, I grabbed a skirt out of the box. "The Fun One."

"The Fun One," she repeated as if that were his name. "And what exciting adventure did The Fun One take you on?"

"We went on a helicopter ride to see the sunset, and then we went to dinner."

She dropped the shirt she'd just unpacked. "What?"

I nodded. "Surprise helicopter ride, dinner at this nice-ass restaurant, and then we went to his hotel downtown for dessert." My smile grew. "It was a nice night."

She wiggled her eyebrows. "I see. Such a good night that it made you late."

I laughed. "I overslept. My intention was to go home after . . . dessert. But that man put me to sleep."

"No wonder he's your favorite."

"You know I don't play favorites."

"You had back-to-back dates, right? The Smart One on Sunday and The Fun One on Monday."

I grabbed the last skirt out of the box and put it on a hanger. "I did."

"And you're not sleeping with The Smart One, correct?"

"Correct."

"So The Fun One is the only one you're sleeping with?"

Just the thought of it created a flashback and caused me to clench. "Yes."

"Your answer plus that look on your face tells me everything that I need to know." She pointed a hanger at me. "The Fun One is your favorite. I rest my case."

I burst out laughing. "In my defense, he's kind of hard to compete with. It isn't a fair competition." Pausing, I put my hand on my hip. "You know . . . it's really because I have a big heart. I don't want to set the rest of the team up for failure. It wouldn't be right."

"Oh my God, Nina! I can't with you!"

Charlotte always acted appalled by my dating life, but she hung on to every word and lived for my updates. I always assumed part of it was because she had been with her boyfriend for so long and she missed the excitement of dating. She never outright said it, but she was living vicariously through me, and I didn't want to disappoint.

We spent the next four hours talking as we opened boxes, scanned in merchandise, and rearranged the floor display. Finally, I put my boxcutter in the drawer and took a last swig of water.

"And with that, my job is done," I said, tossing the empty bottle in the trash. I swept my eyes over the replenished shelves and racks, the updated outfits on the mannequins, and the new signage posted around the store. "It's ten o'clock, and even with me being a little late, we're done on time. We did a good job. The store looks incredible!"

"Yeah, we did. And it does." She put her hands on her hips. "This look that you put together in the window—perfection!"

"You did the shopping. I just worked with the materials you gave me," I complimented her back.

She gestured to the stack of clothing on the counter. "And you racked up."

"I sure did." I glanced at the five items that I'd gotten for my services. "So, the hard work put in was well worth it."

"Good! Now I'm going to treat myself to something small before opening. Will and I are going to lunch at noon."

"Oop!" I made a face. "Okay, afternoon delight!"

She laughed. "No, it's just lunch!"

I grabbed the clothes from the counter and gave her a look. "And here you were judging me about my activities last night while you were planning your own midday activities."

Flushed, she sucked her teeth. "Anyway, what are you doing today?"

Snickering, I answered, "I'm making content for the rest of the day. Not as exciting as a midday sex session, but it'll be fine."

Squealing, she opened the door for us to leave. "Stop it!"

"I'll see you soon," I said in a singsong voice. "Have a good morning. I already know the afternoon is going to be a good one."

"Nina!" she protested, amusement raising the pitch of her voice.

Waving my hand, I said goodbye.

I had a lot to do that day, so I picked up breakfast on the way home. I was running on adrenaline and vibes with only three hours of sleep. My night of fun had really taken a lot out of me. But I was going to rally. I had content to create and money to make.

I entered my two-bedroom loft-inspired space and immediately exhaled. For the last two years, I'd called the converted warehouse home. From the polished gray concrete floors to the brick accent wall, I was impressed by how cool the place looked. But it was the spaciousness that sold me.

Every time I walked in, I couldn't help but smile. The sleek appliances and open floor plan made it modern and luxurious. The abstract artwork, the unique shelves, and the high-end furniture replicas showcased my style and my creativity. It was tastefully colorful, with vibrant throw pillows on a white couch and effervescent art that leapt from the walls, and the sweet smell of lilac lingered in every room.

It was so me.

Although at least once a week, I questioned why I was so committed to the white couch.

My home was my sanctuary and filled me with peace. And since I believed that people carried energy with them, I rarely allowed new people over. My family and close friends were the only people I invited into my space.

Walking through the living room to the back of the apartment, I went to the first door.

"Welcome to your new home," I murmured to the clothing slung across my arm.

The second bedroom was meant to be a guest room, but since I didn't have many guests, I converted it into a closet. The extra-large arch mirror, custom-built vanity lights, personalized shelves, and the extended rack made the room the closet of my dreams. It was color coded, labeled, and organized. Once I put the clothes in their proper place, I headed to the en suite bathroom.

I'd taken a shower at the hotel after the first round with Russ. I had every intention of leaving after I got myself together. But that man decided to join me in the shower and fuck me again.

With a smile pulling at my lips, I shook my head at the memory.

As I lathered myself up, I couldn't help but have flashbacks. It was always like that after a night with Russ. It was hard to shake how completely he handled my body. We started sleeping together after the second date, and my body had been calling for that man ever since.

We'd seen each other weekly since we'd met. Sometimes our schedules didn't align, and we'd only get a night together. Most of the time, we'd get a whole twenty-four hours. Twice, we got the entire weekend. But every single day we'd either talk or text. Our relationship was fun and free, so the sex seemed better because of it.

But then last night . . .

"Mm, mm, mm," I intoned under my breath.

He'd always fucked me like he had gotten his degree in my pleasure and graduated summa cum laude. But last night was different.

Maybe it was because I was still heady from watching the sunset from that altitude. Maybe it was because I was feeling territorial because of the waitress's disrespect. Maybe it was the realization of how well he knew me, how closely he paid attention to me, and how well he took care of me. It truly could've been any of those things that resulted in the best sex I'd ever had.

I ran the washcloth between my legs again, cleaning myself and reminiscing at the same time. I was tender from the work that was put in all night long. I shivered as I let the water run over me and wash off the suds. My stomach tightened as I remembered the feel of him on me.

Now that *is some good dick.*

The only issue with getting dick like that was it made it harder to want someone else.

Tyrell and Dru didn't stand a chance at getting anywhere with me while Russ was a contender. James and I were having sex up until Russ and I had sex, and then I never looked back. I would've needed at least a few days to shake Russ off before I could even consider sex with someone else. But since he raised the bar with each encounter, it didn't make sense to get dick from anywhere else. He wasn't my man, so I could if I wanted to. He just fucked me so good that I didn't.

I turned the water off and wrapped myself in a terrycloth towel. Shifting my focus from men, I went over my schedule for the day. I was hoping I could factor in a nap, but I didn't see how it would be possible.

I'll sleep tonight. I have work to do.

Being a content creator, fashion influencer, and social media model was a time-consuming task. I was naturally stylish and got a great eye from my mom, but it was work to create looks. Brands I partnered with would send me clothes, and I had to style them in a way that felt true to me. I put together combinations from the miscellaneous items they sent. I had five brands I currently worked with, and my deals kept me creating content regularly. Every Monday I filmed the bulk of my content for the week. But because of my date with Russ, I still had work to do on Tuesday. So, I pulled out the remaining outfits I'd planned to feature for this week.

People started following my social media pages because I didn't just showcase my style—I showcased my personality. I put together outfit combinations people wouldn't have necessarily thought of. I found pieces that were budget friendly and paired them with luxury items. I recreated outfits at different price points. I got to set trends, feature some of my favorites, and make money doing it. My content worked for the people who followed me. But more importantly, it worked for me.

And as much as I loved my business account, it only featured my professional life. Outside of the stories I told, there wasn't any photographic evidence of my real life.

I had my personal account for that.

I still posted cute outfits on my personal account but mostly while I was doing cool things around the city, traveling the world, and attending fun events. It was a perfectly curated glimpse of my life.

I'll get a few shots in this tonight, I thought as I considered wearing the dress I just got from Charlotte's shop.

Looking at my calendar, I realized it was the last week of content I needed to do for the Good Good brand, so I shot their content first. The dresses were cute, tight, and very much club attire. I did several get-ready-with-me videos and then a mini-photoshoot with each dress. I went to the next designer and repeated the process.

Taking a break from content creation, I spent time focusing on engagement. Liking, commenting, and responding to my followers had helped my audience grow, but it also reminded me why I loved what I did.

> *I've never seen someone with my body type wearing that. I didn't think I could pull it off until I saw it on you.*
>
> *I love how you don't let fashion rules of the past drive your style. Watching your videos has really changed my mind about how I dress and why I dress the way that I do.*
>
> *I've spent my life covering my body and never felt empowered to show skin until I started following you.*
>
> *I've spent most of my life choosing styles that I didn't really like because that's all companies seemed to make. But lately, with some brands expanding their options for fat girls like me, it makes me happy to watch you and curate my new style as a thirty-four-year-old woman.*
>
> *I love you so much! You have changed my life and helped me find my style.*

I smiled.

Those kept me going and made me realize the importance of what I do. Unfortunately, they weren't the only comments.

For every ten comments and messages I received thanking me, I'd get two fake positive ones about my content.

> *You're so confident to wear that! I wish I had your confidence.*
>
> *You're pretty now, but if you lost a few pounds, I bet you'd be gorgeous.*
>
> *You're pretty for a fat girl.*
>
> *You're pretty for a Black girl.*

I didn't know they made that in your size. It doesn't look bad!
Go Nina!

For every ten positive comments and messages about what I do,
I'd get three negative ones.

You're promoting an unhealthy lifestyle.
Why do you think it's okay to be a fat, disgusting pig?
Fat whores shouldn't be showing so much skin! Cover up you
big back bitch!
Lose weight! You're going to drop dead any minute from a heart
attack. Instead of going on dates, you should be going to the gym.
I'm not saying this to be mean, but it's not healthy to weigh as
much as you do. I'm a personal trainer who has helped thousands
of people lose weight. I helped them and I can help you. Check your
DMs.

When I first started monetizing my accounts on social media,
the negative comments got to me. Not because it affected how I felt
about myself, but because I thought the brands I wanted to work
with wouldn't want to partner with me if I was receiving so much
hate. Also, because I hated to think that women who looked like
me would read those comments and internalize them. I wanted to
create a safe space.

I soon realized that the harassment I received online didn't impact my relationships with brands who wanted to work with me
because I wasn't alone. Almost everyone received hate. But because I happened to be a fat, Black woman, the messages tended
to be particularly vile. Racist, sexist, fat-shaming attacks about me
and my body would weave their way through a sea of positive comments.

I'd been threatened with physical and sexual violence. I'd been
called out my name. I'd been ridiculed and mocked. My content featured my style and a story about what I wore, why I chose to wear it,
and where I was wearing it to. Most people seemed to like my stories and my style. But there were plenty of no-profile-picture-having

users who would spew such hatred my way. And my only crime was existing.

It was a hard job to put yourself out there to be scrutinized, disrespected, and judged by faceless strangers on the internet. But I'd been dealing with bullshit like that my entire life. I'd always been pretty. I'd always been chunky. I'd always had haters. And even though I grew up knowing I was a bad bitch, I was still human.

My coping mechanism had always been to do what I love and experience joy. From going to the mall or Magic World as a kid, to finding unique articles of clothing or getting my back blown out as an adult, I coped with the negativity by doing what I loved.

I had thick skin and high self-esteem, so the nonsense people would spew didn't change how I felt about me. I stood up for myself. I advocated for myself. I loved myself. In turn, I lived my life the way I deserved to, and I dressed the way I wanted to. And I just wanted to be an example to other people, especially women who looked like me, to live happily in their bodies. When I realized how many people didn't feel confident about themselves because they were fat, I made it my mission to be that representation so they could see it.

And I wasn't going to let haters stop me.

I was genuinely loved and respected by my friends and family. I was admired by plenty of strangers. I was adored by plenty of men. But my confidence and self-worth came from within. My realness, my authenticity, and my zest for life created a safe space for me. My home was a place of peace—and very few people were allowed in. My dating relationships were a place of peace—and everyone played their individual roles. My work was a place of peace—and those who violated it were blocked.

After deleting some of the bullshit in my comments section, I checked my email.

"Holy shit!" I whispered excitedly before reading it again.

Calling Aaliyah, I let it ring three times before I hung up and immediately called Jazmyn.

"Hello?" she answered.

"Hey, Jazz, how are you?" I asked.

Jazmyn's aunt was sick, and things weren't looking good. What started out as a quick trip home for a weeklong visit turned into a summer-long extended vacation. I hadn't seen her since the beginning of June, and I wasn't going to see her again until Aaliyah's birthday party at the end of the month. With each passing week, her voice and conversation indicated that she was making peace with what was going on.

"I'm okay," she replied. "How are you?"

"Just okay?"

"Yeah . . . I'll tell you more later."

I curled my feet under me on the couch. "Talk to me. What's going on?"

"Later," she reiterated. "What's going on with you? I know you called for a reason. I can hear it in your voice." She gasped. "Do you have a date tonight?" She lowered her voice. "Is there a fifth contender?"

"No!" I snickered. "I've learned that four is my sweet spot."

"From the messages in the group text, it sounds like that might be changing."

"What do you mean?"

"The Fun One getting a lot more playing time than anyone else on the roster."

"He's the star player, but it's a team effort."

She laughed and the sound truly made my heart swell. Phone conversations had been mostly short and morose all summer. We primarily conversed via text message. I hadn't been privy to her laughter or her joy on full display for weeks. So to hear her laugh reassured me that she would be okay.

"Well, if it isn't that, what's going on?" she prodded. "I know it's something good—I can feel it."

I grinned. "I was calling to tell you about the email I just got."

"I'm intrigued. Tell me more."

"So, you know the influencer meetup that's happening this weekend in New York?"

"Yes. It's like a conference, right?"

"Yeah, something like that. It's more focused on networking

and photo ops, but there will be a couple of speakers during our brunch on Saturday. But here's what I called to tell you. Bree organized the speakers and the brunch. She just sent an email and confirmed that we're now having a cocktail dinner, and reps from different companies are coming, including social media managers from fashion houses all over the country . . ."

As I read the names from the list Bree sent, Jazz's excitement grew and flamed mine.

"Wait, wait, wait, wait, wait," Jazz demanded enthusiastically. "Are you able to pitch yourself to these people?"

"Yeah, that's what I'm gathering from the email."

"You're so good in situations like that! This is going to be life-changing for you, Nina!"

"I think so, too," I agreed, letting my head fall back on the cushion.

"I'm so proud of you! You're chasing your dreams and making your way through the world on your own terms. I love that for you."

"Thank you." I paused. "I miss you, girl!"

"I miss you, too. And I'm—oh, wait, someone's at the door. I think it's the doctor. But we need to talk before you fly out. I want to know everything."

"I'll give you a call tomorrow so we can discuss that *and* so you can tell me what you have going on," I told her.

We said our goodbyes and then disconnected the call.

5

"I'm about to put it on!" I greeted the camera with my signature opening. "Get ready with me, I'm heading to the airport. The thing about traveling is that you must combine comfort with style. You never know who you might run into." I pursed my lips. "Believe me. Six or so years ago, after some late-night fun, my—ahem—*friend* and I popped into the store on the way home and ran into my supervisor at the time." I leaned into the camera. "And how was she gonna judge me if she was out at four o'clock in the morning, too? Who and what I did off the clock was none of her business."

I grabbed my purple jumpsuit with the belted waist.

"This is a Bowen original. I love the way this color complements my skin," I continued, holding it in front of the camera. "And it is so comfortable. I love the way this spandex blend stretches over my curves but still offers support. The last time I wore this, I was approached by a man on his way to Tokyo for business and complimented by a mom wrangling two young kids fresh off a cross-country flight." I shook the garment off the rack. "This 'fit is versatile . . ."

By the time I finished getting dressed, I'd highlighted all the reasons I loved it and why it was the perfect travel outfit. Even though Bowen was literally paying me to say it, I truly loved their pieces. On the way to the airport, I sat in the back of the taxi, editing the video. And by the time I took a seat at the airport bar, I had scheduled the video to be posted over my social media accounts.

That one video paid my rent for the month.

My smile grew. *Life is good.*

"I just had to let you know how beautiful you are," a middle-aged man with gray streaks in his hair told me from the barstool next to me.

"Thank you," I responded.

"Let me buy you a drink." He lifted his hand in the air and gestured to the bartender. "What would you like?"

"Um . . ." I noticed someone down the bar drinking something that looked pretty. "That looks good," I told him, pointing to the drink.

The man ordered it and then asked for his tab. "So where are you headed?"

"New York. And you?"

"Chicago. Headed back home to the wife and kids." He winked at me. "You look just like my wife when she was your age." He grabbed his briefcase and duffle bag. "Take care of yourself."

I nodded in his direction. "You, too."

A few seconds passed before I saw my free tropical drink being made. The blue concoction with the purple flowers as an accent looked like it would taste good. But I got it because it complemented my purple outfit. As soon as the bartender placed the drink in front of me, I rigged my phone against a napkin dispenser and set the automatic timer.

"You want me to take it for you, shawty?" a man asked me, inviting himself to the empty barstool next to me.

"I think I got it," I told him as I checked the photo and smiled. "Yeah, I got it." My body turned to look at him. "But thank you."

"You're welcome. Your boyfriend isn't going to kick my ass for sitting here, is he?"

I gave him a look. "Boyfriend?"

"That old man that was with you." He pointed in the direction of the exit.

"Oh. Nah."

"Well, either way, I'm glad you got your shot with your Blue Lagoon. Your thirty-dollar slushy."

My brows furrowed at his mention of the cost. "Is that shade?"

"No, no, no. It's an observation. You buying thirty-dollar drinks—"

"You seem obsessed with how much this drink costs."

"I'm just trying to figure out who buys thirty-dollar drinks at the airport."

I tilted my head and gave him a look. "If you can't afford this drink, why do you think you can afford to go back and forth with me?"

His face contorted, and he shifted in his seat uncomfortably. "Who said I can't afford it?"

I took a long sip. "The fact that you keep referencing the price is screaming that you can't afford it."

His jaw hardened. "I just figured if you were going to spend thirty dollars on something, it would be food." He looked me up and down.

I let out a sarcastic laugh and took another sip. "Watch yourself."

You . . ." He stopped, lifted his eyebrows, and then leaned back a little. "Wait, I know you from somewhere. You look mad familiar."

I eyed the big man with the long locs and shook my head slowly. "Nah . . . I don't think so."

"Were you at Hamilton University the other night? At Dr. Reynolds's lecture?"

"I was . . ." I said slowly.

"You almost ran into me and said watch yourself."

My eyes widened as it clicked. "You were on your phone and not paying attention to where you were going."

He pointed toward the exit. "And weren't you with *another man* that night?"

"And?"

He narrowed his eyes and scoffed. "It's just funny."

"Why are you so worried about me and what I got going on?" I asked.

"Because it's crazy how I ran into you twice and both times you were with somebody different." His glare intensified. "I guess you put the eat in cheat."

I put the straw to my lips. "You came over here talking to me, and now you're taking shots at me." Smirking, I shook my head. "It's clear you're broke financially, spiritually, and intellectually, so I'm going to just cut to the chase. You don't have a chance with me. And I don't want you to think it has anything to do with your little smart comment. I want to be clear when I say you never had a chance."

He sneered. "I don't date fat bitches. I don't want your fat ass."

"Oh, sweetie," I said in a saccharine-sweet tone. "What you want doesn't matter. Do you understand what I already told you? You were never eligible."

He got off his stool in a huff. "Like I said, I don't date fat bitches," he muttered under his breath as he stormed away.

I smiled in disbelief. "Okay, twin!" I called behind him, watching his childbearing hips as he walked away. "Sir, you too are a fat bitch!"

He didn't acknowledge what I'd said, but I lifted my drink in the air in honor of his departure.

"I like the way you handled him," the bartender said, tucking her hair behind her ears. She was chubby, with mousy brown hair. "I see idiots like that all the time when there's bad weather and a major flight delay. They come in here, get drunk, and make rude comments if I don't give them any attention. It sucks."

"I believe it. But what someone else thinks of you doesn't define you," I told her, finishing my drink. "Fat bitch is such a lazy insult. Like, where's the creativity? And if that's the worst thing someone can say about me, I'm living my life right."

"You're right. You're absolutely right," she said before tapping the bar. "Thank you."

"You're welcome." I got off my stool and grabbed the handle to my bag. "I mean it. Fat is a descriptor, and bitch usually means you don't take someone's shit. Neither is a bad thing."

"Roxy!" someone who looked like a manager yelled out.

The bartender whipped her head around, startled, and then looked back at me. "Thanks again," she said before scurrying toward the woman who called out to her.

I made my way to my gate.

I'd never met any of the people I was meeting in Manhattan in person. I talked to a handful of them on video calls over the years, and I would even consider a few of them friends. The plan was to have fun, but ultimately, it was a work trip. And since I wanted to grow my platform, I had business on my mind.

"Excuse me," I said as I moved through a group of people crowding the boarding lines.

"They just called business class," a man said in a curt tone, remaining in my way. "Just wait your turn."

My eyebrows flew up as I stared at the back of his head. *Oop! No, the fuck he didn't.*

"Yeah, that's why I was trying to get by," I snapped, walking around him from the other side.

"You're in business class?" he reacted incredulously.

I didn't bother to respond as I made my way toward the ticket agent. And after I scanned my boarding pass, I glanced back at the man who had something to say. With a smirk, I sauntered through the door to board my flight.

We were only in the sky for about an hour and a half, but when we landed in New York, I was excited. As business focused as I'd been, the fact that I was linking with some other fashion content creators was cool. And even though the meetings with different brands were definitely the highlight of the trip for me, I liked networking.

Party me tonight. Professional me tomorrow.

I checked into my hotel and immediately made my way to my room. I avoided the bar area because I knew there would be people there. I wanted to get ready before linking up with everyone at dinner. Our itinerary started with a party bus picking us up for dinner at seven and then we were heading to some trendy new club. The pictures, videos, and collabs were going to be content gold. The last thing I needed was to get caught up in a long conversation and not have my look pulled together on time.

After taking a long hot shower, I had a hard time deciding between two outfits. Ultimately, I decided to put on a gold sequin bodycon dress. Typically reserved for special occasions and New Year's Eve celebrations, the dress stood out and photographed well. It fit my body like a glove and showed off my curves. And if that wasn't enough, when the lights hit me, I was going to be the main attraction.

"This is the one," I murmured to myself, turning around in the mirror. "This is definitely the one."

Pinning my hair with gold pins in a half-up, half-down style, I adorned myself with gold hoop earrings and gold bangles. My lips were slathered in red lipstick and my favorite perfume dusted my skin. The fire-engine-red pumps and the vintage black-and-gold bag from my mom completed my look.

I knew I looked good. But when I stepped off the elevator into the lobby, the catcalls I received confirmed it.

"Yessssssssss, bitch!" Sherita yelled out.

The curvy woman with the long braids and gray contacts greeted me with the warmest hug as soon as she saw me.

"Hey, Sherita," I said, hugging her back. "You look great!"

"So do you! I love everything about this look."

"Can I get in on this hug?" Gabriella Pace shouted, her heels clicking loudly as she approached.

"Gabby!" I shouted to the plus size model with the huge Afro.

She was one of my favorite content creators, and she was one of the sweetest people I'd ever met. She was from the Los Angeles area, and she started growing her platform around the same time as I did.

"Hey, beautiful!" She gave me an extra squeeze before she took a step back. "It's so good to see you again!"

"You, too!" I exclaimed. "And this!"—I gestured to the silky peach dress she had on—"I have this same dress in a different color. It looks fantastic on you!"

"Thank you!" She looked between me and Sherita. "You both look so good!"

"We all do," Sherita confirmed.

"Where's Toni?" I wondered, looking around.

"She missed her flight," Sherita informed us. "She'll be here tomorrow morning though."

"Well, then, let's get to the bus so we don't miss *our* ride," Gabby said, linking her arms with ours.

The three of us had the best night. We laughed, joked, and took pictures all throughout dinner. And then when we got to the after-party, we really let loose.

"I'm going to the bar to get a drink and do some recon," I announced.

"I'll get our spots in the section and check out the talent in the other sections," Sherita replied.

"I have to go to the bathroom, and then I'll walk through the dance floor and see what's what," Gabby said, wiggling her fingers. "See you guys in ten minutes!"

We each went our separate ways. I noticed a few other influencers and content creators at the bar. I didn't know them well, but I was familiar with their content on social media. They weren't anywhere near me on the bus or at dinner, but since the point of the night was to network, I marched over to them and said hello.

"Hi," the tall, slim, fair-skinned woman greeted me. "You're Nina, right?"

"I am."

"I'm Skylar." She stuck out her hand. "But you can just call me Sky. This is Daisy and Jess."

I said hi to the other two women.

"Nina is a plus model," Sky explained to the other thin women.

"Oh, wow, good for you!" Daisy cheered.

"Aww, I love that," Jess cooed.

Their tone didn't hit my ears right, but I didn't want to jump to conclusions. It was loud in the venue, and I wanted to believe they weren't coming at me sideways.

"And you are all fashion content creators, too?" I wondered, tilting my head.

"Yes," they said in unison.

"Good for you," I replied with a wide smile. I shifted my eyes to each of them. "I love it."

"Pretty drinks for pretty ladies," the bartender said loudly, handing the three of them martinis.

They giggled flirtatiously. "Thank you," Sky replied, leaning over the bar to give him a better view of her low-cut dress. "So, sooooo much."

He ran his hand through his stringy brown hair. "Of course." He winked. "It's on the house."

They turned their back to him.

"See you later, Nina," Sky whispered, giving me a knowing smirk.

Wiggling their fingers, Daisy and Jess said their goodbyes as well.

"I'll catch y'all later," I told them as I moved to the free space their absence created at the bar.

Before I could place my order, the bartender had moved down the bar to take someone else's order. Several minutes later, I still hadn't been served.

I glanced over at the feel of someone brushing against my arm. I moved over fractionally.

"Yo, what's your name?" a man with enviably thick eyebrows asked as he continued squeezing himself next to me.

I met his gaze. "Why?"

He was clearly inebriated as he shifted his body toward me. His breath was coated in liquor as he leaned forward. "You don't want to tell me your name?"

"You don't want to tell me why you want to know?"

"Come on, Jelly Belly," he said with a slight drawl.

I narrowed my eyes. "Jelly Belly?"

"You pretty though. You got a belly, but you pretty."

I shook my head. "No. I'm not interested."

"Let me take you home tonight. You look like you need some dick to turn that frown upside down."

"If I did need dick, you'd be one of the last ones to qualify for an interview for the position," I retorted.

It was a common misconception that big women had low self-esteem and low standards. Because some assholes spread that rumor around, fat women spent good dating years fending off men looking for quick and easy sex—or worse, money. Too many people thought fat equated to desperate and had the audacity to be offended when we didn't welcome their advances or jump at the chance to entertain them. It was that same audaciousness that made the man in front of me think he could talk to me like that.

Hell, it's audacious for him to think he has a chance with someone like me in the first place.

"You're gonna let that big back bitch carry you like that?" a voice on the other side of the man asked.

Before I could even address either of them, the bartender came over and took my order. After I told him what I wanted, I found the man next to me was staring at me.

"You think you're bad, don't you, Jelly Belly?" he asked, sneering.

He had one more time to say some slick shit or to call me Jelly Belly before I got petty with him.

"I know I am," I replied. "And you know it, too, which is why you're still staring in my face."

"You got a big-ass ego to match that big-ass body."

"Get her," his friend egged him on.

I curled my lip in disgust. "He can't. That's why he's mad now."

"You got a mouth on you," his friend commented. "If you keep running it, I'll give you something to put in it."

"I'm not taking any recommendations for what to put in my mouth from you. Your side tooth is on hospice," I retorted.

"Oh, damn," the man beside me snorted, unable to hold back his laugh.

I lifted my drink to their stunned faces before walking away.

Pleased with myself, I made my way to the section and spent the night partying with the other influencers. It was a good time. My encounter with the man at the bar wasn't an indication of how the night would be. I drank and danced the night away. I gave my number to two men, but I didn't plan on linking up with either of them before I left town. By the time we got back to the hotel, I was feeling tipsy.

I wasn't sure how I made it on time for the conference part of the weekend, but I did. Everyone was going to be dressed to impress so I refused to be outdone. Wearing a green pantsuit with a cropped black-and-white houndstooth top, I felt like a sexy fashion industry professional. My hair was brushed into a high Afro puff and my makeup was soft and pretty. I was proud of how quickly I'd gotten ready.

Since I was ahead of schedule, I made my way to the small coffee shop in the lobby before the workshops began. After grabbing a specialty coffee, I wandered to the hotel event space located next door.

"Nina, you look great," Bree greeted me as I entered the large room.

"Thank you! So do you," I complimented the woman, who was wearing a black pencil skirt and a gray eighties rock band T-shirt that had been cut up.

"The workshops are in the other ballroom—behind the front desk." She put down her clipboard and gave me a hug. "But I'm glad you're here. Every time I went to go talk to you last night, you were dancing."

"I couldn't help it! The DJ was playing hit after hit. You should've come out there, too." I took a step back and checked her out again. "I love how you put that together."

"Thanks! And girl, my man would've lost his mind if I'd been out there with another man," she snickered.

"Do you have a lot more to do before the workshop starts?" I wondered, checking the time. "You want to walk over together?"

"I would, but I'm waiting for—hey!" Bree's eyes shifted behind me.

I turned around and saw a woman who had that air of importance to her. She strolled up to us wearing a red minidress with the matching oversized red blazer. From the expensive shoes and the confidence in her stride, the woman was clearly in the fashion industry. I couldn't help feeling like there was something very familiar about her.

Is she a model? An influencer? I wondered silently as I took in her entire look. *She's definitely a boss.*

And from Bree's reaction, I could tell she was important.

"Remedy, hi!" Bree greeted her. "I pulled the paperwork for us to go over everything. But please, take a look around and tell me if there's anything that you need for your session."

The woman glanced at me and then back to Bree.

Bree gasped. "Oh, how rude of me!" She looked back at me. "Remedy Rose, this is Nina Ford. Nina, this is Remedy Rose of RL Fashions."

My eyebrows shot up. "Oh, wow," I blurted, sticking my hand out. "Nice to meet you!"

Giving me a firm handshake, she looked me up and down. "It's nice to meet you as well." My top was an RL Fashions top, and her eyes lit up when she noticed it. Her striking features were highlighted when her lips curled into a smile. "You have style."

"Thank you."

She didn't need to know that I hadn't realized RL Fashions made more than streetwear until a few weeks ago. She also didn't need to know that I'd gotten the top from a thrift shop. I was a lover of fashion, and I spent a good amount of time seeking out cute pieces. So since I'd stumbled upon the top I was wearing, I'd created a list of other items I wanted from their site.

I opened my mouth to tell her I was excited about the upcoming line. But before I could say a word, she'd turned her attention back to Bree.

"I need to speak to you privately," Remedy stated, checking her watch.

"I'll leave you two to it," I uttered, sidestepping whatever was happening between them. "Remedy, it was great to meet you. I love your shoes. Bree, I hope we get more time to speak later."

As I walked off, I heard Remedy say, "Does she model?"

I smiled as I sashayed out of the room and to the other side of the lobby.

Entering the morning workshop, I heard Amber giving the opening welcome and saw Sherita, Gabriella, and Toni at a table near the back. Giving them hugs and then taking my seat, I prepared to learn how to grow my brand and my bank account.

Eight hours later, after the learning portion of the weekend had come to an end, we all went to our rooms to change and get ready for the cocktail party. When I linked back up with my friends, we did a mini-photoshoot before we went downstairs to the networking event.

"This is going to be a big deal," Toni stated, fiddling with her bracelets nervously. "Some of the brands tonight could give us the opportunity to be commercial models. I heard Bowen is going to be here."

Getting a modeling contract with Bowen would be a big deal. They were the biggest plus size clothing line in the country. They were based in Los Angeles but had stores in many big cities. Known for their quality and attention to detail, the line spent the last five years becoming a powerhouse. They hired social media influencers and fashionistas to promote their brand, but they only used established models in their campaigns and runway shows.

I nodded. "A Bowen campaign would add weight to our careers and open so many more doors."

"I know," Gabriella agreed softly. "I'm freaking out a little bit."

"There is nothing to be worried about. We just need to go down there and be ourselves," Sherita assured them.

Toni jostled her bracelets even louder. "I mean, you're right, but I don't understand how you're so calm." She looked up at me. "You look calm. Are you not nervous either?"

I glanced at myself in the plum-colored dress that I got from Charlotte's boutique. The way it showed off my body while completely covering it was elegantly sexy. Depending on the accessories, I could wear the dress anywhere. I felt confident in it. It was great for networking with colleagues and brands or pulling some fine-ass man at the bar.

"Look at us," I told them, rallying the troops. "What do we have to be nervous about? We have built our platforms from the ground up using our personalities, our sense of style, and our looks. We have what it takes to be successful in this industry, and being here proves that. We are all doing the damn thing, and we are all bad." I lowered my voice and took a step closer to them. "I'm going to give you some real talk. Whether we walk away with meetings or not, that doesn't take away what we've already done and how far we've already come. So, we'll go out here and we'll meet some people, collect some cards, make some connections, and we'll have a good-ass time doing it." I pointed around the group. "Don't forget that they have to sell us on them, too. It's a two-way street."

Sherita put her hands on her hips. "Who knew Nina was a motivational speaker?"

"I knew it," Gabby confirmed with a nod.

"Well, damn, you're right," Toni pronounced.

"Let's go down there and have a good time," I said.

"You know who I want to talk to tonight?" Gabby wondered as we walked toward the elevator.

"That dry-ass speaker you were salivating over when he was boring the rest of us to death," Sherita answered.

"Oop!" I laughed.

"Shut up! I was going to say Bowen," Gabby giggled. "But the speaker was cute! Y'all didn't think he was cute?"

We laughed the entire way to the cocktail party. It was nothing but fun and games with my internet friends. They weren't extremely deep friendships, because we only talked about fashion and work, but they were meaningful. And I was reflecting on that when I was stopped by a woman with a short bob and very sharp features.

"Excuse me," the woman said, interrupting the conversation she was having with Skylar, Daisy, and Jess. "Would you happen to be Nina Ford?"

The three of them whipped their heads around in unison. They seemed confused that the woman had interrupted them to stop me.

"Yes . . ." I responded slowly.

She stepped toward me, boxing out the other women. "I'm Lori with RL Fashions, and I have an opportunity for you, if you're interested in knowing more."

Recalling my earlier encounter with Remedy Rose from RL Fashions, I was definitely intrigued. "I'd love to hear more!"

"Great. Do you have a card?" she requested as she pulled out her own.

I opened the bag I'd gotten from my mom and pulled out one of my business cards. "Yes," I said, handing it to her.

"Remedy was very impressed with you," she said before slipping my card into her clutch. "We'll be in touch."

She turned to the other ladies and smiled. "It was a pleasure meeting you," she told them before walking away.

I'd only taken a step when Sky threw out a question. "You know the people at RL Fashions?"

I shook my head. "I just met them today."

She and the other two gave me strained smiles.

"Oh, okay," Sky replied finally. "I just . . . I was confused because

I'd been talking to Lori for months and then you stroll by and—boom—an offer." She forced a smile even though I could see sadness in her eyes. "Congratulations, Nina. Really."

"Thank you. I don't know the offer yet, so who knows what this will be, but I'm looking forward to finding out."

Again, strained smiles.

"Okay, I need to mingle." I took a step back and then turned on my heel.

It wasn't just an excuse. I really did want to mingle.

But twenty minutes later, I was hiding out in the bathroom, making a call to Russ. He'd sent me a picture of the sunset on the beach in California. I smiled, biting my lip as I waited for him to answer.

"You know I love the sky," I said as soon as he picked up the phone. "And I do wish I was there, too."

"The blue in the sky right now is my favorite color." He sounded sexy and relaxed. "I know you're at a work event. But if you feel inclined to hop on a plane and spend the next twenty-four with me in LA, let me know."

"Very, very tempting offer," I giggled. "But, alas, I have to network."

"Okay." He sighed dramatically. "You would be in New York while I'm in California."

"From the looks of the photo, it seems like you're working hard over there."

He chuckled. "Everybody deserves a break. I had a business dinner that got rescheduled for tomorrow, so I came to the beach to relax for a minute."

"Well, one of us has to work, so I should get back to networking. But hurry your ass back to the East Coast."

"Oh, you miss me?"

I rolled my eyes, even though he couldn't see me. "Goodbye, Russ."

Amusement tinged his words. "I miss you, too. Ain't nothing to be ashamed of."

I laughed. "You always take it too far."

"That's you! But seriously, have a good time tonight and hit me up when you're back home."

"I will. I hope you have a good time, too."

We ended the conversation, and I couldn't stop smiling. I was just putting my phone in my bag when I heard three familiar voices.

"I'm tired of losing out on opportunities for diversity hires," Jess complained. "This body positivity movement has gone too far, and taking opportunities from real models is a problem."

"Nina is a real model," Sky corrected her. "And my issue isn't even that she's a plus size model. My issue is the fact that Lori has ignored my requests to partner with them, and then when I finally have her in a conversation, she tunes me out and literally hands someone else the job."

"Well, Nina didn't get offered the job yet," Daisy reasoned. "And maybe there is a plus size line they are launching. You're a size two, Sky. You wouldn't be a good fit for a plus size job."

"You're the size of a model. If they are doing a campaign to celebrate fatness, they went with the right person." Jess laughed. "Oh, come on, you know that was funny! The industry started rewarding unhealthy, fat, and ugly, so we can joke about it."

"I'm serious, Jess," Sky responded, annoyance straining her words. "It's not about anyone else. I just feel bummed out about not being offered the job."

"You didn't get offered the opportunity because brands are trying to include more fat people," Jess said matter-of-factly. "I didn't get that shoe store opportunity, and then when they ran the ad, it was with some lard ass. I lost that deal to a fatty. You lost a deal to a fatty. I haven't had any offers today—hell, I haven't had any this year, from any fashion brands—and it's because we're losing out on opportunities because of this body positivity bullshit. We need to bring modeling back to its roots."

I flushed the toilet and opened the stall door. "And what does that mean?" I asked on my way to the sink. I looked at all of them, and their shocked expressions, then my eyes lingered on Jess. "What does bring modeling back to its roots mean?"

"Oh my God," Skylar reacted. "Nina, I'm so sorry."

I shook my head. "I'm talking to her." I pointed to Jess. "Stand on the bullshit you were saying and say it to my face."

"I, um . . ." She shrugged. "I just meant we work hard to stay in shape for this career, and now we're losing jobs to people aren't in shape."

I washed my hands. "I get deals and contracts because I'm qua ified. But let me get this straight . . . you think being thin is the requirement and that fat models are stealing opportunities from thin models?"

"Yes!" Her voice carried with the force of her answer. She lifted her chin up defiantly. "This body positivity bullshit messed everything up for hard-working *real* models."

"Hard-working real models," I slowly repeated her statement back to her. Grabbing a paper towel, I dried my hands and then cocked my head to the side. "There are a lot of brands out here looking for models and making connections with the people they want." I narrowed my eyes. "How many of them wanted you?"

Her face turned red, and she started sputtering.

Before she could string together a coherent sentence, I made the number zero with my hand. "Exactly. None." I walked toward her on my way to the bathroom exit. "Brands that feature straight size models because they only sell straight size clothes saw you and still opted out. That ain't got nothing to do with me or other plus models. That's all you, boo. When you're ugly on the inside, that shit starts to seep through your pores."

"I'm not ugly," she screeched at my back as I moved past her.

Grabbing the door handle with the paper towel, I glanced over my shoulder. "Neither am I."

"You're fat though."

I smirked. "Yeah, I sure am. I'm a beautiful, fat, *working* model."

6

"... was your trip?" Aaliyah asked me when she picked me up from the airport.

My smile grew. "It was a lot of fun!"

"Well, give me details!" She merged into traffic and then glanced over at me. "Why are you holding out?"

I sat back in my seat and sighed. "I don't know where to begin . . ."

I told her about the expensively bland dinner and the underground club on Friday night, all the things I learned during the workshop, followed by the cocktail hour, and then all the amazing content I secured at the Sunday brunch. But I saved the best bit of news for last.

"Bowen wasn't there, but I made some really good connections," I told her. "There's a lingerie company that wants to do some stuff with me. They said they were going to send some paperwork for me to look over this week."

"Nina!" Aaliyah gasped. "That's amazing! Oh my God!"

Her excitement only fed into mine. "And that's not even the best part . . ." I leaned forward, the seatbelt restricting me, but I wanted to see her whole face when I told her. "When I got off the plane, I checked my email and RL Fashions sent me a brand ambassador modeling offer that includes participating in a national campaign and a commercial."

"What?" She looked over at me with wide eyes. "Nina!"

"I know!"

"Nina!"

"I know!"

We both screamed.

"What did you say?" she asked excitedly. "What happens next?"

"I didn't say anything yet. You called and I came outside, so I haven't responded. But . . ." I looked down at my phone, exhilaration causing my hands to shake. "RL Fashions is growing into something big. This brand is . . ." I exhaled.

"I've heard of them. They do T-shirts, right?"

"That's what I thought!" I exclaimed. "Up until a few weeks ago, I thought RL Fashions was just a T-shirt brand. I saw a couple of casual pieces, but I didn't research anything more about them. And now, I want to get their contract and hear them out before I look up anything. I don't want to be swayed before hearing them out first."

"I like that plan," Aaliyah agreed. "Do your research after you gather the information from them."

I nodded. "I'm going to formulate my thoughts and opinions, meet with them, and then research other people's experiences with them." I sighed. "But if everything is on the up-and-up . . ."

"You were born to be in the limelight, Nina. This is huge, and I can't wait to see how this and every other opportunity you get continue to grow your brand, your success, and your bank account."

I threw my hand in the air. "Amen!"

We squealed excitedly.

"Okay, now tell me what's going on with you," I insisted, changing the subject. "What's going on with your dating life?"

She sighed loudly. "I'm not any closer to getting a boyfriend."

"What about—"

"I know what you're going to say, and no," she interjected, but her lips curled into a smile. "We're just friends."

I rolled my eyes. "Yeah, okay."

"I'm serious."

I stared at her with my lips pursed until she glanced over at me and laughed.

"Well, then, who is at the top of your list?" I inquired.

"No one," she whined. "I'm starting to think my soulmate was swallowed."

My head fell back, and I let out a loud cackle.

Aaliyah dropped me off at home and after kicking off my shoes, I sat on the couch with my laptop.

"Here goes nothing," I mumbled as I pulled up the email that I'd quickly read after landing.

Dear Nina Ford,

RL Fashions is a brand that is continuing to evolve from streetwear to casual chic styles. As we grow, we want our marketing to do the same. Your style caught our attention and then reviewing your stats on social media confirmed that you would be an asset to our team. We would like to invite you to be a brand ambassador model with RLF. In an official capacity, we would like to speak with you about being a model and exclusive style consultant. We understand how exclusivity may impact any current deals or contracts you're a part of, so we would like you to review the contract attached. Please take the week to consider and then meet with our fashion scout Lori Smith on Friday to discuss further. If you accept the offer, I look forward to speaking with you soon.

Sincerely
Remedy Rose
Chief Creative Officer, RL Fashions

I had an even bigger smile on my face than I did the first time I read the email. Taking my time and absorbing the words, I was a mixture of excitement and nerves. Most of the email filled me with happiness. But the word "exclusive" made me nervous.

If I fulfilled my contracts and then went with the RL Fashions deal, I'd only have one source of income. Putting all my financial eggs into one basket felt risky. My first instinct was to decline the offer. But I didn't know if I was operating out of fear or logic, so I pushed down my initial reservations and opened the attached contract.

"Whoa," I breathed as the fifteen-page document popped open on my computer screen.

I spent the rest of the night going over everything in the contract, taking notes on what I read, and marking anything I had a question about. I reviewed the brand deals I had currently, and all of them required me to film fashion content for them. I still had content to film before I'd fulfilled my duties. I was almost done, so it would be about the time I'd look for additional work. But it had been a while since I'd had just one stream of income.

RL Fashions was paying well. The contract alone would provide me approximately the same amount as the five deals I had, combined. So for similar pay, I would be doing a little less work. There would be less organizational stress from running my own business, but a lot more oversight because I'd be working for someone. I would get exposure in a way that would take years to do on my own. But because of the fact that there was a no-compete clause, a nine-month commitment, and an intellectual property element, the deal gave me pause.

I didn't know what to do.

I'd ignored all calls and texts and climbed in bed. I wanted to sleep on it before I made a decision. I spent Monday batch creating content. I went through all of the clothes that were sent to me, and I created videos until close to midnight. I started back up first thing Tuesday morning. It threw off my typical schedule, but I didn't feel like I could fully consider the RL Fashions offer until I got things off my plate.

By Wednesday afternoon, I took a brief break from editing and scheduling my posts to return text messages from Aaliyah and Jazmyn. After dinner, I confirmed my comedy-show date with James for Thursday night. It was on my calendar, but I'd almost forgotten about it.

It'll be a good way to clear my head before my meeting on Friday, I told myself.

But Thursday night as I drove to the comedy club, the meeting was the only thing I could think of. And since I didn't talk about work with my dates, I picked up my cell and called my best friend.

"Hey," I said as soon as Aaliyah answered the phone.

"Are you okay?" she wondered groggily.

My face twisted in confusion. I glanced at the clock to make sure it was before eight o'clock. "Are you asleep?"

"Yeah. I'm exhausted. Between trying to date, having these pointless-ass conversations on the app, and going to work, I'm beat."

"Oh, sorry! Go back to sleep. I didn't mean to wake you. The sun was still out so I thought you might be up."

She let out a sleepy laugh. "What's going on with you? Is everything okay?"

"You know what . . ." I shook my head as I turned at the light. "I'm fine. I'm meeting The Funny One downtown to watch a comedian he's into."

"James is The Funny One, right?"

James Stansfield was a little younger than me at twenty-seven years old. He was an electrician by day and a comedian by night. He kept me laughing, and he was really handy. I never allowed him in my space; however, when I needed the lights in my closet, I consulted with him about how much something like that should cost. He was hilariously helpful, and I appreciated the role he played.

He was funny. He kept things light, and nothing was ever serious with him. With me still struggling with my decision and what I wanted to do about the job offer, I needed to just laugh the night away.

"Yeah. That's him. The Funny One."

"Well, don't stay out too late," she advised. "You have a big meeting tomorrow."

"Oh, I definitely won't. He wanted me to go back to his place so he could cook for me when the show was over, but I already told him I was making it an early night."

"If the show is at eight, it sounds like you would've gotten back to his place at ten o'clock." She sucked her teeth. "He was planning on feeding you more than just food."

I nodded. "He was definitely hinting that he wanted to feed me dick."

"I'm proud of you for saying no. I know you say sex is the great stress reliever."

"It is. But I wouldn't jeopardize my work for The Funny One," I scoffed. "Can't let a man get in the way of money."

"Weren't you late to work because of your date with The Fun One?" she countered.

My mouth dropped as I parallel parked.

"That's different," I protested.

"How?" she pressed

"Because . . ." I started, racking my brain for an explanation.

"Because you like The Fun One," she teased.

Even though she couldn't see me, I shook my head. "I'm not doing this with you."

"Mm-hmm." Aaliyah's intonation let me know she was calling bullshit. "You know what's interesting . . . Since having sex with Russ, you've completely lost interest in The Funny One."

Feeling my cheeks heat up, I shook off the realization. "I don't know what you're trying to insinuate—"

"You know exactly what I'm insinuating!"

I burst out laughing as I got out of my car. "I've never denied liking Russ. But if I had a big meeting in the morning, I would prioritize that meeting."

"I hear you," she said in a tone that made it clear she didn't believe me. "You're full of shit right now, but I hear you."

She wasn't wrong, but I needed clarification. *Is it that obvious?*

Slightly amused and extremely curious, I wondered, "Why don't you believe me?"

"Because the way you go on and on *and on* about Russ, I don't think you'd turn that down."

Just the thought of Russ and all the ways he took care of me sent a chill down my spine. Because it wasn't just the dick that was magical. Every single thing about that man was magical.

I could not resist him.

Even though I wanted to deny her claims, the truth nagged at me. I smoothed down my black-and-lavender romper and collected myself.

"Of course I'm not turning him down!" I exclaimed. "The dick is exquisite."

Aaliyah cracked up. "I'm gonna start calling Russ by his real name because there's something between you two. And you called the dick exquisite . . . that's high praise."

I cleared my throat, looking around even though my cell phone was pressed to my ear and no one could hear Aaliyah's end of the conversation.

I made my way to the entrance. "You are making this a much bigger deal than it needs to be."

"All I'm saying is that you've never used the word 'exquisite' before."

"A bitch can't use a thesaurus nowadays?" I continued over her snickering. "And at the end of the day, I don't play favorites. No one is getting chose. It's all for one and one for all . . . and I'm the one."

"What is wrong with you?"

"Not a damn thing!" I walked into the club, my eyes sweeping the room until they landed on my date. "But I just got here. I'll talk to you tomorrow."

"Call me after your meeting," she directed.

"Call me before your date," I responded.

We said our goodbyes just as James glanced over at me.

Six feet tall, with a goofy smile, James Stansfield had boyish good looks. His humor and confidence were why I kept him around, but I couldn't deny that he was very attractive. His deep-set dimples and curly high-top fade made him adorably cute, and his thick build and toned arms made him a sexy combination of soft and muscular at the same time. He always wore jeans and a T-shirt on our dates, and I would've loved to see him in something a little more fashion-forward. But the man looked good—basic, but good.

I'd spoken too soon.

What does he have on his feet? I wondered as I took in the orange-and-brown sneakers.

Flashing him a smile, I slipped my phone in my handbag and pulled out my ID for security. James was at my side in seconds.

"If it ain't Disappearing Acts herself," James greeted me, pulling me into a hug.

I laughed as I squeezed him. "Hi."

"It's good to see you." He slid his hand down my back to pat one of my cheeks. "Real good. I missed your fine ass."

I pushed him off with a giggle. "You missed me?"

He put his arm around my shoulders and pulled me back into him. "You know I did. You need to stop playing and spend some real time with me."

"What do you think I'm doing now?"

"I've been trying to see you for the last few weeks."

I gave him a look. "And I'm here now."

He escorted me to our seats. "You changed your mind about us spending the night together?"

"No."

He put his hand over his heart. "Damn!"

James and I spent most of our time together bantering back and forth. He was confident enough to take a joke and funny enough to make them.

When we got to our table, he pulled out my chair for me. I had a question before I took my seat.

"James, what's going on? Why are you so pressed to take me home?"

He grabbed my elbow and leaned so his lips were right against my earlobe. "You've been avoiding coming back to my place for the last six weeks, and I miss the way you feel on my dick." He exhaled so his breath tickled my neck. "And I'm willing to beg for it."

My nipples instantly hardened. My eyes swept the crowd before I slowly turned to face him. "That's a lot of energy for some pussy you're not going to get," I whispered.

"That's a lot of denial for some dick you came on six weeks ago."

I twisted my lips and tried not to laugh as I sat down. "Yeah, okay."

Once he sat across from me, he flashed his goofy smile.

"You look good as hell," he told me.

"Thank you. You look good, too." I glanced at his shoes and then back at his face.

His smile grew even as his brows furrowed. "What?"

I shook my head. "I didn't say anything."

"Your eyes are saying a lot." He gestured to me. "You got something to say about my outfit, let's hear it."

"If you like it, I love it."

He sucked his teeth and shooed me away. "Nah, say what's on your mind. What do you think of my shoes?"

"You're asking my opinion?" I questioned carefully.

"Yes."

I shrugged. "Okay, well, they look like big-ass pumpkins on your feet."

He burst out laughing. "Just because you overdress to everything we do doesn't mean you can shit on what I got on."

"I'm not shitting on you." I gestured to his feet. "Your shoes are doing that on their own."

"Wowwwwwwwww!" His voice carried his amusement. "You don't know style if you don't recognize these are the new Glizzy joints everybody wants."

I frowned. "In that color and shape?"

"Yooooo, you're an asshole. You think just because you're all put together, I don't have heat for you?"

Grinning, I nodded. "Bring it!"

"What's this right here?" He pointed to my hairline. "What's going on with your hair right there?"

My smile grew. "I laid my edges."

"No, the swoop thing."

"Yeah, my baby hairs."

"Nah, not those big swoops." He shook his head. "Those aren't baby hairs. Those are adult hairs. They got bad knees and a pension."

My head fell back, and I laughed. "Shut the fuck up!"

He chuckled along with me. "I'm just playing with you. You look good. Swoops and all."

We were still laughing as the lights dimmed.

"I have a surprise for you," he told me as the DJ started playing music.

"What's up?"

He rose to his feet.

"Guess who is hosting . . ."

My mouth dropped. "Oh shit!"

He leaned down and kissed me. "I'll see you in a minute."

The DJ lowered the volume fractionally. "Put your hands together for your host, the winner of the open mic new-comedy showcase, James Stansfield!"

The crowd clapped and yelled out in support as James jogged up to the stage.

"What's up? What's up? What's up?" he started as the applause started to die down. "How many of you out here are on dates?"

Half of the crowd seemed to raise their hands, yelling their affirmative answers.

"The thing about dating is that shit is unpredictable. I'm a good-looking dude. My mom tells me all the time, so fuck what you think, I know that shit is true. So anyway, I'm on these apps, swiping left and right, and these bios are terrible. *Must be over six feet to ride this ride*—then you look and she's four feet eleven inches tall herself. Ma'am, five feet five inches is plenty." He pointed into the crowd at a man laughing and clapping hard. "We see you, short king." When the crowd finished laughing, he continued. "*Looking for the Jim to my Pam*—ma'am, Pam is a cheater, so now you're telling on yourself . . ."

Laughing, I looked around at the crowd cracking up. When my eyes went back to the stage, my heart swelled. I was so happy and proud of him. If I didn't have a potentially life-changing meeting in the morning, I *might've* stayed for the entire show.

7

Dressed in a black pencil skirt and a white blazer with black piping, I felt interview-ready. Even though the email said it was a meeting and not an interview, my nerves were telling a different story.

"I got this," I whispered to myself as I got out of my car.

My outfit was stylish, my makeup was flawless, and my hair was kinky, coiled perfection. I looked good. I just wished I felt as good on the inside.

I was more nervous than I'd ever been. All I could think about was the contract.

I would be getting a lot, but I would be giving up a lot, too.

I shook off the thought the moment I stepped off the elevator.

"Hello?" I called out as I entered the business suite on the third floor.

"I'm here," a voice called back. "One moment."

I swept my eyes around the mostly empty space until I heard footsteps making their way toward me. When she rounded the corner, I smiled at the familiar face.

"Nina, hi," Lori Smith greeted me.

The fashion scout that had stopped me in the networking event extended her hand to shake mine. She was followed by a woman with oversized oval-shaped glasses.

"Hi," I replied, smiling at both women.

"Sasha Beaman, this is Nina Ford," Lori introduced us. "Nina, this is Sasha. She's with HR, and I asked her to join us so we could discuss this opportunity with you and answer any questions you may have."

"Hi, it's nice to meet you," I said to the woman.

"It's a pleasure," Sasha replied.

Lori beckoned to us as she turned to the right. She started

walking toward a large glass-encased conference room at the end of the hall. "Follow me."

We fell into step behind her, and I listened intently as the two of them chatted about the space. We passed several offices on the way. I glanced behind me, wondering what was down the other hall.

"The RLF brand has continued to grow," Lori informed me, pulling my attention back to her. "Our unofficial headquarters has always been here in Richland. Our founder started the business here while in college. But the action was in the big city. So, RLF grew its wings in New York, but it was birthed here. And as we've grown, we've needed to accommodate that growth. And since real estate in New York is tight, it was decided that we'd just open a dedicated space here in Richland"—she opened her arms—"so this is our new corporate office."

"Well, that's amazing that the company is doing so well. The fact that it's growing so fast that you needed to expand is a huge deal," I responded as we had a seat at the conference table.

"It is," Sasha agreed. "Thank you. I'm proud to be part of this company. RL Fashions is built on integrity from the top down."

Lori took over with a beaming smile. "We're expanding into casualwear, and Remedy was impressed with the way you styled one of our intro pieces. We premiered four pieces last season as a trial run, and you were wearing one of them. Was that intentional?"

I shook my head. "No. We weren't told who would be in attendance, but we were told that we should do our own spin on business chic."

"And you chose well," Lori complimented. "So let me tell you about the position. Each of our models and brand ambassadors are hand chosen. We were set with four, but Remedy saw you and believes you are the missing piece we need on the board."

She opened a portfolio and showed me the concept of one of their print ads.

"I like that you want to have an array of body types," I commented.

One of the male models appeared to be on the larger side, with a thick build. He looked good—like the sexiest offensive lineman I'd ever seen. The three other models had different body shapes but were all straight sized. Every single one of them was beautiful, and so were the garments they had on.

Lori nodded. "Our clothing is size inclusive, and our models should reflect that. Our customers are real people with real bodies, so our models are real people with real bodies. We're doing the first of a few photoshoots for print ads in a couple of weeks and we want all of that reflected."

"I like that," I acknowledged, continuing to listen to her pitch.

She pulled out a stack of papers and slid them across the table to me as she detailed the content creation and modeling expectations and requirements.

Lori flipped to the second page of the contractual agreement. "If you take the job, you'll be featured in the national campaigns. And although you're not guaranteed a feature in our commercial, as a spokesmodel, you're in the running."

So basically, I get paid a lot to do the same things I'm already doing, I thought as I stared at the paper contemplatively. *Hell fucking yeah!*

Keeping my poker face straight, I looked up at Lori. "This sounds great. Truly, it does. But how long is the exclusivity clause?"

"For the full nine months, you'd be exclusive to our brand. And at the end of the nine months, there is a bonus and a possible option to renew."

Nine months. It's not even a full year, I reasoned with myself.

"This contract is like any other—if you violate terms, you'll be terminated. And if you decide you don't want to participate anymore, you can terminate. However, if you are the one to terminate, the no-compete clause would remain in effect for the duration of the nine-month period."

I exhaled slowly. "Okay."

Lori continued going over the duties and highlights of the position. There were too many pros and only one con that I could come up with as I listened carefully to what she had to say.

"Now, this right here is your actual employment contract . . ." Sasha started as she went over the human resources paperwork in front of me. She reviewed typical stuff regarding code of conduct, fraternization, breach of contract, pay schedules, and direct deposit. "And finally, you'll be paid at the end of each month. You follow everything so far?"

I nodded. "Yes."

"Great." She opened a folder and placed papers in it one at a time. "These are the pages you'd need to sign if you decide you want the job. This is everything we just went over. If you get home and you have any questions, my card is here. You can email and ask away."

As soon as I took the folder and placed it in front of me, I knew I had already made up my mind to accept the job. "Okay, thank you."

Lori sat back in her chair and smiled. "So now that you've heard everything in detail, we'll need to know by Monday morning if you're interested in accepting the position. Because if you accept, you'd need to report here on Monday at noon."

"I don't need until Monday," I told them. "I'm interested. I accept."

"Wonderful!" Lori clapped happily.

"Yes!" Sasha pumped her arm with glee.

Their excitement was infectious, and the smile I was trying to control stretched across my face. "Thank you!"

Sasha leaned forward, pushing a thick booklet toward me. "You need to read over this employee handbook. You aren't an employee, per se. Your role functions as more of an independent contractor. But read through everything so you know how we do business. The primary function of the contract is the exclusivity."

Lori nodded. "Yes. This year is a big one for us—especially as we roll into the fall season. For the time you are under contract, you will represent RL Fashions."

"I understand," I responded, looking between the two of them.

"There's a semiformal event all of our models are encouraged to attend tomorrow," Lori added, standing up. She reached across the table to shake my hand. "The Player's Ball. All the fashion and business industry players are invited. I know it's last minute;

however, now that you're one of us, it would be a pleasure to have you there. You'll get a chance to meet everyone and celebrate as we kick off our countdown to Fashion Week. You don't have to wear an RLF gown, but if you can add a piece, it'll go a long way."

"Thank you," I said as she let go of my hand. "I look forward to it."

"The details will be sent to your email," Sasha informed me as she extended her hand. "And be sure to review the code of conduct and fraternization policies."

"We have a lot of fun, but we don't do drama," Lori added. "We know what can happen when you put a bunch of beautiful people together and in order to protect our investments—the models—we like to avoid any lovers' quarrels before they can begin."

Sasha nodded. "It's all in here." She pointed to the paperwork she'd given me.

"You'll have a plus-one though." Lori gave me a knowing look. "Make sure he or she is as fashionable as you. Since we are debuting our models, there will be eyes on you."

Overwhelmed, yet overjoyed, I felt a ripple of excitement as I looked between the two of them. "I guess I will see you tomorrow."

"Indeed, you will," Lori said. "Thank you for coming out."

"Bring those papers to me on Monday so I can get you processed," Sasha reminded me.

With a wide smile, I said goodbye to the two of them. I kept my composure until I got into the car. "Yes!" I screamed, banging my fist against the steering wheel.

I had so much to do in order to prepare for tomorrow's event. I needed to figure out what I was going to wear. I needed my hair done and my nails done. I needed to figure out who I was taking with me and what he was going to wear. And even as thirty-five different things rearranged themselves on my to-do list, excitement shot through my system.

The first thing I did was call my mom.

"Guess what?" I cried as soon as she answered.

"What?" Her tone matched mine. "What's going on? Nina!"

I grinned. "I just accepted an offer to be a model for a brand. I'm going to be in their national campaign."

My mother's squeal pierced my eardrum, and I couldn't do anything but laugh.

"You're going to be a real model! *This* is what you deserve. *This* is what I've been talking about, Nina. You're too beautiful and too fashionable just to be modeling online. You need the world to see you. You deserve for the world to see you."

"Thank you." I grinned. "But just so you know, what I do on social media can be seen by people all over the world. But I get what you're trying to say. And this will take my platform to a whole other level."

"So, what's next? What do you have to do first? When do you start? Do you need anything?"

Her rapid-fire questions and giddy tone made my smile bigger. "So I guess I start tomorrow. Technically, I turn in the official paperwork on Monday, but I get to meet everyone at this event tomorrow."

"I'm so happy for you, Nina! This is such a big deal!"

"Thank you! I have to make some calls, but I wanted to tell you and Dad first."

"I'll let your father know you have some news for him as soon as he gets a minute."

"You can go ahead and tell him. I'll call you both before the event tomorrow, and I'll send you a picture of my completed look."

"I can't wait!" she squealed. "Nina! I'm so happy for you."

"Thank you, Mom. I love you."

"I love you, too."

We said our goodbyes and I was still buzzing from her energy. Her excitement and pride were palpable. My parents were always the boost of serotonin I needed.

I had several things to do and one of the first was to nail down my date.

I called The Romantic One as soon as I stopped at a red light. "Hi, Dru."

"To what do I owe this surprise?" he replied.

"Are you busy?"

"I have two minutes before I'm about to walk into a meeting. Can I call you back in like an hour?"

"Yes, but can we reschedule tonight's date?" I asked him quickly.

"Oh, uh . . ." I heard the papers stop rustling in his background. "Is everything okay?"

"Yeah, a work thing came up and I need tonight to prepare. Are you available tomorrow night instead?"

"I could be . . ." he stated slowly. "Yeah, yeah, I'm free."

"I have an event that just came up and I think it would be fun to go with you. I *want* to go with you."

I could hear him smiling as he said, "Send me the details. I'll make it work."

My mind already started running through outfits he'd look good in. "Sounds good, thank you."

"No, thank you for inviting me to this . . . event. It's cool that you'd want to go with—oh shit, I gotta go. Send me the details so I can come correct tomorrow."

"Okay, thanks, Dru! Bye!"

Of the four men on my roster, Dru was the best candidate to take to The Player's Ball. Dru lived locally. He was willing to change his schedule to do what I wanted him to do. He was full of romance and passion, so he'd dote on me and fawn over me like a good date should. And with his handsome face and swimmer's build, made for semiformal attire, he would make me look good. All that energy and charm was exactly what I needed for my debut event with the company.

But he was also the biggest risk.

Dru seemed to be growing weary of being one of many. He denied it when pressed, but he was starting to express deeper feelings than what we'd originally agreed upon. Although I'd checked him on it, I could tell he was still fiending for something more. And I just wasn't interested in anything more with him. He assured me he was good, but something told me he wasn't.

But he was my only option.

James—The Funny One—was hilarious and kept me cracking up, but he was not fashionable at all. He would've been the worst candidate for a fashion event. He would've worked the crowd, and then they would've talked about me and him the moment we walked away. If there was more time, I might've been able to style him. But he was too far gone for a last-minute date.

Tyrell—The Smart One—had model good looks but I could see him being overwhelmed in a fashion environment. He wasn't socially awkward, but he would've found a corner somewhere to stand and observe. He seemed most comfortable in the academic world and might've inadvertently dampened the fun party mood. He would've looked the part though.

And then there was The Fun One.

Russ—The Fun One—would've been the best choice. But because he didn't live locally, it was unrealistic to invite him to a last-minute event. He was such a good time. It didn't matter what we did, we always had a lot of fun and we just enjoyed each other. He was fashionable and we looked good together, so that would be good for my brand. He had a similar personality type, so he would be great in a social situation like that. There was no denying it: Russ Long was my first choice. But no matter how much fun I could imagine having with him both during and after the event, I knew he wasn't a real option.

A time would've been had with that one, I thought as I pulled into my parking spot.

My phone dinged and my eyes lit up when I saw the name that flashed across the screen.

Speaking of the front-runner . . . I thought before picking up my phone.

> Russ: I have some things lined up that'll put me in Richland. Please tell me you're free on Sunday so I can take you out.

A flashback to the last time we were together sent a ripple through my body. Our conversations between dates were great, but I always found myself anticipating our next meetup. Even if I wasn't free, I would clear my schedule for him.

> Nina: Depends on what you have in mind, me and my schedule can be wide open for you.

Amused, I got out of the car and made my way into my apartment. I'd barely gotten my shoes off when my phone rang. A smile stretched across my face as I answered.

"Nina . . ." Russ's thick, deep tone sent a chill down my spine. I loved the way he said my name.

"Hi, Russ," I greeted him back.

"I'm going to be in Richland, and I couldn't think of a better way to spend my time than with you."

"What do you have in mind?"

He let out a short, low rumble of a laugh. "Well, that depends on how much time you're giving me."

"How much time do you want?"

"All of it," he answered flirtatiously.

My stomach flipped. "I think you like me a little bit," I teased.

He just let out a light chuckle in response and then continued. "I would say I'd just scoop you on Saturday, but I don't know when I'm going to be done with everything and I don't want to keep you waiting."

"Well, I appreciate that."

"So, if you let me get you first thing Sunday morning, can I have you all day and night? I have a meeting Monday afternoon, so we have to be back first thing in the morning. But I'll make it worth your while."

I bit my lip as I made my way down my hallway. "If you have me back by nine, ten at the latest, I think I can accommodate your request."

"Good. It's been a hell of a week, and when I realized I needed to be in Richland, seeing you was the first thing that crossed my mind," he admitted.

I smirked. "I'm glad to hear that. It has definitely been the kind of week that would warrant some fun with Russ."

"I'm making the arrangements now."

"I look forward to it."

"I'm staying downtown, at the same hotel since you liked it. Anything specific you need to know, I'll hit you up later with the details, okay? I have a couple of meetings this afternoon and then I need to pack for my flight tomorrow."

"Okay, you go do what you need to do. I have a busy afternoon as well."

"So it sounds like we're both due to let out a little steam."

"Yeah, it sounds like it."

"Well, I got you."

My lower body clenched. It wasn't necessarily the words he said but the way he said them.

"Yes, you do," I murmured instinctually.

I didn't mean to say it, but his sexiness pulled it out of me.

"I like the sound of that," he whispered. "You know what else I like the sound of . . . ?"

"What's that?"

"You coming for me."

My panties were soaked.

"Russ, please. You're not about to get me all hot and bothered and then not see me until Sunday," I reprimanded him playfully.

He chuckled. "The minute my assistant said Richland, I thought of you and my dick got hard. So the feeling is mutual. Trust and believe."

"Oh, I believe it. But if you aren't here to do anything with that hard dick, I need you to stop teasing me."

"You're right. There will be plenty of time for teasing on Sunday."

I giggled. "Goodbye, Russ."

We ended the call and I almost let myself get caught up in what Russ could have in store for us. Just imagining it put a smile on my face and a flutter in my belly. There was something about him, about our time together, about the way he made me feel that was indescribable.

I like him.

The thought took me by surprise.

It wasn't that it was untrue. I did like him. But unlike the other times, it felt different. It felt deeper—almost like the feeling was embedded in me.

That made me uncomfortable.

Immediately, I backtracked, explaining the thought away.

I'm just excited about the event and the job and the opportunity . . .

I had a few things in my closet that I could wear to The Player's Ball, so I wasn't worried about finding something. I just needed to figure out how I could find an RL Fashions piece to work with something I already had. Then I had to figure out what Dru was going to wear so I could send him his information. Then I needed to book my appointments.

"I have so much to do," I mumbled aloud as I made my way into my closet.

But surprisingly, it didn't take long.

I thought it would be easier to find something to go with the elegantly sexy black-and-white cocktail dress I'd gotten last year. But I'd been dying to wear the showstopping red dress I'd yet to find a place worthy enough to debut. The cups that held my breasts and the skirt of the dress were made of red layered mesh. The space that covered my torso was red lace. Even at my height, the length of the dress, in heels, brushed the floor, and it even had a slight train. And like a hidden surprise, the split that stopped mid-thigh only exposed my leg when I stuck it out.

After having my outfit figured out, I felt like the rest of my list was light work. I figured out what I wanted Dru to wear and called Charlotte to see if she had what I was looking for. Because she did, I sent Dru the information I'd gotten from the email Sasha had sent me, and I told him to pick up his shirt from Charlotte's Webb. He called to confirm pickup and I checked him off the list.

I made all the appointments I could, but I wasn't able to book a hair appointment at the last minute. Instead of worrying about it, I spent the rest of the night trying out different styles. It was time-consuming, but worth it when I came up with my final look. I washed and deep conditioned my hair, twisted the thickly coiled strands, and sat under the dryer for an hour. It wasn't until after I climbed in bed that I checked my phone.

> Russ: Everything is booked, and I'll pick you up seven o'clock Sunday morning.
>
> Nina: Seven o'clock in the morning!
>
> Russ: I know it's early, but we have to be on time. I promise you it'll be worth it.
>
> Nina: It always is with you. I'll meet you at your hotel at seven. What do I need to wear or bring?
>
> Russ: Wear sneakers and something comfortable. And as long as you pack some shoes you can dance in, I'll take care of everything else.

A chill ran down my spine.

This is the energy I like, I thought as I wiggled my toes under the covers.

8

My heart raced with excitement as the car slowed to a stop in front of the abandoned train station that had been converted into an event space. I went to a wedding there a few years back, but it looked different. As I climbed out of the car and looked up the twenty-five steps that led to the front doors, my stomach fluttered with nerves. The realization hit me hard enough to knock the wind from me.

I'm part of this.

There were so many people wearing unique cocktail dresses, fashion-forward suits, and just colorful expressions of style. I felt like I was in my element, and I hadn't even entered the building.

My hair was twisted into the most perfect Bantu knots, with gold wire gently woven through each. My red dress fit my body flawlessly and showed off my curves. My gold shoes peeked beneath the skirt of my dress with each step and matched my gold clutch. I put my perfectly manicured hand against my belly and took a deep breath.

"You look gorgeous," Dru gushed as he walked up to me on the sidewalk.

I took a step back and looked him up and down. "So do you!"

Wearing a black suit and a white, black, and gold RL Fashions T-shirt, Dru looked good. I rolled his sleeves up a little to show off his forearms and then I grinned. "Yes." I eyed him appreciatively. "Yes!"

He offered me his elbow and I accepted.

"What is this?" he asked me in awe as we headed toward a man with a clipboard. "I've never been to anything like this before."

"It's a party celebrating a clothing brand's launch."

"And you work here?"

With pride, I nodded. "Yeah. I do."

After the couple in front of us walked through, we were stopped by security. "Name, please?"

"Nina Ford," I answered.

He found my name and gestured to the red carpet. "Enjoy your night, Ms. Ford."

The doors opened and the music pulsed out. There had to be at least five hundred people milling around, dancing, talking, and enjoying themselves. There were food stations and bars. There were photographers and 360-degree-photo booths. The lights were bright, and the energy was electric. Everyone looked good.

"What do you do?" Dru asked, still taking everything in as we headed to the bar. "I thought you worked at that place I picked this shirt up from."

"I do," I answered in a noncommittal way.

It was my first time doing anything work related with a date. I didn't talk to any of the men I dated about what I did for work. I talked about my life, my interests, and the things we had in common. None of them knew about my real social media page; they followed the private friends-and-family page with less than a thousand followers. If any of them knew about the other page, no one had ever said anything.

"I was going to take you dancing under the stars last night, but this . . ." He pointed to the glass ceiling. "This is much better than what I'd planned."

"I'm sure you had an incredible night planned," I told him, pulling him a little closer.

He brought my hand to his lips. "You're still going to get your incredible night. Don't you worry about that."

We made our way to the first food station and got a small plate, and then we started mingling. We met so many people. Everyone was so friendly. Hellos were exchanged every couple of minutes and before we finished our first drink, we got sucked into conversation about our outfits.

We'd been there for almost an hour before I ran into Lori.

"Nina! Wow!" she greeted me, clasping her hands together.

She had on a navy blue formfitting trumpet dress that clung to her like a glove.

"You are wearing that dress!" I complimented her as she gave me air kisses to both cheeks.

"This isn't an RL Fashions design, but it is"—she kissed the tips of her fingers—"chef's kiss!"

"Thank you. Thank you." I pointed to Dru. "This is my date for this evening"—I put my hand on his shirt and snuggled my body next to his—"and my accessory."

Her eyes widened as she saw how the shirt complemented my dress. "Nina!" she gasped. Looking around, she waved over a photographer that was nearby. Taking the drink out of my hand, she pointed. "Take their picture."

I adjusted Dru's sleeves and unbuttoned his jacket to show off the shirt before lifting my chin and putting my hand against his chest. I posed, doing my model thing, and Dru just stood there smiling, happy to be included.

"Yes! Yes!" a woman cheered as the photographer snapped a few photos. "Work it!"

"I like the way you did this, Nina," Lori told me as the photographer moved on. She checked her watch. "I'm going to wrangle up the others and introduce you all in about an hour. Until then, enjoy yourselves!"

She walked off, and it wasn't until she disappeared into the crowd that I realized that she'd taken my drink.

Dru jumped into action. "I'll get you another drink. What would you like?"

"Rosé champagne, please."

He kissed my hand. "Anything for you."

As soon as he walked away, I dug into my clutch to pull out my phone. I had every intention of texting Aaliyah and Jazz in our group chat when I saw a text waiting for me.

> Russ: I'm going to cut out of this thing I have to do early tonight. How early is too early to start my date with you?

A grin spread across my face. Looking around, I located Dru in line at the bar nearest us. I turned my back so he couldn't see me texting.

> Nina: I'm not home or available until morning, but I do like the way you think...
>
> Russ: If I told you what I was thinking, if I typed it out, there would be no way I'd be able to sit through another conversation. There's some work associates I need to impress and all I can think about is pressing up against you.
>
> Nina: Your mind should be on your money and not me.
>
> Russ: Both of those things stay on my mind constantly. I'm able to multitask.
>
> Nina: Oh I know... I'm very familiar with how you multitask.
>
> Russ: Nina...

My heart beat between my legs as I imagined the way he said my name. Just reading it, I was able to hear it in my head and it stirred something up in me.

> Nina: How are you able to focus on winning over these important people if you're thinking about sliding deep inside me?
>
> Russ: Are you trying to make my dick hard? Because it's working. Now I have to excuse myself.

Just knowing my words were having an effect on him made me want to say more. But I knew I didn't have much time. I didn't want to be rude to my date, so I'd have to end the conversation soon.

> Nina: Lucky for me, no one can see how wet my pussy is for you.
>
> Russ: Nina...

Nina: In less than twelve hours, you can put your face in it and see for yourself.

Russ: I'm about to walk the fuck out of here and come get you now. Don't play with me.

Nina: Please play with me.

Russ: Nina, say the word and I'll leave here and be wherever you are. I'm not even playing anymore.

Nina: Soon.

"I knew you were a great fit for us," Remedy Rose commented as she ripped my attention away from my phone.

Hoping she didn't notice my hardened nipples pushing through the mesh fabric of my dress, I stuck my hand out and shook hers.

"Remedy! Hi! It's so nice to see you again." When I let go of her hand, I gestured around. "This is a beautiful event. Thank you for having me."

"Thank you for being here. And I love what you're wearing. You have quite the eye."

"You do, too! Is this one of yours?" I asked of her purple dress.

"Yes." She puffed out her chest with pride. "This is an RLF original, and it is a prototype of one of the pieces shown during our runway show."

"It looks incredible on you."

"Thank you." She turned and pointed to some people across the room. "There are some pretty important people here and they are taking everything in. There are tons of models, actors, athletes, business associates, investors, retailers, in addition to the design team, the corporate office, and the board. This isn't an audition to walk during our runway show, but . . ." She raised her eyebrows and made a face. "Treat it as such. Work the room. Have a great time tonight. Enjoy yourself. But also know that you should be on at all times. I'll find you later. I knew you'd make a great ambassador."

"Wow, thank you!"

"Don't thank me yet. Show me."

I nodded, understanding exactly what she meant.

Remedy's eyes lit up as something behind me caught her attention. "And is this your boyfriend?"

Before I could respond, Dru handed me my drink and then extended his hand to her. "Dru Robinson," he introduced himself.

"You two look really good together." She smiled at his shirt and then winked at me. "I see what you did there."

Someone called her name and she turned and waved. "I'll be seeing you." She tossed the words over her shoulder before heading to the person.

"Who was that?" Dru wondered.

"This whole thing is basically for her," I answered, taking a sip of the champagne.

It was gross.

"If you don't like it, I can get you something else," he offered, staring at my scrunched-up face.

I giggled. "Nah, it's cool."

"Well, then, tell me what you want."

"Actually . . ." I dragged the word out with a smile. "You said you wanted to dance with me under the stars." I gestured to the dance floor. "I want to see your moves."

He licked his lips and held his hand out to me. "May I have this dance?"

I laughed. "Absolutely."

We got on the dance floor, and I was surprised by how well he moved. He didn't just allow me to shake my ass on him. He danced with me. He moved his body in sync with mine. He twirled me around and shifted us from one side of the floor to the other. At one point, he put his arm around my waist and dipped me. I kicked my foot out and the split in my dress showcased my leg and I swear I heard applause.

"You two make a good-looking couple," an older lady remarked with a twinkle in her eye.

"Thank you," we said in unison.

We were having a good time. There were other couples on the dance floor. Some were making out, some were dancing to the beat, some were dancing off the beat, but everyone looked like they were having fun. When the beat dropped and the song changed, Dru spun me and my dress fanned out, and then he pulled me in so we could dance close. It felt like we were the center of attention and that all eyes were on us.

"You are so beautiful when you dance," Dru commented with a moony expression on his face. "So incredibly beautiful, Nina."

I was hoping he would stop there. But what I'd been afraid of was coming to a head. I felt it.

We were having a good time and I wanted to deny what was right in front of me. But it was his tone and the way he was looking at me that shifted the energy between us.

"I really like you," he whispered as we moved to the slow song that filled the space. "This is our seventh date and I really feel like we have something special."

"We have a good time together. We enjoy each other's company, Dru. You're a great guy and I'm glad we've agreed to keep it casual."

His lips grazed my cheek before he looked into my eyes. "I want more with you. And the fact that you invited me to this event lets me know that you feel it, too."

Shit.

I knew the risk.

I assumed the risk.

And now I was going to have to eliminate the risk of further disaster.

We hadn't even been at the ball for two hours, and I didn't want a scene. It was my debut as part of the RL Fashions team. It was my first official event as a *model* for RL Fashions. I just wowed everyone on and off the dance floor. So having my date break down or make a scene would really undo the work I'd done thus far.

I ran my hands over his lapels and patted his chest. "Do you remember when you took me for that picnic on that giant raft down the river?" I asked him.

"Our fourth date," he confirmed. "We watched the sunset."

"I told you I wasn't looking for anything serious and you said you weren't either. I told you I wanted to keep it casual, and you said you were cool with that." I let him spin me and pull me back to him before I continued. "This date doesn't change that for me," I explained, ignoring the hurt in his eyes.

"But when that woman said I was your boyfriend, you didn't say no."

"I didn't say yes," I reminded him.

As the song faded into something different, I gently tugged him off the dance floor.

I knew I didn't want to be in a relationship with him and I had no intention of hurting him—or any other man. There was no way one man would be able to give me all that I needed to be happy and satisfied in a relationship. So whenever men got too caught up, I knew it was time for our situationship to come to an end. And when I first saw the signs of this with Dru, it was the exact reason I decided not to sleep with him. I saw it coming, but I just didn't think it would be this soon.

I slowed to a stop when we were near the exit. "You and I don't want the same thing and I don't want to give you the wrong impression."

"So what are you saying?" He shifted his eyes to the door.

I put my hand on his arm and squeezed compassionately. "I'm saying we should probably call it a night. We can have a longer discussion about this next week, but for now . . . let's say good night."

His eyebrows shot up. "You . . . you want me to leave?"

I nodded. "I have to give my card and meet a couple more people and then I'm leaving, too."

"I have flowers in the car for you," he told me quietly. He pulled me in for a hug. "I would've given you the world, Nina."

I let out a soft breath, sadness pulling at my heartstrings. "You're so sweet, Dru. A gentleman and a romantic," I whispered, holding him tight. "This is why we have to end things. You're ready for so much more than what I am ready to give. But the woman for you is going to be able to commit one hundred percent of her time and energy to you and only you—like you deserve." I pulled out of the hug and stared him in the eyes. "You deserve everything you want."

"I want you."

I shook my head. "I'm not her. But she is out there."

He let out a long breath. "Okay."

I nodded. "Okay."

"Can I kiss you goodbye?"

"Yes," I murmured as his lips brushed against mine.

There was so much emotion in the way he grabbed and kissed me. After a few seconds, I ended the kiss and squeezed his hands.

"Thank you," I told him.

"No, thank you," he uttered before taking a step back. "Good-bye, Nina."

I wiggled my fingers. "Bye."

As soon as he disappeared out of the door, I turned on my heel and made a beeline to the bathroom.

I hope my lipstick isn't smudged.

I also needed to make sure I didn't look a sweaty mess after getting it on on the dance floor. I needed a mirror before the big introduction with the other models. And I needed a mirror fast.

The line for the women's restroom was ridiculously long. I waited for a few seconds before I knew I needed to find another. I really just needed a mirror.

I'd overheard a woman saying there was another bathroom on the other side of the building, so I headed that way. The crowd thinned as I got farther away from the DJ and the main event. But as soon as I turned the corner where the restrooms were located, I saw a bit of a crowd had gathered.

They must've heard about the other bathroom, too, I griped silently.

Out of the corner of my eye, I saw a man climbing a stairwell. The signage was small, but I was pretty sure I saw a bathroom emblem on the second-floor wall. Quickly changing directions, I scurried across the old train station toward the back wall. I grabbed the handrail and then made my way up the steps. When I reached the top landing, I smiled at the arrows directing me to the bathroom.

"Finally," I muttered, happy to get some privacy to fix my face.

I was just about to enter the women's room when the men's room door swung open, catching my attention.

I glanced over and then did a double take.

"Russ," I gasped.

9

"What are you doing here?" we said in unison before we both burst out laughing.

"Mostly networking. What are *you* doing here?" He shook his head. "You always dress your ass off, so I shouldn't be surprised you're here." His eyes swept down my body. "God, you look beautiful."

"Thank you," I replied softly. "You look as handsome as ever."

We gravitated toward each other, looks of shock and awe on our faces.

"Come here." He wrapped his arms around my waist and pulled me close. "I thought I wasn't going to be able to see you until tomorrow morning." His lips dipped to my ear. "But this is a nice surprise."

I inhaled deeply; his cologne infiltrated my nostrils and filled me. His scent and his presence reminded me of the promises he'd made via text message and sent a chill down my spine. Running my hands up his arms, I linked my fingers behind his neck.

"A very nice surprise," I murmured.

"What are you doing way over here when the party is way over there?"

I felt his question against my skin and shivered again.

Hoping to have the same effect on him as he had on me, I whispered my response. "I had twenty minutes to spare and decided to go to the bathroom to freshen up. The one over there was packed and I overheard someone talking about the one on this side. But when I saw a man heading upstairs, something told me to follow him. As luck would have it, that man turned out to be you."

After his lips brushed my neck, he pulled his head back and stared into my eyes. "Sounds like this was meant to be."

"Sounds like it."

His tongue slid from one side of his mouth to the other. "Do you know why I came up here?"

"Why?"

"Because I couldn't stop thinking about what you texted me." With his hands slowly coasting down my back, he waited until he reached my ass to pull me flush into him. "And I felt my dick getting hard all over again."

My heart thumped in my chest and between my legs. "So, you came over here to rub one out?"

He chuckled lightly. "Nah, I came over here to call you."

My hands gripped his broad shoulders and I exhaled shakily. "And what were you going to call me to say?"

His smile grew. "This probably isn't the time or the place."

Looking around the hallway, I felt confident we were alone. "We're on the second floor . . . on the opposite side of the building as the party. We're hidden in the cut and I'm standing right here." I cocked my head to the side. "That's time and place."

He let out a sexy chuckle and he dug his fingers into the red lace that covered my back. "Nah . . ."

I quirked an eyebrow. "Oh, but I thought you were about to call me."

"Calling you and telling you what I want to do is completely different than standing in front of you and telling you."

"And why's that?"

He glanced around before slipping his hands over my ass and grabbing each cheek. "Because if I have you in front of me, it's not going to be just talk."

"Oh, so you're about that action . . ."

He leaned down, his mouth hovering over mine. "You already know."

I tipped my chin upward, brushing my lips against his. "So, what are you waiting for?"

"Don't tempt me, Nina."

I opened my mouth to respond but before I could, he kissed me hard and with enough passion to take my breath away.

I moaned in response.

"Show me," he whispered against my mouth as his tongue met mine.

I was so drunk off his kiss, I had no idea what he was talking about. "Show you what?" I murmured, gripping him tighter.

"You said your pussy was wet for me." Pulling away fractionally, he rested his forehead against mine and moved his hands to my hips. "Show me."

Something deep in my gut tightened as his words rang in my ears and his touch washed over me. My body clenched in anticipation. Even if I wanted to, I couldn't resist him. Even though we were tucked away from everyone, we were at an RLF event, and it was my first event with them. I didn't want to run the risk of being caught and jeopardize my opportunity.

I opened my mouth to tell him it was too big of a risk, but the words didn't come out. Instead, I pulled his face to mine.

Our mouths met again passionately and the noise that escaped him caused me to curve my body into him, deepening the kiss. It was as if the more we kissed, the more I wanted him. That kiss was lust in its purest form and my entire body felt it.

I slipped my hand down his chest and his firm core until I reached his erection. With each meeting of our tongues, I felt him get harder. Just thinking about him filling me up with his big dick spurred me on.

"If you keep doing that, the whole party is going to get shut down," he warned me, forcing me back a couple steps.

I gasped as he backed me into the wall next to the women's-room door. My ass and then my shoulders hit the wall with a light thud. Sandwiching me with his body, he let me run my hand over the length of him. As soon as I palmed the head, he groaned, "Nina."

Just hearing him say my name like that was too much for me.

"Yes," I exhaled, increasing the pressure against his erection.

He let out a low, sexy growl as he grabbed my wrist and pinned it above my head. "Don't start something we can't finish."

I lifted my leg, rubbing it against the outside of his as I curved my body into him. His hand shifted from my hip to my thigh and his fingers followed the split in my dress. The minute his fingertips slipped underneath the hem, the silk panties I wore were soaking wet.

Using the wall for balance, he angled me so that I remained steady as he gripped the underside of my exposed thigh. I grabbed his shoulders for leverage, and he made the most of my new security. Slowly, his hand slid forward until he was cupping my bare ass.

The ball was going strong on the opposite end of the large building. We were on the second floor, down a hallway. The way our bodies were positioned, no one who happened to be on the second floor would think we were doing anything but kissing. But the fact that at any time someone could walk up on us excited me. The stakes were higher. It wasn't the back of a movie theater or on a private helicopter or even in the bathroom at a club. We were at a semiformal party that cemented my first work appearance for the brand. It was a huge deal, and yet, with his hands on my body, unadulterated lust clouded my brain and nothing else mattered.

"Russ," I moaned against his mouth, pulling him closer.

I wanted him in the worst way.

"Are you going to show me?" he whispered between kisses. "Are you going to let me feel it?"

"Yes," I panted.

"Good." He kept his hand underneath my dress as he let my leg slide down the side of his. When my shoe hit the floor, he moved his hand to my inner thigh. "Spread your legs."

I did as I was told.

As soon as his fingertips traced my panty line, I sucked in a sharp breath.

"You weren't lying . . ." He ran his fingertips over the damp material, pulling it away from my skin. "Is this all for me?"

The yearning I felt was so overwhelming that my voice was barely audible. "Yes."

His fingers slipped underneath the damp lace and made contact with my waxed flesh. "You know the effect you have on me." He gently brushed against me. "So, when I came up here to call you, I was going to tell you that I couldn't wait to touch you . . . to taste you . . . to fuck you."

I closed my eyes. "Oh God."

His finger grazed my clit before tugging my panties down. When they hit my ankles, they got caught on my shoes. Crouching down, Russ lifted one of my feet and then the other, removing my G-string from me completely.

Looking up at me, he licked his lips. "You know what you do to me, don't you?"

Running my hands over my breasts, I tried to soothe my aching nipples. "The same thing you do to me."

Stuffing my panties in his pocket with one hand, he wrapped the other hand around my calf. "Nina, Nina, Nina." He repeated my name softly as he rose to his full height. "Keep your legs open just like that for me."

I placed my hands on his shoulders to keep my balance because he made my knees weak. His fingers coasted over my kneecap and up my thigh until they got to the end of the split in my dress. His touch inflamed my skin as he slowly moved toward my inner thigh.

My lashes fluttered closed, and I swallowed hard. Just knowing where he was headed caused my insides to quiver.

I didn't just want him to touch me. I *needed* him to touch me.

"Open your eyes," he demanded, forcing my eyes to meet his again. He brushed my wet slit. "Look at me."

I let out a small shuddering breath before opening my eyes.

"I love the sounds you make," he rasped, just before he spread me open. He pressed the pad of his finger against the hood of my clit. "Mmm."

Holding his shoulders tight, I exhaled his name wantonly. "Russssssss."

"You know how bad I want you right now?" he whispered hoarsely.

He didn't give me a chance to answer as he continued. "It doesn't matter where I'm at or what I'm doing, I think about you constantly." His finger moved in a slow, methodical circle against my bundle of nerves. "So you can't tell me your pussy is wet and waiting for me and think I don't want to touch"—his lips met mine—"and taste"—another kiss—"and fuck." A longer, more urgent kiss followed. "I want you. Can I have you?"

A shiver ran down my spine and I nodded. "Yes."

The word was barely out of my mouth when he slid two fingers into my wetness.

Digging my nails into his shoulders, I let out a desirous cry.

He smothered my outburst with his lips.

He had me so keyed up that I knew I would come quick.

Slowly moving in and out of my pussy with his fingers, he broke our kiss. "I was talking to someone I want to partner with, and you had my dick so fucking hard I couldn't concentrate." Using his fingers and his palm, he began rushing me toward my orgasm. "Is that what you wanted? Did you want me to think about blowing off everything I have to do tonight so I can stick my tongue in this pretty pussy of yours? You wanted me to think about eating this wet pussy and then sliding inside you, huh? It feels like that's exactly what you wanted. You ready to grip my dick the same way you're gripping my fingers?"

"Yes," I moaned loudly. "Yessssssssss."

His fingers spread my wetness over my clit. "I want you to come on my fingers the same way you're going to come on my dick later."

Watching him watch me, feeling him touch me, hearing him talk dirty to me was all too much. My entire body shuddered.

"Ohmigod," I cried out.

"Listen to how wet you are," he groaned, plunging his fingers into me. "You hear yourself? You hear how wet this pussy is for me?"

I couldn't hear anything except for my heart beating rapidly and the sexiness of his words.

Desperately grinding on his hand, I felt my orgasm quickly approaching. The deep ache that overwhelmed mc was reaching the point of no return as he skillfully worked his fingers in and out of me. I panted wantonly and unabashedly.

"Russ," I gasped as our mouths devoured each other. "Russ, yes, that's it."

"You know how hard you have my dick right now," he grunted. "This pussy stays so fucking wet for me. Let me taste you, baby. Let me stick my tongue right there and eat you until you come all over my face. Let me fill you with this dick so you can come hard on it for me. You know I love to feel this tight pussy cream all over me."

"Ohmigod, ohmigod, ohmigod," I whispered repeatedly as I felt myself surrendering my power to him.

"I beat my dick before this shit, thinking about how it feels to be inside you," he grunted.

Desire flowed through my veins and spread through every inch of me. My head spun. My breathing hitched. My body was on fire. And the gorgeous man dirty talking between kisses consumed me.

I came hard.

Quivering with pleasure, I pulled Russ forward, trapping myself between him and the wall. I didn't realize how hard I was holding on to him until my orgasm had subsided and I felt the tightness in my knuckles. Opening my eyes, I relaxed my grip. My knees were weak, my skin was tingling, and my heart was racing.

He pulled his fingers out of me and then stuck them into his mouth, licking my juices. "Mmm."

My stomach fluttered. "That was so fucking sexy." I reached for his dick again. "I want more."

"So do I, baby." He dropped a kiss against my lips. "But I don't have a condom with me . . . You know my job is to keep you satisfied."

Job.

Hearing the word job brought me back to the reality of where we were, what we were doing, and what I was supposed to be doing.

Oh shit!

My eyes widened and I pulled him into the women's restroom with me.

"I'm supposed to be meeting some people in like two minutes," I hissed as I ran over to the nearest sink.

He checked his watch before washing his hands. "Yeah, I've been ignoring calls since I laid eyes on you, so I know people are looking for me." He stared at me in the mirror as he yanked paper towels from the dispenser. "But my priorities shifted."

I couldn't help but smile as I finished cleaning myself up. "I can't believe that went down out there." I bit my bottom lip and stared at him in the mirror.

"Yeah, that was unexpected." He chuckled lightly. "I just came up here to call you. And then—boom—you were right here in front of me. Looking like this." He licked his lips. "And it's like I can't resist you or something."

"I feel the same way." Distractedly, I glanced at the bulge in his pants.

He grabbed it, squeezing the thickness covered by fabric. I watched his hand move over it and lust twisted my core.

"I'm going to have to wait a couple of minutes before I go down there." His eyes swept up and down my body. "And I'm definitely going to have to stop watching you do that."

I finished patting myself dry with a paper towel and gave him a rueful smile. "I'm going to need my G-string back."

"Oh." He chuckled to himself. "I almost forgot." He pulled it out of his pocket and brought it to his nose. Inhaling deeply, he closed his eyes. "Mmm . . . Nina, give me about half an hour to wrap some shit up and then leave with me. Forty-five minutes, tops. I want you to come back to my hotel room with me tonight."

Grinning, I took my panties out of his hand and pulled them on. "I don't have anything with me, and I still have to pack for our trip tomorrow."

"You don't need anything tonight." He licked his lips while staring at mine. "You just need—" He pulled his phone out of his pocket before he continued. "You just need to be there. I'll take care of everything else."

I smoothed my dress down with a laugh. "I think that's your dick talking, because you made it very clear that we were on a tight schedule, and I needed to be on time."

"I'll run the risk of us being a little late if it means more time with you." He lifted his shoulders. "What can I say? You make everything better and I'm trying to lose myself in you tonight."

Warmth spread through my chest and crept up my neck. His words struck a chord with me unexpectedly. Fixing a couple of my Bantu knots, I met his gaze in the mirror.

"Give me forty-five minutes and I can leave all the bullshit behind." He lifted his vibrating phone to his ear and answered it gruffly. "Hello?"

Ignoring my flushed cheeks, I dug into my bag to pull out my phone.

> Lori Smith: Introductions in fifteen minutes behind the DJ booth.

I checked the time and realized that the text came in five minutes prior.

I have ten minutes!

Pretending I wasn't listening to his call, I took the opportunity to do what I had originally come to the restroom to do and fixed my lipstick. It was basically nonexistent from my time with Russ, so I reapplied.

"Well, first, calm down," Russ instructed into the phone. "It's fine. I ran into someone and didn't hear the phone while we were catching up."

Smirking, I made eye contact with him in the mirror, and he winked at me.

"Yeah, I'll be right there," he continued. "Fine, yes. Yes. Give me a couple minutes. Stall them. Let them know that I'm on the way." He smoothed down his jacket, yanking it to mask his bulge. "Stall them!"

He ended the call but kept the phone in his hand.

"Everything okay?" I asked, turning toward him.

"Yeah, first my assistant, and now my sister." He shook his head. "I'm late for a meeting with some people who are interested in giving me money," he explained.

My eyebrows shot up. "You need to get out of here! Don't lose money on my account."

He grabbed my arm and pulled me into him. "If I were to lose money, it would be on me." Leaning down, his lips brushed mine softly. "But I don't plan on losing anything."

"Good." I reached up and clasped my hands around his neck. "I wouldn't want you to take a loss."

He stared at me for a moment. "Then come back to my hotel with me."

"I have people I'm supposed to meet up with in a few minutes." I planted a quick kiss against his mouth. "And I don't know how long that's going to take."

He shook his head slowly. "You're going to make me wait until morning, aren't you?"

Before I could answer, his phone started vibrating loudly.

Sighing, he took his hand off me to look at it. "I have to take this."

"And I have to get to my own meeting," I told him with one final look at myself in the mirror.

"Nina," he called after me as I headed to the door.

I put my thumb and pinky to the side of my face. "Call me," I mouthed to him as he started to put his cell to his ear.

He winked at me before answering the call. "Hello?"

I grinned as he followed me out of the bathroom.

"Where are you? I'm headed that way now," he told the person on the phone.

I scanned the area. We'd left the little hallway and I was able to see the first floor. The party seemed to have grown, and more people were milling around on the far end of the event space. I looked around and fortunately, no one seemed to be on the second floor.

While giving instructions over the phone, Russ grabbed my arm and assisted me down the steps. When we reached the landing, his fingertips trailed from my elbow to my wrist. A smile played on his lips as he tenderly touched the bracelet he'd given me. For a moment, I thought he was going to hold my hand.

Instead, he brushed his fingers against mine and then removed his hand completely.

"Yes, I'm aware. I got this. I'll be there in a couple of minutes," he said bitingly before ending the call.

The shift between his professional tone and the way he talked to me was slight. There was no code-switching, which I liked. There was just a dry firmness that didn't exist in our conversation.

The large clock high on the wall caught my eye. *Shit.*

"Do you know where you're headed?" he asked me as I picked up the pace. A chuckle rumbled out of him. "I guess so with the way you're running."

"I've been gone for almost thirty minutes!"

He had long legs, so it was easy for him to keep up with me. "You want me to come with you to explain to them what kept you?" he offered.

"Yeah, that'll go over *real* well," I replied sarcastically, rolling my eyes. "You're just asking for security to put us out, huh?" I elbowed him gently. "You need to worry about your own meeting."

"You're right," he agreed.

The music got louder, and the crowd became thicker as we got closer to the main event. His hand rested on the small of my back as we navigated the density of people. I shook my shoulders to the beat as we moved.

Russ slid his left hand to my hip and drew me into him. "I need to head that way." He pointed with his other hand toward the right side of the room. With a squeeze, he put his lips to the shell of my ear. "See you soon."

I giggled, playfully pushing him away. "Text me when you're done."

"Give me an hour, tops," he said before turning and disappearing through the crowd.

Pushing my feelings to the back burner, I switched gears. I'd barely taken a step toward the DJ booth when I saw a vaguely familiar face.

"Every time I see you, you have a good-looking young man on your arm," the older lady I'd seen on the dance floor remarked, wiggling her eyebrows. "Your boyfriend might get jealous of that one."

Oh shit!

I forced a laugh in response as I continued on my path.

Linking back up with Russ while at the ball was not going to happen. I'd spent almost two hours, half of that on the dance floor, with Dru and so many people saw us together. The narrative about me would shift quickly and harshly if I walked out hand in hand with Russ. Technically, I could do whatever I wanted to do. But because I wanted to see where the RLF partnership could take me, I knew I shouldn't do it.

I'll meet up with Russ at his hotel later, I decided silently.

"And this is Nina," Lori stated as I approached.

Four beautiful people of varying shades, sizes, and heights turned around to look at me.

"Nina," Lori continued. "This is Taisha"—she pointed to the dark-skinned, slim-thick woman closest to her—"Jacqueline"—she pointed to the tall, slim, pale-skinned woman with blond hair.

Both women flashed bright smiles and lifted their hands in a wave. "Hi!"

"Hi," I said back.

Lori turned and gestured to the six-foot-two-inch, brown-skinned, muscular Colombian man with the shaved head who had stuck his hand out toward me. "That is Matias."

"How are you?" he asked, shaking my hand.

"Good, thank you. You?" I replied to the good-looking man.

"And this is Jonah," Lori continued, patting the shoulder of the six-four, thickly built man with the close-cut Caesar fade.

"What's up, Nina?" Jonah greeted me with a smile, showing off his dimples.

"What's up?" I responded to the sexy man, who was most certainly checking me out.

"It's so good to meet all of you," I added.

"Nina is the newest addition to the RL Fashions brand ambassador team. Most of you came on at the beginning of the summer so you know the ropes. Remedy herself saw Nina and knew she would be a perfect addition to the team."

They gave me a warm welcome and she facilitated small talk for a few minutes. I got good energy from each of them.

"The five of you will represent RL Fashions as we burst onto the scene with our first full line," Lori told us over the music. "The coming weeks will be busy. You'll have appearances in addition to your other duties. But one of the things that came up tonight with some of the people from the executive team is the idea of a group shoot, with all five of you being showcased. So as a team-building activity, your first assignment is to come up with a photo idea and demonstrate it on film. You have fittings on Monday. On Friday, I'll meet with you and give you the schedule. At that meeting, if we like what you've come up with in the photo, we'll share that with marketing. Once all that is over, if there's time, you'll meet the board."

It was a lot of information and I felt overwhelmed.

"All of this will be in an email that if you haven't already gotten, you'll get tomorrow," Lori concluded. "But I just wanted to let you all know what some of the executive team had decided about the group picture so you can all exchange contact information and plan accordingly. There's still plenty of time left in the party, so get to know each other, mingle, have a good time. I'll see you on Monday!"

Lori damn near danced away as the beat to the next song dropped.

"I didn't know coming to this thing was going to result in homework," Jacqueline complained. "I can't enjoy myself knowing we have work to do."

"We can do both," Taisha responded expressively. "Let's exchange numbers. I'll start a group chat."

"Is anyone available tomorrow?" Matias asked. "We could get together before I catch my flight."

"I have plans tomorrow," I replied quickly.

Taisha nodded. "Yeah, so do I."

"I can only do tomorrow," Jonah pointed out. "My schedule is kind of tight this week. But I'm free Thursday night."

"I have a class on Thursday, but it's over at seven," Jacqueline mentioned.

"What if we just go somewhere and plan something out tonight?" Taisha proposed. "We're all here now. We're all available now. It shouldn't take that long. Let's finish up here and then meet somewhere to plan this out."

"We could go to Al's Diner," I suggested.

Matias's eyes lit up. "I love that place!"

"I see you have good taste," Jonah flirted, not taking his eyes off me.

My lips curled into a smile. "You would be correct."

"Let's wrap up here in, say . . . thirty minutes?" Jacqueline looked at the time on her phone. "And then thirty minutes to get there and get parked—"

"We meet in an hour and fifteen minutes," Matias interjected. "Some of us may need to make sure our dates get home before arriving at the diner."

I nodded. "Okay, that's cool. So we'll meet at Al's Diner in an hour and fifteen minutes." I looked at the beautiful faces that surrounded me and smiled. "Sounds good."

We said our goodbyes and scattered.

We all needed to use the next thirty minutes wisely before we left, to make sure we talked to everyone who was of importance and networked with the litany of guests whose successes in fashion, television, and/or business got them an invitation.

I made my rounds while also keeping an eye out for Russ. I wondered if his business worked closely with the fashion world or if he was an investor. Either way, I hoped he closed whatever deal he was trying to close.

". . . and that's why it's important to have representation," a woman who said she was on the board finished telling me.

I nodded politely. "Representation is important."

She had made that same point three times.

"I hate to cut this short, but my ride is probably outside waiting for me." I pointed to the huge clock high on the wall.

When she looked up at it, her eyes widened. "Oh, wow! I've let time get away from me. I need to find my husband so we can get home and relieve the sitter."

We said our goodbyes and I headed to the door. Casting one last look around and not seeing Russ, I pulled out my phone.

Nina: A thing just popped up with the people I was
meeting, but I will be at your hotel on time in the
morning.

I was just about to walk into Al's Diner to meet the other models
when I received a text back.

Russ: My meeting ran longer than expected. Let me
know when you make it home. It doesn't matter the
time. Good luck with your work thing and I'll see you in
the morning.

"You have a beautiful smile," Jonah commented, startling me.

His unexpected presence forced my eyes up from my phone to
meet his.

"Thank you," I replied, slipping my phone in my bag. "Where
did you come from? I didn't hear you walk up."

He opened the door to the diner wider. "They gave us that table
right there at the window, so I saw you coming." His lips spread
into a slow smile. "And I wasn't about to let you open the door for
yourself. After you."

I walked through the door, and I could feel his eyes on my ass.

Ordinarily I would've at least flirted and started the process of
roster recruitment with Jonah since I had a freshly opened spot.
But instead, I glanced back and smiled. "Thank you."

"No, thank you."

I wasn't sure what Jonah was getting paid or what his deal was;
however, I knew my contract. And as sexy as that six-four, thickly
built, mahogany-skinned man was, he wasn't worth violating the
fraternization policy. Besides, Russ was heavy on my mind, and
knowing I was going to spend Sunday with him made Jonah easy
to resist.

A flashback caused my lower body to clench.

Seven o'clock can't come fast enough.

10

The early morning sun beamed down on Russ, almost spotlighting his good looks as he started his car. I eyed his profile and then let my gaze sweep over his body. From his black T-shirt that stretched over his broad chest to his dark gray joggers that fit him just right, he made comfortable look sexy. But when I noticed he was also wearing the black-and-white two-tone sneakers, I felt a warm flush roll over my skin.

I glanced down at the matching pair on my feet before I realized our outfits looked purposely coordinated.

"You tired?" Russ asked, pulling me from my thoughts.

"A little. But I'll make it. How are you?" I wondered.

"I'm better now." He programmed the music to his Bluetooth speaker and then looked at me. "Seeing you makes everything better."

My stomach flipped. "I feel the same way. You think I'd be up so early on the weekend for just anybody?"

He smirked. "You ready for this?"

"I'm ready for whatever you have planned."

He hooked his finger under my chin and leaned over the middle console. "Good."

His mouth covered mine, kissing me softly.

I wasn't sure if it was the fact that it was seven o'clock in the morning or if the sandalwood-and-leather scent had seduced me, but the kiss made me heady.

Breaking the kiss, he stared at me for a moment, and I felt something.

Again, my stomach flipped.

I must be tired.

"What are you thinking about?"

"You were wearing that suit last night," I complimented him.

"Thank you," he said as he pulled off the lot and merged into traffic. "I know I told you several times, but you were absolutely beautiful last night. It caught me off guard."

I feigned offense. "That I was beautiful?"

"That you were there," he quickly clarified. He looked over at me. "You are always beautiful. But I've never seen you in something like that. I'm going to have to find somewhere to take you to so I can get you dressed up like that again." He paused for a second. "Somewhere that's not for business. Somewhere that can be all pleasure."

"Speaking of business and pleasure . . ." I shifted my body in his direction. "I know that we don't talk about work. But our bathroom break didn't mess up the networking you were doing last night, did it?"

He shook his head. "Nah." Reaching over, he grabbed my hand and brought it to his lips. "But thanks for asking."

"Of course! I definitely wouldn't want to be the reason why you lost any money."

"I don't want you to ever worry about that. But now that you bring up business and pleasure, what were *you* doing there last night?"

I quirked an eyebrow and twisted my lips into a smile.

He didn't know I was a model or an influencer. He definitely didn't know about my new contract with RL Fashions. He only knew about my work with Charlotte, and I left it at that.

"Mixing and mingling," I answered in a noncommittal way. "I'm a fashion girly. You know I like to be on the scene."

He laughed. "This is true. You said you had to link with some people. Were you late?"

I shook my head. "Nope. Right on time, and then we spent two hours coming up with a really cool idea."

"What kind of idea?"

I bit down on my bottom lip and considered the question for a second. "It's for a work project. I'll tell you if it works out," I told him.

"What—oh!"

"Okay!"

We reacted at the same time as a song we hadn't heard in a long time blasted through the speakers.

"I forgot all about this song," I cried before I started rapping along with it.

Russ also knew all of the lyrics and joined me.

By the time the song ended, we were both out of breath.

"I did not think you were going to know all the lyrics," he said with a laugh. "What do you even know about them?"

"I know every song on that album," I retorted. "Before streaming, I got the CD when it first came out and played that thing on repeat. I might've been a little young to know the lyrics, but they were rapping so fast, my parents didn't know what they were saying anyway."

"My older brother had the CD. He's eight years older so I heard and saw a lot of shit I was too young for."

"You have three siblings, right?"

"Yeah. I'm the second of four."

"Ah." I nodded knowingly. "So, you're the middle child."

"I mean . . . I'm in the middle."

Pulling out my phone, I typed something in the search engine. "As the second born, it says that you demand respect."

"Yeah." He chuckled under his breath. "That's true."

Nodding, a memory hit me. "I remember you saying that disrespect makes you mad."

"Disrespect me or anyone I love, and I have to shut that shit down."

"Noted." I looked down at the list. "And that kind of ties in with the next one because it says that you're the peacemaker. Is that true?"

"My family has big personalities, so I was always keeping the peace."

"It says you have a large social circle, and you thrive on friendships."

"Yes and no. I know a lot of people. I am in a lot of social situations. But my circle is small."

"So, you're around a lot of people socially, but you don't spend a lot of time with a lot of people personally."

He nodded. "Exactly. I value my time, so when I get some free time, I only want to be around a select few people. That's always been the case. Everyone I spend time with is someone who adds value to my life in some way, shape, or form."

"Sounds like I should feel special," I teased.

He glanced over at me. "You *are* special."

The smoothness of his delivery caused a flutter in my belly. Eyeing his profile, I smiled. "And don't you forget it."

"Never that."

Shifting my attention back to my phone, I continued to read. "It says you're somewhat rebellious." I looked back over at him with a smirk. "I already know that's true."

He snickered. "Yeah, that's gotta be a trait you have, too . . ."

"We're not talking about me right now," I laughed, deflecting. "And lastly, the list says you're a people pleaser."

"Now that one isn't true."

"Really?"

Licking his lips, he switched lanes. "The only person I'm trying to please is you."

The heat crept up my neck and inflamed my face. "Oh, really?"

"Honesty is too important to me for me to be a people pleaser. That's why my circle is small. It's why I run my business the way that I do. It's why my mom has been mad at me for the last few weeks."

"Wait." I put my phone in my lap. "Why is she mad at you?"

He let out a short, dry laugh. "They were on my ass about settling down. I told them they need to worry about what my siblings got going on and leave me out of the nonsense. The whole table went off." He smirked. "Apparently my brother is going through it with his wife again. One of my sisters is pregnant and the other one has been married for five years and will tell them they are being antifeminist by asking her about her womb." He glanced over at me. "That's a direct quote from the weekend."

"If everybody has something going on, why are they mad at you for not settling down?"

"Oh no, they stay mad about that. But currently, my mom said she's mad that I ruined a nice pleasant dinner."

My jaw dropped. "No! You ruined dinner?"

"I didn't ruin it. Everybody was just hype for the rest of it and loudly defending what they had going on. I didn't even mean it the way everyone took it. All I meant was that they have three other kids to focus their attention on."

I snickered. "So, everybody took what you said the wrong way and got in their feelings?"

"Everybody! I was the one trying to make peace, but it was too late."

"And you ruined dinner." I shook my head. "Damn shame."

"That's the same shit my mom said." He snickered. "It isn't often all four of us are home, so she felt a way."

"How are you going to make it up to her?"

"I'm going to head to Michigan next month for Sunday dinner. The oldest and the youngest are already there. Once I get my other sister to confirm this week, I'll smooth things over with my mom."

"Have you talked to her since then?"

"Yeah, I talk to her every week. If I can either bring home my future wife or get all four of us home for dinner, she'll be satisfied."

I don't know why the statement surprised me, but my eyebrows shot up. "Really? You're ready to settle down?"

"For the right woman, absolutely." He glimpsed at me. "Why does that shock you?"

"I don't know." Shifting in my seat, I racked my brain for understanding. "You are always jetting off. It just felt like you had a certain lifestyle."

"You trying to call me a fuckboy?"

"I was going to say a rolling stone, but I mean . . ." I gestured at him with my hands. "If the shoe fits. I don't know what you do in these other cities!"

He let out a chuckle. "Wow, Nina! Why the hell would you think that?"

"You like to go out and have a good time—"

"So do you!"

Exactly.

"We have fun together. That has always been our thing," I explained. "We enjoy life. We like to be out and about. And you're always on the move, so I assume you keep the fun going when I'm not around."

"Nina," he started, picking up speed to go around a truck. "It's not even like that."

"Okay, my bad, Bubba Wallace," I joked as I tugged at my seatbelt.

His amusement burst out of him as a deep rumble. The way his laugh filled the car simultaneously filled me. Warmth spread through my veins as the sound ricocheted around the car.

"I had to get around them," he explained. "You know I got you. There's nothing for you to worry about."

"I didn't say I was worried. I was just acknowledging that the speed limit isn't ninety-five."

"Yeah, aight. What does your little article say about you being an only child?"

"Don't try to change the subject, Speed Racer." I picked up my phone and scrolled down. "It says lonely, spoiled, high sense of independence, poor social skills, high achievers, and highly sensitive to criticism," I read. Looking over at him, I shrugged. "Three out of six are true."

"I can probably guess the three." He counted them off with his hand. "High achiever, sense of independence, and spoiled."

I smirked. "Correct. How did you guess?"

"From the way you carry yourself, I know you're not lonely. Seeing the way you worked the room when we first met, I know you have social skills. I don't know if you're highly sensitive to criticism because I haven't had any complaints." He glanced over at me. "So, there's no criticism here."

I bit my lip to keep from grinning. "Good to know."

"So spoiled had to be the last one."

I propped my elbow on the middle console and rested my chin on my fist. "Let's talk about how and why you think I'm spoiled."

"Am I wrong?"

Trying not to look as amused as I was, I narrowed my eyes. "That's not the point. What's your definition of spoiled?"

"There are a few different definitions, but with you . . . I can tell that you're used to getting your way; you're used to getting what you want."

My jaw dropped and I reacted indignantly. "What? Whatchumean?"

"It's not a bad thing. It's clear you've been taken care of and there's nothing wrong with that. You know what you want, and you go for it. There's a confidence that comes with that, and it's sexy as hell." He slowed the car as we approached standstill traffic. "So, who spoiled you?"

"My parents. There's nothing my dad wouldn't give me. There's nothing my mom wouldn't do for me." Thinking about my parents, I smiled. "They really are the best. I'm blessed."

"You never really heard the word no, did you?"

I shook my head profusely. "I've heard no so many times in my life! I wasn't the 'I can always get my way' type of spoiled. I was spoiled with love, attention, and generosity. My parents always made sure I was good. They still do. They poured into me so that I could grow up and pour into myself. So, when dating, I know what I want, what I need, and I only allow men who pour into me into my life."

"I see the way you are with people. The way you pour, I can see why you want it reciprocated."

A smile tugged at my lips as I reflected on his observation.

"That's exactly what I'm talking about," I replied. "Reciprocity. I don't ask for anything I can't give."

"So, you always pour back?"

Smirking, I gave him a look. "Don't you feel poured into?"

"Yeah, but I'm trying to figure out if everybody gets this treatment."

They didn't.

Russ was different than the others. While he was fun and the sex was amazing, the way he was present with me made him stand out from anyone I'd ever dated. He stayed in the moment with me.

His energy matched mine and we fed off one another. All of the men poured, but it was the way Russ poured that made me prioritize time with him over the others.

But I wasn't about to tell him that.

I wiggled my eyebrows. "Wouldn't you like to know?"

"Yes. That's why I asked," he deadpanned.

I cackled.

When our amusement died down, he glanced at me before he got into the other lane. "Nah, but for real . . . all I'm saying is that if you're pouring like this you need to always make sure whoever you're pouring into is pouring back with the same energy." He put his hand on my thigh. "Make sure they earn this shit."

I spread my legs wider and moved his hand into the crotch of my black yoga pants. "This most definitely needs to be earned."

Pressing his fingers against me, he chuckled. "What am I going to do with you?"

"Anything you want."

"Nina," he groaned. Pulling his hand away from me, he grabbed the bulge in his gray joggers. "Don't do this to me."

I looked over at him and grinned. "What?"

He shook his head and didn't answer me. Instead, he put both hands on the steering wheel. "I gotta stay focused," he said more to himself than to me. "We have a long day and I have plans for you."

"Plans for me? Do tell."

"Let's just say you're going to sleep good tonight."

My smile grew. "I like the sound of that." I sat back in my seat and stared out the window. "When is your place going to be done?"

I wasn't sure where the question came from, but it surprised me.

"If all goes well with my inspection tomorrow, I'll be able to move in at the end of the month," he said with a glance over at me. "I'll be in your neck of the woods on a more permanent basis. What do you think about that?"

"I think that'll be cool. What do you think about that?"

"I love Richland. I always knew I was going to build a house in Richland, so I love it. And I can't lie . . . I love the idea of seeing more of you."

A slow smile pulled at my lips. "Once a week isn't enough for you anymore?" I teased. "You want more?"

He was quiet for a second. "You know exactly what I want."

The sexiness in his tone caused me to squeeze my thighs together. "No . . ." Licking my lips, I stared at his profile. "Tell me."

"I—"

His phone rang over his Bluetooth speaker. The number flashed on the display.

"I'm sorry," he apologized. "I need to take this."

"Go ahead," I whispered as his finger touched the screen to answer the phone.

"Hello?" he answered.

"Hi," a perky female voice rang out. "Is this Mr. Russell Long?"

"Yes."

"I just want to confirm your arrival today at four o'clock."

He paused for a second. "Confirmed."

"Okay, thank you. We look forward to seeing the two of you later today."

He looked over at me. "We look forward to it, too. Thanks."

I had no idea what was in store for the day, but excitement rippled through me as he disconnected the call.

We spent the next hour joking with one another until we had tears in our eyes. I was so distracted by our conversation that I didn't realize we'd made it to our destination until we turned into a massive parking lot. He started looking around with a goofy grin on his face as he pulled into a parking spot.

My eyes widened as I took in the large sign on the horizon. "Are you serious?"

He nodded as he turned the car off. "Very serious."

"I was just talking about this place with my parents a couple weeks ago. I used to come here every summer with my family—at least three times a summer."

"I remember."

My brows furrowed. "I told you that?"

His smile grew. "You did. And you told me you hadn't been as an adult."

I'd told him that weeks ago as an offhand comment. I didn't even remember until that moment. My heart thumped against my chest, and I shook off the feeling that washed over me.

"That's right." I cleared my throat lightly. "That was when you told me you were scared of E.T. as a kid."

His smile dropped as he opened the door to get out. "I was four, and that muthafucka was an alien!"

Giggling, I put my hands to my face as Russ walked around the car to open my door. Staring over at the large sign, I felt a sentimental tug on my heartstrings.

"Magic World Amusement Park," I whispered to myself, just before he helped me out of the car.

His eyes danced as he studied my face. "I love when you get that look."

I smiled up at him. "What look?"

He cupped my cheeks. "That one."

"I never know what to expect from you," I explained gleefully. "You're always full of surprises."

"I do it to see your eyes light up like this." He leaned down so his mouth was hovering over mine. "And I feel the same way about you."

I inhaled deeply.

Before I could say anything in response, he dropped a kiss against my lips and then slipped his arm around me.

"You ready for this?" he asked as we headed toward the entrance.

I didn't even answer with words. A childlike glee rippled through me, and I let out a little squeal.

Russ laughed.

My excitement was genuine, and when he collected our wristbands from the man at the gate, I was bouncing on my heels.

"This is incredible!" I exclaimed. "Everything looks like it did fifteen years ago, but at the same time, it looks completely different."

"I've actually never been here before."

My eyes bulged. "What?"

He shook his head. "It's my first time. My family isn't from here. I only moved to Maryland when I got to HU."

Grabbing his hand, I tugged him toward the gate. "Well, then, come with me. There's a lot I want to show you."

He smirked. "There's a lot I want to see."

From the moment we walked through the gates of the amusement park, I knew we were going to have a good time.

And we did.

We rode almost every rollercoaster, and he made fun of my exhilarated screams down each hill. We competed at the ring toss, and we playfully talked shit the entire time. When we got hungry, we tried different foods from different stands, and rated each item like we were food critics. We watched a band's musical performance and danced like they were playing our song. For almost seven hours, we didn't just enjoy each other's company. We had fun.

We even got into a spirited argument with a man who incorrectly guessed an answer for trivia.

"I didn't know you knew so much about the government," I marveled, truly impressed.

"The only way to work the system is to know the system," he replied.

"Let me find out you're as smart as you are pretty."

He chuckled. "I could say the same about you. You swept that planet category. Were you an astronomy major or something?"

"I minored in astronomy."

"Really?" He gave me a look. "Let me find out you wanted to be an astronaut."

The laugh that erupted out of me was so loud and boisterous. He had been cracking me up all day. So, it caught me by surprise that he was staring at me like it was the first time he'd ever heard me laugh.

"Why are you looking at me like that?"

He shook his head. There was a little wistful smile that played on his lips. "No reason."

I narrowed my eyes suspiciously.

Before I could say anything, he cleared his throat.

"What made you pursue astronomy?" he asked.

"It was by accident. I thought it was an astrology class I was signing up for as an elective. But the first class was so interesting, and since I've always loved the sky, I stayed." I lifted my shoulders. "But it worked out."

"Yeah, I see." He pointed back to the booth where the trivia took place. "We almost took first place back there."

Amused, I bumped him with my hip. "We were robbed, and you know it."

"Okay, okay." He lifted his hands and relented. "We were."

"They said they were asking ten questions and they asked nine."

"Well . . ." He pulled a face.

I stopped in my tracks. "What?"

"There *were* ten questions."

"No." I shook my head and starting walking again. "There were nine."

He ran his hand over his beard. "There were ten."

"No!" The look on his face gave me pause. "Are you joking with me?"

He frowned. "I'm afraid not."

"When I argued with that guy, you had my back the whole time!" I argued.

"And I'm going to always have your back in public." He grabbed my hand and brought it to his lips as we made our way toward the Ferris wheel. "And I'll call you on your shit in private."

I bit my lip. "Okay."

A woman walked by, loudly talking on her cell phone about her skyrocketing rent while corralling her three kids.

"That's one of the reasons why I can't wait for my house to be done," he declared.

"Yeah, rent is wild. I don't understand how they are justifying the hikes. My rent went up almost three hundred dollars, and they've done nothing different."

"It's been cheaper for me to live in a hotel since my lease was up in July than it would've been for me to do a month-to-month lease until my house is ready at the end of the month."

"You've been traveling so much anyway so it wouldn't have

made sense to pay rent and pay for a hotel if you have the option to let go of one."

He nodded. "Yeah. I don't mind spending money. But I need it to make sense and that doesn't make sense to me."

We launched into a conversation about financial literacy and capitalism.

"—and don't get me started on credit scores," I complained, rolling my eyes. "That's the most made-up shit."

"Hell yeah," he agreed. "You can pay the minimum balance or the full balance, and it does the same thing to your score. Paying off a loan hurts your credit score, but getting more credit cards can build it." He shook his head. "The score is contingent upon borrowing money, but you need a score to borrow money. And you need a borrowing history to get a score."

He spoke with such elegant passion, I found myself staring up at him. Realizing he was done speaking, I quickly nodded in agreement. "It's wild."

"And they don't teach enough about that when we're young. The whole thing is a setup."

A preteen kid tripped his mother up, and our conversation immediately deviated to the shenanigans in front of us. Once she got up and it was clear that she wasn't hurt, I tried not to laugh. But I shifted my gaze to Russ and the moment our eyes met, we both cracked up. I had tears in my eyes when he said she looked like she was on ice. We joked our way to our last ride.

"Look at the sky," I marveled, standing in line for the Ferris wheel. The sky was the prettiest shade of powder blue. The streaks of sunlight burst from behind huge fluffy clouds. "It's beautiful."

"Yeah, it is," Russ responded quietly.

I glanced at him and found him staring at me. I grinned. "You're not looking."

"Oh, I'm looking."

I giggled, bumping him with my hip. "I meant at the sky!"

"Can you blame me?"

My stomach fluttered. Cocking my head to the side, I gave him a look. "Are you trying to seduce me?"

He leaned down, putting his lips against the shell of my ear. "Always."

I nodded, placing my hands against his chest. "Well, it's working."

Moving his head so our foreheads touched, he stared into my eyes. "Oh, really?"

I nodded again, slowly. "Yeah," I whispered as his lips came closer to mine.

Our mouths connected lightly. It was a sweet, chaste, quick kiss. And it put a smile on my face. But when I opened my eyes and saw the way he was staring at me, the breath left my lungs.

"You're holding up the line!" the Ferris wheel attendant called out.

Breaking apart and looking around, we realized he was talking to us.

I covered my mouth to stifle my laugh.

"My bad," Russ apologized to the man before ushering me forward.

Snickering, we made our way to the rusty blue-and-white Ferris wheel car with glass windows all around. Classical music pumped through the small speaker as we climbed aboard.

Locking the door with a firm click, the attendant's thin lips were pulled into a tight line.

He was not amused.

"You know he's cussing you out in his head," I told Russ as soon as we started moving.

"As long as he gets us off this thing when it's over, that's fine," he replied with a laugh.

"Oh, look," I gasped, pointing to the way the sun was peeking over a thick stretch of clouds.

He draped his arm around my shoulders. "Yeah, that's sick."

We were both quiet, staring at the sky as we slowly ascended.

"Today has been so much fun," I murmured.

"It really has. I didn't know what to expect, but I knew it was going to be a good time with you." His fingers danced over my shoulder. "Thank you for being here with me."

"Thank you for planning this."

"I planned it for you, but I enjoyed every minute of it."

"I'm glad you enjoyed your first Magic World experience. Would you come back?"

"I would." He ran his free hand over his short beard and chuckled to himself. "But I don't think this place would've been half as much fun without you."

My lips spread into a smile. "I was just thinking that I don't know if I've ever had as much fun here as I have with you."

Pulling me into him, he flashed a self-satisfied smile. "Oh, really?"

"Yeah. Before today, my favorite memory at this place was with my childhood best friend Leah, my cousin Ashlyn, and Ashlyn's best friend Stephanie."

"Why was that your favorite?"

"We were sixteen, maybe fifteen, and my uncle, Ashlyn's dad, dropped us off. It was a random, hot summer day. We were here from like ten o'clock in the morning to seven o'clock at night. It was my first time being here without my parents, or any parents supervising. We rode all the rides, flirted with all the boys, and spent all of the little cash we were given for the day." I giggled at the memory. "We all had a change of clothes with us, and I changed into this cute little outfit I'd put together. I got so many compliments on my style. It was one thing to hear it in school or at the mall, but it felt bigger here. That's when I knew fashion was my passion."

That was the moment I knew fashion was my life.

"So that's why you look so good all the time," he observed.

I grinned. "Yeah, pretty much." I sighed. "Like I said, it was a great day. But then it started pouring down raining and we had to wait in the rain for an hour to be picked up. We danced in it and laughed about it, but I think three of us ended up sick. It was a mess. But it's still one of my favorite memories."

"Sounds like it."

I looked out at the vast sky. We were so high up on the Ferris wheel that it felt like we were in arm's reach of the clouds. "It was a good day, but this day . . . this day has been perfect," I murmured, still mesmerized by the sky.

You're perfect.

"Why is that?" he wondered.

When I turned my face up to him, our eyes locked.

"You." The admission spilled out of me in an unexpected breath. I ripped my eyes away from him and stared out at the sky. "The thought put into it."

It wasn't just something he thought would be fun for us to do. He heard me mention how I hadn't been since I was a kid and he got us tickets. It was sweet. It was thoughtful. It somehow felt simultaneously nostalgic and new.

Using his forefinger and thumb, he turned my head toward his. He didn't say anything. He searched my face and smiled in a way that made me warm inside. I felt open and vulnerable under his gaze. It didn't scare me so much as it made me feel exposed.

He brought his mouth just above mine. "You are always a thought."

My stomach fluttered.

His lips had just brushed mine. "You—"

The Ferris wheel jerked unexpectedly, and we both startled apart.

"Whoa," Russ reacted, looking around. "The fuck is this?"

The ride kept moving but we were swinging harder than we were to begin with. "I knew this was a setup when I saw the rust on this thing!"

"And you laughed in that man's face, so he put us in this rust bucket."

My head fell back, and I let out a loud cackle. "You laughed, too! You think I wanted this? You think I wanted us dangling in the air on a rusty cord?"

Shaking his head, he ran his hand down his face. "The cord *is* rusty as hell."

I snickered. "I think your boy is doing it on purpose."

"All because you laughed in his face." He shook his head. "You wrong for that."

"There he is right there, mean mugging you."

When we looked to the right and saw the attendant staring at us, we cracked up. Twisting so my back was to him, I tried to hide my face. "He's going to think we're laughing at him."

When our amusement died out, we were cuddled up with one another. Russ pulled me into him, my back to his chest and his arms around my waist as we stared out the window. His head rested against mine and I felt his breath against my cheek. I was comfortably content as I enjoyed the view.

The gentle sway of the ride as we ascended combined with the classical music playing over the speakers to create a vibe. The sun kissed my skin through the glass, and being in his arms, I was just as warm on the inside as I was on the outside.

"I never thought dangling precariously from the sky could be so peaceful," I murmured.

"It is." He kissed my cheek. "Are you tired?"

I languidly shook my head. "No. Just"—I smiled—"relaxed."

"I like seeing you like this."

"Like what?"

"Like you don't have a care in the world."

"With you, I don't," I admitted.

The words were true, but they slipped out of my mouth before I had a chance to swallow them down.

"Good," he uttered, holding me tighter. "Because that's exactly how I feel with you." He paused for a moment. "You're my escape."

I repeated the statement. "Your escape."

That wasn't the first time he'd said that.

"Yes," he confirmed. "I can forget everything and just be . . ."

His sentence trailed off, and we sat in a comfortable silence for a few seconds. His last words hung in the air as I pushed myself up so I could face him.

"Just be what?" I asked him.

He caressed my cheek with his forefinger. "Just be me."

The sincerity and openness in his eyes pulled at my heartstrings. An unexpected sensation swept through me. I didn't have the words to express how what he said made me feel. So instead of a verbal response, I leaned forward until my mouth met his.

He pulled out of the kiss just enough to speak. "Once we get off this ride, are you ready to head out?"

I nodded, letting our lips meet again. "Yeah."

My arms wrapped around his neck, holding him closer. His hands grabbed my ass, pulling me into him. Our tongues caressed one another, devouring one another, and I lost myself in him.

Without warning, the door to our car swung open. "Not again," the Ferris wheel attendant complained under his breath. "Hope you folks enjoyed your ride." The annoyance in his tone was evident.

We pulled apart, and my face was flushed as I flashed a smile to the attendant.

"We did, thank you," I answered.

"Please come this way," he directed us with a little bit of an attitude. "Have a good day."

As we exited the ride, Russ smirked. "Yeah, you too." Draping his arm around my shoulders, he guided me down the sidewalk.

"I think he was a little bit of a hater," I mumbled. "But I'd hate, too, if I had to work on a beautiful day like this."

"Nah, he was mad because your fine ass was with me."

Giggling, I rolled my eyes. "While I agree that I'm fine, that man was not checking for me."

"You didn't see the way he was looking at you."

"I saw the way he was looking at *us*."

He chuckled. "Yeah, okay."

We made our way out of the park.

"Saturday after next, are you free?" I asked seemingly out of nowhere. "It's almost three weeks from now."

"That's the weekend after I move into my place. I don't have anything planned yet. What are we doing?"

I grinned. "My best friend is having a birthday party at Dowdy Lake, and I'd love for you to be my date."

"Say no more. If you want me there, I'm there."

"It'll be a good time."

"We always have fun together." He kissed the top of my head. "No matter what it is."

"That's what I like about you. We could be doing absolutely nothing, and I'd still have the most fun with you," I admitted.

"I was thinking the same thing when we were driving here. I hate the idea of a road trip. But a road trip with you would be a good look."

"I think you like me a little bit."

Chuckling, he shook his head.

For whatever reason, I didn't notice that his arm was still around my shoulders until he removed it to open the passenger-side door to let me in. He walked around to the driver's side and when he got in, he smiled at me. Without a word, he started the engine.

"Where are we going?" I wondered.

His smile grew as he pulled from the parking spot. "You'll see."

"Russ!"

"Do you trust me?"

"As far as I can throw you."

He laughed. "We'll be there in thirty minutes."

He got us there in twenty.

11

I didn't know where we were when we pulled up to the white building with fountains and colorful flowers. It wasn't until I climbed out the car that I saw a sign.

SERENITY'S WELLNESS RETREAT.

My lips spread into a smile. "What is this?"

"You mentioned you had a big week and I also have a lot going on this week so"—grabbing my hand, Russ brought it to his lips—"I thought we could relax together."

I licked my lips. "I like the sound of that."

We walked in and we were greeted by a woman with her hair pulled back into a tight bun.

"Welcome to Serenity! How can we be of service to you?"

"We have a four o'clock appointment under the name Ford."

Her eyes lit up. "Mr. Long!" She turned and grinned at me. "And this must be Ms. Ford."

"Yes," Russ replied. "Thank you for accommodating us."

"It is my pleasure." She leaned forward. "And soon to be yours." She grabbed two wristbands and then gestured for us to follow her. "You will start down here at the showers. Your spa attendant will bring you your robe and slippers and they will escort you to the mud room." She pointed across the hall to the brown door. "Your couple's mud bath will take place in here. After that, you'll rinse off and then you'll be escorted"—she walked a few steps and gestured to the blue door—"to your ninety-minute couple's massage. And then you'll end the session with chromotherapy"—she pointed to the green door—"and refreshments. Do you have any questions?"

I shook my head. "No, I think I got it."

"Yeah, we're good," Russ added.

She flashed a smile. "I'll let Tessa and Byron know you're heading into the shower. They will come to get you to start your experience in fifteen minutes. I hope you enjoy your romance package."

She took a few steps away to speak into a headset.

I waited until she was out of earshot before I looked up at him. "You got the romance package for us? I think you like me a little bit," I teased.

He leaned down and whispered in my ear. "I do."

A chill ran down my spine.

"Go right through these doors," the woman directed us. "Tessa and Byron are expecting you."

"See you on the other side," Russ said with a wink before disappearing through the door.

Biting my lip, I walked into the shower room.

"Oh, wow," I mumbled as I eyed every amenity I would need to shower.

I expected them to have a towel and soap. I didn't expect them to have different types of luxury bath products. They had it all! Impressed, I grabbed the moisturizing soap, shower cap, disposable shower shoes, and facial cleanser. Stripping off my clothes and removing my shoes, I put it all in a locker and then went into the first stall with just my bath products. My hair and feet were protected as I stepped into the rainfall shower.

I hate these, I griped silently.

The water felt good, but I didn't know if the shower cap was going to be enough protection for my hair. Trying not to focus on that, I lathered my body and got myself clean. I didn't think I was taking too long, but I heard a soft knock against the stall's frame.

"Ms. Ford?" a woman called out.

My washcloth stopped mid-swipe. "Yes?"

"I have your bathing bottom, robe, and slippers. Your mud bath is awaiting you."

I rinsed off and then quickly dried before wrapping myself in the towel. It didn't quite cover my entire body so when I stepped out of the shower stall, I had my right breast in my hand to give a semblance of modesty. I exchanged my shower shoes for white terry cloth slippers and my towel for an oversized terry cloth robe. I wiggled into the white swim bottom. The elastic bit into my skin, but overall, it fit.

Once I was fully covered, the petite woman with her hair in a slick bun flashed me a smile and picked up my shower shoes. "I'm Tessa. I'll be your guide for today. Anything you need, let me know." She handed me a swim cap. "For your hair."

We headed out the door and met Russ and his guide in the hallway. We were taken into a room with lots of greenery hanging from walls and draping from the ceiling. The space wasn't that big, so the décor truly looked like a rainforest. The sound of heavy rain, waterfalls, and exotic animals only added to the illusion. The lighting was dim, with uplights strategically placed to illuminate the greenery. In one corner of the room, two huge stone beach chairs sat in a glass enclosure. In the center of the room sat two long, white, oversized tubs elevated on a platform and surrounded by large gray stones and plants.

It was beautiful.

We were ushered around to the other side where there was a small stone bench. There was also a stone trail that led to the corner of the room. I didn't know what to expect but I was grinning.

"These are your mud baths," Tessa told us. "A mixture of hot mineral water, clay, peat, and volcanic ash make up the mud. These ingredients are known for their traditional health-giving properties. It's heated to about one hundred degrees, and you will instantly feel the soothing effects. We will give you your privacy while you remove your robes. Once you're settled in the mud, we will be back to get you started."

"Is my hair tucked in?" I asked after putting on the swim cap. I turned in a circle so he could see.

"Yes."

As soon as the door closed behind our attendants, Russ took my hand. "Let me undress you."

Turning to face him, I held my arms out and allowed him to untie my belt. When my robe parted, I watched Russ's eyes darken. When our eyes locked, he stepped a little closer and placed his hands around my neck. He licked his lips, and his thumb applied slight pressure to the center of my throat.

I swallowed hard.

He ran his hands down my chest, belly, and hips before grabbing my ass. Taking his time, he worked his way back up, over my breasts, before wrapping his hands around my neck again.

"Nina."

The sexy rasp in his voice as he uttered my name caused me to clench. My nipples were rock hard.

"Russ," I responded quietly.

"Mmm."

The soft moan he let out curled my toes in my slippers.

His fingers seared my skin as he moved them over my shoulders, pushing my robe off. He let it fall down my arms and when he bent down to pick it up, he was eye level to my throbbing pussy. He planted a kiss at the apex of my thighs, and I instantly wished I didn't have the bikini bottom on.

"Russ," I gasped.

"Don't say my name like that." He kissed me in the same spot but for longer. "We still have like three hours until we get to the hotel."

"Then stop teasing me," I whispered.

"Then stop saying my name like that."

He slowly stood, tossing the robe onto the stone bench next to us. He stepped back, eyeing me up and down.

My heart pounded in my chest under his gaze.

"You know why I like being with you?" he wondered as his hands caressed my skin.

I exhaled as his fingertips skated over my breasts, lingering on my nipples. "Why?"

His hands traveled over my belly before circling around to my ass. He pulled me into him, and I felt his bulge. My lips parted and I was momentarily distracted.

"Because you feel good," he answered, pulling me back to the conversation.

"I feel good," I repeated softly.

"You're—"

"Are you ready for us to come in?" Byron interrupted as he cracked, then knocked on the door.

As if a starter pistol went off, we startled apart.

"Give us a few more minutes," Russ immediately shouted back, taking off his robe and throwing it with mine.

Damn.

The swim briefs Russ wore stretched deliciously over his erection, constricting him from displaying the full length and girth of his dick. The bulge showcased what I planned to sit on before the day was done.

"Get in first," Russ commanded, snapping me out of my trance.

My gaze shifted from his dick to his eyes to the mud bath. I nodded.

We went as fast as we could, but we had to slowly ease our way into the mud. It wasn't scalding hot, but it was an adjustment. It didn't take long to shift from hot to cozy.

Russ and I were barely submerged when Byron knocked again. "Permission to enter?"

Checking to make sure my body wasn't exposed, Russ called out. "Yes!"

My headrest faced the east wall and Russ's headrest faced the west wall so when we sat back in the tubs, we could see each other. Sitting in mud up to our chin, we grinned at one another.

Tessa and Byron came in and situated themselves beside our respective tubs.

"Your bath is an opportunity to relax, release, and rejuvenate," Tessa started. "The heat draws out impurities and toxins, thereby nourishing your skin. The regenerative and antiseptic properties of mineral-rich mud leaves you with softer, fresher skin. Soaking in this mud and its minerals can help alleviate aches and pains, as it relaxes sore muscles and joints. The soothing properties also do wonders for your mind. As your body releases, your mind also releases and detoxifies. For the next fifteen minutes, you are urged to let go of everything and allow the mud to work. Are you comfortable? Is it too hot?"

After we answered her, she nodded. "Your time starts now."

They stepped away from the tub, and due to the platform and where they were hiding, I couldn't see them. I looked over at Russ and he looked just as confused as I felt. I lifted my eyebrows to communicate silently, and he smiled. I was sure he had no idea what I was trying to say, and that made me smile back.

The rainforest noises echoed through the room, and I suddenly felt extremely relaxed. Closing my eyes, I allowed the nerves surrounding the exclusivity with RLF to fade away. I didn't fall asleep, but I felt like I wasn't fully conscious.

When I opened my eyes again, I peeked over at Russ. His were closed, and he seemed to be in the same zone I was in. As if he could feel my eyes on him, he opened them. It happened so quick; I didn't have the opportunity to turn away.

Staring at each other, we soaked in the hot mud. The way he looked at me held me captive, and a wave of emotion rocked me. I wasn't sure if it was the mud or the detoxification process or what, but my eyes started watering. Still, I couldn't turn away from him. I didn't want to cry in front of him, especially when I had no reason to. It didn't make any sense. His gaze felt like he was speaking to me in a language I didn't fully understand. But I understood enough to have a physical reaction.

I didn't know what he had going on or what he had to release, but my heart went out to him. I'd never wanted to hug him more than I did in that moment. It wasn't sexual. It wasn't based on our intense attraction. It wasn't based on our chemistry. It wasn't even based on our connection.

It was spiritual.

"And that's it for the soaking portion," Byron announced, snatching me from my thoughts.

I looked over at the man with the bald head and then back at Russ.

Russ was staring straight ahead, a contemplative look on his face.

"Let me help you," Tessa offered, reaching for my hand.

As I rocked forward, she handed me a towel to cover my breasts. She pointed out my shower shoes to slip back on before we made our way to the glass enclosure. Mud dripped from our bodies and I didn't look back, but I just knew we were making a mess.

"Stand near this wall," Byron instructed. "You will spend five minutes being heated and letting the mud dry. When the drying process is done, you will spend ten minutes sitting on these stones. When the door is closed, the glass will become opaque, so there is a speaker for us to talk to you. Hit this button if you need us." He pointed to a black button. "And this one if there's an emergency." He pointed to a red one. "If you feel overheated at any time, let us know."

He looked between us before stepping out of the enclosure. Without warning, dry heat blasted us from all angles.

"Oh my God!" I cried.

"What's wrong?" Russ asked.

"I was caught off guard by the desert-air blast."

He snickered. "I was more caught off guard by how hot that mud bath was. I felt like we were being cooked. Like the spa was a front for some cannibalistic shit. I was feeling a little too much like beef stew in that thing."

"We were in a Crock-Pot."

"Talking about it was one hundred degrees. Mannnnn, that shit was easily three fifty."

I giggled. "And now here we are . . . in the microwave."

We were laughing as the mud dried on our skin. I felt the tightness, but it wasn't until the fans slowed to a stop that I noticed how different I felt.

"I think there really are rejuvenating properties in this," I told him. "Look."

We looked like we were covered in clay, not like we'd just stepped out of the mud.

He shook his head. "Gravy."

I burst out laughing. "I was going to say sauce!" I exclaimed.

Tessa knocked on the door before she opened it. Without

hesitation, she pointed to the two stones set up like beach chairs. "Use the ten minutes on the stones to reflect on how you feel with the mud on you. Listen to the sounds of the rainforest and connect with yourself and your body. Instead of talking to each other right now, talk to yourselves."

We sat down.

"You got us in trouble," I whispered playfully.

"That was you!"

We snickered quietly before relaxing into our stone chairs. The mud made my limbs tight and a little more difficult to bend. It felt like I had on a full-body mask. Tessa placed cucumber slices on our eyes and the sudden darkness quieted our amusement. My mind cleared.

"And now, it is time for the mineral shower," Byron told us over the speaker, startling me.

Has it been ten minutes already?

"Brace yourselves," he said before water gently started to fall over us.

With the combination of the rainforest soundtrack and my cucumber-covered eyes, it felt like we were in a heavy rain. Water washed over us gently at first and then increased in pressure. When it stopped, I thought it was over.

"Now please remove your cucumbers and stand," Tessa commanded over the speaker.

Sitting up, I had to blink several times to adjust my vision, but the low lights made it easy. Russ got up before me. Looking up at his sexy, muscular frame, I bit my lip. He was dripping wet and illuminated by the gentle green glow. Although I'd seen him in the shower, I'd never had him tower over me while he was soaking wet.

I liked it.

I liked it a lot.

"Let me help you," Russ suggested, reaching for me.

I allowed him to pull me to my feet. "Thank you."

"For the next few minutes, hold your partner's hands," Tessa instructed.

Russ's fingers intertwined with mine and he gazed at me with such tenderness. I squeezed him and ran my thumbs over the sides of his hands. Even though I knew there were two strangers outside of the room watching our shadows, I was very tempted to kiss him.

"Look into each other's eyes and sync your breathing," Byron guided us over the speaker.

We were already standing close. But I took a step forward so my breasts were pressed against his chest. His lips spread into a smile, and I just knew he was thinking something dirty. I smiled back as he put our interlocked hands behind my back and then brought me closer.

Holding my gaze, he began breathing in time with me. My stomach fluttered with each inhale and my heart pounded with each exhale.

Seconds later, the water started drizzling down on us.

Squinting, we continued to stare into each other's eyes until the water came down harder. I couldn't keep my eyes open any longer, so I squeezed his hand tighter and rested my head against his chest. Hearing his heart thump drowned out the rainforest noises. His chest rose and fell as I leaned into him.

When the water slowed to a light sprinkle, Tessa's voice came in over the speaker.

"You've just experienced our hot-springs mineral shower," she told us. "Hot-springs mineral water heated to . . ."

Russ let go of my hands and grabbed my face. Leaning down, he moved his lips over mine powerfully. I wrapped my arms around his neck and pulled him closer. Our mouths met hungrily, and it wasn't until I moaned that I remembered where we were.

"—so make sure you don't have any more mud on you. We'll be in to bring you your robes and slippers in two minutes."

Leaning down so his lips were against my ear, Russ whispered, "I'm going to sit on this stone . . . and I want you to sit on my lap . . . and ride my dick."

A chill ran down my spine.

"Russ . . ." I was glad I was already wet because the way that man had me dripping, it would've been obvious in my swim bottoms.

His hands slipped down every curve of my body until he had a two-handed grip on my ass. "I want all this ass on me. I want—"

Tessa and Byron knocked before entering. Their presence interrupted the sentence, but he didn't take his hands off my ass. I kept my body pressed against Russ so they couldn't see my bare breasts, my taut nipples, or his hard dick. I turned my head to watch the attendants as they placed our robes and slippers at the door.

"Now it is time for the final stage," Byron announced. "Get dressed, and we'll take you to the cooldown."

"Okay, thank you," I called out.

They left and I looked up at him. "You need to stop. I almost pulled your dick out earlier."

He let out a low, rumbling chuckle. "There's still time."

"No, there isn't," Tessa replied over the speaker.

My jaw dropped and my eyebrows shot up. *Could they hear us the whole time?*

"We'll be right out," Russ replied, looking around.

"You're always getting us into trouble," I teased as I slipped on my robe and removed my swim cap.

He put his on as well. "You started it." He stepped into his slippers and grabbed me by my waist. Lowering his voice, he uttered softly, "But once we get done here, I'm going to finish it."

I let out a trembling breath.

Giggling, I scurried from the glass enclosure, with Russ on my heels.

Tessa and Byron exchanged a knowing smile before the four of us left the mud room. We traveled down the hall and entered a white room with plush white chairs and a couple of love seats facing a glowing statue. I inhaled deeply and looked around. The peppermint scent was prominent but not overbearing.

"This is the cooldown," Byron told us. "This is to rehydrate your body and reset your mind. And because this is a couple's session, this is also an opportunity to reconnect."

"This room utilizes aromatherapy, so the peppermint improves mental function and reduces pain and stress." Tessa ushered us to our seats as she pointed to the light structure in the middle of the room. "The room is lit by the large Himalayan salt lamp, which will boost mood, increase energy levels, and increase the flow of oxygen to your brain. And we have fruit-infused water that will not only rehydrate your body, it'll also flush out any remaining toxins."

We sat on the love seat and propped our feet up on the footstool as we listened. I hadn't realized how thirsty I was until my first sip of water.

"Lastly, you are going to use this time to silently reconnect. Since you've released all the toxins and negativity, use this time to rehydrate your relationship as well."

When they left us alone, we finally took a break from drinking.

"Somebody is thirsty," Russ said, taking another sip of water.

I giggled quietly. "I know you ain't talking! Not the way you just took down that whole bottle."

"I let out a lot of toxins and negativity in that mud. I had to replenish."

I gave him a sidelong glance. I started to make a smart-ass remark, but then I remembered the look that was on his face when we were in the mud.

"What were you thinking about when we were soaking?" I asked, staring at the salt lamp.

My question was met with silence. After a few seconds, I looked over at him. He was fixated on the lamp, so I took in his profile. His tongue wet his full lips before he started to speak.

"What I saw for my life." He looked over at me and gave me a tight smile. "And what I see for my life."

I nodded contemplatively. "Is what you saw for your life lining up with how you're living your life?"

"Yeah. In some ways."

With a tilt of my head, I requested more information. "In what ways?"

"Time. Money. Freedom. Connections." He paused, searching my face for a moment. He looked like he wanted to say something else.

He didn't continue, but the way he was looking at me caused my stomach to flutter.

I cleared my throat lightly. "I know we agreed to not talk about work, so I won't take it personally if you don't want to answer. But I noticed you didn't put your work on your list."

Hesitation flickered across his face.

It was the first time I'd ever seen him hesitate and that intrigued me more. But I didn't want to pry. I reached over and squeezed his hand.

"Never mind," I said quietly. "It's okay."

I started pulling my hand away and he stopped me. Bringing my hand to his lips, he kissed it before allowing me to retreat.

"I love what I do," he began. "But I miss being creative. I miss designing my own shit. I miss getting hands-on with my work. I don't get to do that as often as I used to. And that's been weighing on me. This summer, spending time with you, made me realize that. I have too much going on at work right now. But one day, I'm going to move some things around and make it happen. I hadn't really said anything to anyone until now."

I smiled. "So you're going to get back in your creative bag?"

He nodded. "I am. Creating always made me happy. I'm good with numbers and business. But creating was my shit."

"Then that's what you should be doing. Even if it's not full-time or every day yet. Life is too short for you not to be doing what makes you happy."

"You're right." He ran his hand over his beard and let out a short, dry laugh. "It's going to shake some shit up at work, but I have to. Even if it's only one day a week, I need to get back to my roots."

"As you should," I agreed. "If it's been on your mind to do it, you should do it. If it's going to make you happy, you should absolutely do it. We have one life to live so we have to live it to the fullest."

A ghost of a smile tugged at his lips. "What makes you happy?" he inquired. "Are you doing what you love?"

"I am." I felt myself light up as I thought about how blessed I was to do what I'm passionate about for work. "I'm living my dream. I have my dream job and I've just recently taken it to the next level. I'm . . ." I stopped myself from telling him more. "I'm happy with what I do."

He reached over and stroked my cheek with the back of his fingers. "I can tell."

"I want you to be happy like this, too."

"Thank you." He fingered a coiled strand of my hair. "Tell me how you feel."

My stomach fluttered with nervous energy. "About work?"

Silently tracing the shell of my ear, he didn't say anything for a few moments. "You're open and private at the same time."

"What do you mean?" I murmured, shivering from the gentleness of his touch.

"I know you." His fingertips trailed down my neck. "But there are parts of you that you keep to yourself."

I took in a shuddering breath as his touch continued its path, following the collar of my robe. "Yeah," I murmured in distracted agreement.

"There are things that you don't say with your words, but you say it in other ways."

I averted my eyes briefly. "Hm."

The silence that surrounded us was loud.

"I've always been surprised you don't want to talk about work." He sat back and stared at me. "You light up when you do."

Oh! The knots in my belly loosened.

"Well, it's not just you. I've made it a point to not talk about my career with anyone I've dated," I explained.

"Why?"

"A few years ago, I went on a first date with a man who asked me what I did. After I told him, he called me big money." I shook my head. "Red flag!"

That guy also sexualized the fact that I modeled, insisted on looking me up on social media, and then told me that I thought I was hot shit because I had a lot of followers. He called me big money, but he also started acting like he was in competition with me. Just overall jealous behavior, but I wasn't going to go into all that.

Snickering, he leaned forward. "What?"

I lifted my right hand. "I swear! I never brought up my job with a man again. Calling me big money and 'joking' about me paying for dinner was enough for me."

He tipped my chin up. "Well, it's a damn shame because the way you look when you talk about what you're passionate about is sexy as hell."

I bit my lip to tame my smile. "Well, I'm not the only one." I pointed at him. "I'm surprised you don't talk about work. Since you're always working, I figured it would come up."

"That's exactly why I don't talk about it," he laughed. "It already takes up so much of my time."

"Yeah, but you can't spend as much time working as you do and not love it. It's your business. It's your baby."

"True. But I like to separate business and pleasure. That's why when I do something for myself"—his eyes swept down my robed body—"I like to leave work where it's at."

I shivered. "You might leave it there, but even without talking about it, I know how you get down at work."

He smirked. "Is that right?"

"I might not know all the specifics, but I know you're good at what you do because of how successful you are. I know you're an ambitious go-getter because it's your business and you built it from the ground up. Your attention to detail is"—I kissed the tips of my fingers—"chef's kiss, so I know you're thorough, thoughtful, and focused. You make time to enjoy yourself so that means you delegate freely, and you trust your team—which also means you're a good judge of character." Fighting a smile, I leaned closer to him. "And I've seen the way you take charge, so I know you handle business." I quirked an eyebrow. "See, I know you."

Amused, he grabbed the back of my neck and pulled me to him. "Let me do you next."

I leaned forward, letting him guide my mouth to his. "You can do me now."

"You're funny and smart and"—he kissed me gently—"interesting and unexpected and"—another kiss, longer—"passionate and perceptive." His voice lowered as he continued. "I know fashion is your thing. I knew that when I met you. But you're so effortlessly sexy. Your style, your personality, your conversation, your look, every fucking thing."

My stomach fluttered. "Like I said, you're a good judge of character."

The serene quietness of the room was broken by his hearty chuckle.

"And that concludes your mud treatment," Byron announced, entering the room.

"We hope you have enjoyed your time to replenish," Tessa added, motioning for us to follow. "Now that you've relaxed your mind, come with us so you can relax your body."

We got up and followed the pair into a different part of the building. Soft ambient music coupled with dim lighting created a relaxing atmosphere in the massage room. The white marble flooring shone with fresh wax and white musk scented the air. Sheer white panels of drapery decorated the wall and ceiling, softly hanging above two white chairs. The two tables were side by side, with a couple of feet between them. The mirror-lined wall made it appear as though the room went on forever.

Looking around, I took in the environment. A small smile played on my lips as we were introduced to our masseuses. I wasn't sure if it was just me, but the room was both sterile and sexy at the same time. After being instructed to undress and get under the sheet, we were left alone.

We took off our robes, and while I was hanging mine up, Russ came up behind me.

"What are you doing?" I asked as he slid his hands over my belly and pressed himself against my back.

He ogled me. "Enjoying the view."

I reached back and grabbed his neck, bringing his head lower. "The view is nice."

"It's perfect." His fingers brushed my nipples before he cupped my breasts.

Staring at our reflection in the mirror, there was no denying how good we looked together. I wasn't just focused on the physical either. It was the intimacy, the energy, and the comfortability between us that looked good. But more than that, everything between us felt good.

He kissed my cheek and then my neck. "What's on your mind?"

Turning around, I pushed up on my toes and gave him a soft peck against his lips. "How long until your hard dick is in me."

With a grin, Russ squeezed me tight. "After our massage, I promise—"

The knock at the door startled us apart.

Snickering, we ran over to our tables and covered ourselves up. By the time the door opened, we'd just barely gotten situated.

"Ready to begin?" the masseuse asked.

12

"Russ!" I screamed his name as his fingers dug into my thick thighs.

"Tell me again," he grunted forcefully.

"It's yours. Oh my God, it's yours." My body shuddered as another intense orgasm ripped through me. "Ohmigod."

"Fuck," he swore as I clamped down around him.

He felt like he was deeper than ever and the growl that came out of him sent a tingle down my spine. I felt hornier, wetter, as I ground against him. The dick had never felt so good. I didn't even think I could come again, but I was chasing it. He must've felt what I felt because the way he started fucking me was reckless. His long, deep strokes were coming faster and faster, as if he was losing control.

"Wait," he groaned hoarsely as I locked my legs around his waist to pull him closer.

I opened my eyes just in time to see his handsome face contort as he stiffened. With three violent jolts, he grunted through his release.

It was sexy as hell.

The sunlight poured into the room, casting a glow behind his muscular frame. His chest heaved and his biceps flexed. Just looking at him in the aftermath of his orgasm caused me to clench.

Breathing heavily, he fell forward, caging me with his arms. "Shit," he breathed before covering my mouth with his.

When he finally rolled off me, I brought my hands to my racing heart. "Good morning," I murmured.

He reached for one of my hands and brought it to his lips. "Any morning I get to wake up to you is a good morning."

I bit my lip to keep from smiling. "You're getting soft on me?"

With a smirk, he looked down at his semihard dick, slick with my juices, and then back at me. "We both know you keep me hard."

I giggled.

And almost simultaneously, we both jerked our heads back to his dick.

"What the fuck!" he exclaimed, sitting up.

My eyes bulged. "Where the hell is the condom?" I asked frantically.

I attempted to sit up, but he put his hand on my belly to keep me in place. With his brows furrowed in worry, he commanded, "Let me see if it's in you."

I parted my legs, and I could tell something was up by the way his eyes widened.

"Shit," he muttered.

"What?"

The pressure of his fingers against my still-tender flesh caused me to suck in air sharply. He pulled out a beaten and battered condom. When he held it up, the hole in it was painfully obvious.

I squeezed my eyes shut. *No, no, no, no, no, no.*

"Are you, uh . . ." Russ tossed the tattered condom toward the trash can with his right hand. "Are you on any type of birth control?"

I pushed myself up into a sitting position and took a deep breath. "Yeah, but we should also pick up an emergency contraceptive on the way home."

He nodded. "We can do that. Are you okay?"

"I mean, it's not ideal, but I'm okay." I paused for a moment. "Obviously, this means testing needs to take place."

He nodded. "Yeah, yeah, of course." He scrubbed his face with his hands. "I can get it done today. I'll get my assistant to set something up."

Staring straight ahead, my mind was going a mile a minute. "Yeah. I'm going to call my gynecologist to make an appointment."

"I leave town tonight for a meeting tomorrow morning back in New York. I'm back here on Thursday for some stuff with the house. The results should be in by then. My last test came back negative. I expect it to be the same."

"Same."

We were both quiet.

Sunlight filled the room as the stark silence surrounded us. When I looked over at him, he was staring at me.

"I should've fucking known." I shook my head. "It always feels good, but it was feeling extra good and . . ." My sentence trailed off.

He reached over and put his hand on my thigh. "I was lost in it . . . in you."

"I would've never locked my legs around you if I was thinking clearly."

He licked his lips. "When you locked in, I lost it."

The conversation shouldn't have made me tingle, but it did. Shifting uncomfortably, I said, "As good as the dick is—and believe me, it's good—I'm trying to avoid pregnancy at all costs."

"Hell yeah. I'm right there with you." His phone rang but he continued holding my gaze. "We'll get the emergency contraceptive on the way, and then I'll get you home on time, as promised. You'll get to your meeting. I'll get to my meetings. Everything will be fine. I'll handle it."

I climbed off the bed and stood on wobbly legs. Pointing to his phone, I quirked an eyebrow. "You can get that," I told him.

He exhaled, reached for the ringing device. "It's work."

"Take it. I'm going to take a shower so we can get going. I have that meeting at noon."

Instead of answering his phone, he followed me to the bathroom. Leaning against the doorjamb, he watched me in the mirror.

"Getting my essentials," I told him, even though he didn't ask. I moved the bodywash and face scrub from the counter to the bathtub ledge.

"I meant what I said about seeing you more since I'll be local," he stated.

I grabbed the towel and washcloth and sat it on the counter. "I meant it, too. I enjoy being with you."

"I enjoy you, too." He gestured to his dick, hanging long and thick between his strong thighs. "And I don't just mean sexually.

It just so happens that when I look at you, over there jiggling like that, I react to it."

I giggled, rolling my eyes. "You're so ridiculous."

He just stared at me with this look that made goose bumps spread over my skin. "I'm serious though. I enjoy your conversation"—he took a step forward—"your company"—he got behind me and wrapped his arms around my middle—"and the way you think."

Sighing, I leaned back into him. "I feel the same way."

"You do."

It wasn't a question. It was more of a clarifying statement.

We gazed at each other for a moment, letting the admission settle around us.

He broke the silence first. "I'm not having sex with anyone else."

"I'm not either," I murmured.

Moving his hands from my belly, he gripped my hips. "Let's keep it that way."

I cocked my head to the side. "What do you mean?"

"Let these other dudes know you're not available anymore."

A chill ran down my spine as I felt the emotions I'd been avoiding bubble up. "You want to be exclusive?"

"Yes. I want you exclusively to myself." He ran his tongue from one corner of his mouth to the other. "And I don't share what's mine."

I bit my lip and tried my hardest not to grin. "What if I'm not looking to be in a relationship?"

With his eyes trained on our reflection, he kissed me behind my ear. "What if you found one anyway?" he whispered.

"So, you're telling me you're my man now?"

He leaned down and whispered in my ear. "Are you telling me I'm not?"

A chill ran through my body. "Russ . . ."

Nuzzling his nose into my hair, he inhaled deeply. "Are you mine, Nina?"

My heart, stomach, and pussy thumped in response. "Yes."

The answer burst out of me in a quiet huff.

Turning me around, he grabbed my face. "Say it."

I inhaled shakily. "I'm yours."

"Good." He planted the sweetest, most tender kiss against my lips. "I love to hear you say it."

Do I . . . have a boyfriend?

The only thing that would change on my end was that I'd have to let The Funny One and The Smart One go. But in that moment, I realized that didn't feel like a loss. The two of them combined couldn't compare to Russ.

This is really happening.

I was in a state of shock.

Within thirty minutes, we were in the car, making our way back to Richland. With one stop at the local pharmacy and then another at a coffee shop, we battled Monday rush hour traffic. Even though I was still in a state of shock, I was surprisingly sure of my decision. And I could only attribute that to the realization that while everything happened so fast, nothing changed. We agreed to exclusivity and then everything was the exact same as it was before.

It was the same fun-filled road trip that it was on our journey there. I typically would've avoided allowing a man to drop me off at home. But it was Russ, and apparently, he was my man. So, I gave him my address and allowed him to bring me through the gate and into my complex.

"Okay, I see you," he acknowledged appreciatively. "This is cool."

I smiled proudly, even though I'd had nothing to do with the gorgeous architecture of the converted warehouses, the beautiful landscaping surrounding the artistic marvel of a fountain, or the resort-style pool that peeked from the side of the first building.

"Thank you." I pointed out the building on the corner. "That one is me."

"When you said you lived in a converted warehouse, I didn't imagine this."

"Some of the buildings were designed to look like they were

part of the original tobacco warehouses. Mine is new construction, but it still has the cool feel."

"I look forward to seeing it sometime," he said as he pulled in front of my building.

"And I look forward to seeing the house you've built," I returned.

He chuckled as he parked illegally. "You're right. But I gave you the address so, even though I haven't moved in, you know where my house is."

"True." I reached in the backseat to grab my bag and he tried to stop me.

"What are you doing?" I wondered.

"I got your bag. I'll walk you to your door."

"You can't park right here, and security does not play. And for me to get the guest parking pass would take too much time." I leaned over and kissed him. "I promise I won't think you're less of a gentleman. But I really have to go."

He opened his door at the same time I did, and as I grabbed my bag out of the backseat, he pursed his lips. "Nina."

I nodded my head behind him. "See?"

He glanced in the direction of security and made a face. "Gah-damn, I've been parked for sixty seconds."

I smiled ruefully as he met me on my side of the car. "That's all it takes."

"I'm going to tell him I'm dropping off my girlfriend. He'll understand."

Girlfriend.

Hearing the word roll off his tongue gave me butterflies. It was coated with love and lust and reverence. It flushed my skin and increased my heart rate. I didn't think anything had changed, but him saying the word thrilled me and scared me at the exact same time.

Grinning, I shouldered my bag and then allowed Russ to take me in his arms. He brought his forehead down to mine and gazed into my eyes.

"This was exactly what I needed," he whispered against my lips. "Thank you for this weekend."

"For escaping with you?"

"*You* are the escape. We could've been anywhere, and it would've been exactly what I needed."

"So, if I'm understanding you correctly, it sounds like you're saying *I'm* what you needed," I teased.

With seriousness and sincerity, he caressed my cheek. "That's exactly what I'm saying."

Our lips met hungrily as I tasted the sweet perfection of his words. Lifting up on my toes, I gripped the back of his neck tighter.

"Excuse me, folks," the security guard interrupted. "You can't park here."

Exhaling loudly, Russ pulled out of my arms. "Aight, man," he replied irritably. Grabbing my face, he stared at me. "I have something I want to show you on Thursday. Can I see you?"

"Yes," I answered automatically. "I mean, I have to get my schedule figured out, but at some point Thursday, yes."

"Good. I'll send you my flight information and you just let me know your schedule. I'll plan something based on what you have available."

"Okay, sounds good."

With a quick kiss, we said our goodbyes and then I lightly jogged to my door.

Pushing my feelings to the back burner, I needed to switch gears. I had a little over an hour to get to my RLF meeting.

Once I decided what I was going to wear, I did my makeup and called my girls.

"—and after the massage, we checked into a suite at a nearby hotel, ordered room service, and then fucked until we were exhausted." I sighed happily during the morning three-way call with my best friends. "This weekend was everything I needed," I concluded.

"I love this!" Aaliyah squealed. "He's giving you fun, conversation, laughs, romance, and bomb sex, what else could you ask for?"

"Is he a drug dealer?" Jazmyn asked.

Ignoring Aaliyah's question, I burst out laughing. "No, Jazz!"

"He doesn't want to talk about work, but he takes you on these expensive dates, so you know he has money. I'm just saying . . . I just rewatched *Power.* I know the signs of a kingpin."

"He's a legitimate businessman," I said.

"Have you seen a business card?" Aaliyah wondered.

I shook my head even though they couldn't see me. "No, but—"

"Because drug dealers don't have business cards," Jazmyn interrupted. "I rest my case."

My laugh turned into a cough. "Liyah, back me up!"

"I mean . . ." Aaliyah dragged the statement out. "Drug dealers *don't* have business cards."

"I can't stand either of you!"

We cackled loudly.

Amused, I pulled on the wide-legged magenta pants. I wanted to catch them up on the weekend's events before I headed into my first official day with RLF. But I should've known they weren't going to be serious.

"All jokes aside, I really like this for you," Aaliyah said wistfully. "You sound so happy."

"I am," I told them, checking out the way the pants hugged my butt. I tucked in the sleeveless silk top and smiled at how professional I looked. "He makes . . ." My stomach fluttered. "I am very happy."

"Are you finally ready to admit that there's something real between you two?" Aaliyah questioned.

"Fine!" I exclaimed in exasperation. "It's real."

The two of them squealed and the mixture of disbelief and delight ricocheted. There were a million questions flying at me at once.

My heart pounded with the same panic that hit me earlier. I'd never felt compelled to be with a man before Russ, and it was as frightening as it was exhilarating. I was more nervous about my feelings and my unexpected title than I was starting my first day with RLF.

"I go in and pull pieces today. I find out the photography and the appearance schedule today." I let out an excited noise. "Happy is an understatement."

"This opportunity is amazing," Jazz pointed out. "Your career is just going to keep growing and elevating. This is just the beginning."

"You said you wanted to take things to the next level, and now, a few months later, here you are," Aaliyah marveled. "So proud of you."

I felt my heart swell with their words. "Thank you both so much." I slipped into my cream-colored sandals. A wave of excitement fluttered my belly as I took in my final look. "I'm so ready for this."

"Are you nervous?" Jazmyn questioned.

"No, not really nervous. I know I have what it takes. It's more first-day jitters than anything."

"Once you walk into that building, you'll be fine," Aaliyah assured me. "And after your *satisfying* weekend, you're going to carry that energy into the day."

"That's true," I agreed. "I do feel like I'm on a high right now."

"So, you have the job of your dreams, the man of your dreams, and—"

"And he's so perfect, we will overlook his kingpin status," Jazz interjected.

Laughing, I decided not to tell them that Russ and I had made it official. They were going to be excited. Hell, I was excited. But I was also nervous and overwhelmed. The idea of dating just one man—even one as perfect as Russ—felt risky. It felt like I was putting all my eggs in one basket. And since it was the first time I liked a man enough to want to be in a relationship with just him, they would make a big deal of it. And admittedly, it *was* a big deal. But once I said it out loud, it would be real.

A smile pulled at my lips as nervous energy swirled in my belly. *I'll call and tell them as soon as I leave the office.*

"Are you denying that you like The Fun One?" Aaliyah's voice elevated two octaves, bringing me out of my thoughts.

With my phone lodged between my shoulder and my ear, I reached for my bag and then made my way out of my apartment.

"Of course I like him!" I answered. "I wouldn't spend time with any man I don't like."

"But I can tell there's something different there," Jazmyn chimed in.

"It's . . ." I couldn't even find the words to argue with her, because it was different with him. "We enjoy each other. We have a lot of fun together."

"You went to a ball as a paid model for RLF and you sounded more excited about your spa date and fuck session," Aaliyah pointed out. "Every time you talk about him you sound so . . . happy."

I rolled my eyes as I climbed into my car. "I had a good weekend. Your overly romantic ass is reading too much into it."

"I can understand why you'd think Aaliyah is romanticizing the situation. She's looking for a boyfriend," Jazz countered. "But I'm divorced and actively not looking for a man, and I also think there's something between you and The Fun One."

"You say you don't play favorites, but he's clearly the front-runner," Aaliyah said with a singsong tone.

I couldn't deny that. He was my favorite. He'd been my favorite from the beginning. And hearing my friends say what I'd finally come to realize was low-key hilarious.

"I enjoy my time with Russ," I simply stated as I pulled out of my parking spot.

They are going to lose their shit when I tell them we're together!

"Oh, he's Russ now and not The Fun One," Aaliyah teased.

I pulled into traffic, trying not to laugh. "I know what you're getting at."

"I have a question," Jazz announced. "What are the cons with Russ? Besides the illegal employment thing."

"He's not a drug dealer!" When our laughter died down, I continued. "And honestly, so far, so good. There are no cons with this man."

"Is it fair to say that he is the whole package?" Aaliyah wondered. "Everything you want and need in a man?"

"He is the whole package," I admitted slowly.

The way they started hooting and hollering was ridiculous.

"He's the one," Aaliyah declared.

"I hate to agree with Liyah on this, but yeah . . ."

Grinning, I rolled my eyes. "How about we focus on the fact that Aaliyah is turning thirty and the three of us will be reunited in a couple weeks."

"It'll be good to see you guys," Jazz said with a sigh. "It's been a long summer."

We talked for the next twenty minutes. Aaliyah had to abruptly get off the phone because she was being summoned at work.

"Where are you now?" Jazmyn wondered. "It's almost time for your meeting."

"I'm in the parking deck across the street." I checked the time. "I'm meeting with Sasha in HR at noon. I have ten minutes before I need to head over."

"Okay, good." She was quiet for a moment. "So . . . I have a question."

I flipped the sun visor up with a snap and braced myself. Jazz being back in her hometown was already a lot for her. But given that her aunt had taken a turn for the worst and didn't have long to live, I knew she was going through it. She was dealing with it privately and wasn't ready to share much about how things were going. So even though I was glad she was finally ready to talk, the fact that she sounded so serious worried me.

"What's going on?" I asked carefully.

"You broke things off with The Romantic One because you felt him catching feelings and you didn't want to hurt him?"

"Oh!" A silent sigh of relief escaped me. I wasn't sure what she wanted to talk about, but I was bracing myself for the worst. "Yeah, that's right."

"How did you know it was time?"

"I could feel it."

"What do you mean?"

"I could tell things were changing between us. When he looked at me, it didn't feel like we were on the same page. Even before he said it to me, I could tell. He's sweet and fine and honestly, a great guy, so I was hoping he'd chill out. But when we were at the RLF event, he asked me to be his girlfriend, so I had to end it."

"You didn't sleep with him though. How do you end it with someone you slept with?"

A smile tugged at my lips as I turned my car off. "Jazz . . ." I dragged her name out curiously. "Are you sleeping with someone?"

"I didn't say that," she replied quickly.

I climbed out of my car. "You didn't have to say it."

"Your meeting is at noon, right? Because you only have seven minutes to get in there."

"I'm crossing the street now. But back to you—"

"Back to you," she countered in a rush. "You stopped talking to The Romantic One because things were changing, but it sounds like things are changing with The Fun One, too. Are you planning on ending things with him?"

"No." I lifted my hand in a wave toward the person who waited until I was on the sidewalk before proceeding through the light.

"Are you planning on making it official with *Russ*?"

"Oop! Not you using his real name to deflect from this mystery man you've been getting busy with in your hometown," I said as I opened the door to the building.

"I'm getting off the phone," Jazz announced, amusement hinting at the truth.

"Well, while you sit in denial, I'm going to give you some real talk. It's about time you got them cobwebs cleared out. And don't be more worried about hurting someone else's feelings than you are about hurting your own. If it needs to end, end it. But don't end it just because you're scared."

She was quiet.

"Jazz?" I headed toward the elevator.

"I'm here," she replied softly.

"Don't be scared," I repeated.

"You don't be scared either."

I swallowed hard.

The elevator door opened, and I walked into it with a handful of people. "I'm feeling really good and confident about today," I declared. "Now that I'm here, I'm excited." The doors started to close. "Oh, I might lose you in the elevator."

"I didn't mean about the job."

My mouth was agape. Before I could even respond, she continued. "Have a great first day! You got this! Bye, girl!"

Even though she'd already hung up, I still had the phone to my ear. "Bye."

I shook off what she said because I didn't have time to analyze it. The doors opened and I got out with a man with a large portfolio.

"Welcome!" a woman greeted us.

I looked around, marveling at the change that had taken place in a couple days. The office looked completely different than it did on Friday. It went from a blank canvas to an actual fashion house. The décor was simple, yet sleek, with chrome-and-black furniture, interesting art in black frames, and enlarged black-and-white photos of models in RLF designs. The RLF logo emblazoned on the floor just off the elevator was the flashiest thing about it.

"You're early," she remarked to the man. "You can go back." Then she looked at me. "How can I help you?"

I flashed a big smile. "I have a twelve o'clock meeting with Sasha."

She picked up a phone and then directed me down the hall to the right. I followed her directions and Sasha met me in the hallway.

"Welcome, Nina!"

For the next half hour, we reviewed and went over paperwork. I signed all the necessary documents. Then I was given my schedule for September and input the dates in my calendar. I kept a straight face, but I was so excited I could burst.

"Now, let's get you over to the showroom," she directed. "Angelica is the head stylist and the person who will be critiquing your social media posts." Noticing the look on my face, she explained further. "Think of her as quality control."

Before I could even respond, Sasha flung the door open, and we entered a space twice as big as the conference room.

"Oh!" I mumbled in surprise.

The showroom was an extremely large open room lined with racks upon racks of clothing. My eyes widened as I took in the impressive display. I didn't know RLF had so many designs. After introducing me to Angelica, Sasha left to prepare for a meeting.

"I'll have a packet for you to take with you and your parking pass," Sasha said. "But right now, I need to get ready for a meeting so I'm leaving you in Angelica's hands."

"It's so nice to meet you, Nina." Angelica shook my hand. With a stern expression, she pushed her red frames up the bridge of her nose. "I need to get your measurements."

She directed me behind a partition to get undressed. A few minutes later, she pulled the yellow tape measure from around her neck and got to work. Quietly, she jotted down numbers and continued to make notes until she was finished. The silence wasn't stony, but it wasn't comfortable. Small talk didn't seem welcome, so I followed her lead. She told me to get dressed and to meet her back at her desk.

And without a word, I did.

She eyed me as I walked across the room toward her.

"You carry your weight well," she said to me. "You would be good on a runway."

Without another word, she turned and headed toward the first rack of clothing. I didn't know what to say so I just silently followed her. She pulled fourteen pieces—a combination of shirts, dresses, pants, skirts, and jumpsuits. I suppressed my enthusiasm and internally oohed and aahed over the clothes.

When we returned to her desk, Angelica broke the silence. "The fashion show is the marquee event to launch. But everything that is posted to drum up the anticipation for this line is just as important."

She looked at me over the top of her glasses. "For you as a model and for the company."

Does that mean if she doesn't like what I post, I'm out? Does that mean—?

"Good afternoon, Angelica," one of the two female models I'd met over the weekend called out. "Oh, hey, Nina!"

The other models filed in and spoke as well.

The brisk hello from Angelica put me at ease. Seeing her interact with the other models with the same firmness and lack of warmth made me feel better.

That's just who she is, I guess.

"As I was telling Nina, this launch is important. Your roles are important. Your different personalities showcase how RLF is for everybody. I've pulled looks for you all. I'll be monitoring to see what you do with what I've given you." She pointed at us. "You are the tastemakers. You are the influencers. Let me see what you've got."

She handed us each a tote full of clothes and then she dismissed us.

Confused, I walked out into the hall.

"Is that it? Do I go home?" I covered my face bashfully. "I don't know what's next."

All six feet, four inches of Jonah came up beside me and draped his arm around my shoulder. "Stick with me. I'll lead you—"

"Astray," Taisha interrupted humorously. "Jonah will lead your ass astray."

The five of us laughed as we made our way up the hall. The noise seemed to alert Sasha we were done. She hurried out of her office and down the hall.

"Leave your stuff behind this desk. I have some people I want you to meet," the HR manager said before beckoning for us to follow her. "RLF executives are here. I know a couple of you haven't met everyone so this will be a good opportunity."

I didn't feel nervous at all. I'd already met Remedy and I knew she liked me. I'd made it through Angelica's silence. I'd already signed the paperwork to bind our contract. Maybe it was the dick I'd gotten last night and this morning.

My smile grew.

She knocked on the conference room door before sticking her head in. "Hi, I have the models here." She nodded and then smiled. "They have their own clothing on." She took a step back and allowed us to walk in. "I'm pleased to introduce you to the face of the company, Chief Creative Officer Remedy Rose . . ."

She introduced us to seven men and women who held executive position with the company. Everyone appeared to be between the ages of thirty and fifty, which was exciting to see. After shaking hands and making light small talk for a few minutes, Remedy took her place at the head of the table.

"Have a seat," Remedy instructed. "This won't take long."

The five of us sat at the far end of the conference table. I clasped my hands in front of me and waited.

Turning to the other executives, Remedy gestured to us. "Our marketing budget has been restructured to add these key pieces to our marketing strategies. Social media is the new commercial, but with more reach, opportunity, and effectiveness. Our marketing team is great and will go through all the traditional channels. But this modeling team"—she pointed to us—"will be key in positioning RLF as a leader in the fashion marketplace." She turned to us. "The more valuable content you are sharing on social media, the higher your chances to be featured in our national campaign and commercial." She turned back to the execs. "These five models have a significant social media following. They have the look, they have the style, and they have the opportunity to grow with us. Not only will they show people the versatility of what we offer, they will build the grassroots type of following for our pieces. So, models, we are the waymakers. We can pave the way in this industry to catapult your already-rising stars. And fellow executives, these are the tastemakers. They can make RLF into a household name. And together, we can all make a lot of money."

The room filled with laughter and applause.

"Thank you for stopping in," she thanked us before politely indicating for us to leave. "We'll see you soon. I'll see you at your in-person appearances. We—oh, perfect timing! Models, there's someone I'd like to introduce you to." She gestured to the back of the room. "Russell Long . . ."

Confused, my head jerked in the direction she pointed and my breathing hitched.

"The president and CEO of Real Life Fashions."

13

Russ took a step forward and when our eyes locked, he froze. His handsome face maintained his professionalism, but his eyes gave him away and I could tell he was surprised.

"We were just leaving," Sasha insisted, opening the door for us to exit.

He stared at me for a moment before sweeping his gaze to the rest of the models. He flashed his perfect smile. "I was wondering who the extra guests were. It's nice to meet you. I'm Russell Long."

He moved from left to right, shaking our hands. When he got to me, he stared into my eyes.

I opened my mouth, but no sound came out. I didn't know what to say.

Should I act like I don't know him? Should I let him take the lead? Should I—

"I thought there were four brand ambassadors," Russ said, sliding his hand over mine.

"We have five now," Remedy responded. "I met Nina at a conference and added her to the lineup. Her style, social media presence, and relatable content make her perfect for RLF. She fits in with the others beautifully. With these five, you are looking at our social media marketing campaign."

Russ cleared his throat as he removed his hand from mine. Looking around, he took a step back from me.

"And now that you're caught up"—Remedy gestured to Sasha—"we need to go over the mid-quarter projections for you."

Sasha nodded. "We are heading out now."

In a single-file line, we followed her out of the conference room. Even though I felt his eyes burning into me, I didn't look back. I was in a state of confusion and disbelief.

Russ is the president and CEO of Real Life Fashions?

"I hope you all have a great rest of your week," Sasha told us as we reached the unmanned front desk. She turned and handed me a folder. "Your information and your parking pass. Welcome to RLF."

I thanked her, grabbed my tote, and then joined the models in the elevator.

"Whew! I thought he was one of the models when he walked in," Jacqueline gushed, fanning herself.

"I met him a few weeks ago when I was first doing my measurements. He's the sexiest man I've ever worked for," Taisha commented.

"I wouldn't mind being his arm candy," Jacqueline joked, wiggling her eyebrows suggestively.

"How's your man going to feel about you talking like this?" Matias asked.

"Talking like what? Telling the truth?" Taisha tossed her hands in the air. "She's just pointing out the obvious."

"And he might be mad, but he'll know it ain't a lie!" Jacqueline added.

Both ladies giggled as we walked out of the elevator.

"We have eyes!" Taisha looked over at me with a full smile. "Ain't that right, Nina?"

I nodded, still unable to find my voice.

The three of them continued their playful conversation.

"You good?" Jonah asked quietly. "You haven't said a word since we left the meeting."

Looking at him, I nodded again. "I'm okay."

"Are you overwhelmed?" Jacqueline asked gently.

I looked up, realizing all four of them were staring at me. Walking slowly and watching me with each step, they were waiting expectantly for my response.

My eyebrows flew up. "Um . . . yeah, something like that."

I was overwhelmed, but not for the reasons they were thinking.

"You don't strike me as the nervous type," Taisha replied, cocking her head to the side.

"And I've done one of these deals about a year ago and it's pretty chill," Matias informed me. "Nothing to worry about."

"But if you need to talk or need anything at all, you have my number," Jonah said, holding the door open for me. "Call me . . . anytime. For anything."

"Damn, Jonah," Taisha reacted, turning all the way around to look at him.

"What?" he laughed.

"You're laying it on thick," Matias answered with amusement.

"And we were explicitly told we can't mix business with pleasure," Jacqueline mentioned.

"That's rich coming from the woman who just said she was trying to get Boss Man to be her arm candy," Jonah retorted.

"I didn't say that!" Jacqueline put her hands on her hips. "I said I would be *his* arm candy."

We all laughed.

My laugh was a little distracted and my smile was a little forced. My head was spinning, but no one thought plagued it. It was several thoughts all at once.

I exchanged goodbyes with the models and as soon as I got in the car, I called the girls.

Neither of them picked up.

I sped out of the parking deck and headed home. I was just about to park when I received a text message.

Russ: We need to talk.

"We sure as hell do," I muttered as I grabbed my stuff and rushed into my place.

I was just about to call him when my phone started ringing.

"Liyah!" I cried as I answered.

"Hey, what's going on? How was your first day?" she replied.

"Tell me why I met the CEO of the company, and it was Russ!" I yelled into the phone.

She gasped. "The Fun One?"

"The fucking Fun One!"

"Wait, wait, wait, wait, wait, wait, wait. Hold on." She sounded as if she was walking, and then I heard two different doors closing. "Okay, what? Run that back from the beginning because what?"

Kicking my shoes off, I paced my living room. "Remedy, the one I thought was the CEO, introduced us to the real CEO—Russ!"

"Stop! You're lying!"

"I swear!"

"That's wild!" She paused. "You know what this sounds like?"

"What?"

"This sounds like a scheme that Todd set up," she joked.

I stopped in my tracks. I wanted to laugh and cry at the same time. "Aaliyah!" I snickered and then groaned. "This is not the time!"

"I'm sorry, you're right. What did he say? What did you say?"

"We didn't say anything! There were like fifteen people in the room. We just kind of looked at each other in shock, and then I was escorted out of the conference room."

"Oh my God!" she screeched. "That's . . . I don't even know what to say because ohmigod!"

"I know!" I pinched the bridge of my nose. "And he just sent me a text message saying we need to talk."

"So, what are you going to do?"

"I have no idea. I haven't even fully processed the situation yet. I don't think I've ever been so shocked in my life."

"I bet!"

"I literally saw every inch of the man this morning, and then I find out this afternoon that I work for his company."

"You're sleeping with the boss," she mused.

"Oh—I . . ." I hadn't had a chance to fully digest it. But hearing her say it stopped me in my tracks.

I am sleeping with the boss. More than that, I'm in a relationship with the boss!

I started pacing again. "We have to end it. There's a no-fraternization clause in the contract that I signed."

"But he's the boss, so he could easily get that clause thrown out."

"Or the board could easily get that contract thrown out."

She laughed. "From everything you've told me, I don't see him letting that happen. And you like him too much to give him up that easily."

My stomach was in knots. "Aaliyah, please."

"What? Tell me I'm lying."

"Russ is great, and we just . . ."

Made it official, I completed the sentence in my head.

My heart was racing.

"The two of you just had the best time together," she reminded me.

"But this is my career we're talking about. And his, too! We're going to have to end it."

"People date at work all the time. You and Russ have something real. I've never seen you like this with anyone," she said, hopeful romanticism dripping from each of her words.

I opened my mouth to tell her she was projecting, but I was interrupted by an incoming call. Pulling the phone from my ear, I stared at it in stunned silence.

"See, you can't deny it," she continued.

"It's Russ. He's calling," I told her, still staring at his name as it flashed across my screen.

"Answer it! Call me back!"

She said goodbye but I barely heard her as I hit the button to answer his call.

Clearing my throat, I took a deep breath. "Hello?"

"Are you home?" Russ asked with a firmness that caught me off guard.

I swallowed hard. "Yes."

He was quiet for a moment. "I'm on my way."

He didn't ask.

He told me.

And due to the circumstances, I didn't question it.

"Okay," I murmured.

I didn't know what else to say so I ended the call.

Ten minutes later, there was a knock at my door. Even though I knew who it was, I peered through the peephole. Seeing him caused my heart rate to spike. Taking a deep breath, I opened the door.

"Russ," I greeted him.

"May I come in?" he asked, a serious look on his face. "Please."

"Of course." I stepped back, shifting from one foot to the other. "Come in." I locked the door behind him and gestured to the couch. "We can talk over here."

There was a chaotic energy between us. It felt anxious and uneasy, unlike every other time we'd been together. While it was strange, it was a little reassuring knowing that the laid-back man I'd grown fond of was just as out of sorts as I was. There was something different about him—an emotion I'd never seen in him was seeping out of his pores.

He got halfway to the couch and then spun around. Running his hand over his beard, he searched my face before he spoke. "You are one of the brand ambassadors . . . ?"

It was a statement and a question all rolled into one. I wasn't sure if he wanted confirmation or not, but I gave it to him.

I nodded. "And RLF is your company."

"So, you weren't at The Player's Ball on Saturday as a guest of someone."

"Technically, as an invited guest of Lori. When I was hired, they told me to come out and meet everyone."

He pinched the bridge of his nose. "So, the people you were rushing to meet with . . ."

"Were the other models," I finished. "And when you said you were meeting with people trying to give you money, you meant investors . . ."

He nodded. "For RLF."

Twisting the bracelet he'd given me around my wrist, I shook my head. "That never dawned on me. I was told there were lots of different people from different businesses there. You being the CEO of RLF never even crossed my mind."

"We met at a fashion event where I was meeting with investors, so I didn't question why you were there. You *working* for my company never crossed my mind."

We stared at each other for a few seconds.

I'd started my day in his arms, and now we were arm's length apart. I was unsure of how to act around him. What seemed so easy and carefree that morning felt hard and complicated that afternoon.

Maybe there's a perfectly logical explanation—

"Did you know?" he asked with a quiet sharpness that took me by surprise.

I know he's not asking me what I think he's asking me.

I gave him a look. "Did I know what?"

"Did you know who I was when you took the job?"

I made a face and took a step back. "Obviously not."

Confusion creased his forehead. "Then how did this happen?" He said it more to himself than to me, but the insinuation got under my skin.

"I don't know."

"You had no idea who I was?"

"No!" I scoffed loudly, frustration getting the best of me.

"Okay. I know you've already signed everything this morning, but you can still break your contract. It's not too late. If that's what you want to do, I could get you out of it."

It wasn't just my personal goals of growing my platform and making more money that made me sign the RLF contract. The opportunity to grow my brand and reach even more big-bodied women was a huge deal. I wasn't just thinking about myself; I was also thinking about my impact. So for him to even suggest that I void the contract was outrageous to me.

I made a face. "You mean the contract I turned down other brand deals to sign? This opportunity is a great move for me and my career. Why would I have to be the one to lose out?"

"I'm not saying you have to. I'm just . . ." His sentence trailed off as he appeared to be warring with himself. "Nina . . ." He chewed his lip for a moment before gesturing between the two of us. "Did you plan this?"

"Did I plan this?" I let out a short, dry laugh as I regurgitated the question in bewilderment. "Are you serious?"

He blinked. "Yes."

My eyebrows shot up. It felt like I was in the twilight zone, because there was no way he was standing in my home accusing me of using him for the job.

"No, I didn't plan this," I snapped. "Did you?"

The crease between his eyes deepened. "No."

"This is your business, but you didn't know who was being hired to promote it? Shouldn't you know that information?" I stepped forward. "Did you know who I was when you got me off at the party? Or when you whisked me away yesterday?"

"No. I didn't."

"So, you see how ridiculous it sounds for you to ask me if I planned it or if I knew?"

He laced his fingers and sat them on top of his head. "What else am I supposed to think, Nina? It looks like—"

"I don't care what it looks like," I interrupted. "I care what it is."

He crossed his arms over his chest. "Then what is it?"

"Well, first and foremost, I didn't seek out this job. Remedy saw me at an event in New York and sought me out." I put my hands on my hips. "Second, I thought Remedy ran things. She was introduced to me as the person in charge. I had no clue you were part of the company, let alone the CEO. Third of all, what would I gain from keeping this from you if I knew this was your company? This opportunity is a huge deal for me, and I wouldn't squander it by playing games with the person who is cutting the checks. That doesn't even make sense." I shook my head. "To come here acting like I was trying to date you for this opportunity is complete and utter bullshit."

His head rocked back, and he scrubbed his face with his hands. When he finally looked at me again, his features had softened and there was a resigned look in his eyes. "You're right," he sighed. "You're right. I'm sorry. I just . . ." He squeezed his eyes shut. "I just don't understand how this happened."

"I don't understand it either." I threw my hands in the air. Shaking my head, I walked past him and took a seat on the couch. "Today was my first day. I didn't know what you did for work, so when Sasha said we were meeting with executives, I didn't expect you to be one of them. The main one."

"Yeah." After a few seconds, a small smile pulled at his lips. "It was all over your face."

My lip curled slightly. "Your eyes bulged out of your head when you saw me."

"I've never been so shocked in my damn life," he admitted, un-buttoning his suit jacket. He joined me, taking a seat on the other side of the couch. "I believe you didn't know. I'm sorry I came at you like that. My gut told me you didn't. But my head has been all over the place and"—he lifted his shoulders—"I had to ask."

"It's a wild situation, but to think I was plotting on you is just . . ." I shook my head. "What have I ever done to you that would make you think some shit like that?"

"Charge it to my head, not my heart. I couldn't make sense of it and I just . . ." His sentence trailed off. "I'm sorry. I should've known better."

"Yes, you should've. But how did you not know they hired me? Don't they have to run these things by you?"

His phone rang and he looked at it but didn't answer.

"Yeah, typically. Remedy's the chief creative officer and I gave her the go-ahead to expand the marketing within the parameters we set. There were four models selected before I went into my last meeting on Friday. I was scheduled to meet them Monday. That's why I was so thrown off."

Before I could respond, his phone rang again.

He let out a deep breath. "I need to take this."

"Yeah, go ahead."

"Remedy?" he answered, causing me to glance at him out of the corner of my eye. "Yeah, I'll check the email. I'm well aware. I'll call you back."

The call took thirty seconds, but afterward, he remained fo-cused on his phone as he started typing and clicking. When his jaw tensed, I broke the silence.

"Everything okay?"

He cleared his throat before turning to me. "Remedy directed me to an email Lori sent on Sunday. It was an update about the brand ambassadors. When I'm off, I'm off so I"—his eyes dipped to my lips momentarily as he licked his—"enjoyed my weekend. I intended to read it this morning. But I went to go get my blood work done before heading to the office and didn't get around to it."

"What does the email say?"

"That they're bringing on a fifth brand ambassador. Nina Ford. Plus size model with five hundred thousand accounts following, two million followers across all platforms, and high engagement." He looked over at me. "I'm guessing this is a different account than the one I'm following."

I nodded. "You have my personal account. It's not linked to my business account."

"Of course," he muttered. He shook his head before tossing his phone to the couch cushion between us. "Shit."

I didn't know what to say so I didn't say anything.

He exhaled roughly. "You know how this looks, right?"

"How does it look?"

"It looks like I fuck my employees. It looks like an HR embarrassment and a PR nightmare. It looks like everything I've worked my ass off for going down in flames and me getting roasted on social media as one of those predator bosses. It doesn't matter what the truth is, what it looks like will cost me. The collateral damage—"

I waved my hands to stop his rant. "Russ."

It hadn't dawned on me that his energy when he walked in was rooted in fear. The heightened emotions in his words and the look on his face when our eyes met made the connection for me. He had always seemed so fearless, and he lived in the moment. I'd never seen him spiral.

It was fascinating.

And humanizing.

And real.

"What it looks like will cost us *both*," I uttered. "You're not in this alone. We *both* have to figure this out."

He shook his head. "You won't lose everything."

"I'd lose money. I'd lose my integrity. I'd lose my reputation." I counted each loss with my fingers. "It's not just you who has something to lose."

"I'm not going to let that happen to you. I'll make sure of that."

A slow smile pulled at the corners of my mouth.

Even with the cracks in his perfection, he still managed to be perfect.

Ignoring the flutter in my belly, I nodded slightly. "Okay."

Looking at me with fierce intensity, he turned his body slightly to face me. "But I need you to understand I spent the last fifteen years building my business. The next few weeks are the most important for my company. There's too much money and too many people tied to these next few moves." He rose to his feet. "So, it doesn't matter what the truth is, as soon as the public finds out I'm involved with an employee, it won't be long before they say it was sexual harassment—or worse. There's no coming back from that. I'd lose everything."

Staring up at him, I stood.

His expression conveyed the same apprehension and worry that coated his words. And I wished there was something I could say to ease the creases from his forehead, the frown from his lips, and the tension in his jaw. But I couldn't deny that he'd lose more than me. I couldn't argue that the impropriety could possibly destroy him, his company, and all the opportunities.

My fingers tingled as I itched to reach out for him. But he was staring straight ahead at the artwork on the wall, avoiding eye contact.

He cleared his throat. "We can't do this anymore."

The floor fell out from under me.

Well, damn.

My stomach twisted. Even though I'd just said the same thing to Aaliyah earlier, hearing him say it was an unexpected gut punch. When I hypothetically mentioned it would be the only solution, it hurt. But the reality of ending things with him rocked me.

"We can't let anyone know that we know each other," he continued.

"I, um . . . yeah," I agreed softly. "There's a lot at stake. It's the only way to protect us both."

He didn't say a word.

His chest rose and fell as he stared straight ahead. "This could ruin me," he uttered after a minute.

Me too.

He swallowed hard before turning to look at me. "I have to meet with the inspector before my flight. But I'll make this whole thing go away. Everything will be fine."

"It'll be like it never happened."

He stared at me with a blank expression on his face, so I elaborated.

"With no evidence of a connection between us, there would be nothing they could find suspicious. It'll be like it never happened."

He shifted his eyes, remaining quiet for a moment.

"I think Remedy is . . . suspicious," he admitted, sliding his phone into his pocket.

His sentence hung in the air as I wrapped my mind around what he had said.

No wonder he was so freaked out.

Staring at him, I willed him to say more words. When he didn't continue, I whispered, "What?"

"After the meeting, when it was just the two of us, I asked her about you. She made a joke about the way I looked at you." He ran his hand over his beard. "About how I seemed *particularly interested* in you. Those were her exact words: particularly interested."

What does that mean?

He wasn't telling the story fast enough.

"Is she going to take her suspicions to HR?" I asked as he headed to the door.

He shook his head, stopping at the front door. "No, she wouldn't do that."

I wiped my palms down my thighs. "So, if we do our part and pretend like we don't know each other, her suspicions won't be validated and we'll both be protected."

And employed.

His hand was on the doorknob, his body still facing me. "Right. We just have to play it cool." His eyes dipped to my lips and lingered for a beat too long. "And keep our distance from one another."

Blinking up at him, I felt the pull deep within. It was the first time I'd been around him, felt the pull, and actually resisted it.

We couldn't continue and we had to keep our distance. I knew it was the right thing to do. I knew it was too big of a risk. But it didn't feel right.

"Well, Mr. Long"—taking a step back, I stretched my hand out to him—"it has been a pleasure getting to know you this summer."

He slipped his hand over mine, gripping it firmly. "The pleasure has been all mine."

Hearing him say "mine" flashed me back to that morning. It was only a few hours ago that he'd asked me to be his.

And I actually said yes!

Now we were pretending that never happened—like none of it ever happened. I swallowed hard, ignoring the burning sensation in my throat.

He looked like he wanted to say something else, but he didn't. Bringing the back of my hand to his lips, he kissed it softly.

A chill ran up my arm and then down the rest of my body.

"A fantasy in the flesh," he murmured.

I couldn't respond. I didn't trust myself. Anything I would've said would've resulted in me with my mouth open. Either a sob would've come out, or his dick would've gone in. Neither needed to happen, so I swallowed my feelings.

He walked out of my place and left my body humming, wanting. I couldn't speak. I couldn't move. I couldn't do anything but stand in the doorway and watch him walk out of my personal life.

When he was thirty feet away and there was enough distance between us, I could breathe. He snatched the ticket from under his windshield wiper blade and shoved it into his pocket. Just as he was about to climb into his car, I yelled to him.

"How do you know for sure Remedy won't say anything?"

"Because she's my sister," he called back.

14

I thought finding the man who felt like home was an impossibility. But it was depriving myself of said man that was proving to be impossible. I could not get Russ out of my head. I tried everything to rid myself of the emptiness that gutted me whenever he crossed my mind. It wasn't just that we were no longer dating. It was the fact that he was my employer and dating would be career suicide.

It was a devastating predicament, and I couldn't remember a time I'd felt this bad. A man had never gotten me in my feelings to the point that I was down, let alone down bad. The only thing I could think to do was stay busy.

I spent the week distracting myself with outfit coordination, business planning, and online dating. My doctor's appointment was quick and easy on Tuesday. Besides them reassuring me that my IUD was still in place, my test results came back on Friday, and as expected, I had a clean bill of health. On Saturday night, I let The Smart One take me out, but I didn't have a good time.

On Sunday night, I sat across the table from Denzel, a man I'd met on TenderFish. We'd had very surface-level conversation online, so I didn't know what to expect. He was a tall, good-looking man with kind eyes and prematurely salt-and-pepper hair. We exchanged pleasantries over appetizers and cocktails. I was distracted, but not enough that Russ didn't cross my mind.

I hated it.

After placing our orders, he leaned forward in his chair.

"What's your favorite verse right now?" he asked.

"Oh, it's gotta be when Megan Thee Stallion said . . ." I went on to rap my favorite lines from one of my favorite songs. I moved my shoulders to the beat in my head. "I've been obsessed with that verse since I first heard it. What's yours?"

His eyebrows were raised. "Uh . . . Proverbs 3:5."

The silence that followed was like a vacuum.

I thought I heard God laugh.

The rest of the date was more of the same as we both realized we didn't have much in common. He was a teacher who enjoyed quiet nights at home. He was looking for a long-term relationship. So, while we enjoyed our dinner and conversation, we ended the night pretty early.

"How was your date?" Aaliyah asked as soon as I answered the phone.

I was already home, showered, and in bed. "Dinner was delicious. We made light small talk but we won't be seeing each other again. He might be a good match for Jazz though," I told her, quickly recapping the night.

"Hm. Have you linked up with The Funny One?"

"No. He hit me up, but I just . . ." I frowned. "I haven't felt like it. I saw The Smart One though."

"You don't really sound too interested in anyone."

"I'm not," I murmured.

"What's that thing you always say? You can't compete where you don't compare?" Before I could open my mouth to respond, she started again. "So, speaking of Russ . . ."

"Oop!" I chirped, making a face even though she couldn't see me. "Not you bringing this conversation back again."

She let out a light laugh. "I'm sorry. I just . . . It's obvious you still want him, Nina."

I didn't immediately respond because I *did* still want him. There was no denying that. I distracted myself with pointless dates and endless swiping, but it was going to take more than a week to get used to the fact that Russ was out of the picture. The void he left was too big, too significant. Everything felt like it was at risk, and I wasn't busy enough to distract myself from the pain.

And this is exactly why I like to have multiple men and multiple jobs!

Aaliyah's voice became softer, as if she were handling me with kid gloves. "I don't think any amount of swiping or dating or denial is going to change that."

The truth of her words made the pit in my stomach grow larger.

"For the next eight and a half months, I'm denying any affiliation with him," I stated.

"Have you talked to him at all?"

I swallowed hard. "Nope."

Outside of him texting me his negative test results, I hadn't heard from him.

"That's too bad," she said sadly. "You liked him a lot."

My heart sank, as it had done all week. "It was fun while it lasted," I acknowledged.

"Are you going to see him this week?"

"I doubt it. We have a photoshoot every day this week and he's always traveling."

"A photoshoot every day? You're going to be busy."

I cracked a slight smile into my pillow. "Yeah, I'm excited. We get a couple days off next week and then September comes and it's go time. We have a trip, then Fashion Week, and then a few other trips."

I needed to be busier. I needed the distractions. I needed the work.

"What are you going to do if you see him?" she asked unexpectedly.

"I'll keep it professional. Say hello. Do my job. It'll be fine." I rolled onto my side, checking the clock on the nightstand. "But honestly, I can't imagine he'd be in town just for the photoshoots."

She was quiet for a moment. "I hope he comes into town, and he has a new contract written up that makes it cool for you two to continue dating."

The burning feeling coated my throat again. "That's not going to happen."

"It could," she argued.

Sighing, I rolled my eyes. "You are such a romantic."

"True. But I honestly thought you and Russ were going to get together. I thought he was endgame for you. You have never gotten excited about a man like you did with him. And I loved that for you! I want you to have more of that. You deserve it!"

I blinked back tears and then just decided to keep my eyes

closed. She wasn't wrong. I wouldn't call him "endgame," but he was special.

I cleared my throat. "Yeah, Russ left large shoes to fill."

And large everything else, too . . .

"But . . ." I continued, shaking off the thought, "the point of having a roster is that anyone can get replaced. And since quality far outweighs quantity, it will take time to replace him."

"What about The Romantic One?"

I frowned. "What about him?"

She giggled. "It's interesting how you never said anything about how hard it would be to replace him."

"Girl, please."

I hadn't thought about that man since he left the event.

As her laughter died down, I changed the subject.

"Your birthday is coming up," I pointed out. "What dates do you have lined up?"

She told me about the men she'd talked to on the app, the predicament she found herself in, and how she still hadn't finalized a date for her birthday weekend. Twenty minutes later, we said good night.

Even though I knew I should've immediately gone to sleep, since I had an early call time, I couldn't shut my mind off. I stared at the TV, but I wasn't focused. I kept replaying the events of last weekend over and over again. As I started drifting off to sleep, two things became clear.

The dates I'd just gone on didn't compare.

The men I'd just gone out with didn't compare.

Would anyone?

I'd had to replace men on my roster before. Finding someone fun had never been that difficult. But finding someone like Russ would prove to be a challenge.

He was more than just fun.

He was perfect.

And I felt the loss.

Russell Long was everything I wanted, and in order to replace him on the roster, I'd have to find someone who was comparable.

And even then, it wouldn't be enough. It hit me that I didn't want someone comparable. I didn't want someone to try to fill his large shoes. I just wanted him—just him. And that thought brought me to tears. I was only in a relationship with him for three hours yet I'd cried more and harder than I ever cried over a man.

And that made me mad.

How did I let myself get put in this position?

My phone vibrated, startling me and waking me up.

> Tyrell: How are you? I'm sorry to reach out to you so late, but I just found out there's an author event for Fumi Davis in a couple weeks and tickets go on sale at midnight. If I get two tickets, would you like to come with me? It's in New York so we'd be gone for the weekend.

There was no way I would be able to do a weekend getaway with him in the mental state I was in. Emotionally, I was not available. Physically, I was not available. And socially, I was not available.

> Nina: That's my best friend's birthday weekend so I'm not going to be able to make it.

> Tyrell: There's another one in Philadelphia in a month. I want to do a weekend with you if you're free in September. Things felt different the other day and I'd like to make it up to you. What do you think?

> Nina: I think you should be planning weekend getaways with someone who is on the same page as you. Things did feel different last time we were together and that was on me. I'm not emotionally available and you deserve that. You're a great guy and I've had a great time with you.

> Tyrell: I don't even know what to say to this.

I didn't feel bad for ending things. But I did feel bad that I did it over text. I picked up the phone and called him, but he didn't answer.

New roster, new men, new everything.

I needed a clean slate. I needed a fresh start.

Sighing, I placed my phone back on my nightstand and closed my eyes. Unfortunately, my mind raced, and I tossed and turned until my alarm went off in the morning. Despite my restless night, I made it to the studio in DC on time. I had to be in hair and makeup by nine o'clock, and knowing DC traffic, I got on the road early.

It felt like it took forever to get there in rush hour traffic. But it gave me plenty of time to shake off the thoughts of Russ that plagued my sleep.

"Good morning," I greeted the room as I entered the building.

I met a photographer, makeup artist, hair stylist, and a bunch of RLF employees. The only people who looked familiar to me were Remedy and Angelica.

Remedy Rose was holding court, speaking emphatically about something. The moment I looked at her, all I could think about was Russ. The siblings didn't look alike, but they had the same eyes. They didn't have the same personality, but they had the same commanding confidence. She was his married sister who lived in the area.

I would've never connected those dots.

I was shook.

Interrupting my thoughts, Angelica beckoned me over and showed me what I would be wearing. Even though she wasn't friendly, she acknowledged me and seemed to be in a pleasant mood as she went over each look.

It wasn't until I saw the clothes that I felt the ripple of excitement shoot through my limbs.

I was the first model there, but the others soon followed. It wasn't long before we'd completed hair and makeup and were camera ready. Dressed in a denim skirt and a deep V-neck RLF sweater, I smiled at my reflection in the mirror. My legs looked good. The sweater hugged me sexily.

"You all look great," Remedy complimented us as we positioned ourselves in front of the large white backdrop. "We're going to do group shots and then individual ones. Let me introduce you to the photographer . . ."

We got acquainted and then old-school rap music came blasting from overhead speakers. There were at least fifteen people at the shoot who were just watching, but I blocked all of them out. The models and I had already discussed what we should do for our group shots, so we moved into position effortlessly.

"Nina, you're up," the photographer called out as I walked over to do my solo shots.

As I was posing, I lifted my chin and looked slightly to the left. The smoldering look I was giving faltered the moment our eyes locked.

Russ!

I was not expecting him to be there. I was not expecting him to be watching me so intently.

It's his job, I reminded myself. *So, do yours.*

My heart beat a little faster knowing he was watching. But I was a professional and I wasn't about to let him get in the way of my bag.

"Yasssssss," Taisha cheered.

When I finished, I went over to where the models were huddled, and we waited for Matias to do his thing. When we were all done, we were directed to change into our second and then third outfits to do the process all over again.

By the time we finished, it was four o'clock in the afternoon. I was hungry and tired.

"You all did an incredible job," Remedy remarked as she approached us.

"Thank you," we said in unison.

"They transformed with each new look," she continued, turning to her brother. "Isn't that right, Russell?"

"Yes," he answered, seeming to avoid eye contact with me at all costs. "You looked good and cohesive. I know they got some good shots." He checked his watch. "If you'll excuse me."

He stole one fleeting glance at me before he turned and walked away. The look lasted two seconds, three at the most. But I felt that shit everywhere.

Swallowing hard, I shook slightly as I watched him walk away. *Mm, mm, mm—*

"The rest of the week will run about the same amount of time," Remedy continued. "Different photographers have different processes, so don't hold me to that. But at least you can estimate a plan. Tomorrow's shoot has a seven o'clock arrival time. Check your email if you need the address."

Tuesday's photoshoot took place in a garden park on the outskirts of town. It was a fun, lighthearted shoot where we laughed the entire time. But it was hot and there were bugs flying around annoyingly. I hated it. The other models were the only thing that made the shoot a good time.

"These jeans feel so good, right?" Jacqueline marveled, smoothing her hand down her slim hips.

I nodded. "I'm impressed."

"I love the way these hug my thighs," Taisha commented.

"Yeah, my ass looks great," Matias quipped, turning and shaking his ass.

"Don't nobody want to see that shit," Jonah complained.

We all laughed.

It was our denim day. We all wore RLF jeans and various RLF T-shirts. The good time we were having was the only thing keeping me distracted from Russ's sexy ass, standing just on the periphery of the area we were working in. Our eyes met a couple of times over the course of the shoot. Each time twisted my gut a little, but we didn't hold each other's gaze long enough to trigger anything else.

I had to admit I was slightly disappointed.

I wasn't surprised though.

He didn't really speak to me on Monday either, so I couldn't say he was acting funny. But it was clear that he was keeping his distance. And every time I looked at him, he got under my skin. So when Jonah would flirt with me, I'd indulge a bit. Anything to stop the tingle down my spine I felt when Russ watched me.

When we were posed for our final looks, Russ moved right next to the photographer. They spoke in low tones and then directions were given to everyone but me.

I stared at him, but he deliberately avoided eye contact with me. Inhaling deeply, I let out a shaky breath. He wasn't ignoring me per se. He didn't talk to any of the models. He interacted with the other executives and with the photographer. Anything he wanted changed with our wardrobe, he directed the changes to the stylist. And he looked at us to make sure those changes were implemented.

But now he's actively not looking at me.

He made another comment to the photographer and then he pulled out his phone and left.

I could breathe easier when he wasn't standing right in front of me.

Fortunately, Russ wasn't there for Wednesday's photoshoot. But every time the door opened, I looked for him. Anytime Remedy took a call, I assumed it was him. But about halfway through the shoot, I relaxed and forced him out of my mind.

Thursday's photoshoot took place in a studio on the southside of town. From the low buzz of conversation and the lack of music and joy, I could tell there was a different vibe from the moment I walked into the place.

It was gorgeous—maybe the most beautiful studio I'd ever visited. The pristine space had a foliage-covered wall, with props situated to give it a jungle theme. The photographer didn't smile or introduce himself like the others had. He stalked around the room with two young people on his heels, assisting him. Everything seemed less fun, but more structured, with that photographer.

There were only five RLF employees, as opposed to the twelve upper management and execs who showed up every other day. They stayed on the perimeter of the room, taking notes on their tablets and laptops. Instead of three outfits, we had five different wardrobe changes. We didn't laugh or joke like we had at the beginning of the week. We got in front of the camera and did what we were instructed to do. It was always work, but for the first time, it felt like it. When a brief break was called to change lenses and adjust the lights, we patiently waited for direction.

"I don't mean no disrespect," Jonah whispered as the photographer took some test shots. "But you were made for those pants."

I glanced over my shoulder at him. "Are you flirting with me?"

"Only if you're into it."

The photographer interrupted the conversation by saying, "I want to try something with Jonah and Nina."

"Okay," I mumbled, taking my place in front of the camera.

Taisha, Jacqueline, and Matias walked to the other side of the camera.

"Line up on those dots," he demanded. "I want you two to face each other and look like you want each other. While keeping the distance between you, convey desire. Be mindful of the camera, but stare at one another."

With a foot of space between us, I stood on my mark and looked at Jonah. It was funny at first. We smiled at each other, and the only reason I didn't laugh was because the photographer didn't seem like the type to take too kindly to that. But as we were guided through the poses, we were told to wrap an arm around one another. Our bodies faced the camera, and our heads were turned toward each other. And then I was instructed to look directly at the camera while Jonah was directed to look down at me.

"Yes, Jonah," the photographer encouraged. "You want her. I want to feel the chemistry. Yes! Yes!"

"Tilt your head up, Nina. Yes, like that!"

"Turn your body toward Nina, Jonah."

"Nina, the chemistry and tension are there. Look at the camera. Now look beyond the camera. Now . . ."

I didn't hear anything else the photographer had said, because beyond the camera stood Russell fucking Long.

My stomach flipped at the unexpected sight.

Russ's handsome face, which I came on a week and a half ago, was hardened. His full lips, which I kissed passionately ten days ago, were pulled into a tight line. His beautiful brown eyes, which used to roam my body every time he'd see me, were narrowed.

Everything muted as our eyes locked. For several long seconds, I was transfixed.

I could pretend I didn't miss that man in the privacy of my own home, but it was hard to deny it in his presence.

Jonah tapped on my back, and I sucked in a sharp breath. Tearing my eyes away from Russ, I tried to focus on my work. But it was too late.

"No, no, no, it's gone," the photographer grumbled. "You had something, but you lost it. Let's try this with Jacqueline and Matias."

I walked toward Taisha, Jonah on my heels.

"You two looked good," Taisha whispered excitedly. "If I didn't know any better . . ." She wiggled her eyebrows.

"We were sharing something special," Jonah replied, draping his arm around my shoulders.

My eyebrows shot up. "Oop! Not you lying!"

"She's just shy," he joked to Taisha in a low tone.

Rolling my eyes, I spun out of his embrace. "Jonah, please."

The three of us snickered quietly, hoping not to be overheard by the photographer or his team.

I glanced in the direction where Russ was, but he was gone. I didn't want to make it obvious, so I watched Matias and Jacqueline for a few seconds before discreetly turning to look behind me.

Russ was staring directly at me.

My gut twisted violently. So much so, I whipped back around.

"That's it," the photographer stated with finality.

His assistants turned off the LED lights and that's how we knew the shoot was over.

"I guess that's it," I murmured as we headed toward the changing areas.

"He isn't the nicest, but he is an epic photographer," Jacqueline whispered. "These photos are probably going to be the best of all of them."

I smiled. "I can't wait to see them."

Trying to play it cool, I looked over toward the back of the room where the RLF team had spent the entirety of the shoot. Russ was in a conversation with Remedy. He wasn't looking in my direction, but she was. Quickly averting my eyes, I filed out with the rest of the models.

My heart thumped nervously.

Even if Remedy saw me looking in that direction, there was no way for her to know that I was looking at Russ.

It's fine, it's fine.

I talked myself down as I changed. By the time I exited the studio, I felt more at ease. I was just about to get into my car when I saw Remedy walking my way.

"Nina," she greeted me with a pleasant tone.

Definitely not the tone of someone suspicious of my past with her brother.

"Hi, Remedy," I said, smiling.

"I was right about you." She pointed at me. "You're a natural. You're a star."

She put her cell phone to her ear and continued walking down the sidewalk.

I watched her for a moment and then I climbed into the car.

A star?

The feelings Russ brought out of me were to be expected—he was one of the good ones. He and I connected in such a significant way *and* the sex was unmatched. But the feeling of being validated by industry professionals who could elevate my career was huge. I thought about all of the women who would be inspired by me, my presence, my body, my style.

The point of having a roster is that anyone can get replaced, I reminded myself. *This opportunity is once in a lifetime.*

I had to make peace with the fact that I wasn't going to replace Russ. Meeting someone fun or smart or romantic would start rebuilding my roster and that was a step in the right direction. But I knew my heart wasn't in it. I just had to hope that being mildly entertained by lesser men would feel a lot better than being down bad over a man I was prohibited from dating.

Just the thought of my last few dates caused me to purse my lips in displeasure. Having to let Russ go gave me no joy. I hadn't seen him on a personal level since the morning he'd left my place. It killed me not to talk to him or spend time with him. To know we didn't have upcoming plans was a constant reminder of how much I actually missed him.

I tried to ignore the empty pit thinking about spending time with him created within me.

Dammit.

15

"Thank God it's Friday, am I right?" Lori asked me and Taisha as we rode the elevator to the RLF office. "First week of photoshoots are wrapping up, and I'm glad our location for today is on the roof because I get to check out the shoot! Are you looking forward to having a weekend off? Any plans?"

"My cousin's having a party this weekend," I told them.

"Oh, nice!" Lori reacted. "We've been keeping all of you so busy this week. I'm sure you're ready for a break."

"It's been a lot of fun," Taisha replied. "I've actually enjoyed it."

"I'm looking forward to seeing the final images," I answered, sidestepping the question.

Hell yeah, I'm looking forward to having the weekend off!

I needed a break, and I needed some time to recuperate. Spending one week not seeing Russ at all, followed by one week seeing Russ almost every day while we pretended not to know each other, was too much. On the surface, it was uneventful—just a few sidelong glances and the unmistakable feeling of his eyes on me when my back was turned. But internally, I was in turmoil. I wanted him. The attraction was intense. The thing that took me by surprise was how I longed for his company just as much as his dick.

If I were being really honest with myself, I missed spending time with him. I missed being with him. I missed the way he made me feel. The Funny One was hilarious—truly a good time. The Smart One was incredibly intelligent—such a good conversationalist.

But Russ—

My eyes widened as I stared out the opened elevator door.

Russ!

"Mr. Long," Lori greeted him cheerfully as we exited. "Have you had a chance to meet Taisha and Nina? I know I introduced you to Matias and Jonah, but the ladies weren't around during that introduction."

He nodded, only briefly glancing over at us with a tight smile. "Yes, I met them last week."

"So, you didn't see them in their outfits for the ball?" She gestured to us with her thumbs. "I was hoping you might've seen Nina's boyfriend. She made him the RLF accessory!" Lori exclaimed, still amused two weeks later.

For the first time, Russ looked directly at me and stared silently for a moment. "What?"

I opened my mouth to respond, trying to figure out how to deny what she was saying without being obvious, but before I had a chance to come up with anything, Lori continued talking.

"She had him wear the shirt from your very first T-shirt press with a tailored suit! It was quite nostalgic and made such an impression! And the outfit reminded me of something you would wear, to be honest."

He clenched his jaw before forcing a smile that didn't reach his eyes. "I missed that."

Oh, he's pissed.

Lori continued as if she hadn't thrown a grenade. "Yeah, and Taisha . . ."

She paid Taisha a compliment that I didn't hear because I was still trying to find my voice.

Russ was a professional, so I knew he wasn't going to say or do anything that implicated either of us. But I was surprised his poker face wasn't better. The clenched jaw, tight lips, and darkened eyes made it evident to me, but I wasn't sure if anyone else noticed. Either way, I knew I needed to clear up the misunderstanding.

I cleared my throat lightly. "It wasn't—"

"I'm sorry to run off in the middle of you telling me Taisha's story," he interrupted me, looking between Lori and Taisha. "But I need to meet with the photographer before we can begin the shoot. We can catch up once everything is set up." Pointedly not looking at me, he said his goodbye to us. "It was nice touching base with you all."

Without waiting for a response, he disappeared through the stairway exit.

"That man is about his business," Lori told us, continuing to lead us to the showroom. "And somebody is in trouble."

"You think so?" I asked, curious to get as much information as possible.

She nodded. "He has a tell. When he's mad, he'll fix his mouth like this"—she made her lips into a hard line—"and then he'll address the problem. He's a good leader and doesn't get mad often. But he does like things to be up to his standard. And when it's not, you fix it or you're out."

Taisha frowned. "He sounds tough."

"He knows what he wants," I stated unintentionally. When I realized I said the words out loud, my eyes widened. "I mean, it sounds like he's cool, but if you don't fix things when you have a chance, that's it."

Lori nodded as she opened the door to the showroom. "Russell Long built this company from the ground up with his bare hands. He started designing and selling T shirts when he was at Hamilton University. He brought in some people and grew that to designing and selling streetwear. And then he brought on his sister and expanded things more, and we're now offering such a cool variety of garments." She opened her arms wide, gesturing to the racks of clothing all around. "He does not play about his business." Lifting her hand to Angelica, she called out, "I have the last two right here for you!"

Once Angelica had us styled to her satisfaction, we were ushered up to the roof. The view of the city from that vantage point was unmatched. We met a photographer who seemed surprised to see me.

It seemed like everyone from the company was up on the roof watching us.

Everyone except Russ.

It was a bit unnerving to have that many eyes on us as we worked and took direction. As the RLF crowd had thinned out, people from other floors had come to spectate. While I didn't mind an audience, they were scrutinizing our every move. We could hear them commenting on our appearance, our poses, and the way the clothes looked on our bodies. To a certain degree, I understood that the RLF employees had a vested interest in the way the product was going to roll out. Their jobs depended on it as much as ours. But the remarks from the other spectators were uncomfortable.

Hearing some of the same comments that I would normally read in the comments section online was wild.

"Even though she's big, she is so beautiful!"

"That top is a little too small for her."

"She's so brave to have the stretch marks on her stomach showing."

"I wish I had her confidence."

Since it was Friday and the afternoon was winding down, the crowd dwindled significantly. And I was ready to go as well.

"Okay, now, let's bring you in," the photographer stated, beckoning me over and positioning me in the back.

Again.

The photographer treated me as an afterthought for most of the shoot. He captured group and solo shots of each outfit. He placed me in the back, hiding me in most of the group photos. He took fewer solo shots of me. He made subtle comments that weren't specifically targeting me, but it felt that way. I maintained my composure because nothing was explicit. And to everyone watching, it would appear as if I was just the angry Black woman, when in actuality, I was a victim of his microaggressions.

I sighed.

During my last solo shot, everything was fine until I was asked to leap.

I looked down at my cropped white RLF hoodie and the high-waisted, acid-washed jeans I wore. Although I looked great, I wasn't wearing a bra that could handle a leap.

"Excuse me," I said to the photographer, moving closer to him. "I don't think me jumping up and down is a good idea due to—"

"Your knees?" he guessed, giving me a sympathetic look and patting me on my shoulder. "Listen, this is the last shot of the day and it's a low-impact jump. Don't think too hard about it. You're fine."

Shocked and slightly taken aback, I made a face. "No. Actually my knees are fine. But since I'm not wearing a bra—"

"Is everything okay here?" Remedy interrupted, appearing on the other side of the photographer.

"Yes, the plus model had some difficulty with the instruction," he told her. "But I think we're all good now." He ran a hand through his graying hair before giving me a thumbs-up.

"No, we're not all good," I clarified. "And my name is Nina." I turned to Remedy. "I'm top-heavy and this bra tape has no support, so me jumping is not a good idea."

"This is my photoshoot. I'll decide what's a good idea for my shoot," he snapped.

"And this is my body," I returned, just as forcefully. "I'll decide what's a good idea for me."

Remedy's eyes were large as she looked between the two of us. "Okay." She clasped her hands together and took a step back. "She doesn't do the leap."

The photographer's face turned red, and I could almost see steam coming from the top of his head.

"Can you lift your arms up and turn toward the sun?" he asked. "I wouldn't want to ask you to do anything you're not comfortable with."

I lifted my arms and let the sun shine on my face. I moved deliberately, playing up my angles.

"Is it too much to ask for you to drop into a squat?" he asked sarcastically.

I squatted.

He sighed loudly. "Lower."

I squatted lower.

"Lift your chest and squat lower."

I was basically sitting in an invisible chair. He had me hold that position for ninety seconds. I know he was hoping I would break, but I was in the gym five times a week. I had one more minute in me.

In a stony silence, he snapped some pictures. When I had to stand after two and a half minutes, he smirked and then unceremoniously stopped.

"Where's Mr. Long? Can you get Mr. Long for me, please?"

An assistant ran toward the exit.

I dropped my arms to my sides and waited. Unsure of what I was supposed to do, I looked over at the other models. They also looked confused. Slowly, I made my way to them.

"What's wrong?" Remedy asked, rushing to his side.

The photographer glanced at me. "The vision I pitched to Mr. Long isn't able to be executed if one of the models is difficult and uncooperative."

My face twisted. "Difficult?" I muttered.

"I just texted him. Difficult how?" Remedy asked.

"Being unable to do the poses necessary to execute the vision."

"I see." She nodded slowly as she checked her phone. "So you can't do your job?"

He looked insulted. "I can do my job. It's her—"

The door opened, and Russ walked our way. His long legs carried him across the roof swiftly, and the photographer turned his back to us in order to address the man in charge.

"Finally! Mr. Long, we need to talk," the photographer called out.

"What's going on?" Russ asked, slowing down a few feet in front of him. His handsome face was unreadable as he stared at the man. "What's the problem?"

"You know the idea I told you about? The one you hired me for? Well"—he turned and gestured to me—"you didn't tell me that there was a fifth model or that she's a plus model—"

"What does that have to do with anything?" Russ interrupted.

"She's making it difficult to get the shots."

Russ looked at me and then back to the photographer. "I hired you to do a job. Are you telling me you're unable to do it?"

"No, no." He shook his head with fervor. "That's not what I'm saying."

"We paid you for the memory card with the images. Let me get that from you."

"Yeah, sure. It's just the raw images." The photographer took the memory card out and handed it to him. "Once I edit the photos, you'll see what I can do. And I know I proposed the idea of the models flying because their clothes are fly. It was going to be a whole thing. And you said you loved my idea. You know I've wanted to work with you for a long time, so I was just trying to give you what you wanted."

Russ handed the memory card to Remedy before he responded. "I said I loved how prepared you were. I didn't realize that was your one good idea."

"No, it's not my only good idea. But it's hard to work with fat—" He hooked his thumb toward me.

"Watch your fucking mouth," he growled, eyes flashing. He stepped forward, getting in his face. "You're fired."

The photographer's eyes bulged as he backed up. "You said if I did a good job here, I could work with you during Fashion We—"

"You think you can disrespect her . . . or any of my employees and stay on with me?" His voice was low and cold. "You're fired."

"But I didn't—"

Through gritted teeth, he uttered, "I don't tolerate disrespect."

"She—"

Turning toward Remedy, Russ ignored the photographer. "Set something up for Wednesday and let Angelica know that we'll be running these same outfits." He pointed to a tall man who was hanging back but clearly listening to the entire exchange. "Pierre, help him get his shit and escort him out. I have a flight to catch."

Without another word, Russ stalked toward the exit and disappeared through the door.

Remedy chewed the inside of her cheek as she beckoned to us. "Go to the showroom and give Angelica your outfits. Everything is still the same for Monday, but I'll email you with details about this new Wednesday shoot." She cleared her throat and turned to the photographer. "When they leave, I need to speak with you . . ."

The five of us silently made our way to the elevator. As soon as the door closed, everyone started talking at once.

"Holy shit!" Matias said before he burst out laughing. "I don't even know what happened."

"Wow." Jacqueline put her hands to her face. "I've never seen anything like that before, and I've worked a lot of jobs."

"I thought Boss Man was about to knock Camera Man out," Jonah remarked.

Taisha asked, "Y'all didn't hear how that guy was being shady?" She turned to me. "Are you okay?"

"Yeah, I'm fine," I answered.

"I didn't hear him say anything shady," Matias responded. "What did I miss?"

"What did he say?" Jonah wondered. "If I would've heard, I would've said something."

"Was it when he asked if you had the right outfit on?" Jacqueline pondered. "I thought that was odd."

I nodded. "Yeah, that was one of the things he said."

Jacqueline pursed her lips. "Adding an extra day onto the shooting schedule when it's already tight *and* losing a whole photography session." She gave me a look. "This *definitely* cost RLF some money."

"Yeah," Matias agreed. "Not to mention he probably still has to pay that dude for shooting, even if he doesn't use the images—even after firing him!"

"You should tell Mr. Long what happened," Taisha suggested.

The elevator opened and we all immediately stopped talking. The statement hung in the air.

Russ was exchanging goodbyes with a man carrying an extra-large portfolio. As soon as we left the elevator, the man entered it. I stared at Russ, hoping he'd look at me. But when he did, a chill ran down my spine. His face was unreadable, his eyes were narrowed, and his mouth was set in a hard line.

The hair on the back of my neck stood up.

He broke eye contact and then headed to the right while we turned left. As we headed to the showroom, I glanced over my shoulder to see Russ entering an office. I felt a pit in my stomach.

"I need to talk to Ru—the CEO," I murmured to the group as I slowed to a stop.

"Do you want me to wait for you?" Jonah asked.

I shook my head. "I need to do this on my own."

"I think it's a smart move," Taisha chimed in. "Get ahead of things. You know people love to call us difficult."

Nodding, I lifted my hand in a wave. "Yeah. I'll see you guys later."

My forced smile dropped the moment I turned my back to them. As I walked down the hall, my heart beat louder with each step. By the time I reached the door with his name on the plate next to it, I was shaking.

Rolling my shoulders back, I lifted my fist and knocked gently against the door.

"Yes," Russ said sharply.

I'd never been nervous around him before, but that was the best way I could describe the sensation I felt as I pushed the door open. I didn't know how he was going to react.

"Hi," I said softly.

It was clear he'd been pacing, because he was statue-still in the middle of the spacious office. His eyes were wide, and his surprise was evident, but he didn't say a word.

"I just wanted to thank you for what you did on the roof," I told him from the doorway.

He shook his head. "He shouldn't have disrespected you and I'm sorry you had to hear that."

"I appreciate it." I put my hand to my chest. "Truly."

"It's not a problem. You photograph well and you're doing a good job."

His response was so robotic. It was professional, but void of all emotion.

Taking a deep breath, I stepped inside and closed the door behind me. "Do you have a few minutes?"

He checked his watch and then looked everywhere but at me. "I need to be out of here in an hour and I have a lot of work to do before I go."

I crossed the room until I was a couple feet in front of him. "You can't even look at me?"

When his eyes met mine, I saw a flash of intensity.

"I'm looking at you," he uttered through clenched teeth.

The coldness was gone. I wasn't sure if it was replaced with passion or fury, but it was intense, and he wasn't masking it anymore. My heart rate went back up, but it wasn't nerves this time.

"Why are you looking at me like that?" I asked, searching his face.

"How do you want me to look at you, Nina?"

"I don't know. But I don't want you to look at me like you have beef with me."

He took a few steps back. "I don't have beef with you. I just . . ."

His sentence trailed off and my insides twisted at the distance he kept between us.

I stepped forward. "You just can't even be in the same room with me?"

He stepped back. "I don't have beef with you. I have a lot of stuff to do before my flight. So, if you'll excuse me."

I was being dismissed.

I exhaled. "Wow."

Embarrassment, hurt, and shock made my chest feel like it was caving in. My eyes stung unexpectedly, and I wanted to cuss him out for making me feel emotional.

I took a step back. "I didn't realize that when you walked out of my place, you decided you couldn't speak to me or look at me or even be in the same room with me anymore. But I get it. You don't have to worry about it happening again. Fuck this."

I turned on my heel and stormed to the door. As soon as my hand touched the handle and pulled it open, Russ grabbed my arm. Spinning me around, he pushed my back against the door, causing it to slam shut.

Breathing heavily, we stared at one another. Seconds ticked by and I got lost—lost in his eyes, lost in my desire, lost in the moment. With both hands flat against the wood, his arms caged my head between them. I was trapped.

My breath was coming in shallow bursts and my heart was racing. His lips parted and his gaze dipped to mine. His tongue ran from one corner of his mouth to the other. I didn't know if he was going to kiss me, cuss me out, or kick me out. That uncertainty made me putty in his hands.

"Fuck me?" he asked in a raspy whisper.

"I said fuck *this,*" I clarified.

"You're the one with the boyfriend, but you're saying fuck me?"

"I don't have—"

"Just tell me it's not that muthafucka that I'm paying to watch push up on you."

"No!" My voice came out as an anxious burst of air. "You have this all wrong." I searched his eyes and the longer I stared into them, the more out of sorts I felt. "I don't have a boyfriend now. I didn't have a boyfriend then. I haven't had a boyfriend since high school. I brought a date with me to the ball and ended things with him before I even ran into you," I explained to him in a rush. "And there's nothing between me and Jonah."

He didn't say anything.

With every inhale, he sucked my breath from me. His presence pressed me against the door. His energy made my stomach flutter. His eyes bore into me.

My heart constricted.

"Is that why you've been keeping your distance from me?" I murmured.

His face twitched and his lips parted.

"Nina . . ." One of his hands left the door and relocated to the middle of my chest. "You really think that's the reason I keep my distance?"

I sucked in a sharp breath. The heat from his hand seared through the material of the shirt and scorched my skin.

I swallowed hard. "If that's not it, why?"

Sliding his hand up my chest, he wrapped his fingers around my neck. "Because every time I see you, I want to touch you." His hand tightened around my throat. "If I look at you, I'm always looking over my shoulder to make sure no one caught me staring.

If I'm around you, all I want to do is put my hands all over you."
He brought his forehead to mine. "When I'm in the same space as
you, all I want is this . . ."

His lips crashed into mine and my entire body instantly caught
on fire. When his tongue grazed mine, my knees went weak. As he
deepened the kiss, my nipples hardened, my panties were soaked,
and the desire that curled in my belly felt like I would instantly
combust.

"Mmmm . . ." I moaned as I grabbed his shirt, pulling him
closer. Feeling his erection pressed against me made me dizzy with
want as I moaned into his mouth for a second time.

Breaking the kiss abruptly, he dropped his hand from my neck
and stepped back.

I could still feel his fingertips on my skin. I could still taste his
kiss on my lips.

"This is why," he uttered, adjusting himself and backing away
from me. "I can't be close to you. I can't look at you. I can't be alone
in a room with you. I just . . ." He shook his head, taking another
step back.

"Russ," I whispered, stepping away from the door.

Even though he was about six feet away from me, when I moved
forward, he moved back.

I stopped in my tracks.

It felt like he was recoiling from me.

My mouth felt dry. "Russ—"

"Nina, please," he interrupted, walking to his large black L-shaped
desk. He took a deep breath and sat down in his chair. "You
should go."

My hand was on the door handle, but I was rooted in place. The
gentle squeak of the wheels rolling back was the only sound in
the room for a moment. Avoiding eye contact, he started grabbing
at files and loose sheets of papers, lifting them, and putting them
down. "Go."

Biting the inside of my cheek, I pulled the door open and left.
Making my way to the showroom, I had several thoughts running
through my head at once.

"I was wondering where you were," Angelica stated as soon as I entered the space.

"I'm sorry," I apologized distractedly as I went behind the first partition and changed out of my clothes.

A few minutes later, I handed her the garments.

Without a smile, Angelica looked me up and down. "I'm going to nominate you to walk the final look in the runway show for Fashion Week."

Her words chased every thought out of my head. My eyebrows flew up. "What?"

"Print modeling and runway modeling are two different beasts. The clothes need to move a certain way. And you have the walk."

"Oh my God," I gasped. "Thank you."

"There's no guarantee," she clarified, turning around to put my outfit on the rack with the others from the shoot.

Knowing Angelica, I knew that was the end of the conversation. "Thank you. See you Monday!"

I walked out of there with the biggest smile on my face.

I'd only made it halfway down the hall when Russ and Remedy came out of his office. The minute I saw him, my body reacted.

His kiss still remained on my lips.

His touch still inflamed my skin.

His words still rang in my ears.

Remedy's back was to me while she talked to him. Russ stood in front of her with his arms crossed over his chest. As I got closer to the elevator bank, our eyes locked. He was listening to Remedy, but he was watching me.

His gaze sent a chill down my spine, and I shivered.

Suddenly, Remedy turned around and looked at me.

Shit!

Not knowing what else to do, I lifted my hand in an awkward wave and then turned right to the elevator.

16

I needed the weekend out of the city to clear my mind. I was ready to get swept up in conversation that had nothing to do with me or what was plaguing me. I was ready to release all my pent-up stress on the dance floor. Friday night was a dinner with six of my cousin Kiya's closest friends. The food was good, the conversation was lively, and something about Kiya's demeanor felt different.

She's either pregnant or engaged, I concluded as we said good night.

Sitting in a VIP club section with those same friends on Saturday, the loud, boisterous conversations and the chaotic celebratory energy made it easy to block out any and all nagging thoughts. We danced, we laughed, and we drank. I wasn't a heavy drinker so I couldn't keep up with the rest of them. When I got back from backing my ass up on the dance floor, I sat down on one of the leather couches in our section.

"I follow you on social media." A short woman with a cute fade haircut sat next to me. "Kiya didn't tell me her cousin was a celebrity."

I laughed. "I wouldn't say celebrity."

"I thought you looked familiar at dinner last night and then it hit me today." She pulled out her phone and showed me that she followed my page. "I'm trying to get my followers up. What would you suggest I do?"

"What do you do? What's your thing?"

"I cut hair."

"I would just consistently post your work. Show your skill. Show your personality. And figure out what you want to say and make sure you're communicating that to the audience."

She opened up a notes app and typed what I'd said. "Thank you. I know you're just trying to chill and don't want to talk work, but I have one more question and then I'll leave you alone about all this. I promise."

I took a sip of my drink. "Okay, let's hear it."

"How did you get into being a social media content creator?"

"I've always loved fashion and I couldn't find big fashion girlies to follow. So, I became what I wanted to see. And then people were in my comments asking about the outfits and expressing a desire to find similar pieces. I was putting clothes together in a way that other people weren't and helping to change the narrative of big-bodied style. I enjoyed the impact of that." I smiled. "I still enjoy that. And I connected with my audience over fashion, style, and my personality. I've stayed true to my brand. And that's why I suggested that you figure out what you want to say and then say it consistently."

"Is it hard to have a relationship when your life is so public?"

"I'm authentically myself, but I am also private. I don't use names or specify the places I'm going to be. I don't share too much. No one I date knows what I do for a living."

Her glassy eyes got big. "Really?"

"Really," I confirmed.

"So, your man doesn't know—"

"Nina doesn't have a man. She has men," Kiya interrupted with a laugh, plopping down next to me. "As long as they stay in rotation, she won't ever settle down."

"What?" the woman screeched. "So you mean to tell me you've never had one that you were so down bad for that you wanted to let everyone else go? One that had everything you were looking for?"

My alcohol-infused brain quickly flashed moments with Russ through my mind, and I shut my eyes tight and shook it off. "Nope," I answered.

"Can I steal my cousin from you?" Kiya asked, interrupting. She grabbed my hand. "Come with me."

I allowed myself to be pulled toward the VIP bathrooms.

"I'm sorry if she's asking you a million questions," Kiya apologized. "Ever since she realized you were my cousin, she's been fangirling."

My smile grew. "It's fine. Honestly, it made me smile."

She freshened her lipstick and then glanced at me. "What's going on with you?"

I shook my head. "Nothing."

"When she was questioning you about settling down, you had a look on your face."

"A look?" I frowned, shaking my head again. "I don't know what you mean."

She eyed me suspiciously. "You had a look. I can't describe it. But it made me think that maybe you were uncomfortable. And the only reason I could think that it would make you uncomfortable is if there was some truth to it."

"What do you mean?" Jerking my thumb toward the exit, I gave her a questioning look. "I just took that man's number on the dance floor!"

"Yeah, but you seemed disinterested."

"We didn't talk much, but he could dance." I shrugged. "If we end up talking more, I'll let you know how he is."

"Something is different." She folded her arms over her chest. "Is your roster full?"

I rolled my eyes and teased my hair with my fingers. "There has been a recent opening."

"Well, maybe this guy will be able to fill the opening." She wiggled her eyebrows. "And I mean that in all the ways."

"I know that's right," I cackled as we left the restroom.

I couldn't shake Kiya's insinuation or the thoughts that ran through my mind, so I made it a point to dance and flirt with every man that I was attracted to. There were only a handful that really fit the bill. But with drinks in my system and two available spots on my roster, I made the most of my night.

At one o'clock in the morning, Kiya made us all lift our lemon drops. "To friends," she said as we drank our shots. Grinning at us, she placed her glass on the table and opened her arms wide. "Thank you for coming out and celebrating with me," she started with a huge smile. "Last night's dinner was elegant and perfect. Tonight has been over-the-top fun. The party bus will be here in thirty minutes, and I wanted to take a minute to tell you how much

I appreciate you being by my side through all of the major moments of my life. And I hope that continues over the next year—as bridesmaids in my wedding!"

We all screamed.

"I knew it!" I called out. "From the way you've been acting the last couple of months, I knew it was coming!"

Crowding her with hugs, the eight of us spent the remaining time on our feet, drinking, dancing, and celebrating. The rest of the night was a blur.

"I'm so happy for you," I told Kiya as we entered her house an hour and a half later. Sitting on her couch, I put my hand to my chest. "My girl is getting married! I love this for you."

"I didn't think you believed in marriage or monogamy," she replied, sitting down in her recliner.

"Of course I believe in marriage and monogamy!"

"You do? I thought you didn't want to settle down."

"I would settle down with someone who fulfilled all my needs," I told her. "We grew up seeing happy, healthy couples. If I meet someone who is the perfect fit for me and I'm the perfect fit for him, I will settle down."

Grinning drunkenly, she sighed. "When it happens, it's going to knock you off your feet."

"How did you know?" I asked. The question bubbled out of me unexpectedly. I was sure I had just thought it until she started answering.

"I knew he was the one almost immediately. We just fit and everything just flowed. But it hit me that he would be the one I would spend my life with when I realized I felt like my most free, my most peaceful, my most authentic self. I found someone who makes life fun. And that's harder to do than it sounds, because it's easy to have fun doing fun things. But to have fun riding in the car, going to the grocery store, just sitting and talking." She swooned. "He brings out this childlike quality in me, and at the same time he brings out the badass woman in me. That type of love is so effortless. When you love someone effortlessly, it's everything."

I didn't remember what I said in response. I didn't remember falling asleep. But when I woke up on that couch a few hours later with a crook in my neck, I didn't forget what she'd said.

Or how I felt about what she said.

I couldn't get Kiya's words out of my head. I showered, slept another few hours in her guest room, and I still thought about it. I returned home Sunday evening, ate a delicious dinner, soaked in the tub, and was still reflecting on Kiya's answer to my question. But it wasn't until I arrived at the RLF building and saw Russ standing at the elevator that I realized why it was nagging me. The time we'd spent away from each other didn't lessen the intensity of what I felt for him, and that made me uncomfortable because of what it meant.

I feel like that about Russ.

The thought hit me like a ton of bricks and rooted me where I stood. The thoughts that crept out of my subconscious over the weekend washed over me at the sight of him.

I know I like him, but it isn't love, I told myself as I put one foot in front of the other. *I like him. I miss him. But I don't love him.*

Our conversation and kiss on Friday mixed with the alcohol and conversation with my cousin and stirred my feelings up. But even if what we had was real, it didn't matter because our work circumstances were what they were. Nothing we had mattered anymore. We could only focus on moving forward. The feelings didn't just go away because not being together was the right thing to do. But we had to work together, so we had to figure it out.

Rolling my shoulders back, I decided to confront things head-on.

I tentatively approached Russ as he waited for the elevator. He stared straight ahead with the kind of unwavering focus that confirmed he knew I was there. Clearing my throat lightly, I announced myself.

"Can we go somewhere and talk?" I asked nervously.

"No."

My mouth fell open. *The fuck?*

A stream of people flowed out of the elevator just as I'd gathered myself enough to respond. Stunned, I entered the confined space with Russ and three other people. I went from shocked to embarrassed to angry by the time we'd reached the second floor. As soon as the others exited, I turned to him. The doors had barely closed before I erupted.

"What do you mean no?" I snapped. "Who the hell do you think you are?"

He glared at me. His mouth formed a tight line, which sharpened his expression. "The CEO of the company you work for," he replied through clenched teeth.

I stepped toward him. "I don't work *for* you. I'm an independent contractor. I work *with* you."

"And the work you do with *my* company doesn't require us to have a private conversation." The elevator dinged as we arrived on the RLF floor. He broke eye contact and focused his attention straight ahead. "After you."

I stared at his profile for a moment and then exited the elevator.

"Everything okay?" Remedy asked as soon as I hit the intersection between the executive suites.

I forced a smile. "Yeah, I just have a lot on my mind. How are you?"

"I'm well, thank you." Her eyes shifted behind me. "Russell, there's an inventory issue . . ."

I continued my way to the showroom. I smiled and greeted everyone, ready to have a great photoshoot. But the opposite was happening on the inside.

A mixture of embarrassment and hurt swirled and filled the hollow space within me. By the end of the shoot, the rejection had fueled my anger, and I was fuming.

"And then he had the nerve to say that he didn't want to talk to me," I told Aaliyah as I prepared for bed hours later.

"Do you think he just meant he couldn't talk to you right at that moment?" she countered.

"He said the work I do for his company doesn't require us to speak," I informed her as I pulled the covers over my body. "So, I blocked his ass."

"Nina!"

"What? If he wants to keep things professional, we can keep it professional."

"What if he needs to contact you?"

"He can email me like everyone else at RLF."

"Ninaaaaaaaa . . ." She sighed loudly and I could almost hear her shaking her head. "Don't do your man like that."

I curled myself into a ball. *He was only my man for a couple hours.*

"He's not my man," I retorted petulantly.

"He should be."

"Aaliyah, please."

"Have you considered the possibility that the stuff your cousin was saying got to you because you feel like that about Russ?"

My heart pounded nervously. "What?"

"You have feelings for him."

"I've never denied that but—"

"It's not going to go away," she interrupted. "Maybe you didn't want to talk to him to clear the air for work. Maybe you wanted to talk to him about the two of you."

"There is no two of us. There hasn't been for the last couple of weeks. And there won't be. I'm going to focus on my opportunity, and he's going to continue doing his thing."

"When are you going to admit you're in love?"

"Oop! When you do," I retorted.

"Wh-wha . . . I'm not . . ." She stammered over her words. "Don't do that. Don't try to change the subject. You and Russ have something real. The way you talked about him and the way you looked when you were fresh from seeing him. I've never seen you that happy with a man, and I've seen you date a lot of men. *A lot.*"

I snickered. "Not too much on me."

"No, but seriously. Russ is the only one you have ever talked about like this. Before this whole work fiasco happened, I could've sworn you were going to say you two declared your love or something. The way you talked about that Sunday with him and started calling him Russ, we already knew something happened on that trip. And then all of a sudden, all of it kind of exploded because of this work thing. You never really got a chance to see it through, and then you never really got a chance for closure. And on top of that, you're seeing him regularly but not in the way that you were."

I closed my eyes and let out a shaky breath. "Yeah," I murmured, focusing on the last thing she said.

I didn't even get a chance to tell my best friends that I took it there with him. I wanted him. I wanted to be with him. I was committed to him. And hours after I gave in to the idea of us together, it ended. So, I agreed with Aaliyah's sentiment—I never got a chance to see it through, and I never got closure. That had to be the reason I felt so reactive and all over the place.

"I'm sorry," I apologized. "Enough about my bullshit. Are you ready for Saturday? Do you need me to do anything?"

"Just thank Charlotte for me. My dress is perfect."

"I can do that. I can't wait to see both looks."

"All I need now is a date."

My stomach sank. "Same. But I'm not worried and you shouldn't be either."

"Taco Tuesday tomorrow?"

"Yes," I agreed quickly. "I'm shooting content all day, so I'll be ready for a night out with my girl."

We ended the call fifteen minutes later.

Talking to Aaliyah helped to calm me down, but when I woke up Tuesday morning, I got mad all over again. More accurately, I was mad at his actions and embarrassed because I felt like I played myself.

And there was nothing I could do about it.

Channeling that energy into my work, I spent the day creating content. I was able to lose myself in the process. Being preoccupied with work actually made me feel better.

"I'm about to put it on!" I greeted the camera. "Get ready with me as I get ready for a girls' night out—Taco Tuesday edition. It's pretty hot tonight and I plan on bringing that same energy . . ."

After I was ready, I called a car to take me downtown to the Mexican restaurant where Aaliyah and I were meeting. I walked into the restaurant in my green-and-gold minidress and smiled as soon as I saw my best friend.

After a quick hug and an exchange of compliments, Aaliyah and I were seated. As soon as the waiter took our order and walked away, we launched into conversation.

"Okay, who are you meeting after this? Because you look good!" Aaliyah commented.

I shook my head. "Unfortunately, I will be heading home after this. I have a photoshoot in the morning."

"Oh, really?" She gave me a curious look. "I thought you were done."

I told her about the incident that happened on Friday. "So, a new shoot was set up for Wednesday," I concluded.

Her mouth hung open as the waiter sat our drinks down. When we were alone again, she sputtered. "So, he kissed you and he *fired* someone for you?"

I swallowed my feelings again. "Not like that—"

"He kissed you and fired someone for you," she interrupted.

"He doesn't like being disrespected. And the kiss . . . the kiss happened because we hadn't been around each other in a couple of weeks."

"Hmm." She lifted her drink to her lips. "That man loves you."

"Aaliyah, please," I complained.

"I love that energy." She swooned, ignoring my protests. "He stood up for you. He had your back. He then couldn't resist you. I knew you two were endgame."

I stared at her in disbelief. "Are you not hearing anything I'm saying?"

"No, I heard you. And this changes everything."

"This changes *nothing*. After he did that on Friday, he turned around and played in my face Monday morning. He ignored me during the entire shoot. He didn't even attempt to make amends. And for that, he's still blocked." I shrugged, trying to appear nonchalant. "I extended that man an olive branch and he rejected it."

"Nina, you're in denial!" She leaned forward. "It's so obvious that he said no to you because he can't be alone with you! He wasn't rejecting you. He was resisting temptation."

I rolled my eyes and waved my hand dismissively. "Speaking of resisting temptation. Run the potential dates you have lined up by me and try to convince me you don't have a thing for—"

"These plates are hot," the waiter said, sliding the fajita skillets in front of us.

The sizzling chicken and fresh vegetables smelled delicious. I took a sip of my drink as Aaliyah asked for chips and salsa. As much as I hated to admit it, Aaliyah's romantic-ass excuse for Russ made me feel better.

Slightly.

". . . so I don't know. It doesn't matter."

I pointed to her. "It does matter. Because you matter. And what you want matters."

"It's been an exhausting summer," she admitted. "I don't know how you do it. My birthday is Saturday, and I don't feel like I'm any closer to what I want than I was two months ago."

"Change your perspective," I told her. "You had a mission this summer and you went for it. You should be proud of that. Dating is exhausting if you're not having fun. So have fun! Line up the rest of your week with dates and see what happens. While you wait to find the one, enjoy the ones." I gestured to her cell phone. "And when you're ready to go after what you really want, you'll get that fairy-tale, happily-ever-after Prince Charming."

She swallowed the bite she was chewing and pointed her fork at me. "You, too."

I almost choked on my fajita.

17

When I pulled up to a large multipurpose art space downtown and saw Russ in a navy suit standing at the door, my stomach flipped.

He looked good—too good.

I watched him open the door for a woman. She seemed to thank him, but then lingered, reaching out to place her hand on his forearm.

My eyebrows flew up. "Oh," I mumbled, intrigued. It was always interesting seeing how women reacted to him. I understood completely how and why he received so much attention. But I never felt threatened, jealous, or bitter because I was secure in what we had.

But now we don't have anything.

He said something and smiled. She moved closer to him and then went inside.

When the door closed behind her, his smile fell. Pulling his phone back out, his thumb breezed over the screen. He slipped his phone into his pocket, but he didn't seem to be leaving his spot near the entrance.

Maybe he's waiting for someone.

Licking my lips, I got out of the car. I'd just closed my door and taken a step when I felt something right behind me.

"Hey!"

I jumped at the unexpected voice, dropping my bag and spinning around. My orange sundress billowed around me from my quick movements.

"Jonah!" I yelped when I realized it was him. "You scared the shit out of me."

"I'm sorry," he apologized, grabbing my bag from the ground and handing it to me. "I didn't mean to."

Once I brushed off my bag, I exhaled. "It's okay," I assured him. "I wasn't paying attention."

Turning toward the door, I noticed Russ wasn't standing there anymore.

It was so busy at the shoot yesterday, we didn't get a chance to talk. "How was your weekend?" Jonah asked as we headed toward the building.

"I celebrated with my cousin and her friends," I answered. "It was a good time. How was yours?"

He told me about some club he went to on Saturday and then a book he read on Sunday. I was listening to him but as soon as we walked into the studio, Remedy was yelling.

"No, no, no! This is not happening! Not again!"

Jonah and I stopped in our tracks.

I looked around and noticed Jacqueline in the room across the hall. Elbowing Jonah, I moved in that direction.

"What's going on?" I whispered.

Matias frowned. "A storm is moving in, and we were supposed to shoot up on the roof again."

"I don't want to do this in the rain, but if that's what they want . . ." Jonah shrugged. "It's their campaign."

I nodded in agreement.

If they wanted to experiment, I was cool with it. I just hoped they had some hair ideas that weren't going to leave me looking a mess after being rained on all day.

"This place is huge. They'll figure something out," Taisha murmured.

"Change of plans," Remedy announced, strolling into the room. "We're shooting everything inside first and we'll be doing roof shots after the storm passes. Ladies, you're in hair and makeup first."

She didn't give us a chance to respond before walking off.

Three hour later, we were finishing up our final outfits in the studio. The storm rumbled over us for an hour, but the photographer just turned the music up. As the storm dissipated, the mood in the room noticeably shifted.

"Okay, it's not raining, you look good, and these are the last shots with this look. Let's have some fun," she called out. "Dance!"

It would've been awkward if I weren't with some of the silliest people. It also helped that Russ had gotten a call and stepped out. So, when the song's throbbing beat pulsated through the room, I started rolling my body. Jonah wasted no time getting behind me and mimicking my moves. Whatever he was doing caused Taisha to burst out laughing and grab my hands. We were having a good time, and the photographer was smiling as she snapped photos.

"Now freeze and look at me," she demanded.

We all stopped mid-move and directed our attention to the lens. Breathing hard, we were posed like human mannequins. Taisha and I were still holding hands. Jonah was behind me with his hands on my hips. Jacqueline was damn near on Matias's back. It was chaotic, but I was sure the pictures were going to look good.

Suddenly, the hair on the back of my neck stood up and I felt Russ's presence. I tried to keep my eyes focused on the camera, but instinctually, my gaze drifted to the right.

And there he was.

His stare was lethal, and to anyone around him, he might've looked like an involved CEO. But I felt the way he was looking at me all day. Each time I was partnered with Jonah, Russ's expression hardened. With each mid-shoot conversation with Jonah, Russ's body language was stiff. But with Jonah's hand on my hip, Russ was outright glaring. He said something to Remedy and then marched out without another look my way.

My stomach sank.

"Got it!" the photographer cheered as she wrapped up. "One more outfit change and then I think we're done."

We thanked her and headed to the designated space for us to change.

"Nina, can I speak to you?" Remedy asked just before I left the main studio. "Jonah, you too."

I looked at the other models exiting and then back at her. "Yes, of course."

"You're doing a great job," she started.

"Thank you," we said in unison.

"I just wanted to remind you of the no-fraternization policy.

It's in place for a reason and the rest of the executive team and I wanted to make sure you were reminded."

I opened my mouth to object, and she held up her hand.

"I don't want to know what is or isn't happening. I don't care. What has happened in the past does not matter. I just want to let you both know that your chemistry is reading very well on camera. I don't know what you have going on, but you need to make sure nothing"—she pointed her finger at us—"and I mean nothing, gets in the way of how the chemistry reads on camera. I don't want any breakups or falling outs ruining the campaign. Do I make myself clear?"

"Yes," we answered in unison.

Jonah and I didn't say a word to each other until we got into the changing room.

"What happened?" Jacqueline asked as soon as the door closed behind us.

"The executive team sees the sparks between me and Nina and wanted to know if we were dating," Jonah told them with a cheesy grin. "Obviously, I told them yes."

I rolled my eyes. "She said they wanted to remind us of the policy."

"That makes sense," Taisha mused. "I saw Mr. Long looking concerned during the second outfit changes, so that makes sense."

Russ.

My stomach knotted as I went behind the partition to change.

"Boss Man do be staring and glaring, don't he?" Jonah chuckled. "Him and Angelica are never happy to see my ass!"

He didn't tell Remedy to remind us of the fraternization policy. He . . . wouldn't have done that.

But I already knew he did.

Closing my eyes tight, I had conflicting feelings. I knew he thought something was going on between me and Jonah, but I told him it was nothing. So not only was I irritated that he didn't believe me, I was also irritated that he would threaten my contract by even insinuating I was fraternizing. But the look of jealousy on his face, in his demeanor, and wafting off him was causing a pull deep within me that was hard to ignore. I squeezed my legs together and ignored it.

Just like he ignored the fuck out of me.

He didn't speak to me during the shoot and kept an almost comical distance, but I kept catching him watching me. We were posing on the roof in our final outfits. There were only a handful of RLF people watching and one assistant with the photographer. The concepts were completely different than what we'd done on Friday. Because it was overcast, it gave a gritty backdrop to the streetwear we were modeling. We were directed to look fierce as a group, and then we were paired up to almost look as though we were ready to fight.

"Your fierce expression is looking less tough and more sexy," the photographer told me. "I have an idea. We're going to lean into the sexy." He gestured to Jonah and Matias. "Get on either side of her."

We did a series of poses that received catcalls and whistles while we executed them. As it started drizzling, all of the RLF team left, except for Russ and Remedy. Remedy stood close to the photographer while Russ hung back, observing from his perch near the ledge. He'd face the city and take calls, but at that moment, he was watching intently.

Correction, he was watching me *intently.*

My body was facing Jonah while Matias stood behind me with his hands on my hips. I stared at the camera while both men looked at me.

"Look beyond me," he directed me. "Just above my head. And your leg. Jonah, grab her leg. Nina, lean back into Matias. Keep the lines clean. Perfect! Yes! Keep your eye line just above my head, Nina. Right there!"

Just above his head was in Russ's direct line of sight. He'd taken off his jacket, but with his sky-blue shirt tucked into his navy pants, he still looked like Russell Long, CEO. With his sleeves pushed up, exposing his forearms and one of his expensive watches, he looked just casual enough to remind me of my Russ.

And both versions of him were sexy as hell.

There was a slight quiver in my belly, but I stayed focused. He met my gaze and locked in. I wanted to look away, but the photographer kept telling me to hold it right there. So, there I was, staring into Russ's eyes, with Jonah in front and Matias in back.

The first half of August, Russ and I communicated every day. The last half of August, we saw each other more, but it was at a distance. The shift was so abrupt, and I never got over it. I never made peace with it. As I stared into his eyes, I couldn't deny it. There was too much that existed between us for us to just end like that. But there was also no way for us to move forward because there was too much to lose.

The photographer had gotten some impressive shots before the sky opened up and there was an instant downpour. We'd worked through the overcast sky and then the drizzle. But it was an unpredictable summer storm at its finest. Big aggressive droplets hit us. The photographer took several more pictures before calling it.

"Go, go!" he yelled, gesturing for his assistant to grab his stuff.

Scrambling, we ran inside and took cover. Our clothes were dripping wet. The photographer said he wanted to get similar shots with Jacqueline and Taisha as well, but all of us were wet. I was able to change into something else completely. The others had to dry out before they could get changed for the day. Because of this, I grabbed a towel and headed to a changing area by myself. Seconds after I got behind the partition, the door opened again.

Pulling my damp shirt over my head, I put the garment on a hanger. "That was quick," I yelled out as I wiggled out of the jeans.

My remark was met with silence.

My nipples hardened from the cold air hitting my skin and I glanced up to the vent. The one in the back corner offered the most privacy, but a rain-soaked body and a high-powered air conditioner made the choice questionable.

I should've picked a different spot, I thought.

I reached behind me, unhooking my bra, and then paused when I heard footsteps drawing closer. I was just about to peek around the partition when a deep, velvety voice finally replied from the other side of it.

"What was quick?"

My stomach flipped. "Russ?" I whispered.

Stepping around the corner, Russ stood in the space between the partition and the wall. His handsome face was expressionless. His lips were parted slightly as he inhaled and exhaled steadily. His eyes locked with mine and we just silently stared at each other.

I was surprised to see him standing three feet away from me. I didn't know what to do. I didn't know what to say. It wasn't until his gaze swept down my body that I even remembered I was standing in an unhooked brown bra and matching satin panties.

My heart rate spiked.

When our eyes met again, I leaned forward slightly and let my bra slip down my arms. The moment it hit the carpeted floor, Russ closed the gap between us. Grabbing my face, he crashed his lips into mine as he forced me backward. My back hit the wall and I gasped.

He kissed me hungrily. His soft lips moved over mine, dominating me, consuming me. I knew I craved him. But that kiss made me realize how deprived I felt without him. And when his tongue grazed mine, I fully gave in. I lost myself in that kiss and I felt everything, everywhere.

I clawed at his shirt, pulling his body closer to mine. Feeling his growing bulge pressing against me, my body shivered. My hand slipped between us and as soon as it slid across the front of his pants, something animalistic took over the both of us.

We pawed each other, deepening the kiss. I wasn't sure when I'd unbuttoned and unzipped his pants, but the moment I wrapped my hand around his thick dick, my knees weakened. Only his boxer briefs separated us, and I knew there was no going back.

I didn't just want to fuck him.

I needed to fuck him.

The desire I felt for him was too much and I couldn't stop myself. I didn't care about the consequences of getting caught. I only cared about getting off.

His hands slid down my neck and chest until he groped my bare breasts. I moaned just as his fingers found my rock-hard nipples.

His touch made the throbbing between my thighs intensify. Unable to speak, I peered up at him through my lashes as I squeezed his bulge gently.

He groaned my name so softly I barely heard it.

I ran my hand up and down his erection as it strained against his boxer briefs. The memory of his dick and how good it felt inside me guided my fingertips through the fly.

"Shit," he growled under his breath as I touched him.

He removed my hand and in one fell swoop, he pinned both of my wrists above my head. With one of his big hands holding them in place against the wall, he used the other to wrap around my neck.

Bringing his face within an inch of mine, he stared into my eyes.

"You were staring at me during your shoot," he murmured against my lips. "Giving me that look . . ."

I didn't know how to respond. I didn't know what he wanted me to say. But I was drunk off the way he was looking at me.

And I was soaking wet.

I leaned forward and pressed my lips against his. The stretch of my arms as I was restrained in my movement only made the desire for him stronger.

He kissed and sucked his way down my neck and chest until he suctioned his mouth onto my waiting nipple. The wet heat of his mouth made me moan as he alternated from one nipple to the other.

"Russ," I said his name softly.

His hands slid down my body. "I've missed that sound," he whispered hoarsely. Hooking his fingers into my panties, he tugged them over my hips. "I've missed hearing it." Pushing them down, he squatted in front of me. "I've missed creating it."

I swallowed hard as I listened to him, watched him. "I've missed you, too. Badly."

"Step . . . step," he demanded, removing my panties completely. He looked up from his position below me. "How bad have you missed me?"

"Real bad," I told him in a whisper.

"Bad enough that you'll let me taste you right here?"

I nodded slowly. "Yes."

Getting closer, I could feel his breath against the wetness. "Is it still mine?"

My breathing hitched. "Yes."

He put one of my legs over his shoulder and wrapped his arm around my thigh to secure me. I could see the desire in his eyes as he buried his face between my thighs. Using his tongue, he opened me up and ran it over my slit.

"Ohmigod," I exhaled.

I buckled against the wall and my knees shook. With one hand on his bicep and the other on the back of his head, I rocked into his mouth.

My reaction only encouraged him as his tongue strategically toyed with me. He started sucking on my clit and I almost collapsed.

"You taste so fucking good," he murmured.

Adjusting his grip, he tilted me forward as he secured a firm hold on me. Moaning something into my pussy, he darted his tongue in and out of me before lavishing my clit.

Pleasure shot through my body, and I was already on the brink. "Russ," I exhaled sharply. I held his head right where I needed it. "Yes. Yes. Yes. Right there. Right there. Right. Fucking. There."

His face was buried in me, and when he flicked his tongue in a steady rhythm, he sent me over the edge in record time.

"Russssssssss," I hissed as I rode the wave that shuddered through my entire body. Holding on to him tight, I bucked against his handsome face.

"That felt so fucking good," I panted.

When I loosened my grip on his head, he trailed fluttery kisses against the inside of my thighs, my pelvis, and my belly.

"Were you trying to make me jealous on the roof?" he asked as he stood.

"Were you jealous?" I cupped his balls before letting my fingers trace over his shaft. Looking down to see how it was straining against the fabric, I licked my lips.

Pushing down his boxer briefs, I wrapped my hand around his dick. He was so thick that my fingertips just barely touched as I held it. Stroking him, I slid my hand up and down his full nine and a half inches.

My heart pounded in my throat as I stared at it in awe.

A deep groan rumbled from his chest, forcing my eyes back to his.

"Did seeing me with other men make you jealous?" I wondered softly.

"Do I seem jealous?"

I nodded.

Wrapping his hand around my neck, he tilted my head upward and kissed me hard. I could taste myself on his lips and it reminded me of the orgasm he'd just given me. He pulled out of the kiss and rested his forehead against mine.

"I was jealous that they were able to touch you out there in a way that I couldn't." He brought his lips to my ear. "So now I'm going to touch you in a way that they can't."

Oh shit.

"Spread your legs," he demanded.

My entire body clenched as I did as I was told. The anticipation to have him fill me up was like nothing I'd ever experienced. Everything about the way his mouth moved over mine was seductive. I was completely seduced and nothing else mattered.

I had no concept of time.

I had no fear of being caught.

I just wanted him inside me.

Hoisting my right leg onto his hip, he tilted my hips forward and pressed against me. My shoulder blades balanced me against the wall. My lips parted and my chest heaved.

"Is this why you were staring at me?" The head of his dick applied pressure against my wet slit. "They might not know what that look means, but I do."

"Russ," I moaned louder than anticipated. Grabbing his shoulders, I felt overwhelmed with want.

"Tell me it's still mine."

"It never stopped being yours. I need—mmmmmm!"

My sentence fragmented into a moan as I felt him entering me.

The growl that emitted from deep within his chest sent chills down my spine. My eyes rolled into the back of my head and my breathing changed. I dug my nails into the shoulder of his shirt, wishing he was as naked as I was.

"Russ," I breathed his name shakily.

There was nothing like the delicious mixture of pleasure and pain as he stretched me out.

"I . . . I . . . shit," I swore.

"I know, baby. I know," he groaned, continuing to fill me up. With each inch, his breathing became more ragged. "I've missed you, too."

His right hand held my thigh up while his left slid from my neck to my breast and then my ass as he buried himself in me.

His touch sent waves of pleasure through me.

I trembled in response. "Oh God, yes."

I closed my eyes tight as his thickness stretched me out.

His thick head pushed against the deepest part of me, and it suddenly occurred to me that he was fucking me raw.

My eyes flew open as I clenched around him.

The thought of it seemed to ignite something in me and goose bumps spread across my skin.

He let out a low guttural noise and stopped moving. Our eyes locked.

As if he were reading my thoughts, he whispered, "You're so fucking wet . . . and warm . . . and fuck—you feel so fucking good."

I shuddered.

Squeezing my eyes shut, I started grinding my hips against him. I worked myself up and down his shaft. My muffled moans seemed to call to him, making him harder. His low grunts punctuated the air, turning me on even more.

Our mouths found each other as we felt each other up. His fingers danced over my skin as his dick speared me. Our tongues wrestled gently, and we talked with our bodies.

Putting my hands underneath his shirt, I held on to him.

When he hit my spot, my head tipped back against the wall, and he peppered kisses across my jawline before trailing kisses down my throat.

"Hold on tight," he demanded quietly.

I did as I was told.

Using the wall as leverage, he tipped me back farther. I was at an awkward angle, but the dick felt so good I didn't care. The new position gave him better access to my clit and forced me to take more of him. That was a lethal combination. With every inch he was able to get into me, he was reaching my depths. Each time our bodies collided, he stimulated my little bundle of nerves. The feeling was so intense that I felt like I was high on something magical, something potent, something godly.

"I need you," he grunted.

Hearing that caused a chill down my spine. Moaning, I pushed my head into the wall so I could meet him pound for pound. The sound of my wetness echoed in the quiet space.

"I—I want—yes, yesssssssssss."

"Talk to me. Tell me what you want."

My shoulder blades thumped against the wall as his hips thrusted, springing my body as he fucked me deep. He made my stomach flutter and my heart race.

"Russ, please, please, please," I panted, warmth spread throughout my core.

"Please what, baby?"

"Please come in my pussy."

"Goddamn," he groaned, fucking me with his entire body.

Saying it out loud did something to me. But his response pushed me to the brink. He moved in and out of me until I felt the tension tighten my entire lower body. I clenched around him and the sound he made gave me chills.

"Shit, Nina." His voice was hoarse and needy. It sounded like he was close to losing control.

His strokes consistently hit the right spot and my body was loving each and every second of it.

"This is my pussy," he uttered softly as I started to lose control.

"Look at how good you take me. Look at how wet you are for me. Look at how tight you grip me. This . . . is . . . my . . . pussy."

Wildly bucking against him, I tried my best to hold it together quietly, but I felt myself coming undone.

"That's it, baby. Come for me. Come on this dick, baby," he whispered roughly. "That's it. That's it, Nina. Let me feel you. Just like that. Just like—oh shit!"

"Yessssssssssss," I cried out. My muscles tightened, my body got rigid, and my orgasm took over. I started clamping down around him. "Yes, yes, yes, yes."

"Fuck," he hissed.

Quivering, I shut my eyes and rode the wave.

He covered my mouth with his as he continued delivering long strokes.

"Nina," he moaned desperately, pulling out of the kiss. "You're going to make me fill this pussy up. Is that what you want?"

Hearing how he was trying to hold back turned me on more. I started gripping him tighter.

"Yes, please," I begged, giving in to my deepest desires. "Don't pull out. Come in my pussy. Fill me up. I need it. I need you." I rocked against him and dug my nails into his back. "I'm yours."

I'd barely choked out the words before a series of grunts erupted out of him. His throbbing dick pumped into me as the raspy need in his voice spoke to me.

A second round of pleasure was about to hit me. "Russssssssssssss!" I hissed, scratching his back.

"Yeah, let me feel you again. Let me feel you, baby," he groaned sexily, fucking me with reckless abandon. "Let that pussy talk to me. Let her tell me she's mine."

He had barely gotten the words out before I dissolved into a puddle of noncoherent ecstasy.

"Fuck," he hissed, fucking me harder.

His body stiffened and as soon as I felt him pumping his load into me, I came again.

Breathing heavily, I closed my eyes and tried to stop my legs from shaking.

My heart was racing, my body was buzzing, and my head was spinning. My mind was in a fog from the best sex I'd ever had. Sex with Russ was always good, but the sex we'd just had was mind-altering. I felt a shift. Slowly and carefully, Russ released my leg so that I was standing on two feet. I didn't open my eyes until I felt the terry cloth towel between my legs.

"Thank you," I whispered as he cleaned me up.

Instead of responding, he leaned down and planted a sweet kiss against my lips.

Pulling away, he stared at me in awe as he finished cleaning us up.

Wordlessly, he pulled up his pants, tucking his shirt back in before he bent down to help me step back into my panties. He kissed my breasts before slipping the straps of my bra up my arms. He turned me around and connected the hook-and-eye clasp.

The intimacy of the act was overwhelming.

He kissed the back of my neck and pulled me into him. Hugging me from behind, he lowered his mouth to the shell of my ear.

"You're my escape," he whispered before turning me around. "And I've missed you."

"I've missed you, too," I admitted with a trembling breath.

He stared at me, willing me to say more. The vulnerability in his gaze pulled emotions out of me, and I felt my eyes starting to sting.

He must've fucked the good sense God gave me right out of my head. He had me ready to admit to feelings I hadn't been ready to confront for myself. He had me ready and willing to risk it all in every sense.

I had to look away.

"Nina—" His phone vibrated, and he pulled it out of his pocket. "Shit."

Running his hand down his beard, he exhaled loudly. "I have to get out of here. They're looking for me. I have a meeting tonight, and then . . ." He shook his head. "Are you free tomorrow night? For dinner?"

I nodded. "Yeah, I'm free. But how?"

Dropping a soft kiss against my lips, he stared at me as if he were seeing me for the first time. There was an adoration in his gaze that gave me butterflies. He backed away from me slowly. "I'll figure something out. Just . . . unblock me."

"Okay," I whispered, literally biting my bottom lip to prevent myself from saying more.

Before he left the confines of the space, he held my gaze. "You said you were mine," he said softly. "And I like the sound of that."

Without another word, he disappeared behind the partition.

My heart hammered in my chest as I listened to his footsteps getting farther away and then the gentle click of the door closing. As soon as I knew he was gone, I placed my hand over my heart and let out a breath.

"—can't understand it!" Jacqueline complained, loudly entering the changing room.

"I agree with you," Taisha said.

I quickly pulled on my orange sundress. "How was the rest of the shoot?" I called out to them.

"Damn, Nina!" Taisha reacted. "I thought you left!"

Rounding my shoulders, I grabbed my handbag and the still-damp clothing on the hangers before I emerged from the partition. "No. It just took me a little while to dry off."

"The rest of the shoot was a soggy mess," Jacqueline said as she went behind the partition closest to the door. "I feel like my hair is messed up from the rain, which would've been okay if we'd continued shooting in the rain, but instead . . ."

They told me about their shoots, what their poses were, the complaints they had about shooting the same "sexy" poses in an unsexy location. I waited for them to finish changing, and then the three of us went to find Angelica to give her our clothing.

"We were looking for you," Remedy stated when the three of us approached her and Angelica.

"I was getting changed and drying off," I explained, hanging my items on the rack.

She stared at me for a beat too long before shifting her gaze to the others. "There's an opportunity on Saturday. I know it's last minute and not part of your schedule, but if you are able to make it, I would encourage you all to be there."

"I'm in," Taisha said quickly.

Jacqueline nodded. "Yeah, so am I."

My face crumpled apologetically as I thought about Aaliyah's party. "I can't make it. I'm unavailable on Saturday."

Remedy nodded. "Okay." Turning to face the other two, she continued. "You two will receive an email and Angelica will work with you on your outfits later this week."

The two of them squealed excitedly.

"Russell, did you get what you needed?" she asked, causing all three of us to turn around. "You left and I didn't hear back from you."

Looking pointedly at his sister, he approached the group. "I did." He adjusted his jacket, looking like the pulled-together professional that he was. "And the table to the fundraiser has been secured."

Remedy pumped her arm. "Yes!" Seeming to realize we were still standing there, she dismissed us. "Have a good rest of the week," she told us.

We turned around and walked away. I glanced at Russ. And even though a flashback flutter churned my gut, I did my best not to stare.

"You are available on Saturday, aren't you?" Remedy questioned.

"No, I'm not available on Saturday," he answered. "Why?"

"*Flavor Magazine* is having an event . . ."

Walking out of the studio, I missed the rest of what Remedy was telling him.

"Did you hear that?" Taisha whispered excitedly as soon as we got outside. "We're going to be going to a *Flavor Magazine* event!"

Jacqueline clapped. "I need to call my cousin!" She gawked at me. "Are you really going to pass up this opportunity?"

I nodded. "It would be cool to go, but I can't cancel my plans. It's important."

They shook their heads in disbelief and then we said our good-byes.

I didn't think saying no to the event would negatively affect my standing with RLF. I also didn't think saying yes to Russ would negatively affect my work with RLF. And although I didn't regret either decision, I had a nagging feeling both would come back to bite me in the ass.

18

> Russ: I'm sorry it's late, but we should talk. Are you still awake?

I'd gone to bed thinking about him. It was sexy and exhilarating to have him fuck me in the middle of a shoot, and the feeling of him coming inside me replayed in my mind every fifteen minutes.

Squeezing my legs together, I let the thought consume me once again before I responded to his text message. I knew I needed to be strong and not let that man get under my skin. We hadn't actually had a conversation and there was so much we needed to discuss.

Thursday, 7:41 A.M.

> Nina: Good morning, I was knocked out. I agree, we should talk. Are you free now?

"Russ," I answered my phone ten minutes later. Clearing my throat, I greeted him again. "Hi."

"I only have about ten minutes before I have to jump on a call, but I just . . ." He paused. "I wanted to hear your voice."

I bit my bottom lip as warmth spread throughout my body. Turning onto my side, I rubbed my feet together. "Really?"

"Does that surprise you?"

"Well actually, yeah."

"What?"

I could hear the confusion in his voice.

"I asked you if we could talk on Monday and you played me," I explained.

"I didn't play you. I would never play you."

"Russ, you didn't even give me the courtesy of looking at me. You didn't acknowledge me. You just said no."

"Nina, look what happened yesterday," he whispered sharply. "Hell, look what happened Friday. I told you no because I can't be around you without wanting you. I can't look at you without missing you. I can't . . . I can't act like I don't want to be with you. And I don't understand what you don't understand about that."

"I understand—"

"If you understood, you wouldn't have blocked me," he interrupted.

The vulnerability in his tone triggered something inside me. "I blocked you because I was mad . . . and hurt." Rolling onto my back, I stared at the ceiling. With tears stinging my eyes and my defenses down, I had no control over the words coming out of my mouth. "You bring out all of these feelings that—"

I was interrupted by the ringing of his office phone, and I stopped speaking abruptly.

"That what?" he demanded softly.

I swallowed hard, pushing down the words and emotions that threatened to spill out of me.

His phone rang furiously in the silence between us.

"Nina?"

The soft pleading in his voice almost got me to break.

"Shit," he swore. "Just give me one second." He seemed to move his cell phone from his face to answer his office phone. "Yes? Have the quarter four projections looked at one more time before my eleven o'clock. I have back-to-back meetings until four, so I can't even squeeze that in today. But I have something to take care of before the Hampton meeting. Well, you should've led with that!"

When he ended the business call, he returned to me. "My eight o'clock meeting is here," he informed me. "I'm sorry to cut our conversation short, but can we finish this tonight over dinner?"

I nodded even though he couldn't see me. "Yeah, that's fine. Have a good meeting. Bye, Russ." My words came out in a rush, and I ended the call as soon as humanly possible.

Tossing my phone to the other side of the bed, I buried my face in my pillow.

What the fuck was I about to say?

It was almost scary how little control I had over my feelings when he expressed his. I felt discombobulated. He made me feel things and want things I'd never felt or wanted before. And as impossible as it was for us to have more than we had, I wanted him—badly.

He really did fuck the common sense out of me.

All I could do was shake my head and get my ass up for the day to edit content.

Thursday, 10:56 A.M.

> Russ: I just walked into the conference room. I have back-to-back meetings until 4. Dinner tonight, seven o'clock, my place?

Thursday, 11:16 A.M.

> Nina: I'll be there.

I sat my phone on my vanity and exhaled, committing myself to work for the rest of the day.

"I'm about to put it on!" I greeted the camera with my signature opening for the final time. "Get ready with me as I prepare for a dinner date . . ."

Two hours later, I was dressed, my makeup and hair were done, and the video was completed. I was overdressed for a dinner at his house, but there was so much we needed to talk about and looking my best made me less nervous about it.

I made my way to his address. There wasn't much traffic on Thursday evening, so I arrived a few minutes earlier than anticipated. I slowed, creeping my way toward the house in the developing neighborhood.

"Nice," I breathed pulling into the driveway. I parked beside Russ's car and then climbed out. "Really nice."

I saw the vision of the area, even though it was the only house that existed on the land at the end of the cul-de-sac. I grabbed the rail and eased up the ten steps that led to the front door. When I reached the top of the landing, I hadn't even pressed the doorbell when I heard his voice.

"The door is unlocked. Come in," Russ greeted me through a speaker.

I smiled, knowing a camera was on me somewhere. "You want me to just walk in."

"Yes," he responded with a little chuckle.

I opened the door and stepped inside the foyer. Sexy R & B music hit my ears at the same time as the smell of bacon hit my nostrils. Everything looked new and perfect as I tried to take everything in at once.

I closed the door behind me.

"Russ?" I called out, looking around the brightly lit space. There was a formal room to the right of me, a living room to the left of me, and a hallway in front of me.

"You look absolutely beautiful," he said as he appeared at the end of the hallway. Dressed in a heather-gray T-shirt with black pants, he looked good. He had a fresh lineup and the biggest smile on his face.

I opened my arms wide and spun around in a circle in my cropped T-shirt and pleated miniskirt. The spin further showed off my legs and the cute sandals. "The skirt is RLF."

He licked his lips as he drew closer. "I never could've imagined that skirt looking that good."

I smirked. "You like?"

He stopped in front me. "Oh yeah."

"How much?"

Grabbing my face, he crashed his lips into mine. My arms instinctively wrapped around him, pulling him close. Our mouths moved hungrily over each other. Soft moans escaped us as we kissed harder, deeper.

"Are you ready for what I have for you?" he whispered against my lips.

Reaching between us, I slid my hand over the bulge in his pants. "Yes."

He gave me a peck. "That's not what I meant."

"That's not for me?"

"Oh, that's *only* for you." He took my hand and brought it to his lips. "But I have something else for you first."

"I'm intrigued," I commented as he interlocked our fingers.

"Let me give you part one of the tour." He took me into the formal living room, the den, and his home office. Just as we approached the kitchen, he turned and smiled. "Are you ready?"

I nodded. "Ready for what?"

The moment we stepped into the kitchen, I stopped in my tracks.

"Oh my God," I gasped, bringing my free hand to my mouth.

The kitchen was open and beautiful, with gray flooring and white quartz countertops. It was a chef's dream kitchen. It looked like something out of a magazine. Even still, my eyes kept going back to the biggest bouquet of flowers I'd ever seen.

"These are for you," he told me, gesturing to the elaborate display.

"Wow . . ." I went over to table and touched one of the petals. "These are gorgeous."

"I'm glad you like them." He slipped his hand across my lower back.

Plucking the card from the display, I looked over my shoulder at him. "It's so many."

"Three dozen." He grabbed my hips and kissed the sensitive spot behind my ear. "For the three months we've known each other."

"I like that," I murmured, my skin tingling from his lips and his words.

He kissed his way down my neck. "Oh, you like that?"

I grinned. "Yeah, I do."

"Good," he replied as I pulled the note from the envelope.

You are my escape.

As I turned to face him, his hands rested on my hips, and he stepped a little closer to me. Our bodies were barely touching, but we were close enough that I could feel the heat emanating from him.

"This is really sweet," I murmured. "Thank you."

"I have plans for you. Don't thank me yet."

My stomach flipped and I took in a shaky breath.

Before I could say anything, the oven timer started beeping.

"Dinner is ready," Russ told me as he made his way to the sink. He washed his hands and then looked at me. "I hope you're hungry."

I watched him as he pulled bread out of the oven. Seeing him move effortlessly through the kitchen was sexy. He carried a tray into another room and then promptly returned with a big smile on his face. I put my nose against the flowers one more time before I headed his way. My stomach growled hungrily as I drew closer to the food on the stove.

"It smells great in here," I told him after washing my hands. "Do you need any help with anything?"

"Everything is done. I just need you to follow me."

He placed his hand on my lower back and escorted me through a door that led to an elegantly designed dining room. He'd blocked me from going in during the tour, so I was genuinely impressed with the look and aura of the room. The table was big, able to seat twelve, with a chandelier hanging above and running the length of it. There was a big window that overlooked a small body of water. The two table settings were side by side, facing it.

"Is that a lake? A pond?" I guessed.

"It's a man-made lake." He pulled the chair out for me. Once I got in place, he scooted me in. "I just thought it would make for a good view."

"You were right."

He kissed the top of my head and then filled our glasses with wine. "I'll be right back."

While I waited, I looked around. There wasn't much in the room outside of the white walls, the gray flooring, and the polished wood table. But the main décor came from the chandelier and the unique high-back chairs.

"It is beautiful in here," I commented when Russ returned with two plates of pasta, salad, and bread.

"I appreciate it. My mom is an interior decorator, so I have her to thank for a lot of this. I can't take all the credit."

"Well, tell her she did an excellent job." I pointed to the chandelier. "This is stunning."

Grinning with pride, he took the seat next to me. "That's the only thing that I picked out."

"I'm impressed."

"I hope you're just as impressed with your meal."

I eyed the plate. "It looks as good as it smells," I told him before I took my first bite. "Mmmm."

"You like?"

I nodded as I chewed. After I swallowed, I looked over at him. "This is really good. What is this?"

"Penne carbonara. Instead of pancetta, I use extra bacon."

I knew I smelled bacon. "It's so good."

"It's my best dish." He ate a forkful. "It's my only dish."

I snickered as I ate more. "This is the only thing you know how to cook?"

"I can cook some basic things, too. But this is the one meal I perfected. My dad said I had to have one in the artillery before I went to HU. So, my grandma taught me some tricks, and now I break this out for special occasions."

With my eyes glued to him, I licked sauce from my lips and tried not to smile. "And today is a special occasion?"

"Any day with you is a special occasion."

My stomach fluttered.

"Look," he commanded suddenly, pointing out the window toward something in the water.

I squinted until I saw what he saw. "What the hell is that?"

"I don't know," he said with a laugh. "It has to be an animal. It doesn't look like a person. I saw it a few days ago and it went underwater for too long to be a human."

"What in the Loch Ness Monster is going on here?"

He chuckled. "Yoooooo! What is wrong with you?"

"Nothing!" I exclaimed. "I'm not the problem. You have the

beautiful home and the pretty view, and then you have the shape of water out there."

He burst out laughing.

"The real problem is out there, lurking," I continued. "And I'm just trying to figure out what type of horror movie setup this is so I can plan my next move accordingly."

"This isn't a horror movie." He shook his head even though his shoulders still shook with amusement. "The place isn't haunted. There isn't some creature in the water. It's—"

"It's built on a burial ground," I interrupted.

He cracked up. "No, it wasn't!"

"How do you know?"

"I checked before it was built!"

"Then, explain that." I pointed to the large figure floating in the water in the distance.

Amused, he shook his head. "I can't. But—"

I lifted my hands. "I rest my case."

We laughed and joked our way through our meal. We drank wine as we watched the sun set in the distance.

He opened his mouth to say something, but a loud noise rang out from the woods on the other side of the lake. We both swung our heads in the direction of the window.

He rose to his feet and walked around the table. "The fuck was that?"

I stared at the lake. "The Meg."

Laughing, he peered out the window, scanning the area. "What is wrong with you, yo?"

"Nothing! You got me in this haunted house on this cursed land."

"Oh!" He sucked his teeth. "People are out there on the other side of the lake."

"Mm-hmm."

He pointed and I saw the flicker of flames. "Look!"

"I see it. I'm still not convinced though."

His laughter filled my spirit and my lips curled into a smile. I eyed the way his T-shirt stretched across his broad shoulders as he closed the blinds and pulled the curtains.

The delicious food, the home tour, the lively conversation, and the picturesque sunset were all working together to create a perfect evening. I was apprehensive to bring up what we needed to talk about. But I knew it had to be done. As the night unfolded, everything that we weren't saying inched its way to the forefront.

I lifted my wineglass to my lips and took a sip. I could feel his eyes on me, and my body tingled.

"We need to discuss the elephant in the room," Russ announced in a low tone.

Caught off guard, I almost choked on my wine. "Which one?" I placed my glass on the table and turned to him. "It's about ten elephants in the room."

He smirked. "It's a gahdamn zoo."

I stifled a giggle as my lips twisted into a smile.

"Nina, I owe you an apology for . . ." His sentence trailed off.

"For Monday," I offered.

"For yesterday," he finished at the exact same time.

We looked at each other for a second.

My brows furrowed. "Yesterday?"

He nodded. "Yeah. I shouldn't have come looking for you. But I just . . ." He looked like he was searching for his words. "I've been trying to keep my distance, but Friday just reminded me how hard it is to be around you. You'd blocked me and I needed to talk to you. I needed to figure out how we could work together. But then you were looking the way you were looking."

He sat back in his chair and ran his hands down his face. "And you were looking at me the way you were looking at me and I lost focus," he continued. "Then I got in there and you were standing there . . ." His eyes slid down my body before returning to my face. "My dick got rock hard at the sight of you and I forgot the plan."

"What was your plan?"

"To set up a time for us to talk. You'd blocked me, and yeah, I admit, seeing you looking at me during the shoot had my head in a different space, but I really did come back there to talk to you. But when I saw you, it was like I had no fucking control." He shook his head. "I'm sorry I put you in that position. It was unacceptable and unprofessional for me to approach you on a shoot like that."

That wasn't what I was expecting at all.

"Russ . . ." I searched his face. "If I didn't want to do it, I wouldn't have done it. It was just as unacceptable and unprofessional for me to participate."

"I came into a designated space where you were changing," he reminded me, letting his eyes drop to my lips. "And you deserve better than to be fucked in a changing room."

I clenched at the memory.

"We could've gotten caught," he continued. "I put a lot of stuff in jeopardy by not being able to keep myself in check, by not being able to resist you." He put his hand to his chest. "And I sincerely apologize."

"Yeah, it was reckless, but . . ." I licked my lips. "I'm not mad it happened. You have nothing to apologize for. I wanted it, Russ. I wanted you."

Reaching out, he caressed my cheek. "You mean a lot to me, and I would never want to put you in a position to compromise you, your money, or anything you have going on."

I leaned into his touch. "I appreciate that. Thank you."

As he sat back, his fingertips slid across my cheek ever so gently. I shivered.

"You really didn't need to apologize for yesterday," I continued. "I thought you were apologizing for playing me on Monday."

He shook his head and let out a groan. "This again? I didn't play you. I *wouldn't* play you." He scooted to the edge of his chair and leaned forward so that he was inches from my face. "But I'm sorry I made you feel played. I'm sorry I made you think I didn't want to talk to you."

My mouth twisted into a smile. "Thank you. I'm sorry I blocked you."

"Now that I think about it, I feel played," he teased. "You played me!"

Pushing his chest, I stifled a laugh. "Shut up."

He caught my hand and brought it to his lips. "So, are we good?"

"Yeah, we're good."

The humor drained from his face as he held my gaze. "I hope you know I would never play you. I would never hurt you," he said with earnestness. "You are my escape."

"You've said that before, but what does that mean? I'm your escape from reality?" I guessed, searching his face.

"When we first met, I was cool with brushing it off as an escape from real life. But it was never that. You're not an escape from real life. You *are* real life. And I escape from everything else to have real life with you."

My breathing hitched.

"When I say you're my escape, I mean you're my freedom." He cupped my face. "When I say you're my escape, I mean I can be myself with you." His mouth hovered over mine. "When I say you're my escape, I mean that whenever and wherever we're together, it's the only place I want to be."

Crashing my lips to his, I kissed him with the overwhelming emotion that was bubbling inside of me. Our mouths moved hungrily and in perfect sync as soft moans escaped us. Tugging me from my seat, he pulled me into his lap. I straddled him in the chair and my skirt rode high on my thighs. Wrapping my arms around his neck, I drew him closer and deepened the kiss.

Pulling away fractionally, he looked up at me. "I wish I would've handled things better. I would've made it work."

"How?" I wondered. "The contract I signed was clear."

"There won't be too many reasons for you to have to come to the office, so I'll figure it out. Because I can't stay away from you. I don't *want* to stay away from you."

My breathing became shallow. "I don't want to stay away from you either."

"So, we'll figure it out," he decided. "We have to. These last few weeks, I realized a lot."

"Like what?"

"Like I don't want you sometimes. I want you all the time."

"Because I'm irresistible," I joked softly.

He didn't laugh.

He grabbed my ass, squeezing as he situated me on his lap. "Yes. You're irresistible." He slid his hands to my hips. "And I don't just mean your beauty or the sex." He leaned forward, his face an inch from mine. "*You* are irresistible. Your mind . . . your conversation . . . your company . . . your heart . . . All of you is fucking irresistible. And I'm tired of resisting you."

My stomach did somersaults. "Then don't resist . . ." I said in barely a whisper.

He held my gaze. "Then tell me how you feel."

"I've never felt like this before," I answered, breaking eye contact. "I . . ."

My sentence trailed off as I tried to figure out how to put my emotions into words that would make sense to him.

He moved his head, forcing our eyes to connect again. He didn't say anything. He just stared at me, willing me to be transparent.

"I've never craved someone like I crave you. I've never wanted to be in a relationship before I said yes to you. You have burned your way into my heart, and these last couple of weeks . . ." I shook my head slightly and then rested my forehead against his. "I've never had someone's absence feel as distinct as their presence."

He grabbed my face with his hands. "I'm not letting you go. I'm going to figure this out for us."

I heard the conviction in his voice. I saw the earnestness in his eyes. I felt the stirring of his dick beneath me. And I wanted to believe him. I wanted to believe that we had a chance to make it work. But there was too much at risk for the both of us. So instead of responding to him with words, I pressed my lips against his.

19

"Russssssssssssssssssssssssssss," I moaned his name, lifting my hips from the bed as my body quivered in ecstasy.

My thick thighs clamped around his handsome face, and I grabbed at the pillow as I rode the wave. His arms held me in place as I squirmed.

Gasping, I pushed his head, unable to take anymore. His beard tickled my skin. His tongue slid all over me, cleaning me up.

"Shit," I swore loudly.

I felt his lips curl into a smile against my inner thigh before he looked up at me.

"You had me in a vise grip," he said proudly, pushing himself off the bed.

I giggled as he kissed his way over my belly, between my breasts, until he planted a sweet kiss on my lips.

"I love that shit," he whispered before kissing me again.

With my eyes closed, I sighed giddily. "You're not going to be able to wake up for work if you don't get some sleep. Why are you out of bed?" I opened my eyes and noticed his muscular bare chest, his sculpted abs, and the bulge in the front of his dress pants. "And already halfway dressed?"

"I have to get to the office," he told me, heading across the room and picking up a light blue shirt.

"This early? It's like four o'clock in the morning." I rose up on my elbows and reached for my phone. "Oh my God!"

"It's seven o'clock," he told me. "I have a meeting at eight, so I'm going to head out."

"Oh shit, I can get ready—"

He shook his head. "No," he interrupted, walking over to me as he fastened every button and tucked his shirt in. "There's no rush. You can stay as long as you'd like."

"I'm not going to stay here without you. Why didn't you wake me?"

"I tried before my shower. You didn't even kind of wake up until I kissed you and asked if you needed anything. You spread your legs and said you wanted me to eat you. And you know I can't resist you, so I did."

I burst out laughing. "I thought I dreamed that!" I pushed myself up into a sitting position. "I'm sorry. I'm not trying to make you late for work."

"It's really not a problem. I got some stuff for you in the bathroom and"—he pointed to the nightstand—"I left the extra key for you."

I'd noticed the key next to my cell phone, but I didn't realize what it was. I glanced at it again and my stomach fluttered.

He grabbed his wallet and put it in his pocket. "You can leave when you get ready. I can set the alarm from my phone."

"I appreciate that." I shook my head, still debating if I was going to stay or go. "We went to bed less than three hours ago. How are you up?"

Leaning down, he kissed me long and hard. When he pulled away, he adjusted himself. "I got you, so I'm always going to be up."

I rolled my eyes even though I was grinning up at him. "Goodbye!"

"I'll see you tonight."

"Yes." I paused. "Russ, are you sure?"

"Of course. Just let me know when you leave and I'll set the alarm." He grabbed his blue jacket and draped it over his arm as he headed to the door. Checking his watch, he shook his head. "I have to get going."

"I won't be here too much longer."

He turned to look at me from the doorway. He eyed me silently, a small smile playing on his lips. "I like this."

"Having me naked and in your bed?"

"Having you."

My cheeks heated as he disappeared down the hall.

Falling back against the plush pillows, I looked around the

room. From the dark brown wood grain headboard that rhythmically knocked against the white wall throughout the night to
the plush sand-colored carpet, Russ's bedroom looked like it was
straight out of a catalog. There was no art or decorations on the
wall. While blue was his favorite color, outside of the blue com-
forter that matched the blue curtains, there were no personal
touches that made it stand out as his.

I closed my eyes for what felt like two seconds and woke up an
hour later.

"Oh shit," I grumbled groggily as I pushed myself out of his bed.

Stumbling to the bathroom, I gasped when I entered. There was
an entire basket full of toiletries waiting for me. Soaps, bodywash,
lotion, sponges, exfoliating nets, deodorant, facial scrub, tooth-
paste, and an electric toothbrush were sitting on the sink with a
note attached.

"Nina's essentials," I read aloud.

I brushed my teeth, washed my face, and took a long hot shower.
When I emerged, a feeling washed over me. I looked over at the
items on the counter and then I noticed my reflection. The smile on
my face was big and bright. It was almost embarrassing.

Not me grinning to myself.

> Nina: I just got out of the shower. When did you have
> time to put together this gift basket? I didn't see it last
> night.
>
> Russ: You had me distracted last night and I didn't even
> think about it until this morning. Did it have everything
> you needed?
>
> Nina: Every single thing. And it's the right brands and
> everything. How did you know?
>
> Russ: I pay attention.

I felt my entire body flush with his response. Giddily, I dried
myself off and pulled on a pair of his sweatpants and my shirt from
the night before. I made his bed and then grabbed my bag and
headed downstairs. I left his place a little before nine o'clock.

> Nina: I'm leaving now. I locked the door and turned off all the lights.

After sending the text, I immediately went to my group chat with Aaliyah and Jazmyn.

> Nina: Is anyone available?!
>
> Jazz: I'm packing and then getting on the road. I can call you when I start driving.
>
> Nina: Oh yeah, I forgot you had to pack a whole summer's worth of stuff. You focus on getting back here safely and we'll talk when you're free.
>
> Aaliyah: Call you soon!

I stopped by Charlotte's Webb to pick up my dress for Aaliyah's party. I was just saying goodbye to Charlotte when I received the text from Russ.

> Russ: Thank you. Alarm is on. Keep the key. It's yours.

By the time I got home, I knew I was going to drive myself mad if I didn't talk to someone. I needed to have some different perspectives regarding the situation I found myself in, and with lovestruck Aaliyah and jaded Jazmyn, I knew I'd be able to figure out a way forward. Their differing perspectives would help me make sense of things. But since they weren't available, I had no choice but to call the one person I knew was going to have the exact same reaction as me about the whole thing.

"Hello?" my mom answered in a singsong tone.

"Hey, Mom. Do you have a minute?"

"Of course." Her voice became serious. "What's wrong? What's on your mind?"

"Nothing is *wrong*, per se." I started pacing the living room as I spoke. "But there's been some changes."

"Since earlier this week? You're not changing your dress for Aaliyah's party, are you? I was looking forward to seeing you in that."

"No, it's not that. I actually just picked it up from Charlotte's shop."

"Did you decide who you were going with?"

I cleared my throat. "I did."

"It's The Fun One, isn't it?" she guessed.

I stopped in my tracks. "How—why do you think that?"

"You always sound different with that one. You seem more excited about dates with him. So, it would make sense he would be the one you would take around your friends. Is it him? Or is it someone else?"

I resumed my pacing, slightly faster than before. "No, it's him."

My mom's musical laugh erupted from her. "Do I know my daughter, or do I know my daughter?"

I smiled slightly. "Yeah, you do. Which is why I wanted to talk to you about what's going on."

"What's going on?" She paused for only a second. "Nina!"

My mouth was open, and I was about to speak before she yelled my name. Her urgency made me laugh slightly. "Mom, I'm trying to tell you."

"You're taking too long!"

I plopped down on my couch and sighed loudly. "I'm going to the party with Russ—The Fun One. But things have been different for the last couple of weeks with him and I think . . . I know I want something . . . more."

"Something more like . . . ?" Confusion stretched the question out. "A boyfriend?"

"Yeah," I admitted quietly.

"I thought you didn't want to settle down?"

"I know."

"I thought you wanted to wait until you found a man who gives you everything you've ever wanted and needed before you settled down?"

"I know."

"So, what does this mean?"

"I'm settling in."

"Oh my God!" she exclaimed. "Are you sure? What does this mean?"

"I don't know."

"You don't know?"

"I don't know!"

After a solid minute of us both hysterically talking at once, we stopped and burst out laughing.

I dropped my head into my free hand and held the phone to my ear with the other. "The situation is complicated," I complained.

"Does he feel the same about you?"

"Yes," I answered with complete certainty.

"Does he know what you do for work? And more importantly, is he supportive of it?"

"Yeah. He is."

"Then what's complicated?"

"You know how I got that modeling deal? The Fun One, Russ, is the CEO of the company. So that's how it's complicated. Because if it comes out that we are together, that could ruin this opportunity for me."

Mom let a long exhale. "Oh, Nina."

"I know."

"What are you going to do?"

"I have no idea."

"This is tough."

I shook my head in amusement. "I know."

"Well, how much do you like this man? Because I already know how much the modeling contract means to you. How much does this man mean to you? And is it worth the contract? Is it worth everything you worked hard to do?"

I squeezed my eyes shut. "That's why I was calling you! I need clarity."

"Well, sweetheart, you're only going to get that from within."

"I know," I wailed, knowing she was right.

"Mm, mm, mm."

We sat in silence for a minute.

"If he's the man you're meant to be with, it's going to work out," she assured me. "When I met your father, I wasn't looking for a husband. But I found him. It doesn't matter what you plan for when God's already got your plan in motion. So, the job and the man will both work themselves out. I know it."

"Thanks, Mom."

As we said our goodbyes and ended the call, I got off the couch and grabbed my stuff for the gym. The conversation with my mom didn't provide any clarity. In fact, it made me feel even stronger about my connection to Russ and to my opportunity with RLF. So, I planned to spend the day thinking about anything and everything else but that.

No such luck.

I had an intense workout and every muscle in my body ached because of the acrobatic positions Russ had put me in. I had a delicious lunch and thought about how when I was full the night before, Russ rubbed my belly. When I spent the afternoon posting content on social media and responding with comments, I couldn't help but think how it was Russ's brand that I was representing.

I can't escape this man, I thought with a rueful smile.

Refocusing, I put my phone on do not disturb, turned the music volume up high, and worked diligently. My stomach grumbled and when I looked at the clock, I was surprised. Grabbing my phone, I made my way to the kitchen, checking my missed calls. There were quite a few people I needed to follow up with. But there was one in particular I needed to take care of.

"If it ain't Disappearing Acts herself," The Funny One greeted me. "Where has your sexy ass been?"

I smiled. "Hey, James. I've been doing a lot, honestly. I've been meaning to get in touch with you."

"Well, I have a show tomorrow and I'd love for you to come. We could reconnect. Afterward, I can take you out to dinner and then take you home for dessert. And don't immediately say no. It's been a minute and you've been depriving me all summer. I'm starting to think you got a man or something?" he joked.

I listened to his light chuckle in silence before clearing my throat. "That's what I've been meaning to talk to you about."

"Oh shit . . . you got a man? Like, one man?"

"Something like that."

"I thought you didn't want anything serious or exclusive."

"I didn't think I wanted anything serious or exclusive either."

"And this is what you really want?"

"Yes." The ease with which the word rolled off my tongue surprised even me. "It is."

"Wow." He seemed genuinely shocked, letting out a long breath. "Does this mean you're not trying to get up with me anymore?"

I looked at my phone quizzically. "Correct."

"Oh, that's . . . wow!" After a moment, he continued, "You don't even want to cheat?"

"What!" I almost choked. "Why would you think I would cheat?"

"You remember when you wore that one pair of shoes to that show, and then you changed into a different pair of shoes for dinner? Yeah, that's cheat energy. You can't even stick with one shoe for the night, you definitely not sticking with one man."

Covering my mouth, I held in my laugh. "James. Please."

"Are you going to deny you give off cheat vibes?"

"I'm categorically denying it! I've never cheated in my life."

"You ain't never had a relationship in your life."

I nodded even though he couldn't see me. "Valid. But I'm not a cheater."

"Fine." He sighed dramatically. "But listen, if you change your mind, I'm here. Give me a call."

I sucked my teeth. "Bye, James."

"Nina, I'm serious. Think about it. Bye!"

I disconnected the call and shook my head.

The ending with The Funny One was lighthearted, like everything else with him. That was a stark contrast to the heartbreak I caused with The Romantic One and the stony silence I received from The Smart One. The diverse roster I'd built was pretty elite.

And I gave it all up for Russ.

The thought gave me a funny feeling. I wasn't nervous or uneasy about the decision. But the realization that I had completely wiped my slate clean and gotten rid of all my prospects to focus on one man was a testament to my feelings.

And I really don't know how this is going to work.

Hours later, after finishing my work for the day, I had a conversation with Jazmyn. I told her I'd be bringing Russ as my date on Saturday. Because of Aaliyah's birthday-date crisis, I didn't have to worry about either of them prying too much for more information. But as soon as I got off the phone with Jazz, I looked at the photo again of Aaliyah's date for the night and then called her up.

As she was catching me up with what was going on, I got a text from Russ letting me know he was on the way to my place. Even though a chill ran down my spine, I decided that I wasn't going to let the dick distract me. We needed to talk.

Clearing my throat, I refocused on the conversation with Aaliyah.

"No, but he looks like someone specific," I told her as I studied the picture she'd sent me. "Ugh! It's going to bother me until I remember the man's name." It was on the tip of my tongue, but the name was escaping me. I sighed loudly. "I'll let you know when I think of it."

"Okay, sounds good," Aaliyah responded, amused. "And have fun on your date tonight."

"It's not a date. We're just linking up," I corrected her. "Unlike you, I plan to have my needs met tonight."

"Mm-hmm. Well, have fun linking up with your *date* tonight."

I rolled my eyes. "Goodbye, Aaliyah."

"Byeeeeeee," she sang in return.

I ended the call and went to get dressed. It wasn't a date. It was an important conversation. But the lingerie I put on under the charcoal-gray tank dress made it clear that the night was going to end with sex.

Grabbing the visitor pass, I approached my front door. Even though he hadn't knocked yet, according to his text, he should've been parking. I didn't want him to get all the way up to the door and have to go back, so I went outside.

"Fuck!" Russ yelled before stuffing his phone into his pocket. When he turned around, he seemed surprised. "Hey, sorry about that."

I eyed him quizzically as I handed him the parking pass. "Everything okay?"

"It's work bullshit. It's . . ." He shook his head, hoisting his duffle bag strap on his shoulder. "You know what? I'm off, and I'm with you. I don't even want to think about that right now." He unlocked his car and put the pass on the dashboard. When he made his way back to me, he smiled. "When I'm with you, all the bullshit disappears."

I rose up on my toes and planted a kiss against his lips. "Well, I have a surprise for you when we get inside."

He grabbed my ass and shook it. "I like the sound of that."

I made a face as I turned around and led him inside. "Yeah, okay."

As soon as the door closed behind him, we took off our shoes.

"How are you?" he asked, following me to the living room.

"I'm glad you asked," I replied, patting the seat cushion next to me.

He sat his bag on the floor and then sat on the couch with me. "What's up?"

"So last night we established how we feel about each other and that led to a really, really good night."

He grabbed my hand and kissed the back of it. "It was so good it was hard to concentrate today."

I bit down on my bottom lip and nodded. "Same."

"When you did that thing with your throat . . ." He let out a breath and shook his head. "I had to start a meeting a couple minutes late because I had to calm down before leaving my office."

I almost let myself get caught up as the heat spread over my body. But I shook it off.

"But before we circle back to that, we need to talk about us."

"The fact that we're in a relationship?" he guessed, running his thumb across my knuckles.

"No." My cheeks felt warm, and I knew my face was flushed. "The fact that if I'm going to be in a relationship, I want to be in it."

His brows furrowed. "What do you mean? We are in it. I'm all the way in it. It's us."

"How are we going to be an us if I'm technically working for you for the next eight months?"

"I'm still working on that. I'm trying to figure out a way that it doesn't blow back on either of us."

"In the meantime, I don't want to feel like we're hiding out."

He shook his head. "That's not the case. We're . . ." He struggled to find the words to complete his sentence.

"We're hiding," I finished for him. "Last night, we were at your place. Tonight, we're at mine. And since we aren't going out because we can't, we're hiding."

"We're going to go out next week."

"How?" I wondered.

"I'm taking care of it."

"I don't understand how though." I intertwined my fingers with his. "I want you. I also want to be out and about. *And* I want us to keep doing work we love. I don't know how all of those things can happen."

"There is a way. I just need time to make it happen."

"As badly as I want this"—I gestured between the two of us— "all of the points you made when you sat right here three weeks ago are still valid today. I don't want either of us to lose anything."

"And we won't," he said with a quiet intensity. "I'm not losing you. I'm not losing what we have. I'm not losing my company. I'm not letting you lose this job." He brought my hand to his lips again. "I don't get a lot of off time. But when I do, I want to spend it with you, focused on you, enjoying you. Let's have fun this weekend and then on Monday, I'll put things in motion."

"Okay," I relented.

"You good with that?"

"Yeah."

He scooted closer to me and leaned into my personal space. His beautiful brown eyes bore into mine and he put my hand against his chest. "Do you trust me?"

I felt his heart beating under my palm. The spell of his gaze caused my stomach to flutter. Overwhelmed with a flood of emotion, I answered honestly.

"Yes," I breathed.

20

For the life of me, I couldn't understand how we could get around the fraternization policy. I read the clause backward and forward. The language was clear. But because Russ was the CEO of RLF, I had hope that he'd figure something out. He asked me to trust him, and I did. But the reality was that I didn't want to lose my job and I didn't want Russ to lose his company. It scared me to think that one or the other would need to happen in order for us to be together.

I wouldn't want him to resent me.

"Did I mention how good you look?" Russ murmured in my ear, pulling me out of my thoughts.

I rotated my ass against his semihard dick on the dance floor. Leaning back into his chest, my lips pulled into a smile. "You did. But I don't mind hearing it again."

His fingers gripped my hips, and he nuzzled his nose into my neck. "You look so fucking good in this dress."

I closed my eyes momentarily.

The mocha-tinted dress with crystal embellishment gave the illusion of sheerness and fit my body like a glove. The G-string that I wore was soaking wet as I listened to the complimentary words he whispered into my ear. My nipples strained against the fabric as I turned around in his arms.

I looked up into his handsome face and smiled. I placed my hands on his cheeks, gently scratching his beard before bringing his lips down to mine.

"Thank you," I purred as our mouths connected again. "You should see what I'm wearing underneath it."

"Why are you doing this to me?" he groaned, pulling me closer. "You've been trying to get my dick hard since we finished dinner."

I wiggled my eyebrows. "Is it working?"

He laughed against my mouth, allowing me to taste his joy, to swallow his happiness. The happiness I felt in him and with him caused me to shiver. I couldn't remember a more perfect night.

There were about forty or fifty people on the dance floor, so it was crowded but not ridiculously so. We had enough privacy that we weren't overheard, but I was tipsy enough to not care if we were, and the other half of the guests were under a tent or by the lake.

"On the count of three, turn to the birthday girl and yell 'Happy birthday, Aaliyah!'" the DJ shouted. "One! Two! Three!"

"Happy birthday, Aaliyah!" I yelled out with about a hundred other people.

"Now make your way toward the lake—we have something special happening in two minutes," the DJ continued. "Two minutes."

Russ intertwined his fingers with mine. "There's more?"

"Yes," I replied as he spun me in a circle.

Pulling me close, he tucked me into his side. "Your girl knows how to throw a party."

"She's been planning it for a year, and it's turned out so good. The dinner was perfect—"

"The chef did the damn thing," he interrupted, escorting me toward the lake with the rest of the guests. "Every course was good."

"Every single one!" I agreed. "The food, the music, the vibe. Everything has been amazing. I hope she's having a good time." I looked around until I saw her with her date and smiled. "It looks like she's satisfied with how the night turned out."

He glanced over. "From that smile on her face, I'd say so."

I looked up at him. "And what about you? Are you having a good time?"

"Yeah, I am. I always have a good time with you. But it's been real cool meeting your friends and seeing you with your people."

"They love you."

A smile pulled on his lips. "Oh, for real?"

"What's not to love? You're perfect," I blurted out.

His smile grew. "You think I'm perfect?"

Stepping back, I rolled my eyes and gestured to him. "Look at you. You're smart and sweet and charming and funny and sexy . . ."

My eyes swept up and down his body as my sentence trailed off, lingering on the last adjective.

Russ looked good in his navy blue pants and matching shirt. His dark brown tie, belt, and shoes pulled his look together and kept him from looking too matchy-matchy. The quality and tailored cut of the expensive threads fit his sculpted body perfectly. The colors complemented his dark caramel complexion, which seemed to glow under the moonlight.

I forced my eyes back to his. "And the dick is immaculate."

He burst out laughing. "Yoooooooooo!"

The fireworks exploded in the sky, and I shifted my focus. The elaborate display over the lake was so pretty. Bright streaks of white danced high above the trees. The sky was so dark it looked black, except where the moon peeked over the trees and made it look purple. There weren't many visible stars in the sky, but the fireworks made up for that.

"Did you see that one?" I asked excitedly, pointing to the "Happy Birthday" formation. "It's so beautiful."

"You're so beautiful."

I glanced over at him and saw his eyes were on me. Grinning, I bumped him with my hip. "You're missing the show."

"I'm watching the one that matters."

A new flurry of fireworks went off, but my eyes stayed trained on him.

He studied my face. "I love when you get that look."

I smiled up at him. "What look?"

He cupped my cheeks. "That one."

"Why?" I whispered.

"I love seeing you happy." His fingers skated across my skin as he moved down to my neck. He held my gaze and his thumbs slid down my throat. "And I'll do anything to keep you happy."

My heart skipped a beat. "I like the sound of that."

He brought his lips down to mine and gave me the sweetest, most romantic kiss. I felt that kiss throughout every inch of my body. When he pulled away slightly, his face hovered over mine. There was such adoration and love in the way he looked at me, and

I felt emotionally raw. I wanted to tell that man I'd be his girl-friend, that I loved him, that I was ready to suck the skin off him.

My lips parted.

"Nina!" Jazmyn called out, pulling me from my trance.

I've had too much to drink, I thought as I swallowed my feelings and turned toward my best friend's voice.

Jazz and Aaliyah waved me over to where they were near the dock.

"Go be with your friends," Russ told me, brushing the back of his hand against my cheek. "I'll be right here."

My stomach fluttered.

Oh, he's about to get sucked and fucked, I thought as I made my way to my girls.

I looked between my two best friends as I approached, and I couldn't help but smile. Aaliyah was stunning in green, but it was the way her hair indicated she'd gotten fucked earlier in the night that really made her shine. Jazz was beautiful in black, but it was her smile and the way her eyes danced that made her glow.

"The two of you look happy as hell," I commented, stopping right in front of them.

"I am," Aaliyah admitted, practically gushing. "I really am!" She pointed at me. "But clearly, I'm not the only one. You're smil-ing from ear to ear."

"Right?" Jazz added, putting her hands on her hips. "And you're one to talk, Nina. You damn near floated down here!"

I laughed. "I've had a good amount to drink tonight."

Aaliyah pursed her lips and cocked her head to the side. "You're really going to say it's the alcohol when it's clear that you and Russ are a thing."

I shook my head. "We're not a thing . . . not officially. He says he has a plan to solve our problem. So, for right now, we're . . . we're friends with benefits." I looked over my shoulder to find him standing with both Jazz's and Aaliyah's dates. "No, we're col-leagues with benefits."

"Does he know you're in love with him?" Aaliyah asked.

My head snapped back, and I stared at her. My heart raced as I processed her question. "Wh-what?"

"Don't deny it. It's written all over your face. He's the one."

I looked at Jazmyn for help, but she smirked. "I have *never* seen you like this. And if I'm being honest, seeing Nina Ford locked in with one man and settling down almost makes me believe in love again."

I shook my head. "Just because the man is literally perfect for me doesn't mean we're in love." I glanced over my shoulder to make sure we wouldn't be overheard. "Until he puts this plan he has in motion, we're just . . . colleagues with benefits," I explained.

"And unofficially?" Jazz wondered. "Because he's been looking at you like you two are together."

Grinning, I looked up at the sky. "Unofficially, that's my man."

"The way the two of you have been carrying on, you might as well admit you love him and propose," Aaliyah teased.

"Propose to a man?" I frowned. "I wouldn't even propose a toast!"

They burst out laughing.

"But in all seriousness, I really am tipsy," I admitted. "I almost told that man I loved him earlier. He was looking at me, touching me, saying all the right things. So, I'm drinking water for the rest of the night because that damn drink got me in my feelings and almost got me caught up."

They were cracking up.

I meant what I'd said. With Aaliyah's signature drinks running through my system, my inhibitions were lowered, and my heart was on my nonexistent sleeve. But they were delicious. So, when Aaliyah's cousin, Tamara, and Tamara's wife came by with a tray of drinks, I took one.

"We want to toast my cousin," Tamara said with a smile. "Where are your dates?"

We all gestured to the three handsome men huddled together in conversation. Her wife took the rest of the drinks and went to go get them.

"So, which of you will be the next to be married?" Tamara teased before taking a sip of her drink.

"Aaliyah," Jazz and I answered simultaneously.

All of us burst out laughing.

"Her lovesick ass," I commented, shaking my head.

"I know you ain't talking!" Aaliyah exclaimed.

"She's right, Nina," Jazz agreed.

I almost choked on my drink. "Jazz! Not you, too!"

She lifted her shoulders and giggled. "I'm sorry. But you look like a woman in love."

My eyes widened as I looked at her in disbelief. "Hello, pot. I'm kettle."

Aaliyah and Tamara were weak.

Russ and the others strolled up, looking amused.

"What's so funny?" Tamara's wife asked.

"These three," Tamara answered in a rush before giving her a quick kiss. Turning toward the rest of us, she lifted her cup. "I want to toast my cousin. For turning thirty. For having this dope-ass party. For constantly proving that the cousins on the father's side are the best." After our snickering, she continued. "Tonight has been amazing and I pray this is the kickoff to more amazingness in your life. May your thirtieth year be your best year yet. Cheers!"

"Cheers!" we cheered in unison.

Just as Tamara and her wife walked off, Mecca, another of Aaliyah's cousins, approached us.

"Can you get together for a picture?" Mecca asked.

The six of us huddled together and posed. Someone called her name, and she ran toward the edge of the lake.

I watched her scurry off. "I can't remember if she's the nosey one or if—"

"It's her," Aaliyah interrupted me to clarify.

We all laughed.

Conversation flowed for a few minutes, but when a song from our college days pulsed through the air, we darted to the dance floor.

Between the drinks and the nonstop hits the DJ was spinning,

I couldn't stop dancing. It had been a long time since I'd danced that hard.

"I love seeing that smile on your face," Russ said with a grin.

"I can't help it. Tonight has been . . . perfect," I admitted.

"I'm glad you invited me. Seeing you with your people, seeing you in this dress, seeing this smile on your face . . ." He licked his lips. "You're right. Tonight *is* perfect. *You're* perfect."

I squealed after Russ spun me around and then brought me back into his arms.

When the DJ slowed the music down, things heated up between me and Russ. Our bodies moved in sync as slow jam after slow jam rang through the air.

"I don't know if it's the drinks or what, but damn . . ." Russ let out a low groan as I continued to grind on him. "This is new."

I had my hands on my knees, and I was throwing my ass in a circle. "We've danced before." I turned around to face him and then dropped it low in front of him. "And you've definitely seen my ass move like this before."

As I slowly slid my body up his to rise to my feet, he said, "Yeah, but never on a crowded dance floor . . ." Russ leaned down to whisper in my ear. "It's almost like you want me to lift this dress up and slid right in it."

Biting my bottom lip, I pressed myself against him. "Yes."

"Nina . . ."

The way he dragged the second syllable of my name was so sexy that a chill ran down my spine. I clasped my hands behind his neck and rolled my body against him. "You want to lift my dress up, baby?"

He grabbed my hips, making sure I felt how hard his dick was with each dance move. "You better stop playing with me," he warned.

"You better *start* playing with me."

He let out a low chuckle that almost felt like a warning just as Aaliyah got on the mic to thank us for coming and to wish us a good night. We wished her a happy birthday again and then went back to dancing to the last song of the night.

Wrapping my arms around Russ's neck, I pulled him until our foreheads touched. "I think it's time for us to call it a night."

Without a word, he slipped his arm around my waist and escorted me off the dance floor. The DJ was telling everyone to go home as we made our way into the lake house where we were staying for the night. There were a few people milling around in the living room, but Russ and I headed upstairs.

There were three bedrooms downstairs and three upstairs. Aaliyah and her date were in the biggest bedroom at the end of the hall. Jazz and her date were in the room to the left. And we were in the room on the right. A smile crossed my face as the thoughts of what I wanted to do to Russ flashed in my mind.

"Whoa, you good?" Russ asked, grabbing my hips and steadying me as we walked up the steps.

The combination of my thoughts, my heels, and the drinks I'd had made climbing the stairs a little more difficult than normal.

"I got you," he said softly as he held me tight. "Put your arms around me."

I wasted no time draping my arms around his neck.

"I'm okay," I assured him, even though I allowed him to lead me. "Just got a little off-balance."

We were still holding on to each other after we reached the second-floor landing.

"That last drink snuck up on you, huh?" he teased.

I giggled, but I couldn't deny the deliciousness of Aaliyah's signature drinks had me in a chokehold all night.

"I didn't even know I liked Malibu Sunrises," I told him as we entered our bedroom and closed the door behind us.

We hadn't even walked a step from the door before I turned into him, almost pushing him against the door.

"Oh!" he reacted with surprise, but he held on to me.

Wrapping my arms around his neck, I hugged him tight. Resting my nose against his neck, I inhaled deeply. Relishing in the sandalwood-and-leather-scented cologne, I smiled against his skin.

He smelled so good.

We stood in silence as we embraced. I held him tighter, enjoying the feel of him. His hands slid up and down my back and then they rested at the top of my ass. Neither of us made any moves to disentangle ourselves. I wanted to hold on to him for as long as possible. But as a wave of emotion came over me, I realized I was holding on to him as if I didn't want to let him go.

It was the first time in weeks that we were able to be out together, that we were able to have a good time in a public space. It was the first time I felt like we were back to ourselves. It was the first time it felt like we were back to our normal. We weren't hiding out at his place or mine. And I knew I'd missed him and what we had, but I didn't fully comprehend the depth of how much I missed us freely being us.

"You okay?" he whispered. Dropping kisses along the side of my face, he rocked me gently.

I couldn't open my mouth to speak because I was scared of what would come out, so I just simply nodded. Closing my eyes tight, I pushed down the emotion bubbling up inside me.

"Talk to me," he coaxed softly.

"I've missed this," I admitted, pulling out of the hug enough to look him in his eyes. "You're so much fun. I've missed going out and having fun with you."

"I've missed it, too." He searched my face for a moment. "We're going to get back to normal."

His words were etched in confidence, and I was tipsy enough to let myself believe him.

Stepping out of my shoes, I maintained eye contact with him.

"Just let me put a plan together and we'll go out. We'll leave our work at work and just enjoy ourselves. I'll take you wherever you want to go. We'll do whatever you want to do. I'll make sure we get back to nights like this."

I ran my hands up his chest and over his shoulders, halfway removing his jacket. He took it off his arms and then tossed it to the side. I put my hands underneath his newly untucked shirt and stroked his back. I looked up at him adoringly, wanting what he'd just described so badly.

"I wish," I sighed.

His brows furrowed. "What do you mean?"

"Where can we go, Russ? You're traveling, getting ready for Fashion Week, and you'll be gone for days at a time. You'll have assistants and other management people all around you, so even if I went on the trip, I'd have to hide out in the hotel room. When you're here, we can't go out because we will likely be spotted by someone who works for you. This is it. This was our last night of freedom. Our last night to be us," I explained, my face crumpling in frustration. The words just kept spilling out of me. "I have months left on my contract and this opportunity means a lot to me so I'm not going to quit. And I know how important your business is to you, so you can't have a scandal. I don't want to stop this. I love"—I cleared my throat and shifted my gaze momentarily—"what we have."

"Hey." With his hands on my lower back, he pulled me into him again. He pressed his lips against mine. "I love what we have, too."

I took a deep breath. "I know you said you're putting a plan together. I just . . . I've really missed experiencing things with you. Sneaking around can be sexy. But hiding is not."

"I'm not hiding you." He pulled back, looking me up and down. "There's nothing I enjoy more than to be out with you, showing you off. If I could be out with you and resist being all over you, this whole thing would be easier."

I smirked. "Yeah, I feel the same way."

He moved his hands from my back to my cheeks. "The plan I'm working on has some moving parts. But I'm working on it because I don't want us to get caught up in some bullshit. I'm not hiding you or this or us. But when I'm around you, nothing else matters."

"I know. That's why this is dangerous."

"Exactly." He nodded, brushing his lips against mine again. "But I'm sorry we're even in this position."

"I'm sorry, too."

He gazed into my eyes. "But as much as my work means to me, I'm not going to act like you don't mean just as much."

My face flushed.

My stomach fluttered.

My nipples hardened.

Before I had a chance to respond, his mouth hovered over mine. "There's a way for everything to work out and for us to both get what we want."

"How?" I asked breathily.

His tongue wet his lips as he paused. "Just know that I'm not losing you or my business. I've worked too hard to build this company. And I've waited too long to find you."

My breathing faltered.

Feeling slightly off-balance, I gripped his shoulders as his words swirled in my ears.

"I think you like me a little bit," I teased, hoping to mask my accelerated heart rate and the heat creeping up my face.

"It's more than a little bit," he admitted before crashing his mouth into mine.

Fumbling with zippers and buttons, straps and sleeves, we stripped each other down without breaking the kiss. Once he pushed my straps off my shoulders, it didn't take long for my dress to slink down my body, pooling at my feet. I was standing in just a black strapless bra and a matching G-string.

I reached behind me and unhooked my bra. My heavy breasts fell, and he broke our kiss to gawk at the way they hung between us. He grabbed them, allowing his thumb to toy with the tautness of my nipples as our lips found each other again. I moaned into his mouth when he pinched and gently twisted the hard peaks.

"I like that," I murmured.

"I know you do," he whispered back.

"And I know what you like . . ."

I couldn't remove his shirt because he was against the door, but it didn't matter. I'd managed to unbuckle his belt and unzip his pants. I pulled his boxer briefs and pants down with me as I sank to my knees. The cushion of my dress protected me from the hardwood floor. Still hearing the conviction, the meaning, and the power behind his words, I planned to suck him off the bone.

Grabbing his dick at the base, I licked the length of him before swirling my tongue around the bulbous head.

"Nina," he said my name roughly as his shoulders rocked against the door. He damn near ripped his shirt off and threw it somewhere behind me.

I stared up at him, watching lust pull his handsome features. His chest rose and fell as he took me in. It was always sexy to see and hear him succumb to me. Opening my mouth wide, I took as much of him as I could, coating his dick with my saliva. With our eyes locked, I kept my lips wrapped around him and just held him there.

"Mmmmmmmmm," I intoned. Making a purring noise, I let my throat vibrate around his girth.

His eyes seemed to darken. There was a deep rumble from his chest as I took him as far as I could go.

I watched his eyes close, his mouth open, and his face twist with yearning. Licking and sucking, I proceeded to bob my head up and down the length of him.

"Shiiiiiiiiiiiiiiiiit," Russ groaned, gripping my hair at the root. He gently stopped me, forcing me to stay still. "After throwing that ass on me all night and then putting that wet mouth on me, you trying to make me come?"

I nodded. "Mm-hmm," I affirmed, batting my eyelashes at him.

He bit down on his bottom lip and shook his head slightly as I started sucking again. I deep throated him. Holding on to his muscular thighs, I leveraged my body so I could take as much of him as I could.

"Goddamn, Nina," he grunted as I took his dick to the back of my throat.

Gagging lightly, I pulled almost all the way off it and then I did it all over again. Each time, I savored the desire in his voice, the hunger in his eyes, the tension in his body, and the power I had over his breathing.

With his dick in my mouth, I peered up at him through my lashes.

I didn't move.

He had his head against the door, his mouth slightly agape, and his eyes shut tight. I waited for him to look at me.

And when he lifted his head and opened his eyes, I was treated to a look of unbridled lust.

My lips curled into as much of a smile as I could muster with my mouth being so full.

I had him right where I wanted him.

"You look so fucking sexy with my dick in your mouth," he growled. "You know that? You know how good you fucking look?"

I nodded, taking him deeper and playing with his balls.

"I'm stretching that pretty mouth out." A slight shudder rippled through him as I stuck my tongue out. "Fuck."

That's it.

I took as many of his nine and a half inches into my mouth as I could. Bobbing my head on his dick, I listened to his moans and couldn't help wanting to please him. My pussy throbbed for him. Increasing my pace, I sucked him hard and sloppily. Stroking his shaft with one hand followed by my mouth, I took as much of him as I could, applying pressure accordingly.

He groaned. "Nina . . ."

I could only imagine how I looked on my knees before him, mouth juicy with saliva and eyes begging for more.

With my gaze focused on him, I moved my hand. I lowered my mouth, allowing me to take even more of him. He closed his eyes as if it were too much, and that just turned me on more. Slowly bobbing my head up and down, I gagged slightly every time he hit the back of my throat.

"I love that shit," he whispered roughly. Putting his hands on the back of my head, he repeated himself. "I love that shit."

I could sense that he was being rushed to his orgasm when he started to thrust his hips rhythmically.

"You look so fucking good taking my dick in your mouth," he rasped. "You know it's yours, don't you? This dick has always been yours."

I moaned, letting the vibrations tickle him as I performed.

A rumble erupted from deep inside him. "Yeah, throat it again, Nina. Throat that shit."

I was soaking wet.

And the more he talked, the more enthusiastic I became.

"You're going to make me nut if you keep doing that," he grunted, breathing heavily.

So, I did it again and again.

"Nina, shit," he whispered sexily. "It feels so fucking good."

"Come in my mouth," I demanded before deep throating him again.

"Fuck . . ." he swore. "You're going to make me come."

I continued doing exactly what I was doing, and he started to twitch. My pussy throbbed at his reaction to my talents.

"You should stop . . ." He held my head in place. "You're about to make me nut."

I didn't stop because I wanted him to lose control.

And he did.

His hips jerked involuntarily. And with two fistfuls of my tightly coiled hair in his hands, he fucked my face to a loud orgasm.

With a rough grunt and a full-body spasm, Russ came hard.

It was so much I almost choked as I attempted to swallow it all. Wiping the corners of my mouth with my fingers, I stared at his dick, shiny and still hard, pointing at me lazily. A smile pulled at my lips as his body slumped in pleasure.

"That was so fucking good," he groaned, pulling me to my feet. "Come here." Grabbing my face, he kissed me hard and deep. "Now it's your turn."

21

I glanced over my shoulder at Russ. "If that's Remedy again, you can answer it," I remarked as we walked up the sidewalk toward my front door.

"Work can wait," he replied, my bags in his hands. "I'm off and I'm with you. I'll call her back later or I'll talk to her on Monday."

I smiled as I pulled my key out of my handbag to unlock the door. "I get why you didn't take the call while we were leaving the lake house or the one while we were at lunch, but now she's calling for a third time—something might be up. She might need you."

Shaking his head, he entered my place behind me. "She's calling as CCO. If she was calling as my sister, she would've texted me." He dropped the bags off in the entryway and took off his shoes. "And she knows how I feel about my time off."

I stepped out of my shoes. "I hear you. But with that event happening last night, and we both didn't go . . ."

It looked like he was going to dispute what I was saying, but he snapped his mouth shut and nodded. "You're right." He stepped toward me, cupping my face with his hands. "But first . . ."

He kissed my forehead and then stared at me in awe for a few moments. "Thank you for this weekend."

I wrapped my arms around his middle, basking in the way he looked at me. "Thank you for coming with me."

"It was my pleasure." He paused for a moment. "*You* are my pleasure."

Dropping a soft kiss against my lips, he stared at me as if he were seeing me for the first time. There was an adoration in his gaze that made my stomach quiver. The thought that crossed my mind while I was drunk was crossing it sober.

"Russ . . ." I murmured, biting my bottom lip.

"Yes?"

"The pleasure is all yours"—I pushed up on my toes and pressed my lips against his—"and so am I."

The low moan that reverberated through his chest and into my mouth made me smile against his lips.

"You're mine," he stated in barely a whisper.

"I'm yours," I confirmed.

"I love when you say that shit."

I'd never said it outside of us having sex. For some reason, it felt more intimate standing in the hallway of my apartment. With slow, dawdling kisses, I felt the sensuality and depth of our connection. Our mouths were speaking from the heart. With each meeting of our tongues, our emotional needs were being expressed and our feelings were being communicated. That kiss was more than a kiss. That kiss spoke to a deeper connection between us.

"Wow," I breathed when he pulled away. I let my eyelashes flutter open and I was met with a look that made my heart leap from my chest.

"Nina, I—" His phone rang again, interrupting the moment between us. Reaching in his pocket, he shook his head. "I'm about to put it on silent."

I took a step back. My heart was pounding, and I needed to create space between us anyway.

We both saw Remedy's name flashing across the screen.

"Take it," I told him, retreating until my back hit the wall. "It's probably important."

He nodded firmly before answering the call. "Remedy?"

"Russ! Finally! I've been trying to get in touch with you all weekend!" His sister yelled so loudly I could hear her from a few feet away.

His handsome face twisted with a frown. "What's going on? Everything good with Mom and Dad?"

"Yes! Of course, they're okay. Did you check your email?"

He pointed to the couch to let me know where he was headed. "Not since I left the office on Friday."

"What are you doing? Where have you been?"

He exhaled loudly. "I had plans, and I couldn't make it. What's up?"

She said something I couldn't quite hear but it made Russ's eyebrows shoot up. "That's—shit, Rem, that's a good look! Hell yeah!" He stopped in his tracks. "Wait, wait, wait, wait. With who?" He glanced over at me momentarily. "That's . . . that's not . . ." He took a deep breath and continued into the living room. "It's a good opportunity. I'm not saying that at all. I'm just saying . . . Remedy, I hear you, but we already have someone to fill that role." He paused, swiping his hand down his face. "When did I authorize Lori to do that?" he asked. After receiving an answer, he took a seat. "When did *you* authorize Lori to do that?"

I didn't want to seem like I was listening, so I grabbed my bags. Peeking at him out of the corner of my eye, I saw the scowl on his face. He clearly wasn't pleased with whatever information he was getting.

I took my bags into my room, dropped them off, and quickly made my way back down the hall.

"—shouldn't have offered because we don't have the budget for that. No. I don't care how viral it's gone. We're not making a change," he said in a low tone. "That's final." His eyes flicked up to me and then back down to the floor. "Let me catch up with the emails and I'll give you a call back."

He disconnected the call and immediately his thumb moved swiftly over the screen. The serious expression on his face was a complete shift from his mood prior to the phone call. And even though it wasn't my business, nerves twisted my stomach and curiosity tugged at my mind.

I tentatively made my way toward him.

He didn't look up. With his chiseled jaw set and his lips forming a hard line, I immediately knew something was wrong.

"Everything okay?" I inquired softly as I sat next to him.

Seconds ticked by and he didn't say anything. He just stared at his phone. Finally, he tossed the device on the other side of the couch and scrubbed his face with his hands.

"I'd been in talks to get RLF in the Bowen shops and they wanted to see more of what we had," he started.

I can't believe I missed my opportunity to impress Bowen, I thought with slight dismay. I had an incredible night so I didn't regret it, but I was definitely shocked to hear the news.

"And after Saturday, they want to partner with us," he continued. "RLF will have a limited run this fall and a full run in spring."

I gasped. "Russ! That's amazing!"

Letting out a deep breath, he shifted his body to face me. "Remedy found out that they were going to be at the event on Saturday and since you weren't going to be there, she had Lori reach out to another model to be our plus size representation." He cleared his throat. "Bowen loved the dress . . . and the model. And now, they are ready to move forward with partnering with us."

I stared at him and the pained expression on his face. "This is a good thing, right?"

"It is." He nodded and forced a smile. "It is."

"What are you not telling me?"

"Bowen wants the partnership to include the other model."

"Oh! Okay. Well, I mean, there's room for all of us." When he didn't say anything, my heart sank. I hesitated momentarily. "Unless that means I'm out?"

"You're not out," he said emphatically. "But . . ." He frowned. "They want to work with the model they met."

It took me a second to understand what he was telling me. "Oh. Okay."

"I need to look over the paperwork and see how it impacts the overall picture. But nothing is finalized yet. I still have to look at things before any of this is official. I don't want you to worry."

I was very worried.

Forcing a small smile, I attempted to nod. "Okay."

"It'll be fine," he reassured me. "Nothing is set in stone until I sign off on it, so you'll know when I know." He grabbed my face and searched my eyes. "But I got you. You're not being replaced."

"That's what it sounds like," I whispered.

"You represent RLF. Your contract is binding." He brought

his forehead to mine. "And let's be real, no one can take your place."

"According to Bowen—"

"According to *me,* no one can take your place."

My heart fluttered. I knew he meant what he'd said. But he owned RLF; he had no control over what Bowen wanted to do. And Bowen wanted the other model.

Not gonna lie, that stings.

The Bowen deal was a good business move. The fact that Bowen wanted another model wasn't a good look for me. So as much as I wanted to believe Russ would take care of things, business was business.

Pressing my lips against his, I tried to shift the conversation. "You're about to have your first Fashion Week runway show. September is going to be an amazing month."

"Yes, it is," he agreed, wrapping his arms around me. "And I hit my lawyer up. We're meeting on Tuesday to go over the legalities of everything." Lowering his head, he put his lips to the shell of my ear. "We're going to be okay."

I leaned my body into his. "You want to tell me the plan?"

"Once it's ready to be put into action, I'll tell you. Just trust that I'll take care of it. Of you."

I felt his words as boldly as I heard them. Tipping my head, I puckered my lips and waited until he kissed me.

We spent the rest of the day talking, eating, fucking, and enjoying each other's company. We decided to watch a movie, but when the storyline lagged, we both seemed distracted and lost in our own thoughts. But after we showered and got in bed, we were back to ourselves again. Because his hands on my body and his lips against my skin evaporated any and all worry, stress, and doubt from my mind.

Unfortunately, when he left for work in the morning, all the thoughts that he'd pushed away came flooding back. I'd climbed out of bed around eight o'clock and after a trip to the gym, a long hot shower, and a breakfast sandwich that needed a little more spice, I was ready to start my day.

And the first thing on my agenda was to check my email.

My September schedule was set already. I was going to be making appearances every weekend in different cities and a once-a-week Wednesday meeting at the RLF office. And because I didn't have any other contracts, I had a lot of free time for my mind to spiral.

I knew Russ said he had it taken care of, and I trusted him. But without him telling me what was going on and without any work to do, I couldn't help but worry. So, I spent the day going over my contract with a fine-tooth comb. The next step was to reach out to my lawyer uncle to make sure I didn't screw myself by putting all my eggs in the RLF basket.

It was scary to feel so sure about something and then have it ripped away. I was so sure about RLF, and then Bowen swooped in and threw a curveball.

What if that happens with Russ?

I pushed that intrusive thought away.

As if she could feel me spiraling, my mother called.

"Hello?" I answered.

"I've been instructed by your father to let you know that he's taking me on a romantic getaway this weekend," my mom stated in lieu of a greeting.

I laughed lightly. "I'm glad to hear it. Do you know where you're going?"

"No, not yet."

"I'm excited for you, Mom! Okay, I see Dad trying to step his game up. Now you can stop living vicariously through me."

"Speaking of, how are things with you and your boyfriend?" She let out a little yelp. "It doesn't even feel real coming out of my mouth."

"It doesn't feel real hearing it either," I joked, pulling my legs under me on the couch.

"Is everything okay?"

I took a breath before opening my mouth.

That short pause was all she needed.

"What's wrong?" Her voice was a bit more serious. "Did something happen?"

"There was an event that I didn't go to on Saturday because I already had plans to go to Aaliyah's party, and another model went in my place. Apparently, there were some business decisions made and the partnership with RLF and Bowen is linked to the model who went instead of me. I gave up all my brand deals and contracts to do this. It was the kind of opportunity that was worth it though." I shook my head in disbelief. "And after I put all my eggs in this basket, I might get phased out."

"What?" Mom reacted. "And Russ let that happen?"

"Russ was with me. He found out about it when we got back yesterday afternoon."

"He's not going to let them phase you out."

I sighed. "I don't think he'll want to do it, but who knows if that will be the end result."

"What? What do you mean? Is he not the man you said he is?"

I swallowed around the lump in my throat. "No, Russ is perfect. Literally everything I ever said I wanted in a man."

"So, he's not going to let them phase you out. It's his company, right?"

"He's the CEO but he has a board he answers to. He's about to expand his brand. And the executives and board members who were at the event want the new model."

"Well, they have to still honor your contract," she pointed out.

"Yeah, I just got finished looking it over."

"You should call your uncle and have him take a look, too."

"Yeah, I'm going to. I sent him a text earlier about it."

"Good."

We were both quiet for a second.

She took a loud, audible breath. "This is just a minor hiccup, but you don't have to worry too much about it. What's for you is for you."

"I know. I just really wanted it to be for me." I groaned in frustration. "But this is what I get for putting all my eggs in one basket."

"When it's worth it, you take the risk. Is it worth it?"

I nodded even though she couldn't see me. "Yeah." I glanced at the printed version of the contract that was splayed across my coffee table. "It is. And they can't outright fire me. They'd have to pay me out, but they *could* replace me for the national campaign—"

"No!" my mom cried out, sounding as heartbroken as I felt.

"Yeah. And that's why I texted Unc. I've been reading over stuff this morning, wondering if I set myself up."

"Set yourself up?"

"I don't like not having options. If I'm tied to one thing and then that one thing screws me over, I'm left with nothing."

She was silent, and if it wasn't for the faint sound of the radio in the background, I would've thought she'd hung up.

"Nina, sweetheart." She paused. "Are you talking about this contract or are you talking about Russ?"

I swallowed hard. "I guess . . . both," I said slowly, reflecting on what I'd said. "All my eggs are in this RLF basket, so I have no choice but to hope it works out. And all of my eggs are in Russ's basket, too."

"The contract is a matter of business. Your uncle will help you figure out if you're getting the short end of the stick. But you didn't go into the contract lightly. You're smart and you did what was best for you. All of your eggs in that basket made sense because of what they told you. If they do something underhanded, that's a reflection of them, not you."

I nodded, taking in what she'd said. "That's true."

"But with that man of yours . . . that is a matter of the heart. And if Russ is as great as you say he is, all of your eggs *should* be in his basket."

"I know. It's just . . . unnerving."

"That's because you've never done it before."

I let my head drop back against the cushion. "And this is the first time I've ever wanted to do it. *That's* unnerving."

"Sounds like you're in love, sweetheart."

I closed my eyes and exhaled, letting out a noncommittal groan. "Mom, please."

"And if you love him, that means he's earned your love. So, he's not going to let his company do wrong by you."

"I know he's going to do what he can." I sat with that for a moment. "But if everyone wants me gone except for him and he refuses to fire me, then all of the hypothetical quid pro quo, sleeping your way to the top rhetoric would hold some weight, and then that would negatively impact him. And I can't let him go down like that. I won't let him go down like that."

"Do you believe he feels the same way about you?"

"Yes, I do."

"Then what are you worried about?"

"I'm worried because I don't have any control over anything."

"Do you trust him?"

"I do. I trust him."

As the words came out of my mouth, I realized how true they were. I knew it when Russ and I talked about it over the weekend. But as I talked to my mother, I realized the anxiety I felt had nothing to do with him and everything to do with my lack of control.

"Who is the new model?" Mom asked, interrupting my thoughts.

"I don't know."

"Well, whoever she is, she isn't you."

I smiled. "That's true," I murmured.

My mother always poured into me and reminded me who I was. I could always count on my parents. My eyes started welling up as I thought about how blessed I was to have their love and support.

"So how are we moving forward?" Mom asked.

"I'm going to do everything I can do. I'm not going to roll over and just give the job away. If they want to choose someone else, I'm going to make it the hardest decision they ever had to make." I exhaled, feeling lighter. "I just needed to vent and get it off my chest because I was stressing. But now . . . not so much."

"That's my girl!"

"Thank you, Mom."

"You don't have to thank me. Honestly, thank you! My daughter is living her dream, and I am so proud."

My eyes unexpectedly stung with tears. "Mom."

"And not to mention, it has been a treat to see you falling for this man all summer."

She ruined the moment.

Stifling a laugh, I groaned, "Mom."

"I knew it would happen. You just had to meet the right one. When I met your father . . ."

We talked for about twenty more minutes before we said goodbye.

My conversation with my mother was the reminder that I needed. I couldn't control what RLF did or who Bowen wanted to work with. The only thing I could control was what I would do with the opportunity in front of me. If it worked out with RLF, my career would reach new heights. If it worked out with Russ, he would forever have my heart.

I put my hand to my chest and exhaled.

It was unnerving, but the reward was worth the risk.

I got up to use the restroom, and as soon as I sat on the toilet, everything made sense.

"I fucking knew it," I muttered to myself as I realized my period had started.

All weekend I'd been feeling emotional. I had been in my feelings and off-kilter. The highs of rekindling with Russ and getting my back blown out every day for the last four days had me on cloud nine. But the lows of having to hide our relationship, having to put everything at risk, and having no clear way forward got to me. And then finding out not only did I miss the chance to impress Bowen but RLF also planned to cut my workload in half sent me to the pits of despair.

I got myself together, washed my hands, and returned to the living room. With a shake of my head, I grabbed my phone. Two missed text messages flashed across the screen.

Russ: I can't stop thinking about what you said about how nobody is bossier than an Aries.

Jazmyn: In the car and can't talk, but I can text. Is everything okay?

I checked the time and decided to text Jazz first to clarify some things. I was in a completely different frame of mind from when I texted her an hour ago.

> Nina: False alarm! My period came a couple days early so disregard what I said about the eggs and the basket. I was having a moment.
>
> Jazz: You said all your eggs were in one basket ten times last night. I was starting to think you had a literal basket of eggs you said it so much.

I cackled as I read her message.

> Jazz: I never thought I'd see the day that Nina Ford would be in love and ready to settle down.
>
> Nina: I know you're not talking! You said you were going to use this summer to fall on some dick and instead, you decided to fall in love.
>
> Jazz: I have no idea what you're talking about. And unfortunately, I have to go.
>
> Nina: You were smiling at that man so hard I could see your molars! And you only smile like that at someone who is dicking you down. Is this the same man you were talking about a few weeks ago?
>
> Jazz: GOODBYE NINA!

I snickered to myself.

Jazz might've been in denial about her feelings, but it was evident. I wasn't going to tease her too much because I knew broaching a new relationship was a big step for her. But she kept calling him her friend, and there was nothing friendly about their chemistry. They were really into each other, and I was happy to see Jazmyn happy—especially after the last couple years she'd had.

Still amused with myself, I picked up the phone to call Russ instead of texting him back.

"Hello?" He answered on the first ring and my lips pulled upward immediately.

"Hey," I greeted him. "Why are you randomly thinking about astrology?"

"Remedy walked her ass in my office trying to tell me what we're going to do. I had to remind her that this is my shit."

I burst out laughing. "Did she at least have a good idea?"

"Yeah, it was good. But that wasn't the point. She should've knocked."

The warmth spread through me with each chuckle. "You're right. That was very rude of her. But I'm glad she brought you a good idea."

"What are you up to? Everything okay?"

"Yeah, I'm good, actually," I told him as I climbed off the couch. I made my way to the kitchen. "After I eat, I'm going to record some content and then get my bag packed for Atlanta."

"Okay, that's what's up. You need anything? I can send my assistant to the store."

I smiled. "No, thank you. Well actually"—I switched the phone to my other ear—"there's one thing I could use. What's the name of the model that'll be working the schedule with me?"

"Gabriella . . . Gabriella Pace."

22

I hadn't talked to Gabby much since the conference in New York, but I reached out to her after Russ told me she was the model in question. I didn't tell her how the circumstances surrounding her new opportunity impacted me. It wasn't her fault or her problem. So, I just congratulated her and planned to see her when she came back to the East Coast.

Russ's meeting with his lawyer was short, but it gave me hope. Russ was advised to wait until after the success of the runway show to approach the board. The idea was that the momentum of positive press and the uptick in sales would help alleviate concerns. In the meantime, my contract and the company's fraternization policy were being analyzed to see if there was a way around it. When the lawyer suggested a relationship disclosure form and a consensual relationship agreement, Russ had him start the process of drafting it that same day. It seemed a little too easy, but I wanted it to work out. So, I went with it.

If Russ wasn't stressing it, I wasn't going to stress it either.

After talking to my mom, I made peace with the fact that they'd brought on another model to encroach on my workload. After talking to Russ, I was happy to hear that I'd be working with Gabby. It wasn't an ideal situation, but I was genuinely happy for her. After talking to Gabby, I realized that Bowen was also based in LA, so it made sense. But after I arrived at the RLF meeting on Wednesday, I was alarmed by the reaction I was met with when I entered the showroom.

"Nina, I'm so sorry!" Taisha gasped before enveloping me in a hug out of nowhere. One of her locs got tangled in the clasp of my bracelet as she tried to pull away.

"Oh no, wait," I demanded.

She grabbed my wrist. "It's my fault. I kind of ambushed you."

She carefully unhooked herself and then stared at it for a moment. "Fantasy," she read the engraved words. "Aw, this is gorgeous."

"Thank you."

She took a step back and eyed me. "You're okay?"

"Yeah, of course," I answered.

"We heard the news. I can't believe they're replacing you. It doesn't make any sense," Jonah expressed, coming over to us with the two others right behind him.

"You should've been there on Saturday. Bowen would've loved you," Jacqueline pointed out.

"Yeah. They would have," Matias agreed. "Are they getting rid of you?"

"What are you going to do?" Jacqueline asked.

All of them were staring at me expectantly.

"I'm going to do my job," I told them, looking around the group. "I appreciate the concern, but it's all going to work out."

"How are you so calm about all of this?" Taisha wondered.

"Well, what is she going to do? Go to Remedy and Russell and demand they reconsider?" Jonah scoffed.

"That's not a bad idea." Jacqueline chewed her thumb.

"Yes, it is," Taisha asserted. "It's a terrible idea."

"Why would she set her up like that?" Matias questioned.

"Because if they get away with this, it sets a precedent," Jacqueline explained. "If they can get rid of Nina like this, they can get rid of any one of us next."

"We've shot all of the promo footage so no matter what, our pictures are the ones that'll be in stores and on the website and social media." Jonah folded his arms over his chest. "Our contracts protect us."

"They don't protect us," Taisha countered. "But they do agree to pay us out and—"

Jacqueline put her hands to her face. "After the way they were raving about Nina, if they can do it to her, who is next?"

The door to the showroom flew open. The sound of Angelica's heels clicked as she approached. "Why are you standing around?"

she asked in a sharp tone. Then she pointed to the table with paperwork on it. "Let's get started."

The conversation stopped immediately, and we silently rushed over to the worktable. The lead stylist broke down what we were taking with us to wear on our visits to the stores in Atlanta. She took us one by one to the racks and gave us our wardrobe. While I was with her, I heard the others speculating about my time with RLF and being upset on my behalf. After putting the outfits in garment bags, we were sent to the conference room to meet with Lori and Remedy. It was the first time I'd seen them since the last photoshoot, and so much had changed since that day.

"A lot has changed since we were last here," Remedy started, reading my mind. "You were popular content creators and now you are models for the next 'it' brand." She smiled as Lori held up a large posterboard. "You are officially commercial models!"

Seeing the image, I gasped.

It was beautiful.

Wearing white tops and jeans, the five of us looked incredible. The poses, the background, the editing, the clothes—all of it worked. We all started talking at once.

"Oh my God!"

"This is great!"

"Wow!"

"Love it!"

"Holy shit!"

Our praise for what we were seeing seemed to shake off the uneasiness that clouded our meeting since my arrival.

"You'll have a busy couple of days in Atlanta," Lori pointed out. "The images in this series will be in the stores that you're going to. Your itinerary has been emailed to you. You'll all be staying in the same hotel, and you'll be taking the same flight. We have a large market in Atlanta so even though you'll be traveling together and staying in the same hotel, you will be in different stores."

Remedy looked around the conference table at each of us. "You will be representing RLF so please review your contract and the terms and conditions of the role. Please reread the code of conduct and fraternization policies"—her eyes lingered on me for a moment too long—"so we are moving into these new heights with no incidents or issues. We are investing a lot of money into the runway show, so we want to feed off the Fashion Week buzz with these appearances. You'll be in Atlanta first and then New York, Miami, Los Angeles. You . . ." She grabbed her phone and looked at it for a second before excusing herself from the room.

I couldn't help but wonder if the call was from her brother.

"You'll be in New York doing appearances around the city ahead of the runway show," Lori stated, picking up where Remedy left off. "The show will be on Monday, so you'll be able to watch it online. Any questions?" Lori looked around inquisitively.

I shook my head. Someone else murmured a "no" but most of us remained silent.

"You have early flights in the morning, and we still need your content posted on social media, so we'll conclude this meeting if there are no questions," she continued.

We exchanged goodbyes and as soon as we were at the elevator and out of earshot, we started talking again.

"They didn't even mention the new model," Taisha pointed out. "What is going on?"

"Do they think sending us an email with the information is sufficient?" Jacqueline questioned. "Because I think we all deserve an explanation!"

"How are you, Nina?" Jonah asked, rubbing my shoulder.

I opened my mouth to respond but was interrupted.

"Nina, can I speak with you?" Remedy's voice cut through our conversation.

Jonah's hand instantly fell from my shoulder, and we all whipped around to face her. The five of us froze, unsure of how much she'd heard. The elevator dinged, highlighting the silence we stood in.

"I'll see you tomorrow," I told the other models as they rushed into the elevator. Walking toward the woman with the serious expression on her face, I braced myself. "Hey, Remedy."

"I want to be clear that the decision to bring on an additional plus model was a business decision and not a personal one. Your face is still the face that'll appear in the in-store advertising. But in a couple weeks, Gabriella will be joining you in your appearance at the Bowen stores in Miami. Is that going to be a problem?"

"No."

"Good." She gave a definitive nod. "Your response to the email welcoming Gabriella to the team was gracious. Your social media posts have been consistently reaching our target audience. And I've heard that the other models have been speculating about the events that took place this weekend. From what Angelica told me, you didn't engage." She took a step closer. "We have a board meeting on Friday and we're selecting our final look. I'm going to nominate you to walk it."

My eyebrows flew up. "You're going to nominate me?"

"Yes."

I was not expecting that.

"Oh, wow, thank you!" I put my hand to my chest. "That would be amazing."

With a self-satisfied smile, she nodded again. "There will be a vote. But Angelica has been speaking about you to the coordinators as we've been putting together the show. Russell's been speaking highly of you since we brought you on, so even though he doesn't vote on this, if Angelica and I are for it, he'll approve it. And I'll be echoing their sentiments with the board when we finalize the vision. The decision will be announced on Monday and if selected, your events for next week will change because you'll have rehearsal."

"Okay." I nodded. "Thank you."

She picked up her phone and concluded the conversation. "Make it a good trip."

I didn't even get a chance to say thank you or goodbye because she'd already turned her back to me.

"Russell, I have news," she answered as she walked away.

Knowing it was Russ on the phone with her, I felt warmth spreading through me. Trying to shake it off, I pressed the elevator call button.

When I got home, I posted on social media, packed the clothes I'd gotten from Angelica, talked to Russ for about an hour, and then got a good night's sleep.

I had an early flight in the morning.

I got to the airport, checked my bags, and then walked to my gate. I saw Taisha sitting by herself and I approached.

"Hey," I greeted, taking a seat next to her.

"Morning," she replied giddily. She took her headphones off and rested them around her neck. "How did things go with Remedy yesterday?"

"Pretty good actually."

"Did she—hey, Matias!"

I looked behind me and waved at him. Not too far behind him were Jacqueline and Jonah. When the five of us were together, I felt the group's attention shift to me. They all wanted to know what happened with Remedy.

"She wanted to make sure I knew that it was business and not personal," I told them with a shrug. "She said that it'll be fine, so I'm going to choose to believe her."

They mostly seemed satisfied with my answer, and we boarded our flight to Atlanta. They booked me in a seat next to Jacqueline and she managed to talk the entire trip. I'd nodded off for at least thirty minutes and when I woke up, she was still talking. I was thankful they didn't have us sharing rooms.

"I made it safely," I told Aaliyah over the phone after checking into my hotel room.

"Okay, good," she replied, a hint of relief in her voice. "I'm glad you're safe. There's a storm here and I was worried about you."

I glanced toward the window and the sun was shining bright. "It's clear skies over here. But since it's raining, does that change your plans to go to the fair with your man?"

"I think we're still going. He has to work on Friday so today was the only day we could go."

I smiled as I listened to her talk about his plans for her. It made me happy to hear how happy she was. After the summer she had and the dates she'd experienced, she deserved to find a man who would love her right and treat her well.

"And what about you and your situation?" she inquired.

I pulled the dress I'd planned to wear to dinner out of my bag. "Which situation?"

"The Russ being your boss situation. What other situations do you have?" she laughed.

"Well, the Russ situation is the main one. He says he's handling it. Paperwork is being drafted and we actually went out last night. It was a small restaurant on the outskirts of town. Low lights, very intimate, extremely romantic. But I couldn't help but feel like we were hiding in the shadows. Fashion Week is going to be big—possibly for the both of us—so we can't afford to get caught."

"But if he's working on it and y'all are back to going out on dates, his plan must be legit."

"I'm choosing to believe that's going to work out. Especially because I have another situation. RLF brought on another model to replace me."

"What?" she screeched.

I told her about the RLF link to Bowen and Bowen's preference for Gabby.

"I'm so sorry," Aaliyah wailed.

"No, it's fine."

"If you weren't at my party, you would've been at that event and—"

"Liyah," I interrupted. "It's not your fault! There was no way I was missing your party. You're my best friend and it was your thirtieth birthday. I'm glad I was there."

"But I feel bad you missed out on Bowen."

"Bowen should feel bad they missed out on me!"

We talked for a few more minutes and then we got off the phone. I took a shower and then climbed in bed. I briefly texted with Russ before I took a nap. He was in and out of meetings finalizing the runway show and didn't have a lot of time, so I told him we'd talk later. I edited content and responded to comments until I drifted

to sleep. When I woke up from a nap, I got dressed and then went
to dinner with the other models.

We were having a good time, exchanging stories in a more relaxed manner than we had the first time we'd gotten together. A
few weeks ago, after The Player's Ball, we were getting to know
each other. Our dinner was our first time together in a relaxed
atmosphere and free from RLF eyes and ears.

And it was a time!

I'd just finished laughing at something Matias said about his
DMs being flooded when my phone vibrated against the table. I
picked it up and smiled.

> Russ: I'm finally home and the only thing I can think
> about is this place I want to take you. Are you free right
> now?
>
> Nina: You had a long day!
>
> Russ: Yeah, I'm going back and forth about what I want
> to do for the runway show. Work stuff that I'm trying to
> leave at work. What are you up to? Are you free?
>
> Nina: I'm at dinner with the others. Where is this place
> you're thinking about taking me?
>
> Russ: Let me pick you up from the airport on Sunday
> and surprise you.
>
> Nina: I'll be getting off the plane with other people who
> represent your company.
>
> Russ: I'll figure it out. Just be ready on Sunday. And call
> me when you're free.

"—and clearly Nina's got one," Taisha teased.

I looked up from my phone to find everyone's eyes on me. I
wasn't texting for that long, but I clearly missed something.

"What did I miss?" I asked, locking my phone and placing it on
my lap.

"We were going around asking who was single," Jacqueline

answered before leaning forward. "From the way you were smiling and texting, I would guess you aren't single."

"The way she keeps dodging my advances, I'd guess she's not single either," Jonah chimed in.

I laughed. "Y'all are funny."

"So again, dating? Single? In a relationship?" Taisha wondered, pointing at me. "What's your situation?"

"I'm not single," I answered.

"Okay!" Taisha reacted. "You're the only one of us in a relationship."

"I figured you had a man when you didn't want me to take you out. But since you didn't mention him when we were talking about people sliding into the DMs, I feel like I have a chance," Jonah joked.

I laughed, pushing his shoulder. "Shut up!"

"That's a good point," Taisha acknowledged. "How does your man handle what you do? My ex was so jealous. We were together before I kinda of blew up on social media and everything was cool. But the more attention I got online, the more jealous and ridiculous he'd become."

Jacqueline nodded in agreement. "Mine was the same way." She pointed at Jonah and Matias. "If we were still dating, he would have lost his mind because I'm on a trip that includes these two fine-ass men. His jealousy got to be too much."

I remembered the only time Russ seemed jealous. Just the mere thought of how he fucked me behind that partition as a result of that jealousy got me hot. I squeezed my thighs together and refocused on the conversation.

"My ex was like that, too," Matias mentioned. "She hated if I did a collab with anyone she thought I had too much chemistry with."

"I've had women not want a relationship with me because they assume I'm fucking everybody I work with." Jonah shook his head. "I guess I look like I'm a player, even though I'm not."

Jacqueline tapped her chin. "It's interesting . . . Nina looks like a player, yet she's in a relationship. Jonah looks like a sweetheart, yet he's not beating the player allegations."

"How do I look like a player?" I wondered, trying not to laugh with the others.

"You just got this look about you," Matias agreed. "You look like you got a boyfriend, a side-dude, and a husband."

I cracked up. "That's not the case."

"Just the one man, then?" Taisha questioned.

"Yes! And I'm not a cheater," I explained. "I would never have a side-dude or cheat on my man. I believe in being upfront and honest."

Matias looked at me knowingly. "You had hoes, didn't you?"

Everyone burst out laughing.

"What!" I screeched.

He pointed at me. "I know a reformed player when I see one. I know my people. You weren't a cheater because you weren't ever committed to one person."

I was weak.

The waiter placed each of our desserts in front of us. As soon as she left the table, I tried to defend myself. "Does that make me a player?"

"Yes!" they said in unison before we erupted into joyous laughter.

Matias sat back in his chair. "I have the mindset that when I meet the woman I want to be with forever, that's when I'll settle down. Until then . . ." He shrugged.

"How did you know he was the one you wanted to give up your player ways for?" Taisha asked me.

Twisting the bracelet around my wrist, I grinned. "I just knew."

"When we get back, I have a date with a Maryland Monarchs cheerleader," Matias told us. "Maybe I'll just know."

"The professional football team?" Taisha asked.

He nodded. "Yup."

"Are you interested in her or are you interested in her discounted game ticket?" Jonah asked. "Because you were talking about a different woman earlier and you never even mentioned a cheerleader."

Matias looked shocked.

"Oop!" I grinned, looking between the two men.

"Matias!" Jacqueline cried out. "You're really a player? You'd date someone for tickets?"

"I didn't realize cheerleaders got discounted tickets," Taisha mused. "I knew the football players got their one discounted ticket. I guess I didn't realize the cheerleaders did, too."

The line of questioning turned to Matias, and I was relieved to have the heat off me. They all knew a lot more about football than I did so I just ate my dessert. Flipping my phone over in my lap, I smiled.

> Russ: I miss you.

My heart skipped a beat as I reread the text again. Before his house was finished and he moved to Richland, we'd tell each other that we wanted and needed to see each other. We'd said those words jokingly. But we never explicitly said it and I didn't expect the reaction I had seeing it typed out.

> Nina: I miss you, too.

"I love the New York Nighthawks," Taisha said. "I have a player in my DMs right now."

I jumped back into the conversation at just the right time.

"Which one?" I asked.

We sat at the table for maybe an hour longer, talking, laughing, and mentally preparing. We didn't know what the weekend had in store for us, but we were excited about it.

We didn't get back to our hotel until close to eleven o'clock. After a shower and a quick conversation with Russ, I fell soundly to sleep. Friday morning, I jumped out of the bed and got myself together. After hair and makeup, I carefully put on the cream-colored fit-and-flare minidress. I styled it with brown booties and a matching brown bag. The blue denim jacket was heavily distressed and the perfect cropped length. When I took a step back,

I checked myself out in the mirror and smiled. I took a picture to send to Russ and then left to catch my ride to the first stop.

> Russ: You are so fucking beautiful.
>
> Nina: Thank you. Send me one of you.

The image that came back was Russ's sexy ass sitting at his desk. He was holding the phone from a low position, so it showed him at an upward angle. Every time I'd seen him from that angle, I was under him. I shifted in my seat as I complimented him.

> Nina: What I wouldn't do to be under that desk...
>
> Russ: Don't start. I have a meeting in a few minutes, and I don't need my dick hard thinking about you under my desk.
>
> Nina: Or on top of your desk. Or bent over your desk.

My phone rang and his name flashed across the screen. Grinning, I answered, "Hello?"

"Just the thought of you is all it took. You happy?" he demanded good-naturedly.

I giggled. "A little bit, yeah."

"You want my dick hard while I'm trying to get these people to understand my vision and execute it within the budget?"

"I want your dick hard all the time," I whispered, hoping the driver didn't hear me over his radio.

"You would say some shit like that." He let out a light chuckle. "How are you? Are you ready for today? You need anything?"

I smoothed down the skirt of my dress. "I don't know what to expect, but I'm looking forward to it."

"You do you. There's no precedent for this. You and the others are the first to do this for us so you can make it whatever you want it to be. Part of the reason you were selected was because of your personalities. So just wow them like you do everyone else that crosses your path."

My cheeks heated under his praise. "Thank you," I murmured. "How are you? Are you ready for your meeting?"

"We have a lot to do today and a lot of decisions to be made. We probably won't get done until late because it's crunch time. The Fashion Week meeting is in five minutes. The show coordinator from New York that I've been working with comes in today, so it's a lot going on. It's . . . a lot."

"And you have it under control," I assured him. "You literally built this brand and this company from the ground up. You got enough sponsors to make this show a thing. You've invited the right people to give it enough buzz. Everything RLF is, is because of you. And now you're doing a runway show in New York during Fashion Week. It's a lot but you've already done a lot and you will continue to do a lot." I paused, hoping the truth of my words comforted him. "You got this. What you were doing is what got you here, so keep doing it. Don't change up because you're going to a new level."

"You either."

I smiled, feeling his encouragement. "I know you'll be busy all day but talk to you tonight?"

"Let me know how things are going. And let me know when you're done."

"I don't want to interrupt if your meeting is running—"

"I'll always make time for you," he interrupted. "Hit me up when you're free. I want to know how it's going."

My belly fluttered. "Okay."

We said our goodbyes and I put my hand to my chest and exhaled. The warmth of his words eased through my body and reminded me of how much affection I had for him.

I love that man.

I didn't even have a chance to shake off the thought because the driver pulled to an abrupt stop. I looked around and realized I was at the first store.

"Thank you," I told the driver as I stepped out of the car.

With my bag in one hand and my phone in the other, I double-checked the itinerary to make sure I was in the right place.

"Here goes," I breathed as I plastered a bright smile on my face and walked through the double doors.

Over the next forty-eight hours, I visited six different stores. I interacted with the staff, styled customers, created social media content, and became a live mannequin. It went by fast and even though it was fun, I was looking forward to getting back home and seeing Russ.

After grabbing my luggage, I waved to the other models as I headed toward the door. I'd only made it two steps before I realized they were on my heels.

"Anyone heading uptown and want to share a car?" Jacqueline asked.

"I'm parked in the deck," Jonah told her. "I can give you a ride if you want."

She bounced on the balls of her feet. "Yes, please! Thank you!"

He pointed at the rest of us. "Anyone else need a ride?"

Matias nodded. "Yeah, man. Good looking out."

"I have someone coming, but thank you," I told him, stopping just before the exit. I rolled my luggage to the right and stood in front of the large window to get out of the way. The afternoon sun was shining bright in the sky and the heat was evident as soon as the sliding door opened.

"Me too," Taisha answered, slowing to stand next to me.

After we said goodbye to the three of them, she turned to look at me. "You know Jonah is in love with you, right?"

I shook my head. "He isn't. He's just a flirt."

She gave me a knowing look before she pulled out her phone. "He likes you. And if anything changes with you and your boyfriend, keep him in mind."

I let out a confused laugh. "Are you supposed to be his wing woman or something?"

"No. I just know how hard it is to be in a relationship and do this job unless you're with someone who understands the business."

"I can imagine. But I'm good."

She pulled her sunglasses out of her bag and slid them onto her face. "I loved my ex and I wanted to make it work. But he didn't understand the nature of the job. He would get jealous at every message, every comment, every dumbass emoji under my pictures. Then he became suspicious of everything I did, everyone I hung out with . . . He broke up with me because he accused me of cheating on him with this guy I did a photoshoot with." She pulled out her phone and showed me the photo in question and it was a sexy yet professional shot. "So now, I only date models, actors, musicians, professional athletes." She twisted her lips. "But I really did love that accountant."

"The man for you is going to love everything about you." I put my hand on her shoulder. "Including your job and your passions."

She smiled. "Is yours in the limelight?"

"He's very supportive of what I do," I answered, shifting my gaze to the cars pulling up on the other side of the window. "Supportive, encouraging, respectful." Realizing I was gushing, I put on my sunglasses and stopped talking.

Taisha bumped me with her hip. "You sound like you have a good one."

My lips curled upward even though I tried to fight against it. Fortunately, my phone vibrated in my pocket, and I had a reason to distract myself from the giddy feeling talking about Russ gave me.

> Russ: I'm pulling up in a white Jeep with dark tint.

"Look at that smile!" Taisha teased before giggling. "I'm happy for you, girl." She checked her phone. "My sister is here. I'll see you Wednesday."

"See you Wednesday!" I called behind her as she exited the airport.

> Nina: Taisha just walked out so I'm going to wait a minute and then head out to you.
>
> Russ: Take your time. I'm not going anywhere.

Grinning, I put my phone in my bag. There was no one around so I didn't even have to mask it. Pulling the suitcase behind me, I swept my eyes up and down the pickup line until I saw a white Jeep with tinted windows. As I approached, Russ slipped a baseball cap on and hopped out. Wearing jean shorts and a white T-shirt, he stepped onto the curb and grabbed me around my waist. Holding me in his arms, he lifted me from my feet and buried his face in my neck.

I squealed, holding him around his neck.

A horn honked and I happened to look up just in time to see Taisha in the passenger side of a blue sedan. I froze, my body tensed, as she pointed at Russ's back and gave me a thumbs-up before the car continued out of the airport exit loop.

Sliding me down his body, Russ placed me on solid ground and crashed his mouth into mine. The kiss took my breath away and cleared my mind. Everything faded away except him, his hands, his kiss, and his passion. I gripped his T-shirt and pulled him closer, deepening the kiss. We didn't say anything to one another. But what we communicated was full of emotional words and declarations that gave me butterflies.

"You can't park here," a gruff voice yelled at us. "Move it along."

We pulled apart abruptly and I saw a police officer angrily gesturing.

"Move it!" he yelled louder.

"Okay, okay," Russ replied, putting his hand on the small of my back and opening the passenger-side door for me.

After getting me into the car, he grabbed my bags, put them in the back, and then climbed into the front seat.

"It's good to see you," I told him.

He turned the car on and grinned. "You missed me?"

I nodded. "I did."

As he pulled off and headed toward the highway, he grabbed my hand and brought it to his lips. "Good. I missed you, too. I'm glad you're back."

"I'm glad to be back."

We talked about my trip and what he did over that morning. As we turned into my neighborhood, I dragged my fingers over the dashboard and took in the luxury features of the Jeep.

"Did you rent this for our date?" I wondered.

"Yeah. I knew I wanted to be the one to pick you up, but I didn't know if the others knew what my car looked like."

My eyes widened. "You rented this just to pick me up?"

"Well, I wanted to be the one to pick you up, so I made a way to do it and still keep us safe."

My stomach flipped. "Russ . . ." I waited until he parked to finish my thought. "You didn't have to do that."

He swiped his thumb across my cheek. "There was no way I wasn't going to be the person to pick you up." He leaned over the middle console and planted a sweet kiss against my lips.

"That's so sweet. I was trying to figure out what the surprise could be," I murmured between kisses. "But honestly, I don't know if anything is topping that."

He pulled out of the kiss and stared at me. "There's been a change of plans."

I quirked an eyebrow. "Oh, really?"

"The plans I had for us had to be rescheduled because you have an early morning tomorrow."

Confused, I frowned a little. "I don't have anything tomorrow. I have a nail appointment on Tuesday."

"You have a fitting at six o'clock tomorrow morning." He searched my face for a moment. "You're walking in the show."

23

The RLF runway show was taking place on Monday, one week from my first fitting. The models were selected at the beginning of the summer and were measured and assigned outfits long before I was brought onto the RLF team. So, when I arrived for the early Monday morning fitting, I was the last piece of the puzzle.

The pieces showcased were the highlights of the upcoming spring-summer line. Everything I'd worn and highlighted on social media were fall and winter ready-to-wear pieces that were available on the site and in select stores. The outfits I'd seen for the show were cool and interesting, but still wearable. I was fitted for the final piece: a white asymmetrical dress combined with a black sheer trench coat. While Angelica checked the fit of the dress on my body, I learned that I was slated to walk down the runway with Russ.

Excited was an understatement.

I got goose bumps as I imagined being on a catwalk for the first time and then sharing that moment with Russ. I was so giddy I could barely stand still. As I stared at myself in the mirror, I felt overwhelmed with joy, pride, excitement, and love. I was in a gorgeous outfit that Russ designed . . . as I prepared to be in the RLF fashion show during New York Fashion Week . . . where I would be walking down the catwalk with the designer . . . who happened to be the man I loved.

Biting the inside of my cheek, I blinked back tears.

Russ's vision and concept were realized from the wardrobe, set design, runway setup, and music selection. I was so happy for him, and proud of him. I'd spent Monday and Tuesday working with Lori, Angelica, the design team, and the show coordinator. It was a lot, but I wanted to do well—not just for myself but also for him. I wanted to make sure I made his first show a success. But more than anything, I wanted to make him proud.

Russ left for New York on Tuesday and wouldn't be back for a week. He was so busy getting everything ready for the show, we only talked before bed. He told me he wanted me to text him updates, but I didn't want to disturb him throughout the day. But after Wednesday's fitting, I couldn't help myself. I sent him a text message as I walked to the conference room for the meeting.

Nina: This dress is so sexy! I want it.

Russ: It's yours.

Grinning, I started to reply.

"If it isn't Ms. Runway Model herself," Jacqueline remarked from out of nowhere.

I almost dropped my phone.

Regaining my composure, I slipped my phone into my pocket and greeted her. "Hey!"

"Congratulations are in order. I wish it was me, but I'm not a hater."

I nodded. "That's fair. Thank you."

We walked through the conference room doors and Taisha squealed, "Congratulations!"

Her joy was infectious, and I couldn't help but giggle a bit. "Thank you!"

She jumped to her feet and clapped enthusiastically. The three of us were the only ones in there so we were a little louder than usual. When I was close enough, she hugged me.

"And don't think I didn't see you with that tall piece of work at the airport," Taisha mentioned. "He seemed *very* happy to see you."

I laughed nervously as we took our seats. I tried to read her face and her expression, but I couldn't.

She didn't see who I was with, did she?

"Who was happy to see Nina?" Jonah asked from behind me. "Nobody is happier to see her than me."

"Her man," Jacqueline said in a singsong voice.

"Maybe we should've hung around to check out Jonah's competition," Matias joked as the guys took their seats at the table.

"The way that man had her in the air when I drove by, I don't think there is any competition," Taisha speculated. "Sorry, Jonah."

"What did he look like?" Jacqueline asked her.

Panic swept through me.

Russ had kissed me and made me forget that Taisha was driving by, looking directly at us. The same anxiety and worry that tightened my gut on Sunday afternoon returned, with more intensity. And unfortunately, Russ wasn't there to kiss the dread away.

I swallowed hard.

"He's over six feet. I could only see his legs and the back of his neck, but he looked light brown skinned"—she pointed to Matias "—like his complexion. He had on a hat, T-shirt, and jorts."

"What the hell are jorts?" Jonah asked with a chuckle.

"Jean shorts," she answered.

"Is that why you're looking so shook, Nina?" Jacqueline wondered. "Your boyfriend wears jorts."

Everyone looked at me and all I could do was put my head in my hands while they laughed. Even though it was only the five of us in the conference room, I couldn't help feeling like things were getting a little too out of control.

Taisha started rubbing my back comfortingly. "Jorts aside . . . That man was so engulfed in Nina, I couldn't even see his face."

This is good. I lifted my head and looked at her. *Nothing to worry about.*

"His arms were wrapped around her so tight, I couldn't even see them," she continued. "And I told my sister how happy I was for her. And then I get an email Monday morning saying she got picked to walk the runway and I was even happier. Am I jealous? Yes. But am I happy? Also yes."

"We are all happy for you," Jonah told me. "But if anything happens between you and your man, I'm here. Taisha talking about you being hugged up on like that and seeing that you're good is a good thing. Am I jealous? Yes. But am I happy? Also yes."

All of us cracked up.

"I appreciate all of you. Thank you. And I'll represent for us on the runway," I promised them.

"Do you think they picked you to make up for the fact that they are giving away half of your appearances to the other model?" Jacqueline asked.

All of us stopped and looked at her.

"Jacqueline!" Taisha admonished her. "Uh-uh, don't do that."

"Whoa . . ." Jonah reacted.

"That's not cool," Matias muttered.

Jacqueline's eyes got big as she looked around. "What? I didn't mean it like that."

"It's fine," I assured them. "It very well may have been part of their reasoning for choosing me."

I didn't mention the fact that Angelica had noticed my walk a few weeks prior and told me she would be nominating me. Because while that was true, I didn't know the motivations of the others who voted. Remedy had pulled me aside to address the Gabby situation in the same breath as the runway show. And Russ was my man and had all but promised me he would make sure I was okay. Having everyone think I got the runway opportunity as a peace offering was the safest bet.

"What do they have you wearing? What do they have you doing?" Taisha asked, trying to change the subject.

As I answered her questions, people entered the conference room. There was a buzz of excitement as almost every RLF staff person I'd ever crossed paths with filed in. When Remedy and Lori walked in, we quieted and gave them our undivided attention.

"Fashion Week kicks off on Friday, and our very first Fashion Week appearance is on Monday at eleven o'clock," Remedy announced before breaking down everything we needed to know. "Our spokesmodels will be in New York for promotion over the weekend. On Friday and Saturday, they have in-person appearances. On Sunday and Monday, they will be promoting the show. And speaking of spokesmodels, Nina will be walking down the runway for us."

Everyone clapped politely, and grinning proudly, I waved.

After some additional information, the meeting concluded, but Remedy and Lori asked us to stay behind.

"You already know your duties for the New York store visits, just like in Atlanta," Lori told us. "But you'll be in New York on Sunday and Monday for content creation. On Sunday, you'll be talking to other fashion heads about what they are thinking and expecting from RLF. On Monday, you'll be talking to spectators after the runway show."

"You aren't journalists," Remedy reminded us. "No one is expecting you to do interviews. However, you are forward-thinking fashion content creators, so your take on Fashion Week, specifically the RLF show, should be highlighted. Everything you do should be catered to your personality. We hired you for your style and your authenticity." She turned her head to me. "Nina, you will need to report directly to Russell, Angelica, and the show coordinator because you will have rehearsal, final fittings, and other things that may interfere with your ability to be at your store post for long stretches of time."

"Should I contact the store to let them know?" I wondered, confused as to why I was just hearing about the changes.

"No. Lori has contacted them, and Gabriella will be in New York to take over your stores," Remedy informed me. "You just focus on creating RLF content and getting ready for the show. You will have eyes on you."

"Oh . . . okay."

"Angelica is waiting for you all to pick up your clothes for the weekend. See you in New York."

Without waiting for us to respond, Remedy turned on her heel and left the room. Lori gave us a small smile and asked if we had any questions. I rose to my feet and left the room with everyone else.

What does she mean I'll have eyes on me? Because I'm on the runway?

"Do you think they are going to compare you and the Gabriella chick and make a decision on who they are going to keep this weekend?" Jacqueline asked.

"What is wrong with you?" Taisha asked her.

"What?" Jacqueline stamped her foot. "I'm just trying to under-stand what's going on!"

I was lost in my thoughts and barely participated in the conver-sation. Between Jacqueline's conspiracy theories and finding out last minute that my schedule had changed, I was thrown off. It wasn't until I was in the elevator, holding clothes I was expected to wear over the weekend to my chest, that I realized my job might actually be at stake.

What if the runway isn't an opportunity but an audition?

The thought haunted me and there was no one I could talk to about it. I couldn't talk to my man because it was his company, and I didn't want to create strife between us. If it was the best business decision to go with Gabby, I would have to accept that from the CEO, but at the same time, I would feel a way if my man made that decision. I wouldn't want him to do anything that would neg-atively impact his business, but I would also want him to fight for me. It was a complicated situation and I wouldn't even want to put that in the air for him to deal with.

Especially with so much on his plate right now.

I couldn't talk to my family and friends about it because they were going to say the same thing I'd been telling myself: whatever is meant for me is for me. And I believed that wholeheartedly. There was literally nothing I could do but my best so that was the plan. But I couldn't help how bad I wanted it.

The opportunity to walk in a runway show was huge. Being one of the faces of the RLF brand was also huge. But the other factor that wasn't explicitly spelled out in the contract but was just as big of an opportunity was the access. The rooms that I'd be invited into and the people I'd be meeting expanded with each trip, each event, and each photo op. The ability to translate my relatability from social media to real life would increase my capital. It wasn't just about money. It was about further legitimizing my career and normalizing beauty and fashion for all sizes.

I knew what I brought to the table, so it wasn't a me versus Gabby situation, as Jacqueline kept bringing up. It was me versus me. I needed to do my best. I needed to win everyone over. I needed to keep my job.

So on Thursday night, after checking into a gorgeous New York boutique hotel and getting changed for the RLF model dinner, I had a renewed sense of purpose.

"I didn't realize we were dressing up," Matias commented when he saw me.

"Damn, Nina," Jonah added.

I did a little pose in my orange halter dress, making sure they didn't miss my blue stiletto heels and matching clutch.

"It's a work trip so I came to work," I told them as I walked with them to the restaurant next door.

As soon as we walked through the door, Jacqueline and Taisha flagged us down.

"We have a reservation under Lori Smith," Jonah told the maître d', pointing beyond him. He nodded and had us follow him to the table. We were just about to take our seats when I noticed there was a sixth chair. Out of the corner of my eye, I saw someone with a huge Afro coming straight toward me.

"Nina!"

"Gabby!"

We exclaimed at the same time, embracing each other.

"I didn't realize you were going to be here," I told her, completely surprised to see her.

"I got in a couple hours ago," Gabby informed me with a smile. "I told Lori I wanted to surprise you!"

"Well, you absolutely did." I turned to the others. "Let me introduce you to the RLF models. This is Taisha, Jacqueline, Jonah, and Matias."

She shook each of their hands as I said their names. When she stepped back, I put my arm around her.

"Everyone, I'd like for you to meet Gabriella Pace."

"Gabriella Pace," Jacqueline repeated before her eyes got big. "Your replacement?"

The awkward pause that hung in the air seemed to quiet the whole restaurant, even though no one heard her but us.

"What?" Gabby asked, looking at me and then back at Jacqueline.

"You're the one they are giving—"

"Jacqueline, that's enough," I interrupted. "There's room for both of us."

"Barely," a wrinkled old man commented from the next table.

His slim wife laughed along with him.

Still standing, I stared at them until it became uncomfortable for everybody.

"What are you staring at?" the old man asked.

With my top lip curled in disgust, I gave him a look. "Not much."

He started stuttering and sputtering with indignation and I held up my hand as I took my seat.

Looking around at my dinner companions, I shook my head. "I'm not about to go back and forth with someone with one credit hour of life left."

They burst out laughing and the waiter came just in time to quell that situation. Even though I was choosing to move on, Jacqueline's comments were still stirring within me. Because it seemed that even though I wasn't in competition with Gabby, we were still being positioned as competition against one another.

It was an odd and uncomfortable realization.

No matter how I framed it or how I approached it, there were going to be folks who pitted us against each other. No matter what I did, people like Jacqueline were always going to frame it as a me versus Gabby situation. And if insisting that it wasn't a competition wasn't enough for them to believe it, I didn't know what else could be done.

But I'm not about to let them see me sweat.

Dinner went on with minimal incidents. The other models mostly peppered Gabby with questions, trying to get to know her while we ate. I tried to stay present in the conversation. But I was tired. I had to be on from the time I walked into the restaurant until I was back in my hotel room. All six of us had rooms on the same floor so the smile plastered on my face wasn't safe to come off until I'd closed my door.

I exhaled.

> Nina: I'm about to take a shower and then get in the bed.
>
> Russ: I wish I got a chance to see you today.
>
> Nina: Because of the dress?
>
> Russ: Because of you. But don't get me wrong, I wouldn't mind getting a chance to take you out of that dress.
>
> Nina: It sounds like you want me in nothing but the shoes.
>
> Russ: It sounds like you want me to come down to your room.

I squeezed my thighs together.

> Nina: Yes please.
>
> Russ: Let me get rid of Remedy and the rest of them and I'll be right down. Give me thirty minutes.
>
> Nina: I'll be ready and waiting.

Thirty minutes later, I was showered, shaved, and moisturized.

> Russ: I'm heading down now.
>
> Nina: Good.

Knowing he was on the way, I wrapped myself in my silk robe and slid my feet into the cozy slippers. When there was a knock at the door, I put my phone on the charger and then merrily skipped across the room. I looked out of the peephole and my smile dropped.

What the hell?

I opened the door slightly, shielding my robe-covered body. "Hey, Gabby. What's going on?"

"Oh, I'm sorry. I was hoping to catch you before you got in bed."

She looked down the hall, toward the elevator, and then back at me. "Can I come in?"

"I'm not dressed. Can we talk in the morning?"

There was a small flicker of sadness in her eyes as she nodded. "Okay, I'll make it quick. I'm not trying to take anything from you. I don't know what Jacqueline meant by calling me your replacement, but I was under the impression that we were sharing the load. I want this opportunity, but I also want to make sure we're good, too."

"Oh, Gabby, we're good. It was . . ." The elevator dinged, snatching my attention before I could continue speaking.

My heart thumped in my chest.

The hint of impropriety between Russ and one of his employees could result in major blowback at one of the biggest moments of his career. The mere rumor of me in a relationship with Russ would undermine how I got the opportunity to walk in the show to begin with.

I swallowed hard. "There was some confusion in the way it was announced, and then everyone else started fearing for their job security. That's all. Me and you are good. But we can talk tomorrow," I finished in a rush.

She turned her head toward the elevator and waved. "Hey, Jonah!" She turned to me and smiled. "He's so cute," she whispered.

"What's up, Gabriella," Jonah replied. "Aight, Mr. Long, thanks again."

A few seconds later, the elevator doors shut, and heavy footsteps were coming closer. I knew in my heart that it was Jonah. There was no way Russ was going to attempt to come to my room with two RLF spokesmodels in the hallway. So, I wasn't surprised when Jonah appeared in my view.

"Boss Man is pretty cool," he commented as he stopped at my door. He looked between us. "What's going on here?"

"Wait, *that* was Russell Long, the CEO?" Gabby questioned. "I've never met him before."

"You'll get a chance to meet him on Monday after the runway show," Jonah stated. "What are y'all doing?" He turned to me. "Why are you peeking out the door?"

"It's my fault," Gabby explained. "I just wanted to check on Nina, but she's ready for bed."

"You have an eight o'clock call time, don't you?" Jonah asked me.

"Yeah, so I'm going to say good night," I told them before closing the door.

When I ran across the room to my phone, I had a missed call and two text messages from Russ.

> Russ: Can't get off the elevator.
>
> Russ: Too risky. Call me.

I didn't waste time texting him back and dialed him immediately.

"That shit was crazy," he said as soon as he answered.

"I know," I groaned.

"I came out my room and Remedy was at the elevator, too. So, I rode down with her, pretended I forgot my wallet, so I needed to go back up. Then Jonah's ass got in before the door could close and he rode up with me. I had to just abort the mission and come back to the room—especially when I saw there was someone else in the hallway."

"That was Gabby. I thought it was you when she knocked. A couple minutes later, the elevator opened, and it was you and Jonah. I don't know the last time I was that nervous."

"I was so ready to see you tonight that I wasn't even thinking straight. When I ran into Remedy, that should've been a sign. But I brushed it off because I needed to see you. And then Jonah got in the elevator, and I just knew I was about to be caught." He let out a short, dry laugh. "There's gotta be a better way for me to link up with my girl."

His girl.

I didn't know why those words spread warmth throughout my body, but they did. He'd asked me to be with him. He'd called me various terms of endearment. But it hit differently in that moment. I fell back against my pillow and grinned.

"All I kept thinking about was how bad it would be for us if they saw you coming into my room," I told him. "I was nervous as hell."

"I'll admit, when the elevator opened on your floor, it hit me how risky this whole thing was."

I chewed my bottom lip for a moment. "Yeah. Everything we talked about when we first found out about this . . . conflict of interest came flooding back."

"Yeah. Our careers are on the line."

"I don't want to be an HR embarrassment and a PR nightmare for you," I whispered.

"You aren't an embarrassment or a nightmare. You're . . . everything to me."

My stomach fluttered as I let his words cover me. "I feel the same way," I admitted. "I just don't want to look like I fuck for work."

"We were fucking way before you were offered work."

"True. But that would be the perception. And my reputation would take a hit. Both of our reputations would take a hit."

"So, we just lay low this weekend. Play it cool until we get through Fashion Week. We'll get the paperwork on Tuesday and then . . ."

"We'll be free?"

"We'll be free."

We were both quiet.

I exhaled. "I wish we were having this conversation in person."

"I wish we didn't have to have this conversation at all," he countered.

"Do you wish . . ." Inexplicably, nerves twisted my gut. "Do you wish we would've never started?"

"Absolutely not."

"Do you wish Remedy would've never crossed my path?"

"Would it have made my life easier? Yes. But every time you tell me how much this opportunity means to you and your career, I want it for you even more. Watching you do your thing and seeing the photos of you in my campaign make me proud. So, I can't say I wish Remedy wouldn't have offered the job to you. You deserve the job. You're good at the job."

"So are you. You've worked your ass off for your company. The fact that you started this as just T-shirts and it grew into this. You've built something really special and that has everything to do with the fact that you're special. The way you do business and the way you run your business is special. I'm proud to wear your clothes, to represent your company . . ." There was more I wanted to say but my sentence trailed off as a wave of emotion gripped my throat.

"Nina . . ." He paused. "That means a lot. You mean a lot."

"I'm not going to let our relationship cost you," I promised him softly.

"And I'm not going to let it cost you."

I let out a breath. "What are we going to do?"

"After the show, we'll get back to Richland and my lawyer will have the forms ready for us to sign. I'll take it to the board, and we'll go from there. I'm not giving you up."

"I'm not going anywhere."

24

The weekend was a blur. The number of models, stylists, fashion students, celebrities, designers, and buyers that I connected with was valuable networking. Between rehearsals, fittings, behind-the-scenes footage, it was a hectic weekend with little sleep. Because Gabby was doing my appearances at the stores, Lori and Angelica had me creating content with the models as they came for their fittings. I was styling pieces and then getting on-the-street feedback. But on Monday, there was no time for anything except runway preparation.

This is the real thing, I thought, looking around at the stage setup. Lights were being tested, speakers were being queued, and black folding chairs were being set up.

All forty male and female models participating in the RLF show arrived on-site at eight o'clock in the morning. Wearing our own street clothes and the shoes for the show, we strutted down the catwalk to the throbbing R & B beat. The rehearsal felt different than any other time because of the lighting, the music, and the seriousness of everyone involved.

Russ was somewhere, lurking in the shadows. Wearing all black and his black-and-white sneakers, his sexy ass was somewhere, running things. When we'd rehearsed on Sunday, the lights were on, and I knew where he was seated. He corrected mistakes, restarted walks, adjusted lights, changed music, and anything else to perfect his show. With the event in less than three hours, the lighting was show ready, the mirrors were in position, and I could only see the end of the runway. But I could feel Russ's eyes on me.

The final fittings were taking place with Russell, Remedy, Angelica, and the other members of the design team. Afterward, the models were sent to hair and makeup. Then we were sent back to Angelica for stylings and final looks. Photos were taken once the outfit was solidified. We were sent out in the order that we'd appear in the show and since I was the final model to walk out, I went last.

Walking around the corner to where the RLF team sat, I locked eyes with Russ and saw him sit up a little straighter. He shifted in his seat, and his eyes swept up and down my body as I stepped up on the platform. My nipples hardened under his gaze. I glanced at the others, trying to focus on their reactions. I wanted and needed to calm down, but every time I caught the lustful expression on his face, my body stirred.

The white asymmetrical dress fit my body like a glove. The fittings resulted in the dress being perfectly tailored to my curves. The shoes I'd been practicing in all weekend were a pair of high heels with a sheer strap around the ankles. They were beautiful, but they were not functional. They had no support. The thought of me tripping in them clouded my thoughts each time I put them on. But I couldn't deny that the shoes and the dress combined with the black sheer trench coat was fire.

"This looks good," Russ told me diplomatically as he inspected my look. "This is the look we're ending on."

"It's perfect," Remedy commented.

One of the people I hadn't met added, "The decision to use a plus model in this dress was spot on. Whose idea was that?"

"Mine," Angelica stated.

"It was a good choice," the second woman added. "It isn't just the way it fits her. It's the way she carries it."

The man nodded. "It's like Russell designed the trench with her in mind."

Russ cleared his throat as he continued to stare at me. "Thank you, Nina," he said finally as the others were deciding whether I needed a bag in my hand. "You can get changed and then head to hair and makeup."

"Thank you." I told them all, but my eyes kept gravitating to Russ.

I stepped down and headed back to the dressing room to get undressed, and then went promptly to hair and makeup.

It didn't take as long as I anticipated. The makeup artist gave me a really dewy look, with heavily dramatized eyes. The hair stylist opted for Bantu knots for me, and I loved them.

After thanking her, I returned to the dressing room and was instantly taken aback. The space was big, but with forty models getting dressed, dozens of fashion assistants helping to get everyone dressed, and hair and makeup assistants touching up hair and makeup, there was a lot going on. The DJ started playing music, and I knew it was our cue that the doors were open and the show would be starting soon.

That was when I started to get a little nervous.

"We're about to start," Russ announced, getting everyone's attention. "This show is about us. It's about RLF. It's about bucking tradition. It's about carving out our space in the world. It's about reminding people who the fuck we are." Russ looked around the room with his chest puffed up and his head held high as we cheered. When we quieted, he continued. "We don't follow trends. We set them. And while it's an honor to be here, it's an honor for them to have us here. So go out there and let's make history."

I felt so proud and so inspired by him. Joining in while everyone hooted and hollered, I couldn't stop staring at him. When our eyes met, he mouthed something to me that I couldn't quite make out. But just the formation and movement of his lips sent a chill down my spine.

"Things are going to move fast," the coordinator reminded us. "Just like at the run-through this morning, but this is the real thing. Get dressed. Line up in the correct order. You'll get a final once-over by Russell and Angelica before you head down the catwalk. T-minus ten minutes until showtime!"

My stomach lurched.

I was excited. I was nervous. I was happy. I was a mixture of emotions, but above all, I was ready. The last thing I wanted to do was let Russ down.

I went to the rack that had a garment bag with my picture attached to it. The assistant assigned to that rack gingerly took the dress out and then helped me into it. I slipped on the trench coat and tied the belt, cinching the waist. Someone came by, checked her tablet, and then touched up my makeup based on what the makeup artist had noted on the spreadsheet. When I was helped into my shoes, I stood and watched all the decked-out models in front of me.

"Wow," I repeated to myself a few times as I stared in the mirror. I looked so good my eyes started to water.

I'd had my makeup done professionally before and I loved putting my hair in Bantu knots, so it wasn't the look that choked me up. I'd had the dress on a few times as they were fitting it to my body, so it wasn't the impeccable fit that moved me. It was the combination of how I looked, that I was closing out a Fashion Week runway show, and that Russ was accomplishing a big feat in the industry, and I got to share that with him. Everything about the experience was surreal but it didn't hit me until I looked at myself in the mirror.

I got in the back of the line, and from the moment the show music started, everything moved so fast. When it was my turn to go up the stairs, there were still two people in front of me who were waiting to walk down the catwalk.

"Do the walk you did earlier," Angelica advised me.

Russ grabbed my waist and adjusted my belt, tying it in a way that somehow made the garment cooler. "You good?"

I nodded, swallowing hard. "Yes."

He licked his lips. "Good. You're up."

I stepped out and there was a bright spotlight on me. The audience was submerged in darkness. The runway was lined with lights, so I knew exactly where I needed to go. I heard the "oohs" and "aahs" in the crowd and the clicks and flashes of the cameras as I made my way down. I stopped at the end of the runway, shifted my weight from one foot to the other, posed, and then made my way back. I kept my face at ease until I made it offstage and behind the curtain.

The music changed and all forty of us strutted out to do our final walk to a standing ovation. As I was about to step offstage and through the curtain, the back of Russ's hand grazed mine and sent a jolt of electricity up my arm. It was a slight touch, yet it reverberated through me. I kept it together and tried not to react. I just kept going, following the other models.

He took his bow and then quickly caught up to me as I tiptoed down the steps in the heels from hell.

"That looked good," he complimented us, clapping his hands together. "I couldn't have asked for anything better than that."

"Let's fucking go!" one of the male models yelled out, causing him to laugh.

It was a joyous mood as we changed and wrapped things up. All of the models were ushered out, some of them rushing off to their next show. I wanted to hang around and congratulate Russ, but I didn't want to draw any attention to us. He was speaking to the press, and I had no reason to hang around, so I sent him a text and took a taxi back to the hotel.

> Nina: I'm so incredibly proud of you. I can't wait to watch the show in full online. But being in it, I was able to see your greatness, your artistry, your creativity, and your business acumen on display. It was sexy as hell. And it was also inspiring. You inspire me.

Our flight back to Richland was at four o'clock so once I got back to the hotel, I needed to freshen up, change, and pack. I planned to meet the rest of the models downstairs in the lobby at one o'clock so we could make it to the airport by two. Even though it was only twelve thirty, they were eating at the small café, sending me messages, rushing me. The last message I got from them told me that if I didn't come down in the next thirty minutes, they were going to come and get me.

That was fifteen minutes ago.

I was pulling my suitcase and weekender bag to the door when I stopped to check myself out in the mirror. I nodded at my look. The red Bowen jumpsuit with the belted waist fit me well. Instead of black heels, I opted for the black-and-white sneakers Russ had designed and given to me six weeks ago. Paired with a lightweight black jacket and my white-gold jewelry, I looked cute and comfortable. Not wanting to waste professional hair and makeup, I opened the curtains to let as much natural light in as possible. Using my portable tripod, I took some great shots of me to post on social media.

I was taking my last few shots when there was a knock at the door. All I could do was laugh because they *meant* they were coming to get me.

Swinging the door open, I said, "I'm coming—Russ!" My eyes widened and I looked back and forth down the hall and then pulled him inside. "What are you doing here?"

"I couldn't let you leave without a proper goodbye," he said as the door closed behind him. "And I couldn't wait until tomorrow."

"Tomorrow—?" I started to question what he meant but his mouth covered mine, sucking the words, thoughts, and breath from me.

Backing me into the wall, he gripped my hips and trapped me with his body.

Not that there was anywhere else I wanted to be.

"Seeing you and not being able to touch you is always hard. But sleeping two floors down from you has been killing me," he whispered between kisses. "If things weren't so busy, I don't know if I would've been able to be keep my distance."

Breaking out of the kiss, I stared up into his eyes. "It's hard being professional around you off the clock," I admitted. "During the day, I was fine. You were Mr. Russell Long, CEO. But as soon as I got in bed, I wanted Russ . . . my man."

A soft groan emanated from him. "Call me your man again."

I smiled against his lips. "My man."

We devoured each other, kissing with the passion we'd repressed all weekend. My hands grabbed at his shirt, pulling him closer, wanting to feel more of him. We moaned into each other's mouths.

When he pulled out of the kiss, his hands ran from my hips, up my sides, over my breasts, and around my neck. He searched my eyes before he spoke.

"My lawyer sent the paperwork to my email this morning," he told me, his thumbs stroking my jaw. "I'm not trying to keep how I feel about you a secret anymore."

My heart thumped in my chest. "And how do you feel about me?" I asked breathily.

"I love you," he said just before his mouth covered mine again.

It was the first time he'd verbalized it and his words sent shock-waves directly to my core. His soft lips and electric touch created a sensation that coursed through my entire body. As our kiss intensified, I felt the genuine emotion behind his words. Shivers ran up and down my spine when his tongue teasingly met mine, repeating the sentiments.

"I love you, too," I confessed, putting words to the feelings that had been simmering beneath the surface.

My confession was so soft that I didn't know if he had heard it. I wasn't even sure I'd said it aloud or just thought it over and over again.

But when he pulled out of the kiss and stared into my eyes, I knew he'd heard me.

I knew he'd felt it.

I knew he was it.

Still holding his gaze, I tilted my head up to connect our lips again. As soon as they met, my eyes closed inadvertently, and I let out a soft whimper.

My pussy throbbed as his erection pushed against my soft belly. I wanted him in such a carnal way. Everything I felt for him and every emotion he conjured from me created an intense desire that twisted my gut so forcefully that I moaned into his mouth.

Lost in the moment, I was completely consumed by him. Reaching for his zipper, I gripped the solid girth of his dick. Running my hand over the length of it as it remained trapped under cotton.

But the firm knock against the door startled us apart.

"Nina!" Gabby called from the other side of the door.

"You need help in there?" Jonah asked.

Another round of knocks rained down on the door.

"Ninaaaaa!" Gabby called in a singsong tone.

Wide-eyed and frantic, Russ backed away from me and grabbed his dick. There was no mistaking that dick print in those pants. I pressed my nipples, hoping to flatten them out some.

"I'm finishing up a call. I'll be right down," I answered finally.

My heart was racing. My stomach churned with nerves, but I couldn't deny the thrill of it excited me.

"Are you sure? Open the door so we can have proof of life," Jonah joked.

"Are you talking to your boyfriend?" Gabby asked.

Russ and I looked at each other. The look on his face was sweet but I'm sure I looked horrified. The whole situation was so comical that I almost laughed out loud.

"I am. Give me five minutes and I'll meet you downstairs," I repeated.

Russ pulled out his phone from his pocket. His thumb moved quickly over the screen.

"Oh shit. Lori said Boss Man wants to meet us downstairs in the lobby," Jonah announced. "This is your last chance for baggage help."

"See you down there," I called out.

"You've been raving about your boyfriend all weekend. Don't let boo-lovin' on the phone get you fired," Gabby yelped.

My cheeks flushed instantly. "Five minutes!" I yelled.

He cocked his head to the side. "You be talking about me?" he asked in a quiet, teasing tone. "Because according to them"—he jutted his thumb toward the closed door before reaching for me—"you talk *a lot* about this boyfriend of yours."

Giggling, I playfully slapped at his arm. "You play too much. We almost got caught!"

"Yeah." He shook his head, taking a step back. "That's why Wednesday can't come fast enough."

Glancing at his dick print, I licked my lips. "Speaking of can't come fast enough . . . I don't want to get caught, but something about the thrill of it made me want you more . . ." I admitted, ignoring the throbbing between my thighs. "So you should back up some more."

He snickered. "Yeah, because I gotta calm down before I go down there."

"It's a good thing they can't see that my panties are soaking wet," I said with a wink.

Crossing the room, I grabbed my phone and tripod and packed them in my weekender bag. I spun around, looking to see if I left anything. When satisfied that I had all my stuff, I looked up at him.

"What?" I walked his way, stopping right in front of him.

He cupped my cheek, bringing his face to mine. "I'm a lucky man."

"I agree."

He chuckled before kissing me. "Let's go."

"Wait! We can't go down together!"

"My elevator would've had to stop on your floor if we left at the same time." He untucked his shirt to mask his bulge and then grabbed my suitcase handle. "And I'm not letting you carry all this by yourself unnecessarily."

I was going to argue, but that luggage was heavy, so I relented.

We better not get caught.

I stuck my head out the door first to make sure no one was around and then the two of us hustled down the hall.

"I feel like we look obvious," I told him as the elevator opened to the first floor.

The models were standing to the side, waiting. I immediately went to stand with them, so it didn't look like we were together.

After an enthusiastic greeting, Russ looked around the group and smiled. "This was a very successful weekend and a lot of that is thanks to you. I appreciate the hard work and dedication. You represent RLF well. All of you in your own way, you bring something special to the team and I appreciate that. I just wanted to personally say thank you."

"Can I ask you a question?" Jacqueline wondered, causing the rest of us to groan.

My eyebrows shot up. *You never know what the fuck she's about to say.*

"I was asking a bunch of different designers this question and

I realized I didn't know your answer," Jacqueline started. "What inspires your creativity right now? First thing that comes to mind."

"My fantasy," he answered automatically with a quick glance to me.

My heart thumped in my chest.

Clearing his throat, he pulled his phone out of his pocket.

"And what exactly do you mean by fantasy?" she pried.

"I'll tell you what I told the press. Your fantasy is where you escape to be your happiest, freest, truest self. It's where you find your greatest purpose and your deepest love." He smirked. "At least, that's proven true for me. Have a safe flight. I'll see you Wednesday."

We all said goodbye and before he left, Taisha called out to him.

"I like your shoes!"

As soon as she said it, I realized what shoes he had on. A pit in my stomach developed.

"Thank you. I like yours, too," he returned.

She grinned, sticking out her attention-grabbing blue sneakers that she'd paired with her white romper. "Thanks!"

"Those are cute," Gabby told her as we went outside to wait for the rideshare van to pick us up.

As we climbed into the van, Taisha and I went last.

As we waited our turn, she turned to me. "I like your whole outfit. You're a vibe." Looking me up and down, her eyes lingered on my shoes and then she met my gaze. "Your airport outfits have been eating."

"Thank you."

"Is your man picking you up from the airport this time?" she wondered.

"My best friend is picking me up," I replied as we climbed in the van.

She gave me a sly smile. "Okay, girl."

The pit in my stomach grew.

She fucking knows.

25

The paperwork didn't just declare that Russ and I were in a relationship. It stripped my ability to sue the company for anything in regard to the relationship. That was the only sticking point for my uncle, and he advised me not to sign it. And while I understood why they felt the waiver of liability was necessary, I would never sue Russ or RLF if things didn't work out. I would never try to tear down what he'd worked so hard to build. But I knew that it wasn't about me, the relationship, or even protecting Russ. It was about protecting the company. And I had to sit with all of that for a minute because my uncle wasn't wrong. It *was* a risk to agree to those terms.

Is it worth it? Is he worth it? My uncle's questions swirled around in my head as I read the contract for the fourth time, coming to the same undeniable conclusion. *Yes.*

> Nina: I read the paperwork from your lawyer, printed it, and signed it already. Can't wait for you to get back!
>
> Russ: I signed it, too. But I have some bad news.

I stared at the text message for a second and immediately thought about Taisha. Even though I'd thought about telling him Monday night when I got home from New York, I knew he had a big day on Tuesday, and I didn't want to get in his head. So, my plan was to tell him that I thought Taisha suspected when he got home, but his flight got delayed. He was stuck in the airport with at least five RLF employees and it just didn't feel like the right time.

Especially since I don't know if she knows for sure.

Nina: What's wrong?

Russ: My flight just got delayed. Again. Now I'm supposed to land at eleven o'clock. I won't get home until
almost midnight.

Nina: They've delayed it twice. You don't think they're
going to cancel it altogether, do you?

Russ: I hope not. I'm just ready to be home. I had plans
for you. I'm sitting in this airport trying not to be rude to
the team, but all I can think about is getting back to you.

Nina: If you think saying stuff like that is going to get me
to fuck you, you're right.

Russ: Yo, what is wrong with you? I'm laughing my ass off.

Curling my legs up onto the couch, I smiled. He had a long day
with meetings as he concluded Fashion Week. I knew the three
extra hours at the airport didn't help, so I was glad to lift his spirits.

Nina: I'm looking forward to you getting back. I miss you.

Russ: I miss you, too. You have no idea.

Nina: That video call last night gave me some
idea.

Russ: I was trying to do all the things I was talking
about doing to you tonight.

Nina: I had an outfit all planned out for you to make
good on your promises.

Russ: We have that meeting tomorrow and I'll submit
our paperwork. Since our relationship will be on the
up-and-up, I'm taking you out, bringing you back home,
and then fucking you the way I've been wanting to fuck
you for a week.

Nina: I love everything about that plan.

I texted with Russ off and on all Tuesday night up until he boarded
his flight. I stayed awake until he landed and talked to him his en-

tire drive home. He was exhausted so we said good night, but I remained up for another hour. Flipping through the channels, I stopped when I saw a familiar face. The name wasn't on the screen anymore, but I recognized the face.

Grabbing my phone, I took a semi-blurry picture of the image on my screen and then sent it to the group chat.

> Nina: Is this who I think it is?

No one replied before I fell asleep. But when I woke up, I had several text messages.

> Aaliyah: Is that Jazz's man?

> Jazz: To answer Nina's question, if you think this was my date to Aaliyah's party, then yes.

> Aaliyah: Just a date? Because you two looked like more...

> Jazz: We're friends.

> Nina: Now I know a lie when I read it.

> Jazz: It's way too early for you two to be double teaming me!

> Aaliyah: Then just admit that you and this apparently famous man are more than friends. And why didn't you tell us you were dating a celebrity?

> Jazz: I definitely told you both on your birthday that he was a football player.

> Aaliyah: He was so cool and laid-back. I didn't think he was in the league. I thought you meant he was a football player as in he played football for fun or he played back in college.

> Nina: He looks like a football player. That's what I thought you meant. I thought you were describing those broad-ass shoulders. But you meant his job is professional athlete?

> Jazz: Yes, he plays for the Maryland Monarchs.

Aaliyah: I've never heard of him before, but you know I know nothing about football.

Nina: I know enough about football to know Jazz told that fine man to put her backfield in motion!

Aaliyah: She said go deep!

Nina: Jazz let him go ... ALL ... THE ... WAY!

Aaliyah: Jazz said he could tackle her any day of the week!

Nina: I know he's impressed with Jazz's ball handling!

Aaliyah: Touchdown!

Nina: It's a game of inches!

Aaliyah: Let's play ball!

Nina: Aaliyah, no. You ruined it. That's baseball.

Jazz: Are you two done?

Aaliyah: I am, apparently. It was between "play ball" and "goal" and I wasn't confident about either.

Nina: I have tears in my eyes. This was the laugh I needed this morning!

Aaliyah: Same!

Jazz: I can't stand either one of you.

Nina: Jazz got a famous boyfriend and now she can't stand us.

Aaliyah: Can't do nothing with money!

Jazz ignored us for the rest of the morning, but that laugh was exactly what I needed to get my day started. Aaliyah told me about her plans to meet Ahmad's parents that weekend. After showering and preparing for the day, I posted content on social media and then headed to the office. I was a little early and with the HR paperwork in my bag and the date with Russ scheduled for the night, I was on cloud nine. I damn near floated into the building.

"Hey, Jonah!" I greeted him with a warm smile as I approached the elevator. "How are you?"

He gave me an odd look. "I'm cool. How are you?"

"I'm good, I'm good."

"I bet."

My brows furrowed. "What's going on? You sure you're good?"

"I'm just trying to respect the fact that you have a man. I don't want to step on any toes."

"You're going to step on toes by saying hello to me? We're friends!" I stepped in front of him, trying to read his expression. "What's up with you today?"

"I'm just trying to keep my head down and get this money."

I had no idea what he was talking about because my relationship status and lack of interest never stopped him from being friendly before. So, I lifted my shoulders in bewilderment. "Okay . . ."

We entered the elevator with six other people.

He looked at me out the corner of his eye. "I have a question for you," he started. "You watch football?"

"Casually." I shrugged. "I don't really have a team, but I understand what's happening on the field."

My father was a football fan, so I learned the basics growing up. And there was always at least one man I was dating who was interested in football. I was always mildly entertained, but I was never a regular watcher. Which was why it was comical that my entire morning seemed to be centered around football.

He pulled his phone out of his pocket. "One of my favorite players got hurt last Sunday so they put in a backup. The backup got hurt and they pulled up someone from the practice squad for the Monday night game. That practice squad linebacker showed the fuck up."

"That's good . . ." My sentence trailed off and I gave him a confused look even though he was still fiddling with his phone.

"Since Monday, every media outlet that covers sports has been trying to get more information about him," he continued. "And I saw something . . . interesting."

Four people got off on the following floor. We reconfigured in the small space, and I was slightly behind Jonah. He shifted his body so I could see his phone and I saw a familiar face on the screen. It was the man that came to the party with Jazz, but he looked different. It was an older picture, so he had a goatee instead of the beard he had currently. But it was definitely him.

My lips pulled upward even though I tried to fight the smile.

"Everyone is trying to find out anything they can about this man." He paused. "And it turns out, I know someone who knows him."

I opened my mouth to ask him how he knew I knew him but before the words could escape, he swiped to the next picture.

The elevator doors opened, and my legs wouldn't move.

Looking from his phone to his face and then back to his phone, I tried to slow down my thoughts.

"After you," Jonah said, gesturing for me to exit.

Taking his phone from his hand, I glanced at the two people still in the elevator. Forcing one foot in front of the other, I froze right in front of the elevator bank. No one was at the front desk, so it didn't look like anyone else was around.

"Wh-where did you get that?" I choked out as I stared at the picture of me and my best friends with our dates at Aaliyah's party.

"My boy is friends with someone who is dating someone named Mecca. She posted it on social media, and after his game on Monday, it's been shared everywhere."

Fucking Mecca!

"Most of the reshares cropped the photo so it's just him and his girl." He took his phone from me and zoomed in on the picture, so it was just Jazz and her date. "But because my boy shared the photo directly from Mecca's page, I saw the whole group." He narrowed his eyes at me. "And that's how I found out your boyfriend is Boss Man Russell Long."

I looked around quickly. "Jonah, it's—"

"I didn't understand why he spent every photoshoot giving me the death glare and then it all made sense when I saw this shit."

He shook his head. "If we're friends, why wouldn't you give me a heads-up?"

"It's not what it looks like."

"Are you saying you two *aren't* together?"

"No, we are but—"

He shook his head. "So why would you let me flirt with Boss Man's girl, knowing he's writing my checks, too, and not say shit? Was it a setup?"

"No! Of course not!"

"So you let me put my job in jeopardy for shits and giggles?"

"I'm sorry it seems like that because I'm sure that's how it looks. But it's not—"

The elevator dinged and my lips snapped shut. The doors opened and Taisha, Jacqueline, and Matias walked out, giving us a suspicious look.

"What's going on here?" Jacqueline wondered, looking between us.

"Nina decided to finally give Jonah a shot," Matias guessed loudly. "Damn her boyfriend!"

Russ and Remedy happened to walk by just as Matias's words left his mouth. They both stopped and we all looked.

An awkward silence hung in the air.

Russ walked off but Remedy remained, hands on her hips.

"What's going on?" Remedy asked. "The meeting is in twenty minutes in the conference room, not the elevator bank."

"We're on our way," Jacqueline responded. Looking back at us, she waved her arm. "Come on."

Jonah and Matias started walking with her.

Jonah looked back at me and shook his head.

Taisha grabbed my arm and pulled me toward her as we trailed behind them. "What's going on? Why is the vibe off?" she asked me in a low tone.

I swallowed hard. "Jonah asked me about my boyfriend—"

"Russell Long," she stated in a low tone.

My eyebrows flew up. *I knew she knew!*

"Don't look at me like that. I'm not stupid. The matching shoes. The way you two eye fuck each other when you think no one is looking. But what really proved it for me . . ." She lifted my arm and pointed to my wrist. "The fantasy."

I closed my eyes. "Oh my God."

"Girl, please." She waved her hand away. "But what's going on with Jonah?"

"He found out about us and feels like his job is in jeopardy. And it's really not. But he's mad and"—I sighed—"I don't know."

She made a sympathetic face. "I feel where he's coming from though."

"Me too. But his job really was never in jeopardy."

As we walked through the conference room doors, our conversation ended. Taking a seat, we silently joined the other models.

"I need to drop some paperwork off. I'll be right back," I told them, rising to my feet.

"Where are you going?" Jacqueline wondered. "Is it paperwork we need to do, too?"

"No, it's something else," I replied, quickly exiting so I wouldn't be asked more questions.

> Nina: They know.
>
> Russ: I know. Come to my office.

I was talking about the models, but I had no idea who he was talking about. I went to his office, and I lifted my fist to knock when I heard a faint voice.

"But you're the CEO," she stated, sounding far away. "It doesn't matter that the paperwork is signed, it *looks* inappropriate. And while legal may be satisfied with this solution, that paper only covers us legally. It doesn't do anything for the impact it'll have on the other models, the company, the brand, and the court of public opinion. You're the CEO, Mr. Long. This is *your* company and since Nina is getting paid by *your company*, it's . . ." She paused. "This is a risk."

"A risk I'm willing to take," he replied, causing my stomach to flip.

Hearing his words, knowing how much he was risking, I instantly felt a pang in my chest. As much as I loved knowing he would risk it all for me, I did not want him to. He'd worked too hard and had come too far and had so much on the line with the exponential growth RLF was experiencing. I loved him too much to let him risk his company for us. I also loved him too much to let him go.

I felt so conflicted.

I glanced down at the paperwork in my bag and noticed my hand was shaking. When I heard Russ's voice again, I closed my eyes and took a trembling breath.

"I wanted to have this conversation with you before I announced it at the meeting. If you have questions or concerns, we can talk about it. But this is happening and because I value you as part of my team, I want to give you this courtesy. But that's all this is—a courtesy and a conversation. This is not me asking you for permission."

His voice was loud, passionate, and steady. But it sounded as though he was walking from one side of his office to the other. Since I couldn't hear anyone speaking anymore, I assumed he was conducting the call on speakerphone.

Looking around, I lightly rapped at the door three times, hoping whoever was on the phone didn't hear. When it swung open, I was surprised to see Remedy on the other side.

"Perfect timing," she said sarcastically, opening the door wider. "Come on in. We were actually just talking about you."

I tentatively entered the room, unsure of what I would find. Sweeping my eyes around the space, I felt the pit in my stomach grow with each face.

Sasha Beaman from Human Resources, Lori Smith, Angelica, and three people I'd seen before but didn't know were already in Russ's office. Everyone's expression was serious. Russ was standing behind his desk, arms folded. All eyes were on me.

"I was coming by to drop off some paperwork," I said, keeping my eyes on Russ. I felt the heat creeping over my cheeks, but I ignored it. "I can come back or wait until after the meeting if necessary."

"No, come here," Russ responded, beckoning to me. "Bring me the papers."

I pulled them out of the bag as I made my way across the room. No one said a word as I walked around his desk and handed them over. Before I could turn and leave, Russ grabbed my wrist.

I looked up at him and he smiled. His fingers slipped across my palm and then intertwined with mine.

"As I was saying," he began, breaking eye contact with me and casting it around the room. "Beyond the fact that this is my choice, my relationship, and my company, I had my lawyer draw up paperwork to support the already established code of conduct and code of ethics in which this company was founded."

His firm, matter-of-fact tone that he reserved for work was commanding and extremely sexy. I had to look away from him so they didn't see the lovestruck look on my face. Shifting my gaze, I immediately locked eyes with Remedy.

Shit.

"And you've sent these documents to our lawyers here?" the man in the black suit asked. "There's no conflict?"

Russ looked at each of them as he spoke. "There's no conflict. Since we both signed these forms, there's no liability, there's nothing that shines a negative light on RLF."

"I just don't understand how this happened," Lori marveled.

"Nina and I met more than three months ago," Russ replied, running his thumb along the side of my hand. "I didn't tell her what I did for work. She didn't tell me what she did for work. We were just as surprised as you are."

"I get it," Remedy said calmly. "And I want nothing more than to see you happy. But is this the time for this?" She gestured between us. "We just made some of the biggest moves for RLF this weekend. We've invested so much money and we have to ride this momentum. And that means we have to avoid any scandals. We're on the heels of something great and as good as you two look together, this situation doesn't look good for RLF."

"Not to mention how it could appear to other employees," Sasha added. "Specifically, to the other models. It could appear as though she is getting preferential treatment."

He nodded in agreement. "Yes, and I've come up with a solution that would attempt to mitigate that." He lifted his shoulders. "But I'm going to keep it real with you—all of you. Nina and I had already started dating before I knew Remedy offered her a position. I only approved her for hire after it was already set in motion by Lori and Sasha. Our relationship was not a factor in that decision. The six of you nominated Nina to walk in the show—starting with Angelica. I was not a factor in that decision. I only approved it after it was voted on. The Bowen contract that we secured meant we had to bring on another model and actually"—he squeezed my hand—"reduce in-store opportunities for Nina while also propping up Gabriella as the RLF representation for Bowen. I was not a factor in that decision. But when that was the necessary way forward to secure our positioning with Bowen, I agreed to it. Our relationship doesn't affect me doing my job and it doesn't affect Nina doing hers."

Oop! This is what I should've said to Jonah!

They were silent. I bit my lip to keep from smiling because of the looks on their faces.

Everything he said was true. Every opportunity I had was instigated by someone else in RLF as a result of my hard work. I earned everything that had come to me over the last month. No one, especially no one in that room, could make a credible claim that my relationship with Russ benefited me unfairly.

But it doesn't need to be the truth to circulate and cause harm.

It was a sobering thought.

Russ checked his watch and then continued. "We have a meeting, and we have a lot to discuss, so let's get to it."

Murmuring about the information they'd just received, they got up and filed out of his office. Remedy hung back. When everyone else had left she looked at us.

"Are you sure about this?" she asked.

"Yes," Russ said quickly and definitively.

She pointed at me. "I was talking to her. Nina, are you sure about this?"

"I've never been more sure about anything in my life," I answered honestly.

With a small smile, she nodded. "I've never seen my brother like this and I'm happy. As his sister, I love this, and I support this." She paused, looking between us. "As the person overseeing your employment, I hope you don't think this means I'm going to take it easy on you. You'll have to be able to separate business and personal."

"I can and do," I assured her.

"Okay. I support it," she told us before opening up the door. "The meeting starts in one minute."

Bringing the back of my hand to his lips, he kissed it. "You okay?" he asked.

I nodded before I peeked up at him.

The feeling that spread over me as our eyes connected forced me onto my toes. He wrapped his arms around me as I pressed my lips against his.

"Now I'm okay," I breathed.

"I made reservations for us to go to dinner tonight at seven." He dipped his head and put his mouth against the shell of my ear. "And then I'm taking you home to have you for dessert."

I giggled, leaning into him. "I look forward to it."

He motioned toward the door with his head. "You head out first. I'll be right behind you."

I walked across the room and before I left, I glanced over at him. "Russ?"

"Yeah?"

"I love you."

His eyes bore into me. His chest rose and then fell as if he weren't just hearing me and seeing me—he was breathing me in. "I love you, too."

I got butterflies.

Biting down on my bottom lip, I tried to tone down my smile before I returned to the conference room. I didn't want to look *too* happy—even though I was elated. Slowing my pace, I rolled my shoulders back and entered the completely packed space.

"Where the hell have you been?" Jacqueline asked, peering over Taisha to glare at me. "I have so many questions for you."

"After the meeting," I told her.

Russ walked in and took his place at the head of the table. "We have a lot to discuss today. But I have a meeting in twenty minutes so we're going to go ahead and get started."

He flashed his perfect smile around the room as we quieted and waited for what he was going to say. "Honesty and transparency are important, and there are a few things I've been keeping close to the chest."

"Like Nina, apparently," Jacqueline muttered under her breath. I ignored her.

"I never wanted to wear the same thing as everybody else," Russ started. "I didn't just want to follow the trends; I wanted to set them. I wanted to design them. So, I started designing T-shirts. People kept asking me where I got them, so I created Real Life Fashions. I was doing T-shirts, sweats, and hoodies and selling them on campus at Hamilton University. I started making real money with it by my senior year. As my style evolved, so did my vision for RLF. I've always wanted a successful business. But this year has blown my mind. Fashion Week was never a dream of mine. Fashion Week was my sister's dream for me. And what we did on that stage set the bar high. What we do here every day sets the bar high. I can't thank you enough because this wasn't just me—this was all of us. We don't follow the trends. We set the trends."

Everyone clapped and cheered wildly.

"First," he continued, "Remedy and I had a meeting with the buyer for the largest department store in the country on Tuesday morning. They were impressed with the show, and they are interested in bringing the spring-summer line to their stores!"

I gasped.

He'd told me that the meeting had gone well, but he buried the lead of how well it went. Everyone started talking excitedly.

Russ waited until the room quieted before he continued. "Second, I typically keep my business separate from my personal life." He turned his attention to me, staring at me from across the room. "But my personal life now includes a woman, *my woman*, and our relationship is extremely important to me. I've held her in high regard since I met her, and she's inspired me in so many ways over the last few months." He stroked his beard and then took a step forward. "So, I was caught off guard when Remedy and Lori added a fifth model for us in August and it was Nina . . . the woman I'd fallen in love with back in June."

A wave of shocked reactions, mumbled catcalls, and complete confusion swept over the room as they looked between the two of us frantically.

"Which brings me to my third announcement." He looked around the room and then gestured for his sister to stand. "Remedy Rose knocked the ball out of the park yesterday. She has been so instrumental in the successes we've seen. I created RLF, but Remedy has been the driving force behind taking it to the next level. I got into this because of my love of design. When Remedy finished her master's program, she came to me with a business plan. This wasn't a sister asking her brother for a job. This was a businesswoman with a plan to take the company to the next level. And for that reason, I've always said Real Life Fashions wouldn't be where it is today without her."

Everyone in the room clapped. It was a beautiful show of love and respect. Remedy walked to the head of the conference room table and hugged Russ, which just made us cheer louder. He whispered something to her, and her face stilled before she nodded. Her eyes were wide, as if whatever he said stunned her.

He took a step back and clapped with everyone else. When he stopped, so did we.

"With that being said, I love RLF, and I'd do anything for it. I love Nina and I'd do anything for her. I love my sister and I am honored to announce that effective immediately, Remedy will be acting CEO. I'm stepping down as CEO of Real Life Fashions."

26

The collective gasp was so loud it reverberated.

My stomach plummeted. *What does that mean? Is this because of me? Because of us?*

He didn't even give us a chance to process as he kept talking. "Remedy will be acting CEO, and it will be made official at the quarterly board meeting at the end of the month. Now, if you'll excuse me, I have a meeting. Thank you for your time."

With my heart slamming against my chest, my eyes followed him as he strolled out of the conference room.

"Did he just quit for you?" Taisha hissed.

"I don't . . ."

I was at a loss for words. I didn't know he was going to do that. I didn't *want* him to do that. RLF was his brainchild and his legacy. He told me to trust him and that he had a plan, but I would've never gone along with a plan that meant he had to give up his company, his dream.

My chest felt like it was cracking open.

Remedy instructed Lori to start the meeting, but I barely heard a word. Just when I was able to push my emotions down, the models were dismissed to the showroom. As soon as the conference room door closed behind us, the models erupted with questions.

"The boyfriend you were talking about is Russell Long?" Matias damn near hollered.

"Is that how you got chosen for the runway show?" Jacqueline questioned.

"Does he know that I didn't know about him so there's no need for beef?" Jonah asked.

"You two have only been dating since June and y'all already got matching shoes?" Taisha joked.

As we walked to the other side of the office building, I answered them all.

"Yes, Russell Long is my man," I told Matias. Turning to Jonah, I continued. "He knows that you didn't know anything, and he doesn't have beef with you at all."

I eyed Jacqueline, not completely sure if she was being shady or not. "No, Angelica nominated me to walk in the show. Russell wasn't in on the vote for me to walk."

Taisha bumped me with her hip. "You didn't answer my question."

Shaking my head, I laughed. "Because it wasn't a real question." I pointed at her. "I knew you peeped that. I felt it in my gut."

"Should I be worried that you'll get all the runway shows or big opportunities?" Jacqueline complained as we walked into the showroom. "Because I can't compete with someone who's screwing the boss."

My brows furrowed. On one hand, I could understand where her mindset was but at the exact same time, I knew she was being shady.

"I already said that he didn't nominate me to walk," I returned.

Jacqueline frowned. "Well, it feels suspicious that you two are together and then all of a sudden, without a tryout or anything, you're selected to walk. No offense."

"Well, I take offense to that," Angelica stated as she emerged from behind a rack of clothes. She pushed her red glasses up the bridge of her nose as she crossed the room toward us. "I nominated Nina. I pushed for her to be selected. Are you questioning my judgment?"

Jacqueline looked shook. "No ma'am."

"Are you questioning the integrity of this company?"

"No—no, ma'am."

She placed a stack of T-shirts on the table and looked around at all of us. "These shirts will be part of your content creation for this week. It is not for the Miami appearances. Taisha, come with me."

We sat in silence as we waited our turn to get our clothing. My sadness subsided momentarily and was replaced with worry. That was the most I'd ever heard Angelica speak and even though it was in defense of me, I still felt like I needed to stay quiet because I didn't know how she felt about me and Russ. When we left as a group thirty minutes later, we didn't talk until we were in the elevator.

"I'm grown and Angelica wasn't even talking to me, and I felt like she told me to stay in a child's place," Taisha commented.

We all burst out laughing because it legitimately felt like that.

When the humor died down, Jacqueline turned to me. "I'm sorry about what I said. I was being a hater."

"Yeah, you were. The first question was shady, but there was some validity to the concern. The second time, you were being a hater for real."

She pouted. "I was jealous. I was hating. And I'm sorry."

The elevator door opened, and I gave her a smile. "Apology accepted." I pointed at her. "But don't do that shit no more."

We exited the building, exchanging goodbyes.

"See you tomorrow," I called out as I headed to my car.

As soon as I started my car, my cell phone rang. The minute I saw Russ's name flash across my screen, I was immediately flooded with guilt.

"Are you okay?" I answered frantically. "What happened?"

"I'm good. What's wrong?"

The concern in his voice made my eyes prick with tears. *Even when he has just done something so heartbreakingly selfless, he's still thinking about me.*

"You're not CEO anymore."

"It was the only way for us—"

"You should've told me you planned on leaving," I interjected, trying not to break down and cry. "I would've told you not to. I never would've wanted you to do it like this. We could've snuck around for the next seven and a half months if we needed to. We could've figured something else out. We could've—I would've made the sneaking around work if I thought you leaving your company was the only option." My voice broke. "You don't deserve for it to happen like this. You don't—"

"Nina," he interrupted gently. "Where are you? Have you already left the building?"

"I'm in the parking deck across the street." I blinked back tears. "On the third level."

"Don't move. I'm on my way."

His phone was breaking up and I knew he was on the elevator. When it disconnected altogether, I took a shaky breath and climbed out of my car. A couple of minutes later, the elevator opened and the second I saw him, tears burned my eyes.

"I'm sorry," I called out to him.

With each step he took, my heart broke a little more. I couldn't stand the idea of him being upset with me—or worse, resentful. Because he was giving up his dream for me to live mine.

My heart swelled as it was cracking in half.

"I didn't want this," I told him when he was about fifteen feet away. I couldn't read his expression and I was scared to let him talk first, so I kept going. "I didn't want you to lose anything—especially not your company. I don't want to walk away from you or RLF. But I don't want you to resent me. I don't want you to regret us—"

Grabbing my face, he crashed his lips into mine. He kissed me hard, forcing me back against my car. His muscular body pinned me in place as our mouths expressed our feelings for one another. His kiss quieted the noise in my head, the despair in my heart, and the churning in my belly. His kiss was a temporary balm covering the guilt I felt from his loss. And for a full minute, I was given a reprieve.

Russ pulled away fractionally and searched my face. "I would never regret us. I would never resent you." His thumbs stroked my cheeks. "You are my escape . . . my fantasy . . . the woman of my fucking dreams."

My eyes started to water. "But RLF is also your dream and I can't let you give it up for me."

"It's the only way for us to be together."

"I didn't want you to give up everything for me, Russ. Knowing that you did this . . ." My lashes fluttered closed. "I'm sorry if I made you feel like you had to do something this drastic for us to be together. Because you didn't. I'd sneak around with you for the next seven, eight months if that's what I had to do."

"Baby, look at me. Look at me," he insisted. When I opened my eyes and stared into his, there was so much emotion in his expression. "You'd sneak around with me for months even though you hated it?"

"I hate the idea of you losing your dream as much as I hate the idea of losing you. I can survive a few months of us having to sneak around. I cannot survive you giving up everything for me. Let's go to HR and fix this."

Looking at me worshipfully, he stirred something within me. He brought his face to mine and planted a soft kiss against my lips. "I love that you'd do that for me."

"I'd do anything for you," I admitted, my voice barely above a whisper.

"And I'd do anything for you." He stared into my eyes, and I was filled with so much love. "Which is why I stepped down as CEO."

"Russ—"

"It's *my* company. It'll always be my company."

"I don't understand."

His hands coasted from my face down my neck and over my shoulders. When he ran them down my bare arms, his fingertips left goose bumps in their wake. When he got to my hands, he intertwined our fingers and then brought them to his mouth.

"I wasn't just the CEO. I'm also the majority stakeholder." He took a step back and swept his gaze up and down my body. "And what I want is you and to design. Remedy's been the face of RLF for years so having her replace me as CEO made the most sense. Because as CEO, I can't be with you the way I want to be with you. But as head of design, I can."

My eyebrows shot up. "What?"

"My lawyer tried, but there was no way around us being in violation. Even if I wasn't your direct supervisor, you were still my subordinate. I was at the top of the organizational chart. So the paperwork we signed was strictly legal. It was to protect the company's assets. But from a public standpoint, we would've taken a hit. Every move I made would've been open to critique. Every opportunity you earned would've been open to speculation. So, my lawyer concluded that our relationship wouldn't have gotten board approval with me as CEO because me taking a hit would be the same as the company taking the hit. But as head of design . . ." He let his new title trail off and hang in the air between us.

I'd heard what he'd said the first time, but it didn't really hit me until he explained it.

I was at a loss for words.

Launching myself at him, I threw my arms around his neck, and he enveloped me. The heat of his hands seared through the chiffon shirt as he held me tight. I buried my face in his neck. His sandalwood and leather scent infiltrated my nostrils and filled my lungs. "Oh my God," I murmured. "I don't know what to say."

"You don't have to say anything." He paused momentarily. "I remembered when you told me that life was too short for me not to be doing what makes me happy. And when I realized that as the majority stakeholder I could get everything I wanted, I did what needed to be done." He kissed the top of my head, my temple, my cheek, and then he pulled back so he could see my face. "I get to retain ownership of my company. I get to design more. And I get you. So, no, you didn't encourage me to do anything that I didn't want to do."

He leaned in, kissing me softly.

The stress, anxiety, dread, and guilt melted away with each brush of his lips. Pushing up on the tips of my toes, I deepened the kiss to express everything I couldn't verbally. His tongue gently caressed mine in a way that punctuated everything he'd just said.

He groaned sexily and a chill ran down my spine.

My lips curled into a smile before I pulled out of the kiss.

Our faces were still close, and I placed the palm of my hand on his chest. Feeling his heart beating as strongly and intensely as my own made me emotional.

"I've spent the last couple weeks trying to figure out how to fix this," I told him. "I was worried that you were going to resent me."

"The only thing I resent is me not making this move earlier."

"I don't think you understand how glad I am to hear you say that." I exhaled audibly. "At one point, Lori was going over something in the meeting and I was trying to figure out how to get your job back. I was so worried."

He kissed the top of my head before wrapping his arms around me and holding me tight. I felt so safe and secure wrapped in his arms.

"I got you. I always got you," he uttered.

I nuzzled my head into his chest as if we were in bed and not in a downtown parking structure.

"You don't have to worry about anything except what you're going to wear on our date tonight," he said softly.

"Where are we going?"

"On a date."

I lifted my head so I could look up at him. "Russ!"

"When have you known me to ruin a surprise?" There was a twinkle in his eye.

I felt the flutter in my belly and the rush of adrenaline that always hit me before a date with Russ.

"How am I supposed to know what to wear?" I argued.

"Dress like we're going somewhere nice for dinner."

"So, we're going to dinner?"

He smirked. "I'm taking you somewhere special." Grabbing my face, he dropped a kiss against my forehead, and then my nose, and then my lips. "But don't worry, I plan on feeding you tonight." With his lips just barely touching mine, he continued. "Trust and believe. You will be fed."

I shifted my weight from one foot to the other, trying to stifle the throbbing between my thighs. "Russ," I whispered, holding his gaze. "What time are you leaving the office?"

"Right after my last meeting ends. Two o'clock at the latest."

"You're lucky you're worth the wait."

I pushed up on my toes so our lips could meet. I intended for it to be a quick kiss, but as soon as our mouths connected, it was hard to pull away. He wrapped his arms around me and ran his hands up and down my back before parting my lips with his tongue. My entire body reacted, and the sensation consumed me.

"Mmmm," I moaned into his mouth.

I felt his energy pouring into me. I felt his love and lust, respect and reassurance, intimacy and affection filling me.

When we finally pulled apart, I took a trembling breath.

"Two o'clock," he repeated.

He took a step back and adjusted himself. "I gotta calm down before I go back in."

"Yes, please. You don't need to be putting on a show."

He grabbed his bulge. "This show is only for you."

I grinned. "Good."

He checked his watch and then sighed. "I need to head back in, but pack a bag when you get home. I'm coming to get you when I leave here and taking you back to my place. We have a lot to celebrate."

"I don't know what you have up your sleeve, but I'm looking forward to celebrating with you."

"Me too." His phone rang and he pulled it out of his pocket. Running a hand over his beard, he let out an audible breath. "My meeting starts in ten." He shoved his phone back into his pocket and then locked eyes with me. "I've missed escaping with you. We haven't really been able to do that."

"No, we haven't."

"Come here." Scooping me into his arms, he kissed me. "I'll be leaving here in two hours at the latest."

"And I'll be ready and waiting for you."

He'd taken a couple steps backward when a question popped in my mind. I knew he didn't have much time, so I hesitated, contemplating waiting to ask him later.

I swallowed hard. "If I was your escape from work and life, how does that look now that we're working together and in a relationship?"

He stopped. "It looks like my fantasy." He closed the gap between us in half a second. Hooking his forefinger under my chin, he tipped my head up and studied my face. "Nina, I was never running away from work and life. I was only ever running toward you."

My heart skipped a beat.

Before I could respond, his phone started ringing again. He pulled it out of his pocket. "I have to take this." Leaning down, he planted a sweet kiss against my lips. "I love you."

"I love you, too," I murmured.

"Hello?" he answered. "Get the projections together and get everyone in the conference room to review." He pointed to the elevator to let me know he needed to leave.

"Okay," I whispered. "Call me when you're free."

He kissed me and then nodded. "Start without me, I'm on my way," he snapped as he walked away. "Get Remedy . . ."

The events of the day replayed in my mind as I watched him enter the elevator. Before the doors closed, I turned toward my car and brought my hand to my chest.

My heart was racing.

I caught a glimpse of my reflection in the window. Between my glassy eyes and upturned lips, my happiness was written all over my face.

The elevator dinged and I glanced over my shoulder.

And then did a double take.

"Nina!" Russ called out to me as he stepped through the doors. His long stride quickly closed the distance between us. "I forgot something."

"What?" I looked around to see if he'd dropped something before meeting his eyes again. "What did you forget?"

"This."

Grabbing my face, he pressed his lips against mine urgently. Warmth flooded my system as his kiss radiated throughout my body. I fisted his jacket, bringing him even closer to me. Our mouths moved hungrily over each other as he backed me up against my car. Soft, contented sighs rang out from us as we kissed harder, deeper.

"Don't you have somewhere you're supposed to be," I murmured into his mouth.

Pulling away fractionally, he waited until I met his gaze before he spoke. "I'm exactly where I'm supposed to be."

My stomach fluttered. "What about your meeting?"

"They can wait." He leaned into me, his lips brushing against mine. "This can't."

Russell Long was the manifestation of the love I always knew existed, but thought would be impossible to find. I'd been fostering men until they found their forever home. It never occurred to me that they were also fostering me until I found mine.

Acknowledgments

I am so incredibly blessed, and I thank God every day for my loved ones. The people who have picked me up when I was down. The people who clap the loudest in the room for my wins. The people who hold space for me, who take care of me, who love me. I am grateful for my family, friends, and readers who have supported me. The people in my life have loved me, uplifted me, rooted for me, and championed me. I am overwhelmed with thankfulness. I always say that everything happens for a reason, and whenever someone reaches out to me to say that they drew inspiration, knowledge, power, and hope from my work, I am reminded of that.

Curvy Girl Summer was my first traditional release, and it was met with such a warm reception. It became a *USA Today* bestseller because of your support. Thank you, thank you, thank you! To everyone who read Aaliyah's story and realized you are deserving of someone who loves you and wants to see you happy, deserving of a quality dating experience, deserving of boundaries with family, etc., I see you. To everyone who read Nina's story and realized you are deserving of not having to settle, deserving of having your beauty acknowledged, deserving of trusting someone with your whole self, etc., I see you. To everyone who will read Jazmyn's story and realize you are deserving of [redacted], I see you too. Thank you for supporting the Curve series. Thank you for letting these three beautiful, fat, Black women be loved out loud, publicly and unapologetically.

It matters.

About the Author

DANIELLE ALLEN is an author, an educator, and a life coach. Living authentically has been the key to her living her best life. With a background in social sciences, helping people better understand themselves so they can become the best version of themselves is one of her passions. Writing contemporary romance novels that challenge the status quo of the genre is another.

Facebook: DanielleAllenAuthor
Goodreads: Danielle Allen
Instagram: @authordanielleallen
TikTok: @authordanielleallen
BookBub: @authordanielleallen